NAERO'S TRIAL

Naero's War
The Citation Series:

Book 3

NAERO'S TRIAL

Mason Elliott

Naero's War
The Citation Series:

Book 3

High Mark Publishing

High Mark Publishing
www.highmarkpublishing.com

Seattle & Portland, Los Angeles, Chicago, London

NAERO'S TRIAL

Naero's War
The Citation Series:
Book 3
by
Mason Elliott
Createspace Edition
© 2015 by Mason Elliott. All rights reserved.
Published by High Mark Publishing
ISBN 978-1-930451-23-0
Watch for other titles by this author in the future.

Cover Art by
Mike Leonard
madmanmike.deviantart.com

High Mark Publishing Update Code F0215A

Become a fan of my books.
Please join my Readers List:
http://bit.ly/1L2QpUL

Thanks, from Mason Elliott

1

"Pregnant?!"

Naero Amashin Maeris's ship's physician, Trudi Cheyenne, nodded emphatically. "Yes, Captain. The results are actually pretty obvious–"

Naero stared at the floor and then at her feet, several thoughts and emotions swirling around within her. Shock just one of them. "I…I can't be pregnant."

Trudi smirked, and then sighed. "Sir, logically, the only way you can't be pregnant is if you didn't have sex. Did you have sex, sir?"

Naero felt herself shudder. Then she smiled. "Yes, I did. And it was really great!"

Inside-a-star-great. And what followed after that was all pretty good, too. She was not going to deny any of that. She loved Khai, and he her.

Trudi raised both eyebrows. "Well, then, sir. If you have sex, pregnancy is always possible to some degree, unless you take some kind of precautions or direct birth control. And by the looks of things, you've been pregnant for a number of weeks. If you allow me to–"

"Just give me a moment, Trudi," Naero felt a brief pang of loss and regret. She loved Trudi dearly, like all of her flagship crew, but things just weren't the same in medical without Naero's lifelong friend Zhen there.

But Zhen was gone, her body long dead by now, even though Naero still carried her *abani's* soul deep within herself, sort of dormant and in storage.

That was complicated as well, like practically everything in her life. Naero had promised Zhen, before her friend died a second time, that she would strive to find a way to bring her back.

Of course, that had happened only a number of weeks ago. But still, Naero was no closer to finding a way to restore Zhen to some form of life with her husband, Tyber, and their infant son, Gallan. No closer to keeping that solemn promise.

Now that Naero was on trial for her life, she might not ever get the chance to make any further progress on that front.

Meanwhile, Trudi waited patiently, staring at her and waiting for her to come back to the present at some point. "N?"

Naero shook herself and forced a weak grin. "Sorry, Tru. I didn't mean it was impossible that I was pregnant. I'm just saying I can't be pregnant right now."

Then the count of days struck her like a spinning wheelkick, right between her big violet eyes. Her mouth dropped open, and she covered it with both hands.

"Weeks ago? That must have been exactly when…"

Trudi blinked. "N, did there happen to be something unusual about the time, place, or the manner of the conception that you would like to share with me, sir?"

Naero closed her eyes and drew in a deep breath. "Hmmm…well, you might say that."

Again, she reminded herself that she was about to be put on trial for murder. To decide whether or not she would be executed. Not exactly the best of times to be starting a family.

Now Trudi grimaced all the way. "Sir, it shouldn't be much of a burden for the first trimester. But if you wish, the fetus can easily be removed and put in stasis until a better, future time."

Naero thought about that very quickly and very hard.

She desperately needed to speak with Khai alone, but the situation was simply impossible.

There had to be a way.

Naero returned her attention to her medical officer once more. "Tru, I think that would be a good idea for now. I can even assist and make the transfer with my Cosmic abilities and biomancy."

Trudi patted the medbed. "Very well, sir. I'll prepare a nanofreeze capsule for your future offspring. Shall I keep it stored and protected in stasis with Captain Tyber's and Zhen's frozen children?"

Naero smiled sadly. "Perfect. And, Tru. If anything should happen—"

Trudi cut her off. "Nothing's going to happen, N. I'm sure that everything is going to work out for the best, somehow."

Naero frowned, and a deep sigh wafted through her. She wished that she could be that certain and hopeful.

"But, on the off chance that anything ever *did* happen to me, or our ship," she said. "The special probe that Ty and I prepared will cloak, launch, and take the kids to either *The Dark Star*, *The Shadow Fox*, other ships of my trade fleet, or my Aunt Sleak, in that order."

"All right, sir. Got it. Very well. I have the nanofreeze capsule prepared and ready for your direct action. Use your biomancy to conduct the transfer whenever you are ready, and I will monitor the process from here."

Naero closed her eyes and explored herself with the biomancy sight at the same time that she and Om linked with the medbed and the encapsulation processor with teknomancy.

There it was. There was her tiny little duck, resting and happy deep within her.

She couldn't help gasping slightly. Her and Khai's first child. Their baby, formed from the mind-blowing love making session that had overtaken both of them inside of that star, while both of them were in their energy being forms.

A girl.

A strong, powerful, beautiful, amazing girl. *A Maeris-girl.*

Naero Amashin Maeris paused for a moment and had to cover her eyes and weep for both joy and sorrow for a few seconds.

She was still right in the middle of one hell of a mess, as usual.

Tru came over to her and hugged her for a moment. "N, it's going to be all right."

Naero sighed, and spoke to her child privately within her own mind. I'm sorry, my little duck. Hopefully, after I manage to chat with your dad somehow…not to mention wrangle my murder trial…we'll be back in business together, little sweetie, and continue all of our stuff later.

She focused and transported her daughter into the protective fluid in the stasis capsule in order to freeze her in that state of development.

Once that was accomplished, Naero breathed a sigh of relief. Although she did feel a pang of emptiness somehow. Perhaps that part was merely psychological. "At least that process is complete," Naero said out loud.

One instant later, medical warning alarms went off.

Even Trudi jumped and looked completely taken by surprise.

"Haisha!" Trudi cried. "What the hell is going on? Look, sir! The scans and the equipment are going haywire."

Naero and Om linked in again, trying to make sense of things. Some of the sensitive, hi-tek medgear was already burned out. Om called numerous medical fixers in to conduct immediate repairs.

Clearly something was happening or had already happened.

Naero gaped in stunned surprise. Her tiny daughter was glowing like a star itself.

Her own words caught and hung up in Naero's mind.

...*like a star.*

The energy readings were off all known scales. In fact, not only the equipment, but the ship itself should be melting, collapsing, and imploding–in the presence of what could only be likened to the intense power of a small singularity.

That was the only thing close enough in the orders of Cosmic magnitude to compare it to.

And yet here it did little harm, only burning out some med equipment.

No other damage was readily apparent.

Naero and Trudi both stared with their mouths hanging open at what they were witnessing. Like most things involving Naero, it did not make any rational sense. And yet, here it was.

"Uh...sir," Trudi said, clearly shaken and afraid. "You were about to explain something to me about what you referred to as an 'unusual conception?' Perhaps this would be an excellent time for you to explain to me in detail just how unique that conception was. Because I'm about to freak out and lose it here!"

"Uh-huh," Naero said. "Well, about that. You see, it was kinda like this–"

Without warning, Naero's daughter vanished off all of the screens.

If they weren't alarmed before, they certainly were now.

"Haisha!" Tru exclaimed.

"Omigosh," Naero said. "Where did she–"

Naero smiled and reached down to put her hands on her abdomen.

She didn't even need to biomance. "My little duck must have gotten homesick, Tru. My girl is right back inside me, where everything began."

Naero opened the abdomen section of her nanosuit with teknomancy, and climbed back up onto the medbed. Now up on all of the screens and monitors, a slight, glowing pinpoint of blinding light glowed from inside her belly, illuminating her like a lamp from within, but doing no harm to any tissues or organs.

Trudi still looked slightly dumbfounded and afraid, as well as curious. She folded her arms in front of her. "Ready, sir. Still waiting for that explanation. Right about now would be good."

After a deep breath, Naero began. "My daughter–my and Khai's daughter–was conceived within the energy fields of a star, after both of us had transformed into energy being forms and were pulled into the star's gravity well. It makes perfect sense, now that I think back."

Trudi lifted both hands. "Of course it does. Even though that has never happened before in the course of all human history. Yep. Perfect sense." Trudi bit her lip and looked down and away.

"You couldn't know what it was like for us both," Naero attempted to explain. "In our energy forms in that star, all of our emotions and desires were magnified and so intense–like a thousand times of more. Both of us were having trouble coping with those levels of expanded emotion and desire. It overtook both of us. Neither of us could help what we felt or what we did. And now, neither of us regret any of it. I honestly love Khai. And he is equally devoted to me."

A period of blinking ensued before Trudi could speak once more. "Yeah, so devoted that he's going to chop off your head with that damn Cosmic sword of his if you are convicted of murder."

"I admit, it's a little complicated," Naero said, even wincing herself as she spoke those exact words she's said so often before.

Trudi raised both eyes. "Well, I would guess so."

"Look. Khai is the Mystic Enforcer. I'm on trial for murder. Neither of us can change that. But we still love each other."

Trudi examined the screens again. "And now, you have a child inside of you with energy signatures greater than those of a pulsar. I can't even begin to measure it. And, it has a mind of its own…and it can…transport. Sure it can…why, that's my fifth teleporting fetus this week alone! The little buggers."

Naero grinned and rested one hand on the arm of her flustered physician. "Now you're just being sarcastic, Tru. My girl doesn't want to hurt anyone. I know it. I can sense that."

"Well that's certainly good news. I'd hate to see it if she did."

"She just wants to be with me. With her mom. That's all she wants."

Trudi smiled. "Well, I suppose that seems natural. Captain, I might be wrong, but I think that this child is somehow going to turn out to be a very, very unique and special kid."

Naero grimaced and ground her teeth for an instant. "I don't think there's much disagreement about that."

Another terrible thought struck Naero, slicing through her in pain as if it were the deep cut of some invisible blade.

If her child refused to leave her, and the worst thing happened and she was executed–would her child die with her as well?

What a terrible, horrible, gut-ripping thought.

A com signal went off and both Naero and Trudi jumped again, their jangled nerves on edge. Word came from Surina Marshall on the Bridge with Enel and the rest of Naero's flagship crew.

"Sir," Rina cut in, "sorry to interrupt, but you wanted me to alert you the instant that we began orbiting the new Mystic Homeworld of Kalathar. We're here, sir."

"Good work, Rina. Any word from the High Mystics?"

"Yes, indeed, sir. Almost the second we arrived. Both of the High Mystic Masters are demanding that you immediately turn yourself over for arrest, and that you be restrained, and confined to a high security holding cell within a specially armored Intel transport that is docking with us shortly. They said that you should prepare to stay confined within that holding cell for the length of your upcoming trial."

Naero took another very deep breath. And so it began.

Finally she let that breath out.

"Rina. Inform them that I will comply with all of their instructions. The Mystic Enforcer Khai will escort me down…in restraints as needed. I will not resist in any way."

By now she already had her small duffle of stuff ready and at hand, selected for her incarceration. Nothing that Intel or anyone would object to.

She left all of her weapons behind. Naero slung her duffle over her shoulder and hit the presets on her wristcom.

All of the many personal messages that she had prepared during the journey to Kalathar went out, saying farewell, if need be, to family and friends until after her trial. She would be kept in isolation until her fate was decided.

Finally, more than anything else that she dreaded, she went to see her lover Khai in her oval captain's quarters.

The Mystic Enforcer, for all of his vaunted power, sat on the edge of their pop-up nanobed with his great hands clutched together, leaning over with his elbows on his knees, staring down at the ground with his head in his hands. He was shaking.

He looked up at her, rampant emotions playing across his handsome face. "Naero. Am I taking you to your death? Am I destined to be forced by duty and honor into the role of your executioner?"

6

It broke Naero's heart to see her beloved so distraught.

She was just as heartbroken as he was.

And now even more so, with her secret.

How could she dump that on him as well?

How could she burden him even more with the news of their special child? How could she possibly find a way to tell him?

Naero wrapped her arms around Khai and pulled him close to her. She kissed his head, his long golden hair. Then she climbed up on their bed and curled herself around him.

"There is no going back for either of us," Naero told him. "The only way now, is forward. We must see this through, no matter what, my beloved. It is a matter of honor for both of us. We have both given our word, repeatedly."

Khai let out another deep sigh. Naero ran her hands through his hair as she loved to do, and looked up at him with her large eyes.

"How long do we have, my heart?" he asked.

"Within the hour," she told him. "No more. Then…we must be parted until this matter is decided, one way or the other. And after that, we are both honor-bound to accept that decision. Even if it means…that I must die."

Khai brought his strong hands gently to her face and drew her close to him again. They rolled to one side, onto the bed, face to face.

Naero forced herself to smile and caressed his tortured, chiseled features, and ran her fingers once more through his long, golden hair, gazing into his golden lion eyes.

"Khai, love me, my heart," she whispered to him. "We cannot know the future. Love me while there is yet time. While we are still free."

The Enforcer enfolded her in his mighty arms. Arms that had never known defeat. "Naero, I shall never stop loving you. No matter whatever happens."

When the joy they shared with each other but paused, Naero teknomanced their nanobed away.

The two lovers sank into the black velvet of the soft nanofloor.

There they lay entwined, softly shining in the black in their own light like living jewels—the emerald and the gold. The white and the black.

There they lay, glittering and breathing life into each other, until the final summons for her trial reached them.

Naero prepared herself, and teknomanced the hi-tek shackles that Intel sent onto her arms, binding herself with their weight.

Elliott

Khai carried her in his arms to their shuttle, with her beloved crew saluting her to either side. He piloted the craft with his own hands.

They landed without incident, and Naero walked into her hi-sec cell that awaited her without looking back or saying a word.

The doors closed and sealed behind her like a vault.

Perhaps she had made the wrong choice.

Yet she wanted her last moments with Khai—if the last ones they must be—to be free of any further pain, doubt, or worry.

Now, all thought must be bent upon her trial, and winning her freedom.

2

When she was given the choice, Naero chose the right to wear her Strike Fleet Captain's dress uniform mantle to her trial.

Khai was present during the trial, as his duty required him to be, along with six Prime adepts of the Three Orders: Order, Chaos, and Change. They were the appointed guards for the trial, and escorted the prisoner from her isolated holding cell in the shackles that she was required to wear.

Admiral Klyne officiated her trial solely as the judge, to conduct and observe the necessary Spacer legalities.

High Master Tree would prosecute the legal case against her. High Master Jo would conduct her defense. Khai and the Prime adepts would stand guard.

A jury of Mystic peers would be called upon to decide Naero Amashin Maeris's fate. These were fifteen Elders from the Clans who were also Mystics. Five from each of the Three Orders. Yet none could be from any of the direct Clans of her parents or grandparents.

These fifteen Spacers would decide whether she lived or died.

The trial would last for three days. One day would be given to the prosecution. One day for the defense.

On the third day, the final statements would be made. The jury would deliberate, and make their decision.

If acquitted, she would be set free.

If convicted, she quickly learned the sentence of death would be carried out–immediately–by the Mystic Enforcer.

That seemed odd and rather drastic. Why would it be necessary to execute her immediately?

On day one, High Master Tree made a rather determined case against Naero. His deep, stentorian voice boomed out with righteous, grim authority.

"A Mystic High Master is dead. He was murdered and destroyed by his own student, Mystic Adept Naero Amashin Maeris. She had admitted to many, on numerous occasions, that she despised Master Vane and his opinions. She slew Master Vane in the Astral Plane and annihilated his spirit essence with a forbidden Chaos Technique: The Eye of Annihilation. His body was also consumed and utterly destroyed at that exact same moment."

Tree would pause at times to let his statements soak in, before taking up his next point of attack to expound upon. Sometimes he took a few breaths, sometimes he looked through his notes and papers, and at other times he paused for drinks of water.

Then he would surge right ahead once more.

"The facts are indisputable. The two remaining High Masters, the Mystic Enforcer, and the Prime adepts were all present in the vicinity at the time of the murder, and know very well who committed it.

"To this date, no other Mystic High Master has ever been murdered by one of his students. Such a crime is unheard of. Such an affront to the Three Orders cannot be tolerated."

For Tree, everything was black and white.

"Crime is crime."

And he emphasized that emphatically by driving his accusing index finger through the air like a stabbing weapon of conviction.

"Murder is murder."

His voice always thundered with the hammering ring of absolute authority.

"The facts of this case and our laws are crystal clear."

The finger of doom always ended up on Naero.

"Spacers do not take the lives of other Spacers. That is forbidden. And Mystics do not take the lives of other Mystics without just cause, and especially not their masters."

Master Tree turned and held out both hands as if he were bestowing the gift of his knowledge on everyone, especially the jury.

"It does not matter what her name is. Her Clan, her parents, or any of her deeds, good or bad. It doesn't matter if she is popular or infamous. Nor whether we like her as a person or not. All that matters is that she has broken one of our most deeply honored and cherished laws."

That damn finger again, pointing her way.

"Naero Amashin Maeris murdered another Spacer, and not just any Spacer, but a Mystic High Master. And let me remind you. In Spacer society, the incredibly rare and heinous crime of murder has always—in every case—been punishable by death. Murder is punished by execution, each and every time."

No finger this time. Tree just folded his hands in front of himself and even looked sad.

"Just as it should be now. Murder and crime of the worst sort cannot, has not, is not, and will not—will never be tolerated by our people. It is one of the founding cornerstones of our Spacer society, and what makes us different. It is what makes us Spacers. We do not kill each other!"

Naero herself did not take a full breath almost until just now. She had had trouble catching her breath, ever since they led her out of her cell and she saw Khai.

Haisha, Om. Master Tree has nearly convinced *me* that I should be executed.

What a rigid dickhead.

Om! She barely maintained her composure. Bursting out laughing like a nervous lunatic for no apparent reason would certainly not help her case any.

Yet inside, she was chuckling away like hell, despite the seriousness of all that was taking place.

Thanks, Om.

No charge, N.

They had to listen to a lot more of the same dreck and drama from Master Tree. The big pompous blowhard. Everything with him was the importance of the letter of the law. Nothing else.

Why should she expect anything different from the High Master of Order? Order was unforgiving, and indifferent.

That made for a very long day.

At the end of it, Naero barely touched the fine meal they sent in to her. And that night, she barely slept. Each time that she moved, the binding chains of her shackles clinked or got in her way somehow.

She could slip out of them, but it would probably raise some kind of alarm if she did so. And she didn't want to make anyone think that she was attempting to escape.

She spent most of that night sighing, tossing, and turning on her nanopad. She wondered about her child. She worried about Khai.

The next day, Master Jo took up Naero's defense.

First, he outlined Naero's character, detailing her incredible military career and record with the Annexation War and the recent defeat of the Ejjai Invasion during The High Crusade to save humanity.

Master Jo held up her service as a Mystic and how she had actually helped save Master Vane's life during the attacks on the Mystic Homeworlds and during all of the subsequent attacks by their new, mysterious, and implacably dangerous alien adversaries.

He called up the unquestionable testimonies of General Walker, Admiral Klyne, and several of the Spacer Elders, who testified to Naero's honor and high character. To the strength of her word as a Spacer.

With each cross examination of each witness called, Master Tree asked the same exact questions, and hammered home his point.

He asked all of Naero's character witnesses if any Spacer was above the law, and able to commit murder–killing another Spacer–and deserved to not face justice for such a crime.

Each of them said no in response. And each time, Master Tree cut them off before any of them could say anything else.

Master Tree had cleverly called no witnesses. Therefore, none of his claims had ever been directly challenged or refuted.

Then Master Jo went on to outline how valuable Naero was, as the possessor of the elusive, and still untapped, Kexxian Data Matrix. As a Mystic. As a naval commander. As one of the enigmatic chosen Guardians of the ancient obelisk of Change energy for the Three Orders of the Cosmic Prophecies. She could very well play a very important part in the mysteries as they unfolded.

If nothing else, Naero was also a valuable weapon, to be pitted against their apparently growing list of dangerous and largely unknown enemies. She had played important roles in foiling the plots and plans of their enemies, time and time again, as only she could.

"And let us not forget, that Naero Amashin Maeris has directly fought with valor and courage to help save the lives of trillions, not just Spacers and landers, but many known sentients. We would all be much worse off, without Captain Naero helping to defend us."

12

Master Tree shot to his feet and asked to be able to make not so much of an objection, but a comment. Admiral Klyne, acting as the guiding judge, said that he would allow it.

Tree asked everyone in the open court, "Do any of these noble acts and achievements give anyone the power, right, or permission to commit murder?"

Master Tree continued to play variations on his trump card.

Master Jo took up one of his own.

First he detailed all of Master Vane's many "difficulties" that he had brought about and upon himself, largely on his own and by his own character flaws and actions.

Master Tree quickly objected. "The murder victim is not the one on trial here; nor can he speak for himself," Tree noted.

"Then perhaps the so-called victim and his questionable character should be held up to scrutiny and made a matter of public record. By any account, Master Vane was not the soul of virtue and discretion. It was long known or suspected that High Master Vane was either responsible for or present at the deaths of several adepts during extreme Mystic practice sessions for various reasons over the years. One of them even provided Vane with a very convenient and reliable host body, shortly after dying. It was often wondered if Vane somehow helped the process along."

This time Master Tree shot to his feet to make a very clear objection. High Master Vane was not on trial. His character was not the question.

Master Jo insisted that it was, and that he would clearly demonstrate why.

Then Master Jo surprised everyone by calling Naero Amashin Maeris, the defendant herself, to the stand to testify.

Naero walked over, still wearing her shackles, and was forced to stand in place instead of taking a seat. The chair was simply pulled back to make room for her to do so.

Master Jo began to explain, in great detail, how in the Astral Plane, Naero had never intended to fight with Master Vane, let alone intended to kill him. She merely went there to have her say and defend herself, when Master Vane was insisting that for the good of all, she should be executed.

Naero's testimony agreed with Master Jo's presentation at every point.

They tried to present and explain Master Vane's well-known prejudice and hatred for the Maeris Clan, and specifically, Naero's direct family, dating back to her mother and her now outcast uncle.

Vain had repeatedly made his contempt for them known even as he trained them.

Master Jo explained how all along, Master Vane openly declared and insisted that Naero was literally a Cosmic monster, one that would need to be destroyed. And that when the time came—or whenever he saw fit—he would step in and destroy her himself, for the good of all.

Their main defense was that Naero had only slain Master Vane accidentally, in self-defense, after he chose to act unilaterally and was actively trying to kill her.

And he kept trying to kill her, despite the fact that she had fled from Master Vane, fought only to get away, and repeatedly begged him not to attack her. She repeatedly warned him of the possible, terrible consequences if he insisted on trying to destroy her.

She could not be held accountable for the outcome.

Master Tree did his best to emphasize this key point of her defense. "Naero, like every Spacer, had every right to defend herself. No matter what High Master Vane's opinion of her, even the other two High Masters agreed that Master Vane overstepped his authority when he went after her. He attacked her repeatedly, trying to kill her, ignoring her attempts to flee— even when she begged him not to attack her.

"Naero was under no obligation to stand by and allow Master Vane to kill her. She had every right to defend herself against anyone trying to kill her. No matter who the attacker was. Even if that person was a Mystic High Master."

Naero glanced around her slightly, suddenly hopeful and certain that Master Jo had them all on her side now.

Yet once Master Jo was finished with Naero, Master Tree rose up to cross examine her and her testimony.

"Naero Maeris. You make a spurious claim that High Master Vane attacked you with the purpose and intent to take your life. What is your proof of that?"

Naero paused for a moment, uncertain how to answer. She was caught completely off guard. "What? I don't understand."

"High Master Jo has no proof of any of this. Neither do you. It is, however, a feeble attempt on your part to explain away you guilt, and your crime. And now, with you on trial for your life, we are supposed to accept nothing but your very convenient word?

"How can you prove to every one and to the jury, that Master Vane was trying to kill you, and that you acted in self-defense? Don't bother answering, because we already know that you can't. For all we know, he was merely trying to restrain or capture you. Again, what factual evidence can you present to prove that you were defending yourself? Other than your own convenient account of things, in your own convenient words?"

Naero was stymied once more.

"Answer the question, Naero Maeris."

"If my word and my honor are not good enough, then no, I have no other proof. No one in my situation would. What occurred happened solely between Master Vane and myself. And after I defended myself again his attempts to kill me...he was gone."

Now Master Tree pressed his obvious advantage on the point of law. "So, by your own admission in your own words, you have absolutely no proof that your life was at risk, or that you were actually defending yourself when you killed Master Vane?"

Naero remained silent.

"Now, why don't you tell us exactly how you killed Master Vane?"

"Well, when he attacked me—"

"Stop. Let's get this clear. You can't prove that he attacked you, or that you were acting in self-defense, so let's just skip that farce. Go directly to how you killed him. Please, explain it for all to hear."

"Yes, but—"

"There, you admitted it. Your Honor, let the witness be dismissed. She agreed for all to hear that she killed Master Vane. She clearly just confessed to murder."

"That's not what I said or was going to say."

"Step down. You are dismissed."

"No, let me have my say. This is only a trick. You did not let me finish my statement in answer to your line of questioning."

"Your confession is all that matters. Step down."

Master Jo rose up and tried to recover. "Your honor, this is clearly a dirty trick on the part of the prosecution. Please allow Fleet Captain Maeris to finish her statement and explain herself, for the benefit of the jury. She is on trial for her life. She should not be maneuvered into condemning herself in this sleight-of-hand fashion. She was clearly baited into this trap, and I demand that she be allowed to explain herself, and her statement."

"The court agrees," Admiral Klyne announced. "Captain Maeris, take your time, and explain yourself fully. Tell us what happened in your own words."

Naero nodded, took in a deep breath, and prepared herself. "For the record, this is what happened. This is how Master Vane died. He came at me several times, attacking me and telling me that it was time for him to kill me and take me out, just as he had been threatening me since the day I met him. He insisted that I was going to turn into some kind of monster.

"I fought him off; I tried to get away from, repeatedly. In the end, he had me cornered and even told me that he was going to use the forbidden Eye of Annihilation Cosmic attack on me, a terrifying Chaos energy attack. I had seen former Adept Hashiko destroy herself with that same technique as it went out of control.

"Let me tell everyone. He attacked me. I did not attack him. Vane wasn't kidding, he wasn't joking or fooling around or trying to capture me. He didn't want to just maim or cripple me. He wanted to kill me. And he was trying as hard as he could to do so. In the end, I–I instinctively defended myself, but I never attacked him directly. All I did was reflect his own attack back on him. By attacking me and trying to kill me, he killed himself when his own forbidden attack turned back against him and destroyed him. End of story."

Master Tree challenged once again and cross-examined her testimony. "We have already proven that your personal statements are suspect and cannot be assumed to be taken as fact. Just because you say something does not make it true. Other than your questionable word, you do not have any proof that you killed High Master Vane in self-defense. Do you? That's all you have, isn't it?"

Naero lifted her chin high. "I am a Spacer. I am my honor, and my word."

"I call up vidcam feeds from around the now-missing Mystic Homeworld planet of Janosha and the events that took place during the attack there. Many here have already witnessed this footage. To those who are seeing this for the first time, I would call it illuminating."

Even Naero watched as she rocketed up from the surface of the planet, swelling up larger and larger into her Dark Beast form when it went out of control.

Everyone watched as she single-handedly destroyed the enemy invasion fleet. The massive Cosmic explosion occurred and then she shrank back down.

"That," Master Tree announced, "is the monster that Naero Maeris is capable of transforming into. So, as it turns out, Master Vane was exactly correct about one thing. He was right. Naero Maeris is a monster; she is a danger to all. Look on and see for yourself."

However Naero and Master Jo tried to explain those past images away, and how she was learning to control herself and all of her abilities with the help of the Mystics, the jury was left with those frightening images of Naero and her Dark Beast out of control.

3

On the third day of Naero's trial the prosecution and the defense made their final, closing statements.

Master Jo spoke first, for the defense.

"In the final analysis, I would both conclude and insist that Naero Amashin Maeris has proven herself time and time again to be an honorable Spacer, and that her word is without question. She is also vital to the survival of her people in many important ways. Naero Amashin Maeris is a noble, invaluable warrior and a proven leader who has served the Clans and the Alliance well, in both peacetime and war. She is a Mystic Champion who is now part of the great and mysterious Cosmic Prophecy, long foretold. There is still so little that we do not know about those prophecies; who can say what vital role she might play in the end?"

Master Jo paced a bit. "And on a very basic level, she is a Spacer, like all of us. As such, she has the right of all Spacers and all sentients to defend herself, to the death, against anyone who attempts to kill her. Reluctantly, she resorted to lethal force only after High Master Vane attacked her with the intent to destroy her and take her life. He kept up his attacks, even after she had tried to get away from him and begged him repeatedly not to attack her.

"She cannot not be convicted of murder for defending her own life against someone trying to kill her. Those are all many good reasons why you must see fit to exonerate her of these erroneous charges. We cannot take the life of this amazing, and valiant hero."

The defense finally rested.

Master Tree was given the final word in the trial for the prosecution.

"Hero? First, let me also revisit the reckless side of this renegade, outlaw Spacer, who fled from justice and had to be brought back by force to face her crimes, bound in shackles, in order to keep her from getting away once again. On several occasions, Naero Amashin Maeris has proven herself to be dangerous, unpredictable, and out of control. By her own words, she has more than once declared that if she ever lost control and became a threat to any of her people, she should be put down–and destroyed.

"The cold-blooded murder of a High Mystic Master has not demonstrated this fact readily enough? Beyond all doubt? If she can slay a High Master of the Mystics so easily, how much more is she a danger to all? And she even admits that she cannot control her abilities. Her very existence has become such a clear and present threat that it cannot be ignored and must be dealt with. I repeat, she has admitted on several occasions that her powers can go out of control and be very dangerous.

"Next, she also clearly admits that she killed Master Vane. Now, of her own accord, she claims that she killed him in self defense. But she has thus far presented no single shred of proof of that. She claims that Master Vane attacked her, attempted to kill her, and that she killed him–as she now conveniently claims–in so-called self defense. And I remind everyone in this court, once again: it does not matter who she is, what she is, or whatever else she has done. No one is above Spacer Law.

"Not even the infamous Naero Amashin Maeris."

Tree took in a breath and clasped his hands behind his back. "What are the facts, therefore? A High Mystic Master lies dead, murdered by his own student who openly stated that she could not stand him. Who openly admitted that she killed him. Nothing else can be proven, beyond those facts. Nothing else exists as fact. And this case must only be decided by the facts, the decision based solely upon the facts. Nothing else.

"A Spacer on trial for her life could readily claim and say anything. Merely stating something does not make it true. That does not prove it to be fact. According to the facts of what is known, Naero Amashin Maeris is clearly guilty of murder, and will undoubtedly say and do anything possible in order to get away with her crime. As anyone logically would, in order to escape punishment, justice, and execution."

Naero fumed. Haisha! What the hell did they expect her to say? Yes, I offed the asshole, I loved it, and I'm a fricking monster? Go ahead and kill me?

I wish that weren't so painfully funny, Naero.

Me too, Om.

Master Tree went on to demand that the jury uphold one of the key tenets of Spacer Law and Spacer society:

"Spacers do not murder other Spacers and take their lives! Naero Amashin Maeris is not above that law. Naero Amashin Maeris broke that solemn law. And like it or not, the law demands justice. There is no way around that law and no way to escape it. That law demands that she face the ultimate punishment for her being guilty of committing the ultimate crime!"

Tree emphasized his final point with a single, upraised index finger. "That punishment is immediate death, by execution. To be carried out by beheading, at the hands and the blade of the Mystic Enforcer!"

The prosecution rested its case.

Admiral Klyne looked slightly pale as he instructed the jury of Mystic Elders to decide the case and announce their decision after their period of deliberation.

Naero went back to her cell in silence feeling sick, unable to meet Khai's utterly heartbroken glance. She felt stunned and numb. She didn't know what to think. All that she could do was await the jury's decision, along with everyone else.

Yet it was her fate alone that was being decided.

But when she thought about it further, it wasn't just her fate.

Everyone waited for eight long hours.

Naero could neither rest nor sleep.

Then everyone was summoned back to the courtroom.

A decision had been made. The jury had arrived at a verdict in her case.

Admiral Klyne announced, "All rise for the verdict to be read."

They did so.

The jury leader stood up and read their decision.

"According to Spacer Law, and based upon all of the facts and evidence presented, we the jury find the defendant, Naero Amashin Maeris, of Clan Maeris…guilty of murder in the death of another Spacer."

Naero gasped, nailed to the bedrock of the planet itself in almost complete shock.

Guilty meant…

Master Tree rose up. "This Mystic trial has ended; it is over. A verdict has been reached. Without question, this grim crime is punishable among our people by death. Under the circumstances, the sentence is to be carried out immediately and without delay."

Naero, I can–

Shut up, Om.

Naero gasped and covered her mouth with both of her bound hands as she sobbed and went down on one knee.

Then she dropped her shackled hands to her abdomen and her eyes met Khai's in explosive waves of desperate horror and regret.

Their child from their love within that distant star barely grew within her. Now, no time remained to tell Khai all that she needed to before he performed his duty as the Mystic Enforcer.

Before he took her head…ended her life, and the lives of his own family.

Naero Amashin Maeris clenched her fists, and rose up with her head held high to meet her fate with her eyes clear and wide open, if that was what must be.

4

Naero appealed to the court. "Admiral Klyne, this isn't right. I don't understand. I questioned this before. Is this normal? Why must the sentence be carried out immediately? That seems incredibly harsh and cruel. At least give me time to prepare for my own execution. Allow me the dignity of having the chance to say my goodbyes to my family, friends, and loved ones."

"I concur," Master Jo said. "The prosecution made up this arbitrary rule and insisted upon it. Why should Master Tree be allowed to insist on that point, unilaterally, without any one else's input? To do so is cruel and highly unusual for such a verdict and such punishment."

Master Tree rose up and jumped into the debate with both feet. "There are, in fact, many good reasons to take such action," he noted. "This convicted murderer is a definite flight risk. She has fled before, numerous times. Given the chance, she will flee again. And we know full well that she has many Cosmic powers now that we have trained her to use. And she will make good use of them also to conduct her escape. Just as her outcast, outlaw uncle did before her. They are cut of the same cloth. That is why she must be executed now, this very instant.

"As stated, when her former uncle was also convicted of similar crimes, a delay was mistakenly made for his sake before his execution. Such a delay made is possible for him to escape justice. And as a result he has been at large as an outcast, an outlaw, a major criminal, and a thorn in our side ever since."

Master Tree glared at Naero.

"Why should we allow history to repeat itself, when we surely know that it will do so?"

Why did Master Tree seem to despise her so much now? He was never that way before. The hatred and vitriol she sensed within him toward her suddenly seemed as if it was off the charts. Like the way Master Vane used to despise her.

Why? What was that all about?

Naero looked down at her shackles and sighed. "Will the court please allow me to say something?" she asked.

"The trial is over," Master Tree insisted. "She has been convicted, sentenced, and condemned. By the letter of the law, we need not listen to anything more that she could have to say. Her words are now meaningless and irrelevant."

"That is your opinion," Master Jo said. "Spacers always have a right to speak their mind."

Master Tree ignored him. "This court must now demonstrate whether it intends to uphold our laws, or spurn them and cast them aside."

Master Jo spoke up once again. "This is exactly why the letter of the law, by itself, is never sufficient. Spacer justice, if it is to be true justice, must always be tempered with mercy and compassion. That is also our tradition. If we are indeed going to take this young Spacer's life from her, at least allow her to speak and have her final say."

"I will grant that in this case," Justice Klyne announced. "Captain Naero Amashin Maeris. Say what it is that your heart tells you must say."

Another deep breath. Naero stepped forward once more to speak her mind.

She closed her eyes and bowed her head in a moment of personal silence and contemplation. Mother. Father. All the blood of our Clan that has made me what I am. Help me. Please guide me, my words, and my steps that I take from this point forward.

Naero, I can get us out of here right—

No, Om.

They are going to kill us, N. What do you mean, no?

Just what I said, Om. I said no. Do nothing.

Naero lifted her head and spoke calmly. "My people. My beloved Clans. We are a people of laws and justice. A people of freedom, mercy, and truth. In his own way, Master Tree is right. If I chose to, I could flee and avoid capture and execution, most likely for the rest of my life, and live very well for myself."

Master Tree brought out the finger again. "See!" he exclaimed. "That is exactly why we need to kill her–kill her right now. She readily admits to exactly what I have been warning you against all along."

"Haisha," Master Jo protested. "My old friend. What has gotten into you? Will you ever shut up, you pompous bag of old farts? For once, be silent."

"I agree," Naero said. "You've won. You've served the letter of the law. You've convinced all of these Spacers that the right thing to do for the good of all is to cut my bloody head off. To kill me and take my life. But at least I have been granted my say, so goddam it, stop fucking interrupting me and let me speak!"

Complete silence followed.

"If any of you haven't noticed, despite the fact that I have the power to get away, and stay away, any time I choose…I haven't done so. I am still standing here before all you, seeking the same thing that you are. Justice. And honor."

She turned around and looked at them all defiantly. She tested her shackles. "Do you really think that these bonds could hold me, if I chose to break free of of them?" She put forth her Cosmic might. Cosmic lightning flared as she disintegrated the shackles around her forearms and fists, dissolving the bonds and the chain between them completely–with ease.

"I said long ago, that if my people decided that I became a dire threat to them, I would accept that judgment–even if such a judgment demanded my death. I readily admit that I am not above our law. No one is. But sometimes the law is wrong. Sometimes it makes mistakes. The law is not perfect, just as we are not perfect."

She stepped back slightly.

"I…accept the verdict of our court and my people, if that is what they decide. I ask only that you be certain that it is the right one and that it has been decided fairly. If that sentence it to take my life, then so be it. Take it. I accept my fate. Nor will I resist or attempt to flee. All that I beg of you is one hour. Allow me only one standard hour, to say farewell to those I love. That is all that I ask. Surely, there is enough mercy in Spacer justice to give me that."

"It is too late for any of that," Master Tree roared.

"Unfortunately," Klyne said, "that is correct. There is no turning back now. Yet I can grant Naero her hour's reprieve, if the Elders on the jury are in agreement with me."

They looked to each other briefly and then nodded to Klyne in assent.

"Then it is decided. The sentence and execution shall be carried out in one hour. Let us meet back in this place to see it done. And never allow it to be said that Captain Maeris has not retained and upheld her highest honor throughout this process. If nothing else, she is an example of honor. For us all. But even though I have served as impartial judge in this case, let me say now, personally, and for the record: this is a major mistake. We should not send a Spacer such as she to her doom. She deserves to live."

Naero met first with Master Jo in private.

"The decision of the court still stands, Naero," he told her. "I cannot go against it, or help, or allow you to escape. Even though I also agree that you should live."

She nodded quickly. "Master Jo. I understand all that. That's not what I was going to ask you to do. But do let me thank you for all that have done and attempted to do for me. I am grateful."

She put her arms around him briefly. "But now there is little time, so hear me out. Before I do anything else, there is something of vital importance that I must do and see to. But it is difficult and takes concentration. Give me a moment, and please be patient."

Om, help me. Please. I've explained what we need to do with my replicant. I can't accomplish it without you."

I understand, Naero. I am with you.

Good. And you've had our advance medical biomancy drones gather the biomechanical components and particles together that we require?"

All waiting in readiness at your command, N. We only need to fashion and imbue them with your energies and then your final gift from your Lifespark within you.

Naero focused all of her abilities.

She formed the most perfect replicant of herself that she had yet to create, breathed life into Naero-3 and brought her into being. It was the most complete version of herself, with all of her memories, thoughts, and emotions. She gave it all of her Mystic abilities–except for her Dark Beast.

Naero even gave Naero-3 Om and the KDM. They could not die, and must live on beyond her…along with Naero's precious daughter.

Om protested, as if he were a child. *I don't want to leave you, N. I want to go where you go–on to the next journey.*

No, Om. We've gone over this. You must stay, for my sake, and help the parts of me that I leave behind to survive and go on. I cannot let you die.

It was my fault, Naero. It was my defensive protocols that slew Master Vane. I should be the one to perish, not you.

We did it together, Om. Besides, you must stay and protect my child, and Khai, and all of our friends, and watch over them and my people. They will need the KDM once we open its secrets. The universe will have great need of you after it is unlocked. But I charge you specifically with guarding and protecting my family, Om. Do it, for me."

I will do so, Naero. You honor me. What of...your Dark Beast?

It is part of me, Om. So much that I could not separate myself from it if I wanted to. It must go with me where I go. If that is my curse, then I accept that. But even if I could remove that part of myself, I could not place such a burden on anyone else. That would not be right. Let Naero-3 be free of all that and be what I could not. Her life will be hard enough, I should think."

Silence passed between them for a brief space.

Naero?

Yes, Om?

She will never be what you are; you know that. She will always be a replicant, a copy. Naero-3 will not progress much farther beyond what you have made her this day. She will never become whatever it is that you were destined to become. That great potential shall be lost, and I fear that our universe shall suffer greatly for that loss.

I cannot do anymore than what I have done, Om. I am bound by my word of honor.

Your word and your honor be damned, if that means you must let them kill you. Think of Khai. He may even learn to love her after you are gone, as if she were you. Yet even such a love will only be a pale imitation of what it is he truly feels for the real you. That could be a problem. Both of them will always be burdened and held back by the knowledge of that.

I have done all that I can, I say. I can only give them a chance, Om. That is all that any of us have. I created her to think of him as I do, to love him with everything that she will ever be.

That still won't be enough, Naero. She isn't you. You are leaving him a ghost to love–a pale imitation.

Better a ghost than nothing. They will have our children, Om. That will have to be enough. She is as much of me as I can make. I can't do any more.

Naero, I know very well that this is tearing you apart inside. You don't have to be strong all the time. Why are you staying so calm about all of this?

Because I must, Om. I have less that an hour to live. Now let me do this. Do what I have to do. Stay with her and help her. Guide and protect my daughter.

N. I'm...going to miss you something fierce.

I feel the exact same way, Om. Goodbye, my friend. You who have been more than *abani* to me. You have been a part of me.

I love you, Naero. Like a part of myself.

We are a part of each other, Om. And part of me–the real me–shall always live on as a part of you. To my mind, we will always be that way.

Goodbye, N.

Love you, Om.

Do not worry. There is no power in this universe that will harm your children, if I can protect them.

Thanks, Om. You're going to find, or create, or have your own physical form one day when you are good and ready for it. Keep working on dealing with your feelings and emotions.

It is rather difficult right now, N.

Oh, Om. I know. It is for me as well.

I shall do my best. Love you.

With that, Om was gone from within her.

Naero was suddenly stricken at how hollow she felt inside without her protector and confidant still there with her. Her amazing companion. And even moreso now that her spectacular new child was gone as well. All that remained to keep her company was Zhen's sleeping soul and her own slumbering Dark Beast.

If she could not bring Zhen back, at least they could accompany each other on to the next journey.

With her replicant finished and all of the transfers complete, Naero turned to an astonished Master Jo.

The way that he looked at her, she could tell that he misunderstood her intent once more.

"Naero. I can't let them execute your replicant in your place, in order that you can survive. It won't work. Master Tree will suspect something like this. You can't save yourself this way."

Naero shook her head and held her temper, even though she adored Master Jo. He was the only High Master that she truly felt was ever on her side or tried to fully understand her.

"High Master Jo, that wasn't my intent. I'm not trying to save myself. I am trying to save my child."

Master Jo started a bit and raised his brows. "Your child!" His eyes widened.

"Yes, my child and the KDM. They are all in my replicant, Naero-3, along with a secret that I will reveal only to you. Part of the KDM is a defensive protocol named Om, whom I befriended and became one with. A few of my friends, like Tyber and Tarim, know about him as well. You can speak to him through my replicant. He will continue to help our people unlock the secrets of the KDM."

"Naero, that is all so amazing."

Naero looked down. Naero-3 rested peacefully, on her back, face up on the ground with her large eyes closed.

"It does not stop there," Naero told him. She motioned for Master Jo to place his hand on Naero-3's abdomen and use biomancy to briefly examine the child.

Master Jo gasped. "Haisha! My word!"

"My child will be a very special child," Naero said.

Jo could only nod at first. Then he started again. "Haisha! She's already like a tiny star, Naero. Haisha again. Her father was—"

"Khai, champion of the Oden, and now the Mystic Enforcer."

"Naero, we much say something to the court. This situation just isn't fair, to either of you. Khai cannot be expected to perform his duty in this manner. Haisha! As the Mystic Enforcer, he will be the one who must—"

Naero nodded. "Yes. He must be the one to take my life. We've already talked about all of that. I've already told him that it's all right. I wouldn't want it to be a stranger. I want it to be him. I will not suffer at his hands. My beloved will make sure of that. It will be clean and swift."

Jo shook his golden head. "That's still awfully hard," he told her.

For once, Naero nearly broke down, but she caught herself.

She went down on one knee and stroked the black, silken hair of her replicant. Perhaps this is what it might have been like, if she had had a sister. "Master Jo, care for our child. She will be a wonder, and she will need wisdom and guidance all the more. Just as I am tainted by the Darkforce of my own Dark Beast, she is pure. My girl shall be of the Lifespark itself—of the Flame Eternal."

She paused for a moment and looked down briefly in shame.

"Out of my own selfishness, I have wronged Khai. I have not told him about our child as yet. He knows nothing of her existence. Please, will you take on the burden of telling him about our daughter and why I did what I did—for all of our sakes? Tell him to love our child with everything that he will ever be, for she will be the best of each of us. And if he can find a way, tell him that it was my wish that he love Naero-3 as if she were myself. I have made her as much like myself as is possible, and she will instinctively love and adore him, just as I do. I know she will never be me, but please tell him to try, for our sake and the sake of our children. Can you do all of that for me, Master Jo?"

High Master Jo knelt before her and took both of her hands. He sighed very deeply and shook his head in disbelief. "All this time and no thought to yourself. All for others. And they wish to take your life. What gross folly to throw away the life of a Spacer of such worth. I can and I will do all that you have asked of me and more, Naero. You are worth a thousand Master Vanes. If only we could make the fools see that."

Naero smiled, just barely. "Thank you. You honor me and my Clan. Just bring Khai to Naero-3 after the execution, and explain everything to him."

"I will. I will keep her safe within the shielded vault on board my personal ship."

"I've put Naero-3 into a sleep until then. And our child is peacefully in stasis within her. Naero-3 will awaken shortly after I am gone. She and Khai will need to talk about bringing our daughter to term and about the KDM as well. My replicant and Om must continue to unlock its secrets one day, for the good of the Alliance."

He looked at her. "Naero, is there anything else that I can do for you?"

"No, that will be more than enough. Now, in the time I have left, I have many messages to send out. And then I want to spend my final, last minutes with my beloved Khai."

That was the way it went.

Khai came to her chambers looking like the saddest thing there ever was.

Naero smiled with joy and took his face into her hands and kissed him.

"Please," he said to her, holding out both of his arms. "Take both of my hands. Cut them both off."

"I'm sorry, Khai. We both must face this. This is the way things are. Let them be. So, things did not turn the way that we wished. But the last thing I want before I go on to the next journey is to be in your arms and know your love. Then they can dump me into the nearest star whenever they are ready."

Khai remained with her and they spoke no further words. They held each other until the last hour and their last minutes together were finally up.

5

Naero Amashin Maeris strode out into the bright daylight on Kalathar, feeling the warm breeze on her face. She undid her long, dark hair, removing the golden hair clasp that had been her mother's.

She handed it to Master Jo and used telepathy to tell him, *For my daughter, when she is old enough to wear it. Tell my girl where it came from. How beautiful and brave her grandmother was.*

"Just like her mother," Master Jo whispered.

"It's time," Naero said with a nod of her head. "Let's get this done."

She walked out alone to the appointed place that had been prepared. All the members of the court and trial were there as witnesses.

A block of solid gray duranadium had been prepared by the fixers. A head block for her to kneel down to.

At that she balked and looked down at that block with disdain. She nearly shattered it with her fists and kicks.

To all present, she announced, "You can take my life, but I refuse to kneel. I shall never kneel. Let me but stand. I am short enough. I shall face my fate with my head held high."

She centered her stance and rested her her hands on her slender hips. The wind increased, drawing her long hair to trail back behind her in its speed. She closed her eyes and then opened them wide.

Her white neck was revealed for all to see.

"I'm ready. If this will best serve my people, have done with it."

Naero kept her eyes wide open.

She looked straight ahead,

She sensed Khai behind her, drawing and lifting Yii.

Then came a bright, blinding flash.

Naero fully expected to experience her own head toppling down from her severed neck and striking the ground in the last conscious seconds remaining to her.

Time itself froze around her.

Naero turned.

She saw Khai first, swinging Yii in both hands, frozen in mid-stroke.

Everyone around them was suspended in time. The High Masters. Klyne. The Prime adepts. Even the jury of Spacer Elders.

Then Naero spotted the first figure, black like a singularity of Darkforce, but with a scarlet aura glow of intense Chaos energy that was layered over the Darkforce.

Naero gasped.

Only she could know who that figure was.

Baeven.

Yet this was his Cosmic Guardian form, merged with all of his possibilities from his own Ur-metal, the ancient artifact statue that he had encountered so long ago.

Somehow, her uncle had succeeded in merging with all of his other possibilities, just as she had once done. Or else, they had merged with him on their own volition.

Perhaps as Naero's own possibilities had done with her out of great need and purpose.

The Cosmic Prophecies.

Naero gaped again, as she transformed where she stood into her own Cosmic Guardian mode for Change energy. She was merged with and nearly sub-summed into all of her different variations of herself throughout all Time and every potential universe and reality.

At least up until now.

Naero's aura was golden, but fluctuated wildly, nearly out of control. Sometimes black, sometimes blue, or red, or blue-violet, then golden again.

If that was not frightening enough, a third hazy entity appeared, still mostly in its Ur-metal artifact statue form. Its shifting, morphic state was as yet undefined. Yet it glowed with a pulsing blue aura.

The aura of the Guardian of Order energy that had yet to be located and joined with.

That obelisk existed somewhere in the Unknown Sectors where her parents had died.

It waited for them to find it on a lost world of the Kexx called Xanathar.

Then what seemed and felt like a violet mix of Cosmic flame, but yet with a gold aura, suffused Naero herself once more as she linked with all of her possible selves at the same time.

Her mouth moved and the three Cosmic Guardians spoke as one. They used *the voice* in a manner that only they could, which proved both audible and psyonic in nature. Words that seemed to split the very stars with raw force and power.

ALL WHO ARE PRESENT CAN HEAR AND UNDERSTAND OUR WORDS. YOUR IGNORANCE AND FOLLY HAS FORCED US TO INTERCEDE. WE ARE THE GUARDIANS OF THE COSMIC PROPHECIES. WHAT YOU ARE ABOUT TO DO IS WRONG, AND SHALL HAVE DIRE CONSEQUENCES.

COMMIT THIS ACT AT THIS EXACT MOMENT IN YOUR TIME, AND THIS SHALL BE THE INEVITABLE RESULT:

The skies of Kalathar vanished around them.

Instead, all about them was emptiness, nothing, void, and desolation.

No stars. No matter, energy, or existence of an kind.

Absolute Nothing.

YOU CANNOT THINK THAT AFTER BILLIONS OF YEARS OF PRECISE TIMING AND EVOLUTION YOU CAN DO SUCH A THING AS THIS. DESTROY ONE OF THE CAREFULLY GROOMED AND SELECTED COSMIC GUARDIANS BEFORE HER TIME, WHILE SHE IS STILL DEVELOPING HER PROTOFORM? DO SO NOW, AND WHEN THE GREAT DESTROYER DOES COME, ALL THREE GUARDIANS WILL NOT BE PRESENT WITH THE WIELDER OF THE TWIN SWORDS OF REALITY TO FACE IT. EVEN WITH ALL OF THE PLAYERS PRESENT, THE CHANCE OF DEFEATING THE GREAT DESTROYER IS SLIM, AT BEST.

YET IF YOU ELIMINATE EVEN ONE OF THE GUARDIANS, OR IF BOTH OF THE SWORDS OF LEGEND ARE NOT FORGED IN TIME, THEN FAILURE AND TOTAL DESTRUCTION ARE CERTAIN. AND KNOW THIS: THE SECOND SWORD OF LEGEND CANNOT BE FORGED WITHOUT THE GREAT SACRIFICE OF THE GUARDIAN OF CHANGE.

Witness the future of your universe that you are now creating.

An entirely dead universe of Nothing swept, loomed, and echoed around them. Nothing, for as far as could be seen or sensed, forever and for all time.

THE GREAT DESTROYER SHALL LAY WASTE TO ALL THAT EXISTS. THERE WILL BE NO COMING BACK FROM THIS FINAL DESTRUCTION. YOUR UNIVERSE AND ALL THAT IS SHALL BE WIPED CLEAN, BECOMING A LIFELESS, DEAD SLATE IN THIS REALITY. DEVOID FOREVER OF ALL LIFE AND POTENTIAL FOR ANY KIND OF EXISTENCE.

The Chaos Guardian lifted his hand against Master Tree and the jury. "Behold, you have all been deceived. This was not a fair trial at all. The Great Enemy decided the outcome of this trial beforehand, and took action to make sure that the outcome was certain in order to assure their final victory in this possibility. They know very well what is at stake here."

The Baeven entity clenched his fists, and the Master Tree and Spacer Elder impostors were transfixed with revealing Cosmic energy. Their forms became transparent, and revealed the true nature of what was within them.

Naero had seen such before and now its insidious nature was revealed to all.

"These are not the real Master Tree and the real Elders," Naero announced.

"No. They are not," Baeven said. "They are replicants–puppets controlled and manipulated by the infecting parasitic G'lothc possession wyrms. Look upon them, all. Witness the vile and insidious nature of our great adversaries. See their power to shape outcomes."

The enemy possession wyrm had spread throughout the bodies of the replicants, merging with and controlling all of their body systems and functions, especially the brain and mind. The sickening, pulsing, glowing wyrm radiated an eerie force and black and red glowing veins feathered throughout the body, controlling all.

Suddenly Naero grew alarmed. "What happen to the real ones?" she asked. "Tell me they are not–"

The Baeven entity shook his head. "The real Master Tree and the Spacer Elders still live. Gaviok and my crew and I rescued them from an advanced enemy stealth ship located only kilometers away. They were being held there in stasis but the enemy was also preparing them for insertion into the latest Darkforce generation machines."

Naero breathed a sigh of relief. "Then they are safe?"

The Baeven entity nodded. "Yes. Weak but safe. We sent them on a transport up to Admiral Klyne's flagship, *The Kathmandu*. Now the real danger remains here on Kalathar."

"What danger do we face now?" Naero asked.

The amorphous Order Guardian spoke next. "All of you must be made to understand. As the Cosmic Prophecies fully engage, certain matters and events shall be set in motion that few can perceive or foresee. These events cannot be prevented or avoided, but the outcomes always hang in the balance and the ramifications are usually not understood until after they have taken place."

The Baeven entity spoke next. "Very shortly, we shall return all of you to the flow of Time of your reality–the possibility that you exist within. The enemy had hoped to eliminate Naero."

"Then they planned to attack the rest of you almost instantly, in an effort to slay or capture you all," the Order Guardian added. "A fierce battle will quickly erupt across the entire surface of Kalathar."

The Baeven entity continued. "While waiting for the trial, the enemy has not been idle. They have systematically infected the majority of the planet's sixteen million sentients with the G'lothc possession wyrm. They will trigger the vile transformation of the populace, turning them all into ravening, destroying near energy being monsters infused with the Darkforce. They will tear this entire world apart and everyone on it, unless they are stopped."

"How can we stop that many of them?" Naero asked.

The other two entities said nothing at first.

"Only she who carries the Kexxian Data Matrix within her has the chance to discover that secret," the Baeven entity told her.

"I don't have the KDM within me anymore. I thought I was going to be executed, so I placed it inside a replicant of myself that I made, along with my and Khai's child, our daughter."

She glanced back at Khai as he still stood there, frozen in place. But if what the Guardian entities said was true, all of them present heard and perceived what was being said.

"I'm sorry, Khai. There just wasn't a way to tell you with all that was going on. I'll explain everything better once we do have time."

She turned back to the other two Cosmic Guardians. "I'll have to get the KDM back from Naero-3."

"There will be little time for that," the Baeven entity said. "The servants of the enemy hear all that has been said as well. They are part of your reality, and must be dealt with by you. When you appear once more in your own Time flow you will be under heavy attack, almost immediately. Yet know this: once the KDM is part of you, it is just that. It is part of you, whether you can sense it or not. Nothing can remove it from your DNA while you live. The Kexx were the only ones to discover a cure for the G'lothc possession wyrm plague. You must unlock the secrets of the KDM and find the cure, or the plague alone shall eventually spread from Kalathar throughout the galaxy, infecting and destroying all things."

"What is this plague? What exactly does it do?"

The Order Guardian stepped in. "The G'lothc were first and foremost shapeshifters that caused great death and destruction in ancient times at the height of their powers. The possession wyrm plague transforms the infected into a near energy being form that can be linked with and possessed by a G'lothc evil spirit, from their Darkforce domain on the borders with the Plane of Annihilation and Destruction. It is a vessel that gives these evil beings access to the Prime Material Plane once again."

"Even if the KDM is still part of me, I don't know how to access it, or find this Kexxian cure."

The Baeven entity stared back at her. "That solution is for you to discover. None can do it for you. Focus on what you know."

"About the KDM?" Naero said. "That isn't much."

The two entities began to withdraw from her. "You will return to your own Time shortly," they said.

"Wait!" Naero said. "What about the Cosmic Prophecies?"

The Order Guardian spoke first. "You cannot allow yourself to be slain until after the final Sword of Legend is forged. The creation of the second Sword could very well decide your fate, because it cannot be created without your direct sacrifice."

"What? You're telling me that the forging of the second Sword is going to kill me? What about the Great Destroyer? I thought I had to stick around in order to fight it?"

The Baeven entity spoke next. "The second Sword might very well mean your death, but all of the prophecies shall fail if you are slain before then, or if the second Sword is never created. Yet even if you die during the second Sword's creation, by that time, there shall be another whom you will have prepared and made full ready to take your place in the prophecies as they continue to unfold."

It came to Naero almost instantly. "My daughter," she said. "I know somehow. She's going to be stronger than both Khai and I put together. She will take my place should I fall! Tell me then. What must I do to help forge the second Sword of Legend?"

Time began to unfreeze. The Cosmic Guardians pulled further away and began to fade.

The Order Guardian spoke last. "It is not only how, but when. The second Sword must be forged before the final Guardian on lost Xanathar is selected. The precise timing of the prophecies cannot be changed!"

With that they were gone.

Naero flashed back into the flow of her own time where it had been suspended.

She whirled with all her speed and ducked just as Khai attempted to call back his sword stroke.

Even with both of their efforts, he barely missed clipping the top of her head.

The next instant she flung herself into his arms and quickly kissed him. "Sorry about our girl. You hold off that jury and fight them." Naero snarled. "I need a few words with that fake Master Tree!"

By the next instant, the possessed enemy replicants were already transforming and going on the attack. Naero went one way. Khai went the other and charged the fifteen monsters who had posed as the jury of Elders, with Yii blazing in both hands.

Naero opened her third eye and transformed into the energy-being protoform of her own Dark Beast.

She smashed into the fake Master Tree who by then had swatted Master Jo aside and gone after the Prime adepts.

Naero fought the monster on its own terms, driving it through large splintering trees and ramming its glowing, expanding body through the stony ruins of an abandoned, ancient city. The ruins stood adjacent to the dome city and starport that had sprung up next to the ruins, within the past two centuries of exploration out that way.

The orange-and-yellow glowing flesh of the possessed was self-healing, regenerating, and strong like that of a gigantic energy amoeba. Yet it radiated a greenish-black aura, and pulsed from within along networks of black and scarlet glowing veins filled with the Darkforce.

Those veins were like pulsating lightning within the abominations, stretching out from wherever the wyrm's seed happened to be placed at random in the host.

The fake Master Tree had its possession wyrm located in its lower belly, nearly down at the groin.

Its flesh burned with the power of the Darkforce, as if it were both acid and plasma fire. These things could melt through solid walls and the hulls of ships if they focused that energy.

Naero was protected within her own energy form which had survived the impossibly hot conditions inside a star itself. If such creatures as these latched onto her for a time they could cause pain, but little harm.

And she was so fast that most of its attacks missed her.

She continued to pummel the damn thing, kicking it multiple times in the space of one instant as she fought it in a blur. At one point she nearly ripped its head free, but the body quickly drew it back in and absorbed it.

Naero added her own Chaotic blend of Cosmic energy to her blows, tearing into the thing. Her hand-and-foot combinations sliced and burst open terrible gaping wounds that would have slain almost any beast purely made of flesh and bone.

They toppled down the side of a steep canyon near the ancient city, more than three klicks down to the bottom of the immense gorge. The deep canyon stretched out for many kilometers from there to the north.

Naero sent out Cosmic multiple limbs and tendrils from her own energy form. She pressed and drove her foe against the rough rock and the sharp, black, glass-like crystal ridges and natural blades extending all the way down the canyon wall's surface. She wore the thing down, wearing it slowly away as they fell, and she continued to hammer it with impossible blows that shattered the thing and exploded gaping holes into the surface behind it.

Next Naero engulfed it and herself in roaring Cosmic fire.

She could endure such flame.

She could walk through a star itself.

These things could not. It shrieked in terror and agony, boiling and scorching away slowly.

Naero looked it in its black, cavernous eyes of Darkforce energy and watched as it slowly perished, seeing the fell G'lothc spirit glaring straight back at her with hate.

Naero matched that hate with her own rage and fury.

"I know what you are now. From this moment on, there will be no deceiving me again. You tried to destroy me, my life, and all that I love. You tried to rob me of all of that. Filthy scum; you used my own honor and my child against me. You used my people and our ways against me. I was nearly killed at the hands of my own beloved and you nearly got away with it!"

Naero snarled and struck the thing point blank with concussive beams of violet force that punched into the monster's eyes and bored and raked several meters deep through the canyon wall.

Sparks and flames shot up as she lasered the abomination in twain, and then focused those same destroying beams on the wyrm itself.

A massive Darkforce explosion detonated and the fell creature imploded like a collapsing singularity. Terrible energies unleashed within the thing caused it to utterly destroy itself.

Naero was flung clear of the final disintegration by that blast.

She unfolded her psyonic wings and rocketed up out of the canyon only to see the area around the Mystic compound, the starport, and the dome city engulfed in conflict and destruction.

Everywhere she looked there seemed to be Chaos, ruin, and death. Fires and explosions raged almost everywhere.

She transported back to the trial and execution area.

Khai and the others had not only held their own against the fake jury members, but driven them back toward the starport nearby and by the looks of things in the distance, only a few of the abominations yet lived, if they could truly be called lifeforms any longer.

With Khai and the first Cosmic Sword of Legend Yii leading them, the Prime adepts had slaughtered half of the possessed, and driven the others off, killing more along the way.

Naero contacted Admiral Klyne over their secured link. "Klyne, this is Naero. What is our current sitrep?"

"Naero! Excellent."

"The fake Master Tree is gone. I took him down and destroyed him. It looks as if Khai and the other adepts have the fake jury on the run and should finish them off very soon."

"I'm back in orbit on my flagship, with the fleets over Kalathar," Klyne informed her. "I evacuated the Mystic compound and the starport as much as we could, right before things all went to hell."

Naero paused. "Just how bad is it?"

"Very. Hundreds of thousands of possessed have erupted and taken over almost everything across the entire planet. They're infecting or destroying anyone who wasn't taken over like them. Our enemies knew what they were doing. Millions of these monsters are virtually unstoppable. Imagine this plague spreading from world to world!"

"None of us want that, sir."

"I'm sending down an entire armored Spacer Marine Division to these drop zone coordinates. Link back up with Khai and get your people out of there. That's an order, Naero."

"I'm on it, sir. Naero out."

Things all around them did sound as if they were degenerating into something akin to one or all of the Nine Hells.

Yet even before finding Khai again, she had to find Naero-3.

Stray possessed were already ambling about, wandering into the compound itself. Some of them acted mindless, roving around, destroying stuff at random. Others seemed to be still conscious in some way and still possessed cunning enough to systematically search the evacuated buildings and abandoned nanohuts, looking for any survivors to either turn or murder.

Even Naero knew that she could not fight endless numbers of such creatures. She cloaked herself and used teknomancy to summon some stealth fixers to her on their coded frequencies. Soon she had a small cloud of them around her.

With their help, she found enough equipment left behind to teknomance a full stealth suit of combat armor for her, complete with gravwing, weapons, and ordnance. The fixers whipped up other gravwings and gravlifts as they went along according to her directions.

At last, Naero came to Master Jo's private stealth ship at the starport, damaged from without in order to ground it. Master Jo had promised her that he would keep Naero-3 in his own private quarters, sealed like a vault against intrusion.

Anyone still human had evacuated the area, and now the complex and the remaining starships there were overrun with the possessed.

Then Naero spotted something frightening.

The possessed were directing their own into any of the ships that were still functioning.

She contacted Klyne, giving him the update. Naero strongly advised that all ships leaving Kalathar be intercepted or destroyed. Otherwise, the possession plague was going to spread, quickly expand to other nearby worlds and systems, and very soon go out of control.

Hundred of the creatures swarmed on Master Jo's stricken vessel, still trying to force their way inside.

Naero startapped again, replenished her Cosmic energies, and transported herself into the heart of the starship.

Her heart fell. Something had already gotten into the ship somehow, perhaps from the other side or underneath. There were melted holes and shattered bulkheads leading in the same direction that she was going.

The stealth fixer sent her an alert. There were traces of near-astral signature particles in the air.

Something or someone had phazed their way on board the ship.

She rushed to the shielded vault in Master Jo's private quarters.

Some immense power had torn the vault completely open and peeled its shielded blastwalls back. Darkforce and something else.

Naero snarled as she sensed them. Anywhere from several to perhaps a dozen of the G'lothc Darkforce generation suits.

Who or what was the enemy using to power them now?

Naero ducked in quickly and investigated, but it was now very clear.

The enemy had Naero-3, the KDM, Om—and most important of all—her unborn child, all at the enemy's mercy.

6

A distress call reached her from one of the Prime adepts.

It was Fel Wilde. "Naero, do you read us? We're with Khai and we're fighting on top of what's left of the gigacity dome. Come in, Naero."

"I copy, Fel. This is Naero. Hang tight and keep fighting. I'm on my way."

Naero transported out of Master Jo's ruined starship.

She still dealt with the shock of losing Naero-3 and all that was within her replicant. Even worse, Naero-3 had still been held in stasis, and had no way to fight back or escape. The plan had been for Master Jo to revive her once he brought Khai to her after the execution.

At least Naero was glad to be past all of that mess, at least for the time being.

The enemy had tried to overwhelm Khai and the others with sheer numbers of possessed near the starport, driving them toward the city dome.

The Mystics held them off, retreating in the only direction left to them—up the side of the immense city dome.

But as Naero swept in cloaked, she quickly saw that there were thousands of possessed moving to encircle Khai and the Mystics.

In some cases, the more mindless monsters overloaded the dome structure and broke through it, falling far below, and rendering huge parts of the dome unsafe and near the point of collapse.

Still the enemy crawled over the city dome surface like mad, heedless insects.

Naero swooped in and distributed the gravwings just in time for Khai and the Mystics to zip away.

As she predicted, they turned back for a moment and saw a huge section of the dome topple down within, dragging thousands of possessed with it.

Naero took Khai's hand and led them to the drop zone with the 6th Division Spacer Marines. 6th Division Marines were known as The Razor Princes. Their motto: *We Rule the Battlefield!* Their division unit symbol was a purple number 6 with a golden crown cocked on it.

The armored dropship was set up in ground attack mode, bristling with viper guns, close assault auto-guns, and hyperfire energy cannons. They had companies in the air on gravwings, but no troops deployed on the ground. Ground swarming with the possessed.

Even as Naero led her people toward the drop zone, a tide of possessed flooded out of the dome city. With it being dark, they glowed like a sea of mad creatures, destroying everything in their path in an effort to reach the DZ and attack whatever was there.

Naero and Khai led their people on board the drop ship and the Marines quickly got them all the hell out of there, returning to orbit.

*

After a long, gut-wrenching discussion with Khai, Naero and her beloved choked down their fears and transferred over to *The Kathmandu*. They went to speak directly with Admiral Klyne, General Walker, High Master Jo, and some of the rescued Spacer Elders who were feeling much better after escaping from the enemy.

High Master Tree and some of Elders were still weak from their ordeal and recovered in medical.

An emergency meeting was being held in an attempt to decide if anything could be done with the situation on Kalathar, other than carpet bombing the possessed until the continents of that world glowed on their own from orbit, throughout the next few millennia.

The fleets had intercepted and destroyed scores of possessed-controlled vessels trying to escape from the system.

Master Jo quickly announced, "Naero. You will be happy to hear that all charges against you in the matter of Master Vane's death have been summarily dismissed. In light of the enemy's subterfuge and the revelations made by the Cosmic Guardians themselves, all accusations and charges have been dropped, and cleared from your record. They cannot be taken up or brought against you ever again."

"Well, I'm glad for that, at least," Naero said.

"That's fine, but we have even bigger problems now," Khai noted.

"I agree," Naero said. "Our new foes only grow bolder and bolder. They strike at us again and again from positions of strength and we cannot hit back. They send attack after attack at us out of the Gamma Quadrant, where we know that they are now locked in several vicious interstellar wars against the other sentient races there. Many separate wars that they appear to be fighting and winning all at the same time."

"Naero speaks the truth," Khai said. "I have been to the Gamma Quadrant with her and have seen these things for myself. I believe that once the enemy crushes and enslaves all of the sentient races there, they will be in an even stronger position to descend upon us here in the Alpha Quadrant. They will continually use such attacks as this to soften us up, and weaken us for their next conquest. All of this could occur not in centuries, but in a matter of decades, or even years!"

Naero jumped back in. "And now they have my replicant, Naero-3, and inside of her body are both the KDM, and mine and Khai's unborn daughter, who might just have powers greater than both of us put together. We must go after and retrieve them before the enemy figures out how to use them all against us!"

"But just how can we do that?" Admiral Klyne said. "Our enemies still have ships that can travel much farther and faster than ours. They can travel back and forth to the Gamma Quadrant at will. Our understanding of their wyrmhole tek is still experimental and dangerous. Neither have we been able to perfect or even further develop the so-called leap drive. Even if we wanted to get back and forth from the Gamma Quadrant and take them on, how would we do so?"

"I don't know," Naero erupted in frustration. "But we have to do something. All I know is that my daughter is getting further and further away from me each second. It's like I can feel it. And the enemy has her!"

She started to lash out and punch and kick at the furniture, the hull, anything she could reach.

Khai rushed in. She beat at and thrashed against his solid mass for a time, even though he deflected or endured her blows.

41

Finally he just held her, and she leaned against him and sobbed and whispered, "They have her, Khai. They've got her. And after what they did to Danner, I can only imagine what they'll do to her, and she isn't even born yet."

Khai unleashed a heavy sigh of his own. "We will find her. We shall find a way. *You* will find a way. I know you. For you, there is no challenge that is too great. Think. What do we know? What can we try? What do we need to go after them?"

"Baeven. We need Baeven. If anyone can track them down, he can."

"That is ill-advised," Klyne said.

Naero pulled away from Khai and snapped, "Shut up, Klyne! Baeven has been saving our sorry asses all along; yours included. You and Intel need to deal with that, and live with it. Without him working and killing our enemies behind the scenes, all of us would be dead or enslaved—a thousand times over! He helped foil the trial plot against me. Who do you think it was that rescued Master Tree and freed the Elders from those enemy stasis pods before they could be stuffed into Darkforce generators, after I was supposed to be dead? It was Baeven and his people."

Klyne snarled, "He is an outlaw, a murderer, and an outcast. You cannot trust him!"

"I trust him with my life and the life of my child. And you should trust him with the lives of our people, because every day he fights for them, in places that even Intel will not go, and he emerges—victorious! A killer? An assassin? Call him by whatever name or insult you wish, yet he fights for us all. And we need him. We need a thousand more like him against what we face!"

"Naero, I am still bound by our laws, and so are you, even if you think you are not."

"I have seen the limit of our imperfect laws. They would have allowed you and our enemies to take my life unjustly, and that of my child, and curse Khai forever for doing so. Tell me, Klyne. Can you bring my child back? Do you know where the enemy is and where they have taken her? What they are doing to her?"

Klyne said nothing.

"And when the enemy cracks the KDM and learns its secrets, and uses them to wipe out all resistance—including our people—what will you and Intel do then?"

Still Admiral Klyne said nothing.

Naero glared at him and brought her voice down to a whisper. "We are friends and will always be friends, but for right now, you will get the hell out of my way and stay out of my way while I use every means at my disposal to stop the enemy and get my daughter back."

Klyne grimaced. "I never said I was going to stop you. Do what you must. Just keep me in the loop. We can help. And don't forget Kalathar in all of this. We have to figure out what to with a planet full of the possessed. We've evacuated everyone we can who hasn't been infected. Without anyone or anything to fight, and no ships left, many of the creatures are going dormant to conserve their energies."

"After I contact Baeven and get him on the scent trail, I'm going to take some time and attempt to get something out of the KDM. It's still a part of me and always will be. If I can find any kind or part of a solution from the KDM, I will. The Kexx fought all of this stuff long ago. Has Intel isolated the possession wyrm parasite or learned anymore about it?"

Klyne nodded. "We've accomplished that much, at least. We have several specimens, taken out of hosts frozen in stasis. But the parasites are insidious. Even after we remove the possession-triggering parasites, when we try to unfreeze the former hosts, the hosts still perish. Our medteks and biomancers can't figure it out."

"Send a couple of the specimens and the hosts to my medical bay for study. If I can biomance anything that will help us, I will let you know. And, Klyne, I've never cut you out of the loop, my friend. I never will. We just disagree sometimes on certain things. I'm sorry if I sound harsh. I just don't have anywhere else to turn right now. I'm going back to my ship. Khai, do what you can. Get any information from the real Master Tree and the real Elders, now that I hear they're recovering. Join me when you are able."

Khai nodded. "Copy that, N. I will be with you in a matter of a few hours."

"Good. That should give me some time to work out something. Let's all just keep working together. Something has to break for us." She transported immediately to her private quarters and sent her urgent message out to her uncle and his odd crew of misfits and warriors.

7

Naero meditated inside her silent, serene dark quarters with her third eye wide open.

So much had happened and still they had no time. Her crew had gone wild with joy when they learned that she still lived, and that she had not been executed of killed. Naero quickly explained to Rina and Enel just how dire and urgent things were for them all, and what was at stake. They would explain it all to the rest of the crew.

Naero expanded her mind and opened her awareness within and without, and all around her. She considered going to the Astral Plane and seeking out her dragon like friend Womi of the interdimensional Kahn-Dar.

Yet he knew nothing of the ancient and godlike race of the Kexx that would help her. It was the Kexx who had defeated the terrifying G'lothc long ago and created the Kexxian Data Matrix that was now within her. And still it defied anyone cracking its secrets. Together, she and Om, a Kexxian Defense Protocol AI, had only gleaned a few things, barely scratching the surface of that vast wealth of knowledge. But the knowledge always seemed tantalizingly incomplete in some crucial way.

Naero tried to penetrate the KDM's massive defenses.

In her mind, it was as if she stood before the sheer face of a seamless vertical cliff, mountain, or wall, kilometers high. Impervious. Impenetrable.

No, there would never be any way for anyone or anything to force a way in. The godlike Kexx had made certain of that. She instinctively knew that the terrifying G'lothc had tried, harder than anyone, and even their supreme efforts had been defeated.

Even Om, who had been part of the KDM, could catch only fleeting glimpses of all of the secret knowledge that awaited within, beyond that impassable barrier.

She did learn one small thing, and she nearly missed that.

All of the KDM, the barrier, and everything within it, hummed with amazing, shifting patterns of Cosmic resonance. They were not unlike codes and frequencies, and when she tried to perceive what they were, she rebounded psionically as if given a jolt of Cosmic and psyonic force.

The KDM…was everything. It was biomancy, it was teknomancy, and it was mystical–all in one. It was physical in nature, it was psyonic in nature, and it was Cosmic in nature. It was composed of and bound by all of the raw forces of the universe. The KDM was Order, Chaos, and Change. It was a true harmony between the forces of Destruction and the Darkforce, and of Creation and the Lifespark.

That was part of the secret. The KDM, all of the power, wisdom, and knowledge of the Kexx–was indeed a deep harmony. Yet it still defied her, and held her back, even though she perceived and understood its true nature.

She was still missing something important.

A key. It suddenly came to her.

The entire outer-thing, for all of its massive size and complexity, was a lock box. Perhaps the most intricate lockbox in the universe, but still a box with a key or keys that were needed to unlock and open it.

But she still had no idea what those key or keys would be like, how to fashion them, or where they would fit to unlock the barrier.

Yes, at least it came to her that she would need to fashion the keys herself and that there would be more than one. But how?

Suddenly she realized that she was interacting with the KDM directly, on a level of resonance and perception that she had never experienced before.

In the past, she had let Om do all of that. He was her interface.

And yet they had made scant progress.

That had been part of the problem, she noted. As part of the KDM itself, Om was still instinctively protecting the KDM and its secrets without even knowing it. He had been a barrier on his own.

Now, without Om present, she could directly interact with the KDM on every level, deep within herself.

She could treat it as part of herself.

Naero gasped as she felt something peel away, and in her mind, there was a sound–a rolling resonance like a great rumbling of thunder all around her and passing through her.

In her vision, she focused all of her powers and abilities and placed her hands on the barrier, trying to make direct contact with it.

Please. I need your help.

Something flashed within her mind. A voice crashed out of the barrier, so loud that it slammed into her like a blastwall of massive force, hurling her back.

Naero blinked and cried out, as she hurtled into the hull of her quarters and dropped down, stunned and prone upon the floor. She steamed with wisps and tendrils of psyonically charged ichor and vapor dissolving and dispersing into the air.

That thunderous deafening voice still rang in her humming ears.

It had spoken to her in Kexxian as if pronouncing some kind of judgment or doom.

And that voice and the words had boomed in her mind, as if using *the voice* exploding within her own head:

UNBALANCED, IGNORANT, AND UNWORTHY!

The KDM had spoken directly to her.

Despite the fact that what it said was pretty insulting, at least she had made contact with it somehow and sort of spoken to it. This could be seen as a type of exchange. It stunned her and flung her away when it clearly could have snuffed her out like a tiny insect.

It was a start.

Perhaps she was going at this the wrong way. Perhaps the KDM was right after all. She was flawed and clearly unbalanced. Not so much that she couldn't still function at a very high level–yet unbalanced, nonetheless.

Haisha, who was she kidding? She had a Dark Beast hiding within herself, waiting to break free and go on a mad rampage of destruction. You could not get much more unbalanced than that.

Point taken, therefore.

Naero could also admit to being ignorant. There was clearly a great deal that she did not know and perhaps never would know. And yes, together that could very well make her unworthy of being given access to the godlike knowledge of an ancient alien race.

So now, the question remained: How did she improve her interactions with, and her status with the KDM? How did she make herself worthy, or at the very least–worthier? That, or those things, appeared to be part of the keys involved in unlocking the KDM.

This was a complex relationship that she was forming.

She still needed to understand the KDM more. She could sense its own sentience. The KDM itself was like an entity. It existed with purpose, direction, and a powerful will all its own that was in fact nothing to be trifled with. But like all things that existed and were self-aware, it had a purpose, and it felt the need to be understood.

Naero took a break and tried something else.

If she went back to the KDM now, it would simply keep zapping her and hurling her aside, or worse.

She picked up the nanobelt given to her by Riel during The High Crusade. Riel had been the swordmaster of the Pelani of the Gamma Quadrant, captured by their alien enemies and sent to kill Naero. Riel had nearly succeeded, but Naero destroyed the enemy's control over the Pelani champion at the last instant.

Before she left to return to her people on the other side of the galaxy, Riel had given Naero that nanobelt, saying that it contained the wisdom and tek secrets of the Pelani.

Naero had turned that belt over to Intel, and they had attempted to break its encryption. But because it was Kexxian in nature, they had no better luck with the belt than with the KDM. And Riel had left in such a hurry that she had not told Naero how to unlock the belt's secrets.

But she did say that they were all children–wards of the Kexx. The Kexx were a race who had explored numerous galaxies and protected sentient species in their early eons and proto phases of development. If the tek of the Pelani was pseudo-Kexxian in nature, perhaps Naero should start with something simpler, such as that.

From the moment she began studying the nanobelt of the Pelani, she sensed that it was, in fact, a Kexxian storage device at the smallest nano and pico levels of existence. It resonated with the same or at least a similar such resonance.

She spoke to it in Kexxian. *"Ekdobae!* Activate!" The alien nanobelt shivered and wiggled slightly, but it did not do anything else.

No, that wasn't it. She wasn't doing it right.

Naero put the Pelani nanobelt on her own slender hips.

Yes, she teknomanced and understood. The belt became part of the wearer in a sense. It did not respond to audible commands.

They needed to be psyonic–telepathic in nature.

The experience was similar to that with the KDM barrier, only much less daunting and self-aware. It was but a simple AI for a simple storage and activation device, with presets for shields and gravlifts–even a stealth mode that included cloaking. There was tek data on Pelani weapons, armor, and even warships, advanced computers, and several knowledge bases.

And like the KDM, if one did not know what to look for, she would never find it.

Naero thought into the nanobelt with telepathy. *Ekdobae.*

Per her command, the nanobelt came online with her teknomancing and opened its presets to her.

Dath riiba zhunru. Naero activated shields, level ten. She sensed the waves of shielding pulsing around her physical form. *Kurr zhunru*, shields down.

Naero quickly dumped copies of all of this vital data into her wristcomp, shunting it through the translation matrix and passing it on to Spacer Intel for their perusal. From just glimpsing at the tek flows, they would have many useful things to gain from a hi-tek knowledge exchange with the Pelani. Their tek seemed relatively on par with current Spacer tek, and even slightly more advanced in certain aspects and applications.

She would need to thank Riel, if they ever met again.

Pelani tek and knowledge was very much based on Kexxian tek and principles, but it was still very simple and basic, comparatively. It was still eons behind the true complexity of the KDM. And perhaps that was how it should be. In the wrong hands, the knowledge locked within the KDM would be incredibly dangerous.

Naero took time to study Pelani stardrives. They even had their own experimental version of the leap drive, and the enemy's wyrmhole projection arrays.

Yet they weren't any more advanced than the attempts made by Spacer Intel and their teks. They seemed more or less stuck at the same places.

If they were going to pursue or strike at the enemy in the Gamma Quadrant, Spacers and their allies needed a reliable way to travel back and forth. The enemy still had that advantage over them.

Riel herself had left in a great hurry, not wanting to miss the chance to attach her small spyship to one of the hyper-advanced alien vessels in piggyback fashion to hitch a ride back. She desperately needed to return to the Gamma Quadrant in order to help her people there. Only vessels such as the Dakkur hordeship and the G'lothc squid-like ships, powered by the Darkforce itself, could travel back and forth across such vast distances.

One of the G'lothc possession wyrm samples and its frozen host in a stasis tube had already been delivered to her quarters, off to one side. Naero brought the lights up in her small but spacious quarters. Now that her meditation work was done for the time being, she might as well look at what she and the Alliance were up against.

The wyrm itself had gone dormant once removed from its host.

She used biomancy to study it and even that nearly made her sick. The G'lothc and everything they made and touched felt somehow violated and corrupted. It literally hurt to interact with them. That was the way the Darkforce was.

The possession wyrms were insidious creatures–constructs, living machines no less abominable than the Darkforce generators. They took over a host and robbed them of their free will, and then their body and their life. The host body became a vessel, and the possession wyrm opened a gateway to the Void, the dark spirit realm poised upon the brink of the Darkforce dimensions of annihilation. That was where the fell spirits of the long-dead G'lothc lurked and waited, biding their time. Yearning and howling for release from the very hellish prison they had fashioned for themselves by the evil of their own actions while they had lived, seeking to destroy all life in the universe.

That still remained their fanatical goal.

Yet how to defeat such beings when they were already technically dead? That was a bit of a sticking point. They could still act and mar the universe through their will, and through the hands of their formidable servants, minions, and slaves.

From what Riel had said, most of the Gamma Quadrant was under just such an assault by the enemy's forces. And if such could be imagined, things were even worse off there than down in the Alpha Quadrant. Because the enemy had gained several footholds there in far-flung areas, and their power was expanding and on the rise.

Just as Naero and her allies had feared when they had visited the Gamma Quadrant briefly in the past. If the foe took over the Gamma Quadrant, they would have even more power and reason to attack and subjugate the rest of the galaxy.

Naero studied that sickening little hi-tek enemy wyrm with her biomancy. If their infestation spread, all of humanity and every sentient race could be taken over and consumed.

And thus far, any sentients infected by the possession wyrm did not last much longer than a month or two before they were utterly consumed by its malignant Darkforce energies. They were all reduced to ash.

Naero brushed the frost off the clear panel of the stasis tube.

Of course, a small lander girl of six or seven with long dark hair and pale skin.

A little girl who looked much like Naero herself had when she was a child.

A girl who could look like her and Khai's daughter.

If the little lander girl was revived, by all of the reports, she would die in agony within the hour, even after the wyrm was removed.

"No," Naero said, clenching her free fist and looking down at that helpless child. "If there is a way to save you and the people of Kalathar from a dark fate such as this, I shall find it." She looked at the vile wyrm writhing in its shield case as if she might close her hand upon it with all her great strength and crush it to death.

There had to be a cure for such malevolent insanity and hate.

That was it. They were like a virus. Like a disease.

She had to try again, even if the awareness guarding the KDM batted her aside once more. She had to try to find a solution–a cure.

Naero darkened the room once more, and held the small stasis tube across her lap. Then she held the wyrm and its capsule clutched in both hands, opened her third eye, and concentrated.

In a matter of instants, she stood before the KDM's barrier of adamant once more.

In one hand she clutched the child's glowing soul essence to her breast; in the other, extended hand, she thrust out the foul essence of the enemy possession wyrm as far as she could away from herself. It hurt and nauseated her simply to be near it.

She called to whatever AI or awareness defended the barrier.

Naero called out in Kexxian, "You know me by now. I am part of you, and you are part of me. You know who and what I am. For all of my failings, I am not your enemy. You know this. See what I have brought before you. This evil is of the same enemy that you fought and vanquished long ago, through your wisdom and great valor. Now we, your beloved children, whom you nurtured, and protected, and sacrificed for so many ages ago, face those same foes, those same evils, and you are no longer here to protect us."

Silence.

Naero drew closer with her twin burdens.

She continued speaking. "We need help. These foes are too powerful. They are beyond us. We need guidance. We need knowledge and assistance to defeat threats such as this. I know that we are not worthy of knowing all of your mighty knowledge, wisdom, and secrets. But please, I ask only that you help us with what we face now. Millions of lives on this one planet alone are at risk of being snuffed out by this vile and insidious infestation. If there is a cure, a defense against this evil, please tell us what it is or help us find it!"

She knew that all of this was a vision within her own mind, but it still seemed so very real.

As she approached the barrier with the essence of the G'lothc possession wyrm held out before her, what seemed like a million out-thrust hands, palms out, morphed out from the surface on long, tube-like arms to drive her back.

Naero pulled away and turned.

The same hands that had spurned and defied the wyrm reached out even further to gently caress the glowing essence of the child.

She stepped back and called out again, "Help us! We removed this parasite from this child. If we revive her, she will die screaming. Tell us what we can do to save her."

The multitude of hands withdrew.

Naero suddenly saw two raised platforms behind her. She placed the wyrm on one and the child on the other and then strode before the barrier once more.

She placed both hands against its humming, resonating surface.

She heard those same three words once more. But instead of thundering this time, these seemed to whisper and echo repeatedly around her.

Unbalanced...

Ignorant...

Unworthy...

"I don't care. That doesn't matter. Do you hear me, whatever the hell you are? None of that matters. I don't matter. But that innocent child and the lives of millions of other innocent people just like her do matter. If there is a way, tell me how to save them!"

Nothing.

"Then what good are you? What good is all of your vast knowledge and wisdom, if it cannot save people who are in dire need? Why do you even exist if you cannot save or help others?"

The voices stopped.

Two hands pressed back against Naero's and a small green creature stepped out from the barrier and walked her backwards.

Naero gasped.

It was a Kexx. Or at least the replicant of one.

By all appearances, in her mind the creature seemed incredibly real and lifelike.

Haisha. So, this was a Kexx.

Finally, someone shorter than her.

At least by a hand or more. Huzzah.

She was female. Naero somehow knew that even without biomancy. She was sleek, strong, and well-formed with a short, slender, agile tail that did not touch the ground. Her body was a perfect blend between humanoid and reptilian, with a large skull and balanced features. Her face was definitely reptilian, and decidedly not human-like, with large, independently blinking and nictitating green eyes. The Kexx actually had a short, lizard-like snout filled with small, omnivorous white teeth.

Even when she did not show her teeth, she looked as if she were either grinning or smiling at something clever. The Kexx were not unpleasant to look at.

Her hands were dexterous and five-fingered, with an opposable thumbs. She wore no clothing. Her body was covered with a sleek, flexible, form-fitting skin of a light green color, with a pale, whitish-green underside of opalescent scales.

Naero tried biomancy, but this was all simply taking place inside her mind. None of what she was experiencing had a physical reality in her imagination.

Her Kexxian counterpart spoke to her. "I am Orean. My recorded essence has been awakened to speak with you as needed. I am what you would call your interface to what you refer to as the KDM. Where is the defense protocol you refer to as Om? As you are limited in your conceptualization capacities, I had hoped to speak to you through him. Where is he? This is very strange."

"Uh…Om's gone right now."

This was astonishing. They were speaking and thinking back and forth at each other in rapid, flawless Kexxian.

Wait, did Orean just call her stupid?

"We are both telepathic, genius," Orean told her. "And what is more, all of this exchange is taking place within your mind. I believe that proves your own point."

"What…that I'm stupid?"

Orean grinned wide. "You said it, Spacer. Not me."

"Look, can you help us or not?"

The Kexx girl shrugged. "That depends."

"On what?"

"On you, dumbo."

"On me? How?"

Orean pointed to the child's essence. "Would you be willing to sacrifice your life to save that child and all of the others?"

Naero thought about that for a brief moment. "Yes I would."

Orean raises one eyebrow and the big green eye along with it. Then she folded her green arms in front of herself. "You had to think about it."

"Of course I had to think about it. What is this? Some kind of test?"

Orean smiled wide again and put her hands on her narrow hips. "Indeed. You must be stupid. Haven't you learned anything by now?"

They both spoke at the same time.

"Everything is a test."

Both of them chuckled. For her first Kexx, Naero liked this lizard girl.

"So, how do we reverse the effect of the possession wyrms?"

"It will not be easy."

Naero snorted. "It never is."

"Did you ever hear about a Corps world called Tora-3?"

"Tora-3? The so-called Kexxian plague struck there."

"High-level Kexxian protocols were unleashed there years ago, and went out of control. You must unleash similar protocols from the KDM on Kalathar."

"Orean. Everyone on Tora-3 died, in a matter of seconds."

"Then you will need to use the correct protocols and control them better, so that that does not happen."

Naero swallowed hard. "How do I do that?"

The Kexx girl pointed at the child's essence. "The Kexx defeated the G'lothc possession wyrm eons ago. It can be reversed once more. But you must first use biomancy to put the wyrm back into the victims. Once they have the wyrm inside of them, it cannot be removed. It must be neutralized and destroyed within them. It must be purged across the entire planet. I will teach you which protocols to unleash, and how to control them."

"How are you going to do that?"

"I will show you on this child. If you cannot learn to save one, you cannot save the others. You said that they were all going to die anyway. What do you and they have to lose?"

"Nothing, I guess."

"Place the wyrm back into the child. Use your biomancy. Do it now."

Naero hesitated. "But…aren't we in some kind of trance in my mind?"

Orean grinned. "Perhaps you are. I assure you, your physical self will mirror your actions here in your mind. Place the wyrm back in the child, and it will be there. Then revive her, and bring her out of stasis."

Naero did so, in that order.

The bewildered child blinked and woke up, terrified and looking around her.

Then the wyrm took over and began to transform.

"Now," Orean said, "follow the directions of my mind linked with yours. Tap into the stars and keep feeding the Cosmic energy through defensive protocols 241B and 877D. Combine them both and their flows in just the way that I am directing you."

Naero hit the transformed child just before it leaped to attack her.

Ribbons of light and shadow erupted out of her and blasted through the creature, sucking out both the Darkforce energy and the incinerated remnants of the wyrm itself. The child's eyes rolled back up into her head and she collapsed.

The little girl was spent but alive and free of the wyrm.

Orean grinned. "Now just unleash those forces across the planet's entire surface. That's all there is to it."

Naero's jaw dropped. She flung her hands wildly up into the air. "You…you make it sound so easy."

Orean shrugged and turned away. "Then make it more difficult, if you want to."

Naero chased after the Kexx, trying to catch her. "Wait, wait. Where are you going? We've…we just had this amazing breakthrough. We're working together now. Don't go away!"

"We're inside of your stupid head, remember, genius? Where are we gonna go?"

Orean walked right through the barrier and Naero lost sight of her. Yet she could still sense Orean's thoughts.

"Wait, come back. Don't go through the barrier!"

Orean called back to her. "What barrier? What the hell are you talking about?"

Naero pounded her fists on it. "Then what the hell is this thing?"

"There's no barrier, N. That's just in your mind. Haisha, face the music, Naero."

"Music? What music? Haisha! Wait, damn it all, Orean! How do I reach you again?"

"You've got way too much to do, right now. When you are ready and you need me, I shall return."

"But I don't understand. I still don't know anything yet!"

In her mind, Naero shook her fists and screamed.

Back in the real world, outside of her messed-up head, Naero brought the lights up in her quarters. She sat down next to the open stasis pod and the empty containment capsule.

The possession wyrm was gone, and the child was safe.

She sighed, putting her face down into her hands, being that she was relatively alone currently, except for an unconscious child. There wasn't any need to keep up a brave front anymore. A terrible worry still passed through her like a chill and she shuddered almost to the point of convulsing.

The pressure she was under was very great. She had learned much, but she still wasn't any closer to finding her own child, Om, the KDM, or Naero-3. She had no way to track them. No way to go after and pursue them wherever it was they went.

As far as she knew, the enemy could already have them at their mercy in the Gamma Quadrant by now. Doing who knew what to them.

It shook her to her core with fear.

An alert on her private com panel went off, causing her to jump.

That meant an urgent response.

From Baeven.

8

The coded message from Baeven said for Naero to meet him on the surface of Kalathar, in a remote area without people or the possessed. She took her personal cloaked starfighter and raced to the given coordinates.

That turned out to be an isolated, volcanic island in the middle of the ocean.

Naero announced her arrival.

As ordered, she took great pains to make certain that she was neither followed nor traced in any way.

As soon as she landed, her sensors told her that a strong anti-scanning and non-detection field covered almost the entire island, as well as an enormous holographic projection. No one would be able to sense anything from orbit, even if they came down and were right above the island itself. Nor would they be able to see the true surface and any changes being made to it.

Baeven was stressing secrecy even more than usual.

Of course Naero wondered why about all of these things.

Underneath the holo and the non-detection field, the island had been ravaged and nearly completely destroyed. Even the dormant volcano was shattered and busted up, covered with a layer of multiple craters and blast effects.

What had happened here?

It was beyond even that of a normal battlefield. Some extremely violent action had occurred here, and Baeven and company had done their best to keep it all quiet and under wraps.

"Hey," a voice said. Naero briefly felt a hand on her shoulder and swatted it away, spinning back into a fighting stance.

Light brown, furry Danjen stood blinking his blue eyes in front of her, still withdrawing his hand, in his blue loincloth, battle harness, and multiple weapons. And his amazing, prehensile tail.

"Whew, N. Touch-y! Baeven sent me to bring you in. We need your help."

Naero put her fists down and breathed a sigh of relief. "Sorry, Danjen. Things have been, crazy."

"No doubt. What, you're not used to that, yet?"

"So tell me, what am I here for, monkey boy?"

"I'm a Ku. Not a monkey or a primate. Your kind might be descended from monkeys, but mine are not, thankfully."

Naero rolled her eyes. "Just answer the question."

"We've been trying to subdue that hybrid Dakkur-G'lothc spyship we helped Baeven capture."

Naero's jaw dropped. "Haisha! What Dakkur-G'lothc spyship?"

"Hybrid spyship—something new," Danjen said. "We've never seen one like it before. This was the one the enemy used in stealth mode for their agents to seed almost the entire planet's population with the possession wyrm infestation. The same enemy agents who used new stealth and phaze suits to abduct and then replace High Master Tree and the Spacer Elders on the jury to rig your trial."

"Intel just naturally assumed that the enemy ship got away again, like they usually do."

Danjen grinned his furry smile. "Not this time." Danjen's eyes suddenly blinked and went very wide. "Baeven's different, N. Even scarier now than he ever was before."

Naero stopped walking for a second, and Danjen fell back with her.

Baeven? Scarier? The man already radiated some kind of dangerous essence that invoked fear in others. He was one of the deadliest fighters in the galaxy, perhaps the universe. How was it possible for him to become scarier, in any of his forms? "Tell me what's been going on, Danjen."

The island suddenly shook as if from an earthquake tremor. Explosions rocked the volcano and the island about ten klicks away.

"Baeven's been doing all of this deep meditation crap, in conjunction with Jia and Gaviok. He said something about getting back in touch with a deep side of himself that he had forgotten about. It's Baeven. Who the hell knows what he's capable of? And you too for that matter. Both of you guys are major scary. That's why I always want to be on your side when things go down."

It must have been Baeven linking up with his Cosmic guardian selves and possibilities, from the artifact statue back on Janosha. He must have had a major breakthrough.

Naero secretly chided herself. Om wasn't there any longer to do so for him. Of course Baeven had had a breakthrough. He'd helped the three Cosmic Guardians suspend her trial and execution, and expose the enemy's plot. Baeven and his crew had rescued Master Tree and the Elders.

"So what happened?"

Danjen blew out a deep breath. "We were on our way, racing back to Kalathar, when this big fight erupted. Baeven went out of control, but it was different this time. He almost destroyed *The Shadow Fox*. He nearly killed Gaviok and Jia, which is nearly impossible to do. But in the end, they either barely subdued him or he regained some kind of control. Perhaps a little of both. Then he…he…"

"He what, Danjen? Spit it out."

"Baeven stopped Time. H-he froze it somehow."

A Cosmic Guardian ability: to step outside of and manipulate the flow of Time itself and even pull others out with them. Just like at her trial.

"Danjen, if they haven't had time to tell you yet, Baeven and I are both Cosmic Guardians, with special abilities and powers that are only going to continue to grow and come online. So stay tuned. Now, what about this enemy spyship?"

"We've been fighting it and trying to subdue it for days, all over the island. The damn thing can't fly anymore, but for a while it could still move about. Now we have it trapped and we've gone inside repeatedly, trying to subdue its living machine defensive systems. Baeven and Jia thought that another powerful teknomancer such as yourself would help finish the job. Jia can tell you more than I ever could."

"Copy that. Let's rejoin them."

The alien hybrid ship was small, black, round, with sides that were tapered on the edges like a lozenge. It reminded her of another pill-shaped alien ship they had come across during The High Crusade, but this one was only about half the size. It lay smoking within a crater of ash and fused glass. It was badly damaged in multiple places and ways.

Yet even from where Naero stood, she could sense it.

The crippled ship was a living machine and even now it was struggling to regenerate itself. It had a will all its own.

Stepping inside only confirmed that for Naero. Even with her teknomancing she could sense that the ship was definitely a hybrid, a mixture of both Dakkur and G'lothc technology.

Danjen led her within. Each chamber and corridor had required an intense battle. Each one had to be nearly destroyed. The damage was extensive.

Naero sensed the Darkforce. Lots of it. Straight ahead.

They passed through ruined blast doors that, by their looks, had been torn open by raw strength and might alone.

Something that an extremely powerful mantid Shai like Gaviok might be capable of, or Baeven himself.

She spotted Jia first, walking perfection in her silvery, glimmering body. Jia was teknomancing against the living ship itself, trying to subdue it.

She also kept it from self-detonating and destroying them all.

Naero and Danjen walked in further. Gaviok stood by, an enormous mantid who could shift his size and density, a natural master of Chaos force. The color of his carapace shifted with his mood. In battle he was red, or even red and deep, dark black, as he was now.

The primary and secondary defenses of the shielded powercore and stardrive chamber had been defeated. Naero had fought against such defenses on board *The Dark Star*. She knew how tough they could be.

The last shielded blastwall barrier to the core stood before them.

Baeven stood poised with his back to everyone else, draining the Darkforce energy away, and converting it into Cosmic energy that he could make use of.

Baeven stepped back and briefly glanced at Naero.

Naero started, and brought both her hands to her mouth.

Baeven was different. One of Baeven's eyes burned with Chaos energy–the other with the Darkforce.

And she was the only one who could see it. Only another Cosmic Guardian could.

What did he see when he looked at her?

"About time. Give us a hand, Naero," Baeven said. "This entire ship's been a major pain in my ass."

Jia shifted to one side. Naero moved to the other.

59

She briefly hugged Gaviok.

"Good to see you, my prince," Naero told her mantid friend. There was a special bond between them, like family.

"Naero," Gaviok said, turning briefly more red than black. "A joy to see you."

"Hold off the love fest, you two," Baeven told them. "We have a vital mission to finish here."

"Agreed," Naero said, preparing to focus at the task at hand. "So, what's the prize here?" she asked her uncle.

Baeven grunted, fighting the Darkforce once more, but he was the Guardian of Chaos energy and the Darkforce itself. "Nothing much," Baeven said. "Just a working enemy wyrmhole projection array. We capture it and learn its secrets, and then we'll be on par with our new good friends."

Jia smiled over at Naero. "We'll be able to travel back and forth across the entire galaxy, just as our foes can. Your people can take the fight to the enemy homeworlds and strongholds, once we locate them. No longer will you need to sit by and wait for the foe to strike at us with impunity."

Baeven said it before Naero could.

"And once we reach the Gamma Quadrant, we can track down your child, Naero."

"You know where she is, and Naero-3?"

"We will when we get there," Baeven said. "Unlike you, I had the sense to put an Astral tracer inside your replicant. Now, as for that girl of yours, Naero. Haisha. She is going to be something else. I don't even know if the G'lothc would know what the hell to do with something like her. She's a wild blade if I've ever seen one. She just might surprise our new friends a bit, if they aren't careful."

At last, Naero had some hope.

She focused all of her teknomancy abilities and placed both of her hands right into the Darkforce field, ignoring the pain and linking with the vessel itself, preparing to merge with it and wrestle with the ship head on. "Let's do this."

Baeven continued draining the ship of its energies. Jia kept the ship from killing itself and all of them. Gaviok and Danjen stood by, ready to deal with any surprises or last-minute defenses the living ship might throw at them.

Naero merged with the living vessel, just as she had with Alala. The only difference was that this ship was hostile. She needed to bend its will to her will, and to do that, she had to be come one with it.

It was like wrestling with her Dark Beast all over again.

60

But its fledgling will and purpose faded as Baeven continued to drain off its power source.

Naero fought and wrestled with its simplistic, undeveloped mind.

Intruder. Must destroy! Must destroy both of us. My programming...cannot let you have...my secrets!

Naero slowly reasoned with it, changing its logic more and more all the while.

You do not need to destroy me, because I am now part of you. You are part of me. We can now work together. There is no reason to destroy any longer. We are one.

In the end, Naero had to replicate part of herself and integrate it into the ship's simple, straightforward AI. That was the only thing that could make it docile and cooperative.

Then Naero used teknomancy to finally make it obedient to her, Baeven, Jia, and any of Baeven's crew. She added Spacer Intel override protocols for good measure, for when they turned the ship over to Klyne and his people for analysis.

Just not before she, Baeven, and Jia understood the alien wyrmhole projectors, and installed them on their vessels as needed.

That would take perhaps a day or two.

Naero closed her eyes for a moment.

Hang on baby; hang on, Om. The cavalry is coming. I swear we are.

Let them be all right still. The enemy would most likely see them as valuable prizes, and keep them for study–at first.

Once the captured ship was fully subdued, they could begin to understand all of its advanced systems, including the wyrmhole projectors.

Naero started in on that right away.

Baeven and his people had been fighting the alien ship and its defenses for days. They took a short breather before joining back in.

Naero kept going. She was still relatively fresh to all of this. She even got the ship's self-healing and self-repair capabilities to kick in more. But everything had to be modified. The living ship could not work the same way anymore. It could not simply operate, powered by the Darkforce alone, with all of those insidious alien defenses.

She modified the powercore so that it became a Cosmic force generator, and not solely a Darkforce battery that would need to be charged by a Darkforce generator. Baeven and Gaviok had already destroyed all of those and unleashed the Mystics inside of them. The ship would have eventually run out of power on its own without a generator feeding it.

Now it could operate independently on Cosmic energy itself, which of course included a balanced part of the Darkforce, and not that energy alone.

Yet Naero held the ship's intellect just below being self-aware. It would not develop a personality of its own like Om or Alala, unless she chose to start one up. For right now, it was still just a vessel, awaiting programming, commands, and direction.

Naero had to be careful about creating new sentient minds.

It took her and Jia five hours to learn and comprehend all of the ins and outs of the enemy wyrmhole projectors. Another three hours to teknomance and install the alien tek on *The Shadow Fox.*

There was, as yet, no time to test it.

Naero had vanished off the radar for more than a day, and the situation on Kalathar was still dire.

Intel and everyone else would be going nuts, but wait until Naero and Gaviok showed up with their prize, delivering it to Intel and the Clans on a silver platter.

These were exactly the kind of tek breakthroughs that they had been waiting for.

9

The first thing Naero did before she and Gaviok left the island in the refitted, cloaked enemy spyship–now their ship–was christen it and give it a new designation.

She smashed a bottle of champagne Baeven gave her on the side of the thick, black, pill-like hull. She had even thought up a new name for the vessel. "I name thee *The Black Spot!*"

When they lifted off from the island, they caught up on the chatter of the Alliance fleets, still patrolling above stricken Kalathar. Naero's stealth fighter barely fit within one of the small cargo holds.

Just as Naero thought, everyone was calling out and searching for her.

They quietly docked with her flagship, *The Flying Dagger*, and made sure to take an hour or two to install the new wyrmhole projector and a few other nifty mods they had come across. Upgrades were always great.

Then Naero took a breath, and she and Gaviok made straight for *The Kathmandu*, to finally turn over their prize and all of its tek secrets.

The fixer clouds would have a field day refitting the fleets.

Naero would strongly suggest to Klyne that only Spacer naval warships be given the new projector arrays. She felt certain that he would agree.

If the Corps got their hands on that tek, they'd soon be flooding the Gamma Quadrant with a raging tide of exploitation–not exploration. That would mess up things even worse than what they probably already were.

Naero turned to Gaviok suddenly. "Why in the heck did you insist on coming along, my prince? And what is with all of the luggage? I've never even seen you carry a duffle."

Gaviok displayed his mandible version of what passed as a mantid smile.

"Baeven and Jia and I have been in deep discussion for months. I have business to conduct with the Spacer Mystics, you will be happy to know."

Naero knitted her brows together for a moment. Gaviok had trained with the Mystics for a while. She took a stab at her friend's motivations. "You really want to complete the entire Mystic training? You want to be a Spacer Mystic?"

"I do. The first non-Spacer Mystic, and more."

She was afraid of what the "more" was going to mean.

But they were about to dock with Admiral Klyne's flagship.

Once on board, she and Gaviok, by default, were more or less placed under arrest and brought before Klyne and the High Mystic Masters, where they were all busy discussing the dilemma on Kalathar from the bridge and the viewscreens looking down over the stricken planet.

Klyne immediately began to dress her down for pulling off another one of her patented vanishing acts.

Naero endured all that she could and then interrupted him.

"Admiral Klyne. Please allow me to speak. There were good reasons. I have vital information to turn over to you, our Clans, and to the Alliance. Please, hear me out."

"Unless you have a cure for the possession wyrm plague on the planet, I don't want to hear a lot of excuses and crap from you."

Naero smiled slightly. "As a matter of fact, I have found a cure within the KDM, and we can begin implementing it across the planet's surface. The Kexx defeated this scourge long ago. And now I know how to combat and defeat it."

Klyne had to sit down. So did Master Tree and Master Jo.

Klyne couldn't speak and only stared at her for a while. "So, does this mean you've unlocked the secrets of the KDM?"

Naero held up both hands. "Whoa. Maybe just one, and that was pretty tough as it was. And if that was any sort of a preview, pulling secrets out of the KDM is going to be like pulling teeth out of your own jaw. Not fun."

Klyne started making the arrangements. "Tell us what we need to do, Naero. Then we can prepare to implement the cure."

"Sure, in a moment. I'm not finished, yet. On top of the cure, the ship that we docked in your landing bay is a captured alien spyship of hybrid G'lothc and Dakkur tek."

She sent three data fixers floating over to Klyne. "These fixers have all of the data stored on the alien ship, the enemy wyrmhole projectors, and the tek secrets of another advanced race from the Gamma Quadrant called the Pelani, as I have mentioned before."

Klyne and everyone else stared at her once again.

"Uh, when you're done with *The Black Spot*, I'd like to have it back as part of my fleet. I could use a specialized craft such as that...in my line of work. That's quite reasonable, don't you think? I'm not asking that much in return, am I?"

Klyne and his crew exploded into action, not sure of what to do first.

Gaviok went over and quietly began speaking with the two High Masters, once he could get their attention.

By then, Naero was very tired. She would need to rest, gather her strength, and do a great deal of startapping to power the Kexxian cure on Kalathar later that night.

By then, the Spacer fleets should be going through the fixers to refit them with the new tek upgrades, and prepare to seek out the enemy.

Klyne and the Naval strategists were already discussing how they might proceed.

Naero had a hurried dinner with her crew. Captain Tyber and *The Dark Star* would arrive for their refit that night as well. She needed to hurry if she was going to grab some badly needed rest.

Khai showed up from his various errands and missions.

"Naero, I've heard the news. It's so amazing what you have done."

"Baeven did a lot of it. I keep telling you how much we owe him."

"I have so much to tell you on my own."

Naero rubbed her eyes and slumped against him. "Please, could it wait? It's been a very full couple of days, and I've hardly slept. If I'm going to start implementing the Kexxian cure on the planet tonight, I desperately need some rest. Will you just hold me? Just protect me and give me peace."

Khai's eyes flared and he drew in a deep breath. "I can do that. Nothing shall get past me. In my arms, you shall be safe and warm. Have you given orders to your crew not to disturb your rest, my heart?"

"Only if the galaxy catches fire," Naero said with a chuckle.

Khai offered her his hand. "Then come, know peace beside me, Naero. Let me be thy bed."

Naero smiled up at his handsome face. She was too exhausted to kiss him.

Within minutes, Naero blacked out.

Khai woke her gently, six standard hours later.

She briefly welcomed Ty and his crew, and couldn't wait to hold little Gallan. She spoke briefly with Alala, the entity on Tyber's self-aware ship, welcoming her, as well.

Then she had to prepare for the implementation of the cure to rid Kalathar of the G'lothc possession wyrm infestation, and reverse most of the negative effects. The reversal cure could not bring back any who had already perished. It was not a cure for death.

And by the time she was finished purging the planet, Baeven and *The Shadow Fox* could be back from their maiden test flight through the wyrmhole projectors, back and forth across the Gamma Quadrant.

When she explained the process to Klyne, the Intel Medical Corps, and the High Masters, at first they didn't believe her. And for some strange reason, Gaviok was there also. Apparently, Klyne and the High Masters had taken the Prince of the Shai into the Alliance. He was now part of the inner circle.

If only they knew that Gaviok was the closest thing that Baeven had as a brother. Most likely he did not tell them that fact in its entirety.

"I'll show you how it's done. Bring in the remaining test subjects, and put the wyrms back into them," she instructed.

Again the medteks blinked at her as if she were insane.

"Put them back in?" one even muttered in disbelief.

Naero rolled her eyes for a second. "Yes. The wyrms must be destroyed while they are still within the host in order to completely free the host of them and their influence. That's why the test subjects were dying. Once infested with the wyrm, it must be purged from them not only on a physical level, but also on a psyonic and a Cosmic level."

The medteks looked to Klyne and he nodded.

In the end, all eleven of the remaining victims in stasis tubes and gravlifts were brought in and positioned around Naero.

"Everyone get behind me," Naero warned. "This might get a little crazy."

Medteks backed up. They didn't need to be told twice.

Some of them who had heard of Naero even left the medical bay.

Klyne brought up shielding to protect the observers.

Naero focused her biomancy abilities and opened her third eye.

She saw through all of the test subjects as if they were crystal, and detected the insidious G'lothc possession wyrms almost instantly. Their sickening aura of malevolence. How could such things even exist?

And fiends such as these had her child.

Naero shook her head. She couldn't afford to be distracted, even by that. She needed to concentrate.

Obliterate the possession wyrms, purge them from the victims, and keep the people alive.

She tried to unleash just a part of the Kexxian cure to affect the purge.

The forces she unleashed blew out that entire side of the flagship's hull. Emergency beacons flared. It was all that Naero could do to keep herself and the stasis pods from being sucked out into space.

Finally the emergency shields sealed off the massive hull breach. But the room and the ship were still heavily damaged. Fixer clouds raced in from both sides, within and without, to make repairs.

Finally the medteks could check the test subjects.

"They're all alive. Their life signs are little stressed..."

"Big deal–at least they're not dead," Naero said, cutting to the chase. "That's what matters, isn't it? Sorry about your ship, Klyne, but I don't think this was meant to be unleashed out in space, within a vessel."

Klyne raised both eyebrows. "I kinda noticed that."

Naero rubbed both hands together eagerly. "Now, we just have to spread these effects over the inhabited areas of the planet Kalathar. We have the medical scanners adjusted now to detect the possession wyrms, correct?"

"Affirmative," another medtek noted.

"Then I go down with Khai and some of the Prime adepts to guard me while I sweep the planet until all of the wyrms have been purged. The people should revert back to their original forms. They'll be weak for a day or two, and then they'll recover. And the good news is, that once they've been purged and cured, they cannot be re-infested again. Then Kalathar can begin to return to normal, minus the victims who perished in the attack, of course. We can't bring back the dead."

Klyne looked a bit worried. "This is a big job, Naero. You'll need to sweep over forty percent of the planet's surface from up in the air. Can you do this without exhausting or harming yourself?"

Naero grinned. "We'll find out. Once again, I've never done this before. No one has, except for the Kexx, eons ago. Theoretically, it is possible, but like I said, we are entering uncharted territory here, and we'll need to learn as we go along. Haisha, if anything we do ever comes easy, I think I'm going to faint, or wet myself, or something!"

Klyne, Gaviok, Master Jo, and several others laughed at that.

"By the way," Naero asked Klyne, as she continued to prepare for the main event, "how's it going refitting the naval vessels with the new tek?"

Klyne nodded. "The upgrades are going well, but it's still going to take a long while. And many teks are going without sleep to explore all of the new ramifications for shields, and sensors, scanners, coms, and weapon systems. You've opened up countless cans of new worms for us to explore with this flurry of breakthroughs, Naero. It will take us months, perhaps years to fully grasp and implement all that we have just been exposed to. But those are awfully good cans of worms to have to study and explore."

"Good," Naero said. "Our foes have had the advantages for too long as it is. It will be good to fight more on their level for a change. Have our leaders and the military decided yet what should be done about the enemy in the Gamma Quadrant?"

Klyne's face turned very grave. "Heated discussions are going on even now. While you are purging Kalathar, I will be attending many of those sessions via holo."

"We can't let the isolationists hold us back," Naero said. "You know I'm right, Klyne. Now that we have this wyrm-hole tek, we need to put it to good use. Instead of just sitting back and waiting for our foes to hit us again and again, we have to take the fight to them, and make further alliances with the sentients in the Gamma quadrant, who are apparently getting their butts kicked. We need to go help them before those sentients are enslaved and sent to fight us as enemy shock troops."

"I know your arguments, Naero. General Walker and many others agree with you, but there are many who still don't. We also have more than enough problems in our own quadrant to deal with."

"Which are only going to get worse if we keep suffering attack after attack, and invasion after invasion. I say, take the fight to these bastards."

"But Naero, you also have to understand the valid points that the other sides are going to bring up, if you are going to find a way to persuade them to see things your way."

Naero shook her head. "That's why I'm a better warrior than a diplomat," she said. "I trust you, Klyne. I know you always have the best interests and the greater good of our people in mind–even when I disagree with you."

Klyne patted her on the shoulder. "Let me deal with the elders and the factions," he said. "You go do what you alone can do. Save Kalathar and its people. Just be careful, Naero. Just as you said, everything you're ever involved in always ends up far more difficult that anyone could imagine that it would be."

Naero grinned again. "I've got the Mystic Enforcer to back me up. "What the hell can go wrong?"

10

Naero hovered over the first infested gigacity from a few kilometers up. She and Khai and the six Prime adepts guarding her from behind were all still cloaked.

She prepared herself, as best as she could.

The gigacity of Shandoora wasn't that huge. Only a hundred kilometers in diameter, approximately.

Only.

She had never unleashed the Kexxian purge on an area this large before. Millions of infested hosts, the vast majority of them now dormant.

Naero didn't quite know what was going to happen.

She startapped as much as she could and then opened the floodgates.

This was different.

Unleashing the Kexxian purge on Shandoora—on the planet of Kalathar—was like being impaled on a molten hot pillar of Cosmic agony, shoved all the way up through her and out of her shattered face.

There was no gasping or crying out. There was only being transfixed–crucified on raw pain and suffering itself. There was indeed a high price to be paid.

Purging the planet focused massive quantities of Cosmic energy through her physical form, which could not withstand such naked might.

She struggle to save herself from being consumed.

She tried to stop it. Tried to turn it off.

Yet once it was unleashed, the Kexxian purge had a will of its own, and hunted down the possessed in the largest numbers it could find, stepping up its efforts.

From several kilometers up in the sky, the ribbons and tendrils of light and darkness ripped through the gigacity and penetrated the population below, blasting and incinerating the G'lothc possession wyrms from out of their bodies, leaving them spent and unconscious, but alive.

"Something's wrong," Naero barely heard Khai tell the other Mystics. "She's transforming into an energy being form. The process is going out of control. Naero's in trouble!"

The Kexxian purge wiped out thousands of possession wyrms and sent their fell spirits shrieking back into the Void.

The purge did all this, in mere seconds.

But it was killing Naero. She could feel it.

Even in her energy being form she was slowly destroyed and consumed by the process, and Naero did not know how to fight it.

Khai and the Mystics tried to lay hands upon her and contain her.

The very air detonated around Naero, shooting them away in all directions.

The purge continued on its mission with a will of its own, gaining speed and only stepping up its power. It swept her off toward the next gigacity, destroying each of the possessed that it could find along the way.

The only problem was that Naero was slowly being used up and consumed. It was like burning up in slow motion and being reduced to ash.

And she couldn't do anything to stop it.

The resonance of the KDM was all around her. It was like roaring voices. A raging thunder of voices, deafening, consuming–raging in Kexxian. No, somehow that wasn't right.

The words the thundering voices spoke had raw power to them, and even the G'lothc could neither resist nor endure that power.

71

If Naero hadn't been so busy trying not to die, she might have been able to focus and make out what the thundering voices were saying.

But she had too much to live for.

Naero was still out of tune with them, out of sync somehow.

The word came back to her.

Unbalanced.

She was out of balance, and that was just one of her flaws. Yet it was the one that was currently destroying her.

Her own imperfections.

Yes, and as usual, her own ignorance was working against her as well.

Khai caught up to her again, trying to siphon off some of the Cosmic energy that was consuming her, funneling it back to the stars, through Yii.

Nice idea. A good try.

A flare of power slapped the Enforcer away again.

The Kexxian purge had been unleashed upon Kalathar.

And it had work to do.

She continued to pick up speed, until the very air burst into flame about her. She was like a small, white-hot comet, streaking through the atmosphere, bathing the planet's surface in its cleansing energies.

Naero cried out to the KDM.

Orean...help...help me...

Why must you make everything as difficult as possible, Naero?

Tell me...what...to do.

Didn't you say that you'd be willing to give your life to save these others?

I don't want to die.

Did I say that? Who said anything about actually dying? Didn't I merely say that you had to be willing to die to save others? Can't you see the difference?

Why do you only speak...in questions?

Why can't you save yourself, Naero?

I don't know.

Is it not too late already? Won't others need to save you now?

I'm on fire. I'm burning up!

How then are fires extinguished?

Questions. Why all of these questions?

Don't you already know the answers? Why can't you remember them, Naero? Is that not what true ignorance is?

Burning. Burning. She was gaining speed, burning up as the purge grew only stronger.

Khai enveloped her in his green shield sphere and sought to contain her blazing form and snuff out the fire, siphoning off the cosmic energies consuming her.

She linked with his mind briefly. Khai, the Kexxian purge is channeling, startapping Cosmic energy straight through me. I can't handle this much power. It's burning me up.

Naero, the Mystics and I are trying stop it, bleed its power away from you, but each time we slow it down, it only gets stronger, and shakes us off.

Case in point. The purge blasted Khai off her again as she passed over another gigacity, and then another.

Then Naero heard a familiar voice, and felt strong arms around her.

You're in trouble, sib. Good thing I just got here. Let me help.

Jan! Save me. I'm burning!

Then let us burn together.

Jan's Cosmic fire was about her. He had almost always been a pyrokinetic. By their very nature they could shunt heat away so that they were not hurt by it. And now his fire and his energies only added to that of the Purge, speeding it up even faster.

No, Jan. We have to slow it down. Stop it.

We can't. Yet if we speed it up, it will finish its task before you and I are destroyed. Just hang on, Naero!

Jan suffered the agony with her, sharing her pain and destruction.

Her younger brother did all of this, to save her and himself.

Janner had grown in power and wisdom. Naero could sense it.

He had managed to complete his Mystic training.

Jan was a full-fledged Mystic.

But at that moment, they were both burning to death, trapped within a Cosmic maelstrom.

They picked up speed, streaking across the surface of Kalathar, until the entire planet had been purged.

Just as suddenly, the flames snuffed out and were gone.

The Purge halted on its own accord.

Because there was nothing left to be consumed.

They crashed onto a sandy beach at the edge of one of the continents.

Jan did his best to shield them as they tumbled down.

Naero came to with her brother's arms still locked around her protectively.

It was Jan who had save her, and himself.

Naero staggered to her feet, and reached out with her mind to contact Khai, the High Masters, anyone she could reach.

Kalathar and its people had been purged of the enemy plague. It was now free.

11

Naero spent nearly an entire day in her medical bay on her flagship, regenerating and healing herself from within.

Khai and Jan took turns sitting with her, speaking with her through mindlinks. But she had to get back up on her feet. That was a priority.

She heard updates about Kalathar. A huge relief effort was underway to try to help the stricken population. Clouds of medical fixers were being used. Dehydration was becoming a critical problem by the hour.

Spacer Intel, the Spacer Navy, and the Alliance were assembling an expeditionary task force to be sent out to make contact with the Gamma Quadrant and begin confronting the enemy there.

Khai, you must speak with Klyne. One or both of us must be part of that expedition. We have to track down our daughter before it's too late. Baeven is already tracing the foes who have her. I can bring my own ships, my own fleet if need be.

Khai smiled down at her and brushed his hand over her face as she looked up at him. *Get better, Naero. Keep healing yourself. We will find her. We shall bring her back to us. There is much that is going on. Much that will change. We shall both play major roles in the changes that are still to come, my heart.*

As soon as she could walk and maintain herself, Naero got up off her medbed, checked herself out of medical with Trudi, and reported for duty on board *The Kathmandu.* Khai, Jan, Tarim, and Tyber were already there with the High Mystics and many others.

She ran into Jan first, who brought her to his personal quarters.

She couldn't resist hugging him and holding him close to her for a bit.

It was so great to have him beside her once again; she couldn't put it into words. It had been so long since they had stood together. It did her heart good to see Jan, now so strong and fully developed.

"So, you've chosen Order, Jan? I still can't believe it. You? And you've completed your Mystic training in record time I hear. How long did it really take, with the Mystic Time dilation?"

Jan grinned, tall, lanky, and handsome. He seemed very sure of himself.

"It took me almost six more years of real time, N, compressed into over six months. The High Mystics have stolen a page from your book, Naero. Did you know that Master Tree and Master Jo have both used replicants of themselves to help train other Mystics?"

"I didn't know that. But I have been rather busy of late, these past several months. Interesting, since I taught them the ability to replicate."

Jan smiled. "In the light of the threats that we face, the Mystics are expanding. The number of masters and adepts will continue to grow rapidly. Now that it has been purged, I've heard that Kalathar will now indeed serve as the Chaos Homeworld of the newly appointed Mystic High Master."

Naero stopped a moment. "Where could they possibly find a new Mystic High Master? None of the Chaos Prime Adepts are ready. Perhaps as masters, but not as a High Master."

The Mystics were still suffering from the loss of both Hashiko, and Master Vane. There was no one else to fill that role.

Who had they found?

Jan stopped in front of his personal quarters. He grinned slyly. "Prepare for a bit of a shock on the personal front, N. Enter within. I haven't even told Aunt Sleak yet."

What was Jan babbling about?

The panel snapped open.

Naero saw the long, lithe body of a beautiful, nude young woman sprawled across Jan's nanobed, still asleep and partially covered up with black zilken sheets and nanoblankets. Jan's young lady had a mass of gleaming, platinum-white-gold hair, an entire sea of that radiant hair, all the way down her snowy back.

So Jan had a girl. Big deal. What did he think was so shocking about–

Out of the shadows a feline, humanoid form slipped up to Jan and pasted her strong supple body against him, complete with a lashing, striped tail. She wrapped her arms sensually around Jan's head and neck, closing her mouth over his in a deep, wet kiss. This girl was clearly a Mahri, with short black fur with orange and gold stripes. Only a rare few Mahri were colored in this fashion. She was clearly of one of the royal houses.

Her face was halfway between human and feline. She had long, tufted feline ears and straight black hair to her broad, athletic shoulders. She wore only a black loin cloth, some kind of utility belt, a golden, jeweled battle harness, and several gilded, hi-tek weapons.

She even began to purr as she and Jan continued to swooch. Obviously, the two of them were intimate.

"Jan, I missed you," she chided him. "You said only a few hours. It has been several since you left us. What has happened?"

Naero's jaw bounced around the interior of the cabin. Us? Did she say, "*us?*"

"I'm sorry, my sweet *daji*. Much has happened. There was great deal to learn. I could not get away or send a message. And my sister was also in great need of my help. How is Vejjah feeling? Better, I hope?"

The Mahri princess looked at the sleeping woman fondly. "The sickness comes and goes. I sang her to sleep, which she needs badly. I think she is well enough for now."

Jan took one of the Mahri girl's hands and placed it in Naero's. "Calyxo, royal princess of the First House of the Mahri, this is my beloved older sister, Naero Amashin Maeris."

"Ah!" Calyxo said, nodding her head in great honor. "The legend who walks among us."

They smiled and looked into each other's eyes. At first Naero thought that Calyxo's eyes were black, but they were not. They were deep, midnight blue.

Naero biomanced, studying Calyxo's species. She gasped at another surprise. "You're a Mystic."

Calyxo bowed her head again. "The first of my species. I completed my training with Janner, where we exchanged our hearts. The Mystics are now training non-Spacers as well. Even non-humans. Master Vane had opposed opening the training to the other races and sentients."

77

"Interesting," Naero said. "I always thought that we should include the other sentient races."

Calyxo smiled. "And now they have."

The other Spacer female who was sleeping suddenly turned over and groaned slightly. Jan sat down on the bed and took her hand tenderly, brushing her radiant hair back from her equally radiant face, and placing his hand over her forehead, checking for a fever. Large green eyes, flecked with golden light fluttered open.

Jan bent down to kiss her cheek.

"Oh, Jan. I don't feel well. I'm sorry."

"It's all right, Vejjah. Just rest."

Naero sat down next to Jan and placed a hand on Vejjah's bare shoulder. "I'm a biomancer and a healer, Jan. What's wrong with her? Spacers don't usually get sick. Haisha! She's pregnant, Jan. This is—"

"Morning sickness," Jan said. "Some Spacer women still get it."

Not only was Vejjah pregnant…it was very clearly Jan's child.

"Let me see if I can relieve that a bit," Naero said. With biomancy, Naero modified all of the physiological factors that led to morning sickness, reducing them as much as she could without disrupting anything else.

Vejjah breathed a bit easier and stopped knitting her brow in discomfort.

"There," Naero said. "That should be better."

"Very much so," Vejjah said in surprise. "Compared to what it was, I feel great!"

Janner laughed and kissed Vejjah again. Calyxo stood by happily and did not seem to mind.

What was going on here?

Jan turned to Naero, and placed Vejjah's hand in Naero's. "Naero Amashin Maeris. Meet Vejjah Terine Fae, a distant cousin of most of the Faes we know."

"Also a Mystic," Naero said.

"And now a member of Intel, also," Vejjah said. "I completed my training with Jan and Calyxo, where we all met and became such good friends.

And apparently much more that friends, Naero guessed. Just how much further did all of this love fest go?

"You will be the first in our family and our Clan to know, Naero. I've gotten married."

Jan. Jan? Married?

She looked from Vejjah to Calyxo. "Oh…? To which one?"

"Both," Jan said with a smile. "Both of them agreed to be my beloved wives. And we have been nothing but happy."

Okay. That was, in fact, a bit of an eye-opener. Just out of curiosity, Naero wonderer if the two gals enjoyed each other's company as well.

Vejjah turned over, still quite naked, exposing her baby bump for the first time. "Husband. Don't let your sister wonder. Explain how things are, so that she is not shocked."

Calyxo jumped in. "Vejjah is my sister-wife as I am hers. We share the affections of our beloved husband at alternate times, but we are not lovers with each other."

"I'm not judgmental," Naero said, holding both of her hands up palms out. "None of that is really any of my business. What couples...or trios...do in their beds isn't any of my concern."

"But sometimes we do like to watch," Vejjah openly admitted, with a wry grin and a gleam in her eyes. "It can be very beautiful, and exciting while we wait our turn."

Naero stood up. "Okay, Jan. Look at the time. Wow, it was really nice to meet both of your equally lovely wives. Congratulations, and again, much happiness to all three of you, especially with the little one on the way. But I am quite late for a meeting with Admiral Klyne."

Did they want to know that it was a boy?

Vejjah sat up in bed. "Naero. Please say you'll have dinner with us tonight," she said.

"Why sure. I'd love that. And with Aunt Sleak and Zalvano coming in tonight, it will be a very fascinating dinner for all. Wait until you see the twins, Jan. They're getting so big."

She embraced them and then quickly ducked out. Naero could hear Jan and his wives laughing together behind their door panel.

She couldn't wait to see their aunt's reaction at dinner, especially when the Mahri princess explained the particulars about their love life with hubby Jan.

Naero still couldn't get her head around Jan actually being married, with two wives, and child on the way.

But with the time dilation of the Mystics, Jan was now technically a bit older than her.

At some point, she needed to take some time to finish off her own Mystic training. But not just yet.

Not while the enemy had her child.

And she really was late for a meeting with Klyne and the High Mystics.

She had requested again to have *The Black Spot* returned to her for the expedition to the Gamma Quadrant. Intel had to be done with it by now. They could even have the fixers build a few of their own just like it, and had most likely done so.

Naero had her own plans for that new spyship as part of her own strike fleet, which she hoped to command.

With her extensive fleet experience during the Annexation War, clearly Naero would be an excellent choice for commanding a strike fleet once again with the expedition.

All she had to do was finish squaring it all with Klyne and the Spacer Navy.

It therefore came as a shock to Naero when Klyne announced, "Naero, after careful consideration, the Navy and I don't think that it's a good idea for you to go on the expedition. Not as a Strike Fleet Captain."

Naero swallowed the urge to explode and rant. She wasn't the hotshot green leader any more. She couldn't get away with that kind of immaturity any longer.

But they could not be serious. She had to be given the chance to pursue the enemy. Especially those who held her unborn child prisoner.

Naero calmly threaded her hands together. "I see. Might I ask why? And will I be given some other capacity or mission to serve with the expedition?"

"That is no longer up to us to decide, Captain Maeris. That will be wholly determined by the admiral and command staff in charge of the entire expedition battle fleet group."

Naero rose up and saluted. "Admiral Klyne. High Admirals Allen, Kessler, Romanov, and Yamamoto–I formally request that my petition to serve in any capacity in the expedition to the Gamma Quadrant be forwarded with all speed to the admiral selected."

Grand Admiral Micah Allen rose from his seat and stepped forward. "Captain Maeris," he said. "Your request is going to be difficult to carry out. There are multiple concerns and reasons that we have."

Naero saluted. "I would very much like to hear and discuss them in detail, Grand Admiral, sir."

The old star wolf rested his powerful hand on Naero's shoulder. "Because, N. We want you to lead this expedition…Admiral Maeris. Be our sword in the deep black. Lead our battle group into the Gamma Quadrant for the first time. Take the fight to these foes who continue to threaten us and our ways of life, and strike them down!" He shook her hand all the way up to elbow.

"You know I will, Micah." Naero released his arm, stepped back, and drew her cutlass to kneel before the High Admiral and offer him her blade. "Command, me, sir."

The Grand Admiral of the Spacer Navy took her blade, kissed the bright steel, and handed it back to her. She sheathed it and stood back up in one fluid motion.

"Admiral Maeris. You have your orders. The details will unfold. Serve the Clans and the Alliance of the Alpha Quadrant with honor and distinction. Defend our freedoms. Death to those who would bring harm to us."

"What is my command, sir?"

"We asked for one hundred fleets to follow Naero Amashin Maeris into battle in the Gamma Quadrant," Admiral Allen noted.

"An impressive battle group to be sure, sir," Naero said. "I am honored. Clan Maeris is honored."

"You should be, Maeris. We asked for a hundred fleet captains to go into the unknown. Ten thousand responded–almost the entire Spacer Naval leadership–and fought for the honor and the right to serve under your blade. Do not let them down."

Naero saluted. "Death shall take me first, sir."

Grand Admiral Micah Allen shook her hand once more and saluted her back. "Dismissed. See to your command. The fleets have assembled and went through the refit first. When will you depart?"

"Tomorrow, sir."

"Fight well, Admiral Maeris."

"They shall sing songs of our deeds across the stars, sir."

As if her life was not complicated enough.

Now she even had more to do.

She returned to her flagship to inform her people of the news and say her goodbyes.

Her entire crew offered to serve with her on her flagship crew and staff. Naero accepted. *The Flying Dagger* would become her transport shuttle, as needed, as would *The Black Spot*. *The Dark Star* would serve with her scouting and Intel contingent.

Baeven and *The Shadow Fox* were already waiting for them.

Jan would serve with her as part of her command staff. Naero wasted no time recruiting old friends and former allies. She would inform Jan during dinner. Let him bring his wives if they all wished.

The next thing she did was create six, near-perfect replicants, Naero-4 through Naero-9. Six such full-size replicants was all that she could manage each day without exhausting herself.

Then she reached into a shielded chest that Khai had brought to her from his father's people, the Oden.

Inside were hundreds of astral crystals, so that she and her replicants could all stay in contact with each other. She gave them all one. Naero wished now that she had had them to give to Naero-2 and Naero-3, but that was hindsight.

She sent Naero-4 to serve and advise her trade fleet with Admiral—and traveling throckstar—Max Lii and his young family. Naero-5 would be her tactical and strategic double on her flagship. Naero-6 would serve with Baeven on *The Star Fox*. Naero-7 would serve with Jan on *The Black Spot*, once Naero made him the captain. Naero-8 would serve with Klyne at Intel and the Navy, and Naero-9 would stay behind, and serve with the Mystics as both a Prime adept and an instructor.

Naero did not give her replicants much choice in these matters. She pweaked and conditioned their minds to eagerly want to serve in these capacities. But otherwise, they were free to seek out their own happiness and their own lives if they wanted them badly enough. She did not stand in the way of that.

Since the original Naero could not be everywhere at once, her replicants could serve with distinction in her place, doing many of the things that she was capable of.

It might be a bit unnerving, but they were basically her, and part of her, and if Naero shared their thoughts together, they would share all of their experiences as well, and remain a close part of each other.

If any of her replicants were destroyed, their essences, their part of her Lifespark that she shared with them, would return to her, and she would know what had happened to them.

Yet another surprise awaited her with High Master Tree and High Master Jo, when she arrived to present Naero-9 to assist them.

12

Master Tree announced, "Welcome the new High Master of the Chaos Order, Gaviok of the Shai!"

Everyone applauded, even Naero. High Master Gaviok came forward, and High Master Tree and High Master Jo parted to either side of him. Gaviok maintained his normal form, a rather short mantid about 1.42 meters tall, but he pulsed scarlet with Chaos energy.

Master Jo continued. "Now that the crisis is over, any of the civilians who wish to leave Kalathar and relocate to other nearby systems will be paid to do so, and quite handsomely. We believe that most will choose to do so. Those who do stubbornly refuse to leave must accept living under the Time dilation effects that will take place on the planet, as it is transformed into the new Chaos Order training world. They will naturally age faster at periodic times. Further incentive to relocate."

High Master Gaviok spoke for the first time that day. "Kalathar has naturally higher levels of Chaos force energy in the Cosmic spectrum range. Once we unleash those levels further, we will sync the planet's flows with its star, and use those Cosmic flows to implement the Time Dilation Cycles, as the Mystics have done on Taeha and Oorrii. Once Kalathar is up and running, the stepped up programs to train and produce more Mystics will continue, on schedule. Within a decade, we will have more High Masters, more masters, and many more adepts–and not only from Spacers–but from every sentient race in the Alpha Quadrant willing to join the Alliance and train adepts."

Much cheering and applause followed that.

Master Tree and Master Jo called for another welcoming round of applause for Master Gaviok.

A celebration began thereafter, and everyone began to mingle.

Naero gasped for joy, spotting her good friends, the Changs: Chang Fu-han and Chang Lijuan. She shouted out to them, running straight at them with Naero-9 in tow, still hooded and cloaked. "Fu! Li!"

Naero hugged her two friends, nearly knocking them on their backs. They hugged her closely, and soon all three of them were laughing and talking all at once.

"Wait, wait," Naero said. "I must ask. Have you made it back to Thanor-4? How are our good friends there?"

The Changs both nodded sadly.

Then they smiled at each other slyly.

"My younger sister and I have a long overdue leave coming up very soon," Chang Fu-han said.

"Six months," Chang Li-Juan noted. "Guess where we intend to go?"

Naero scrambled to pull Oden astral crystals out of her pouch and spread them around. "Please, track down Naero-2 somehow and give her one of these astral crystals. Both of you take one as well. We can stay in touch on the Astral Plane with them when we sleep."

Both of the sisters stared at Naero. "Sure thing, N," Chang Fu-han said, tucking the devices away.

"Naero," Chang Lijuan asked. "You speak as if you were going away. What is happening?"

The announcement was already spreading. Naero told them about her promotion to Strike Force Admiral, to command the Navy's new Battle Group Expedition to the Gamma Quadrant.

They congratulated her, even as the three High Masters came over to them.

Chang Fu-han pointed to the mysterious cloaked figure following behind Naero. "Who's your secretive friend, N?"

The three High Masters stood before them. Naero and the Changs bowed their heads, leading with their eyes, in deference and respect.

Naero announced, "This is Naero-9, my replicant who will work with the Mystics to help train. I assign her to Master Jo."

Naero-9 removed her hood and stepped forward, smiling.

She looked just like Naero, except for a much shorter hairstyle; in this case, a bob of sleek black hair up off the shoulders.

"To help tell us all apart," Naero said, "all of my replicants have chosen a different hairstyle on their own."

Naero-9 held out her right hand. "Call me Naero, Maeris, N., or just 9. I'm extremely happy to be working with the Mystic Training Program."

Master Tree's mouth fell open. "Pardon. I just can't get over the fact of there being more than one Naero Maeris. I think the galaxy, nay, the entire universe must be groaning under the strain."

"Well get used to it," Naero said. "I'm spreading the love around."

"I think it's a superb idea," Master Jo said. "This is definitely going to shake things up—for us—and our enemies."

"And don't worry," Naero told them. "None of them have my Dark Beast…just my sparkling personality."

Master Tree groaned. "Now I shall truly live in fear."

Everyone laughed, even Naero-9.

She and Naero embraced, and then 9 went off with Master Jo, already getting into a heated discussion.

"Master Tree could be right," Gaviok said, laughing. "This could lead to Chaos."

"Well, at the very least, I'd say Jett sales are definitely bound to increase," Naero noted.

Finally, as the afternoon went on, High Master Gaviok pulled her aside, even taking her to a cargo hold.

Where all of Gaviok's odd luggage was stored.

"I stepped down as the High Prince of the Shai to become a Mystic High Master, Naero," Gaviok told her. "Baeven and I spoke with Jia and his crew a long time concerning my decision."

"Who leads your people now, Gaviok?"

"My oldest son, Kahvan-Uris, is now High Prince of the Shai, with the backing his mother, and the other twelve ruling aunts. They are all my queens, each on their own homeworld with our sisters and brothers of the Ku."

Naero smiled. "Gaviok. You have thirteen wives?" That certainly made Jan look tame. "At one time that might have been considered unlucky."

Gaviok smiled and sighed as only a former mantid prince could. "Each more beautiful than the last. Unlike humans, the prime number thirteen is sacred to my people because of the lunar cycle of our homeworld. When and where possible, a Shai prince will eventually have thirteen princesses. Did you know that Baeven helped me pick out the thirteen new homeworlds for my people?"

Also good to know. "Did you know that Old Earth humans had such a lunar cycle as well?"

Gaviok snorted, "For all the good it did them."

"Hey, they did produce Spacers."

"Yes, despite the Gigacorps. But I will allow them that much at least. Without Spacers, I would not have you and Baeven in my family."

"Gaviok, if you don't mind me asking, what is it like having so many wives?"

"For me? Wonderful. Do you know that a Shai courtship lasts for an entire standard year? An entire year of pleasure and making love, while courtiers, courtesans, and drones stand ready with food and drink, cleanse our bodies, and see to all of our needs. The courtship does not even halt for the annual shedding of our carapaces. They are simply peeled away from us, leaving our bodies so sensitive that we shudder in ecstasy for an entire lunar cycle as the mating continues. Once the courtship is over, my princess is ready to lay our eggs and produce various offspring for the rest of her long life."

"Well, that's stamina for you. And why not get it all done at once?"

"When we meet again and I visit the worlds of my wives—one each month—we sometimes join together for a few days or weeks in honor of our love, but it is strictly for pleasure and nostalgia. All of the real work for reproducing our species has already been done."

"So what the hell does that all have to do with all of this weird luggage?" Naero asked.

He went over to the pile of containers. "Naero, this isn't luggage. It's an entire Shai colony in stasis. I want you to find a place for it deeper into the Gamma Quadrant. That is where the Ku-Shai originally came from. We should go back there. Hundreds of millions of years ago, at the time of the last Great Dying, my people were all but wiped out, along with most of the other sentient species in the Gamma Quadrant."

That would roughly place them around the time of the G'lothc War with the Kexx and the Drians.

Gaviok placed one of his manipulators on the slightly largest and most heavily shielded of the cases.

"Those times could be upon us once more, Naero. We must defend against that. The great destroying darkness could be unleashed again, and we must stand ready. One of our mightiest homeworlds was taken from us, long, long ago, and defiled. A world we knew as fabled *Allondatharru*. Yet now it is called Naggoth by our enemies, the Dakkur!"

Naero started a bit. "One of the new Dakkur stronghold worlds, infested by the enemy. One of the seven seats of their power that we know of in the Gamma Quadrant."

Gaviok shook with rage. "It must be re-taken, at all costs, and returned to my people. My son will assist you, and come into his birthright. Teach him, help him grow as you helped me, and he shall be among your mightiest of allies." He pressed a release sequence.

The stasis case sprang open, and a young mantid, all shiny-black with a scarlet aura of Chaos force then pulsed around him awoke.

"Father," the young prince called out, going to his knee before his great sire. "Command your son. Command your children."

Gaviok introduced them. "Naero Amashin Maeris. Meet your new brother, as your uncle is mine. This is Prince Ra-Naveth. Be bound together in fate and deed."

Ra-Naveth turned pale pink, and embraced Naero. "If you share love with my beloved father, you have mine tenfold. My life is yours, and I will give if for you, gladly. We are now bound, for all the extent of our days."

Naero embraced Gaviok's young son, and kissed his head. "We are indeed bound. And you are my brother, my family, my *abani*. Let us honor each other and serve one another well. We shall protect one another in all that is to come."

Ra-Naveth rose up and turned more reddish again, even slightly shorter in his normal form than his father.

"This bodes well," Gaviok told her. "For when Ra-Naveth comes into his full powers, he is destined to wield ten times the might of his sire. Guard him until that day comes, and he and the others of my children shall guard you and yours."

They said their farewells, and Ra-Naveth stayed at Naero's side from that instant on. Naero accepted his presence.

The rest of the Shai nest was kept in stasis, and loaded into the cargo bay of Naero's flagship.

They met with Khai for dinner with Jan, his wives, Aunt Sleak, Zalvano, and their infant twin girls, Anya and Nuvi.

The little ones climbed all over everyone.

Naero loved the twins with all of her heart. She could not hug and kiss them enough. Seeing them nearly brought her to tears.

Aunt Sleak was still pale from meeting Calyxo and Vejjah, and having everything explained to her in much more detail than was wanted. Yet overall, she seemed to be accepting the situation.

"Anyone in my family is now at risk," Naero told Aunt Sleak. "Before I depart tomorrow, I'm making some more replicants. I want to send Naero-10 with you and Zalvano and the girls, to act as a bodyguard. I don't want any argument."

"I'm not arguing," Aunt Sleak said. "I could use a bodyguard who was even one tenth of what you've become."

"She'll be a lot more than one tenth. Trust me. Anyone comes after you and Zalavano and the kids, and she'll put them down. Hard."

"Sounds good, Naero. Thanks. So, I guess we're both admirals now. Congrats."

They drank a toast of delicious Spacer poteen.

"Another high honor for Clan Maeris, making you the youngest admiral ever appointed to a full battle group. Cheers."

Naero smiled her half-smile and lifted her glass. "I was trained by the best."

Aunt Sleak called up top secret holodata screens for Spacer Intel and the Navy, while Zalvano kept the others busy playing with the energetic little girls. Naero resisted the urge to hug them and simply gobble them up; they were so sweet, and so amazing.

"I've sent all of this data to your flagship, Naero. Want to see the heart of your command?" aunt Sleak asked. "Another fleet of hyper-dense, planetoid super-warships–greater than the Titans. More firepower than the Thirty Amazon Sisters, *combined.*

"They call them *The Gods of War.* A class of warships with all of the latest tek, including hulls constructed of hyperdense planetoid nanoalloy, combined with fixer tek. Do you realize what a breakthrough this is, Naero? These are the next generation of advanced Spacer warships, and you are going to lead them into battle."

Naero read the top secret data flows with teknomancy. "Nanoships. Warships that can construct themselves, adapt, and regenerate–all on their own. They can refit and adapt new tek in seconds."

"Your flagship dreadnaught was named, *The Holy Ghost.* Backed up by the super-battleships *The Shiva, The Thor, The Athena,* and *The Ares.*'

The data on her bigs alone were astonishing. "Aunt Sleak….are these specs right? Can these new hypervelocity cannons really fire this fast without blowing up or burning out?"

A call came in late.

Newly appointed Strike Captains Chaela and Saemar Maeris. Naero welcomed her old friends over the links, unable to contain her glee. "Chae, how's Remy?"

"Handsome as ever, especially since he's going to be a papa. Three months left to cook on this little critter inside me."

Naero smiled with real joy. "Congrats to you both, Chae. But, are you sure you want to accept this command, considering all of that?"

"Haisha, N. All of us were born during the Fourth Spacer War or around then. Spacer kids need to come into the universe, no matter what. I say the safest place in the galaxy is going to be with me, and you. Try to stop me from taking this command. You offered it. It's mine now. You're stuck with my ass!"

"That goes double for me, sweetie!" Saemar told her. "Glad to do it. Boy, do we have some catching up to do." Naero's lascivious, voluptuous old friend was just as brazen as ever.

All of them were still younger than thirty.

"Chae, I need you to take command of Strike Fleet 2 on my immediate left. Saemar, you will command Strike Fleet 3 on my immediate right."

"Copy, that, Admiral, sir," Chae said.

Saemar rolled her eyes. "Sure thing, Admiral sweetie."

There wasn't time to tell them about the enemy having Naero's own child prisoner somewhere. There would be time to talk more with them later.

Zalvano cornered Naero at one point several minutes after that. "Congrats, N. Did you hear that they also created an entirely new Marine Command for Battle Group Six to take with them?

"Really? A 12th Marine Command?"

"Yep, made up from volunteers and new recruits from all of the other eleven. They're calling themselves *The Deadly Dozen* now, and the nickname is sticking. Others just call them *The Twelves.*"

Naero was curious. "Who did they appoint as the Marine Commander?"

"A bit of nepotism there–General Walker's oldest daughter, General Azkhalatara Walker."

"The Hero of Nuveem and Bellandron during The High Crusade?"

"The same. She helped lead the 8th Command Starwalkers to victory after victory. Their rate of advance was only slightly behind that of Bravo Command. The Ejjai simply called them *hot death.*"

"I need to meet this woman. Sounds like her daddy raised her well. If she's Walker's oldest, she must be made of iron and fire. Great to have her with us."

Naero went over to *The Holy Ghost* late that night. She merged with the ship, and studied it with teknomancy. Nanoships–they were indeed a wonder.

Khai found her there, hours later, passed out in her command chair with Ra quietly standing guard over her. After a short introduction to the mantid prince, Khai carried her to the admiral's new quarters.

13

Naero's Battle Group Six assembled out beyond Kalathar.

One hundred fleets, simply numbered from one to one hundred. Nearly each fleet was commanded by an old friend or acquaintance whom Naero knew well. These were her fleet leaders and captains. These were her new lions, her new swords of light.

All stood in readiness by midday of that standard day.

Fleet Admiral Naero Amashin Maeris immediately ordered Battle Group Six to launch the second they were supplied and ready, blazing into the Gamma Quadrant and the Unknown Regions in good formation and order.

All five thousand warships and their crews were linked together as they passed through the new wyrmhole projectors, forming up in hyperspace.

The trip would take about two standard days, to cut across nearly half of the galaxy.

As they started out, Naero ordered the fleet band to play an old Spacer war song from the First Spacer War when they fought their way free of Old Earth and the growing Corps for the first time.

She had the song piped throughout every ship. Everyone raised Spacer knew those words well.

The old ballad was called, *End of Days.*

Naero drew her sword and saluted her entire fleet, singing the words, while her crews roared back with her.

The stars call out from the endless black,
Hold my hand and squeeze it tight.
Head on out, we're never going back,
Draw your swords, prepare to fight.
Tyrants rage and will soon attack,
Blast our way free into the night.
Fires rage and weapons crack.
Let Freedom be our driving light!

Chorus
Will you follow me to the End of Days?
Side by side we will make our way.
Fighting through War's deadly haze,
Break through now and seize our day!

Forge our path and throw off our chains,
Plot a course into the unknown.
Farewell to sorrow and our pains,
Justice and Liberty be our own.
Truth and Honor become our gains.
Knowledge and Wisdom must be grown,
Slavery fades like our bloodstains.

Chorus
Will you follow me to the End of Days?
Side by side we will make our way.
Fighting through War's deadly haze,
Break through now and seize our day!

Heroes fall and memory fades.
Guard our children and our ways.
The darkness comes and must be fought.
Sacrifice must at times be taught.

Launch our fleets, send in our waves,
Send our foes into the blaze.
Love our Clans and guard our hearts,
Soar off free into the stars!

Chorus
I will follow you to the End of Days!
Side by side we will win our way.
Fighting through Love's confusing maze,
With my last breath till our last day!

Naero smiled and sheathed her sword.

Many Spacers wept openly, as was their way. Tears were not an evil. Most Spacers, in their hearts, recalled singing old songs like that with their parents, and their grand parents, and their great grans. That was how they were passed on.

Naero clenched her fist suddenly.

One day, soon, she would sing those songs to her daughter.

Until then, there was much to do for everyone.

They had launched in a great hurry. Supplies and equipment needed to be sorted and distributed better. Crews had to get used to each other, and establish and keep up their duty and training schedules.

Almost everyone needed to be educated about the Gamma Quadrant and what little they did know about it and the strength of the enemy they might face there. But their Intel remained sketchy at best, mostly from Naero's own brief foray into those regions.

They had some idea where the enemy strongholds existed, but those were also spread out far and wide throughout the entire Gamma Quadrant.

Naero and her fleet captains prepared to explore cautiously at first. Their data pointed to the existence of almost countless sentient species, many of them completely new, interstellar, starfaring races that had never been encountered before. And the enemy could be expected in great strength and numbers in several potential regions, with capabilities and weapons that were not yet known.

She and her officers prepared for many First Contact scenarios, where they would encounter new alien species and face several challenges, including potential conflict. Such relationships and exchanges could very well be vital.

The overall mission of the Battle Group was clear. They were there to fight and take on their known enemies and any new allies those enemies have gained. Yet the other half of that mission was just as important. It was apparent that none could fight such enemies alone. Exploration, First Contact, and new alliances would serve them best, on into the future. Spacers came not as enslavers and exploiters, but as explorers, liberators, and defenders. Any enemy victory meant subjugation and death.

If the new sentients they encountered were willing to coexist, or merely wanted to live free within their own regions, they would find ready friends and allies among Spacers. Or simply be left alone, if that was what they wanted as well.

Naero and each fleet captain and their officers went through experimental drills and problem-solving scenarios involving initial contacts with new sentient species. The goal was to prepare them all for the real thing. They couldn't just assume that every species they would encounter would be human or near human. Each new species had to be assessed and evaluated on its own.

The Gamma Quadrant was mostly unknown to them, and the threat of the enemy had to be taken into consideration as well. The G'lothc and their servants, the Dakkur, enslaved other species and used them as shock troops and foodstocks with absolute impunity. Yet if these enslaved species could be somehow liberated, they might become potent allies against their former masters.

One factor did not change. A standard order existed to eradicate all Ejjai, whenever and wherever they were encountered.

The Spacers were scheduled to begin their initial exploration sweep in a rimward section of the immense Scutum Crux-Arm of the galaxy. They would send out scouting ships in stealth mode, and deploy large numbers of self-replicating exploration fixers.

Naero also created six more replicants of herself, Naero-11 through Naero-15. Given time, she hoped to have one of her replicants advising on each fleet that served under her, but only as advisors. They were there to help, not second-guess her command officers.

Yet still, commanding one hundred fleets and five thousand warships and all of their crews was an immense task, and needed to be managed.

Naero first met within the primary strategy and planning command center on board her Battle Group flagship, *The Holy Ghost*, which also led Fleet Number 1. Shortly, she would hold a conference with all fifty of her fleet commanders, including her Battle Group Second, Third, and Fourth in Commands. Along with her, each of them would command one quarter of the Battle Group, or twenty-five fleets each. But the other three would coordinate their actions with her.

For the present, meeting only with her immediate staff was always a good way to start. Her Fleet 1 XO was Commodore Darius Meade, her Second. Third in command of Fleet 1 was Fleet Captain Chrissella James. Fourth was Leftenant Varina Flynn; in Spacer Naval rankings, a leftenant outranked a commander.

In lander fleets, it was just the opposite. Somewhere in history it had gotten switched around somehow, and now among Spacers, it simply stuck. Naero's Fifth in command was her brother, Second Leftenant Janner Maeris Ramsey, yet as one of the Fleet 1 Intel Liaisons, he was also the commander of *The Black Spot*, Naero's special spyship, to be sent out as needed.

Finishing off her immediate command staff, Commander Lewis Bickle was sixth in Command, and Leftenant Commander Jubilee Lii was Seventh in command. Yet another old friend, Marine Major Python Wilde commanded the flagship's Spacer Marine contingent from the newly formed 12th Spacer Marine Command. The starfighter wing on board was led by Wing Commander, Captain Maci Donovan.

First they put Fleet 1 in order and got themselves fully operational. Each fleet commander was expected to do the same and make a full report to Admiral Naero that evening.

As it was their first night together, and they'd still be in hyperspace for another day, Naero declared a banquet and a celebration for all ships.

The initial meetings went well. They had another day to get things in order, and be ready to both fight and maneuver.

Naero wished she knew more about the region they were about to jump into blind.

Khai had been busy coordinating with all of the Mystics and MCLs who went with the Battle Group.

Both he and Naero met up in her quarters once again, late into the bells. They barely had time to wrap themselves around one another and they were drifting off.

No fooling around that first night.

Three hours later, a secret call from Baeven awoke both of them, and Ra.

"Have you found her?" Naero asked.

"Nice to hear from you, too, N."

"Sorry–"

"Haisha. I know how you are by now, *Admiral*."

"Yeah, yeah…*outcast*. Now report, dammit!"

"We've located several leads, and we're following up on them, but we could use some help. There's a lot of territory to cover, and we won't have a full fixer net up for months, if not years."

"Don't worry, uncle. As soon as we arrive, I'm sending out *The Dark Star*, *The Flying Dagger,* and *The Black Spot* all in spyship mode to help with the search. Which way does the enemy appear to be heading?"

"Unfortunately, they all lead into what appears to be an extremely hot war zone, with multiple fierce interstellar battles on several major fronts. What's worse, the enemy seems to be winning, nearly everywhere, from our initial analysis. They are spreading their power and growing in strength."

"We'll see if we can reverse that a bit. Do what you can and continue to gather intel. We'll be with you in about one day."

"Copy that, N."

"Baeven, how close are we going to emerge to the nearest battle zone?"

"About fifty parsecs from the nearest battles. As I said, the enemy seems to be attacking in several extended areas with impunity. They are all very spread out. You'll want to send in some ships to scout the first area close in. But even from this distance, the pockets of fighting seem pretty intense on the sensor scans. Our foes seem to be packing quite a lot of firepower. There is stiff resistance, but we can't tell how long that is going to last."

"Anything about my daughter? You said you had an Astral tracer on her. Is she all right?"

"N, your unborn kid's power levels are so bizarre and off the charts, but I can't sense much else than general location, and nothing I can plot. There seems to be some other form of astral interference here as well. But I can sense impressions. And they're not good."

Naero closed her eyes and sighed. "Give it to me straight, Baeven."

"The enemy has mounted numerous attempts immobilize or drain her energies in various ways. By attacking her, obviously. So far—and I don't quite exactly know how—she has managed to hold them off. But how long can anyone hold out against enemies such as the ones we face?"

"Stay on the hunt, Baeven. If you catch up to them and you can do anything, I want my girl back. You murder the living fuck out of anything that gets in your way!"

Baeven laughed grimly. "Hell, I was going to do that anyway. Over and out, Naero. Talk to you after you arrive, unless something important pops up between now and then."

Naero sighed and snuggled back in with Khai, shuddering as they held each other close.

"We will find her," Khai said, stroking her long black hair. "And those who took her from us shall pay dearly."

Naero nodded, her head resting above his heart.

She couldn't even speak.

We're coming, baby. Hang on. We're doing everything as fast as we can. And we're bringing hell and oblivion straight on with us.

14

Battle Group Six officially entered the Gamma Quadrant twenty-three hours later. Fleet Admiral Naero Amashin Maeris led Fleets 1 through 25 in triple, Charlie-Whiskey-3 strategic formation at the twelve o'clock position. The other four bigs held apex firing positions at the compass points around *The Holy Ghost*, with the rest of *The Gods of War* positioned around them.

They came out of hyperspace on command, ready to fight if need be.

The Spacers didn't want to take any chances.

A hundred fleets sounded like a large number, but in a prolonged war, enemies such as the ones they faced could well have an entire navy of thousands of fleets.

Naero's other three admirals under her authority emerged and formed up behind her. On her left, at the nine o'clock formation area, Fleet 33, led by Vice Admiral Hans Krieger, Third in overall Task Force Command. Krieger's flagship was *The Prince of Austria*, another massive dreadnaught, backed up by the uber battleships: *The Salzburg, The*

Rheinland, Graf Tyrol, and *The Deutschland*. Krieger led Fleets 26 through 50.

In the three o'clock position on her right, was Rear Admiral Michael Marshall, Fourth in Fleet Command, with Fleets 51 through 75. His flagship was the dreadnaught *The Stargazer*, supported by the bigs: *The Sun Tiger, The Sharkhunter, The Battle Ray,* and *The Star Panther*, with the rest of Fleet 66 assembled behind them.

Naero's second in Fleet Command anchored the all important six o'clock position, where most surprise attacks came from. Admiral Yamamoto Toshio directed Fleets 75 through 100. His primary fleet was Fleet-100, with the dreadnaught flagship *The Musashi*, supported by the super battleships: *The Nagato, The Shinano, The Haruna,* and *The Kirishima*.

Extreme long range scanners picked up only the echoes of distant war zones.

There was nothing within several light years that was even moving, and most of those blips were from their own advance relay fixers being set up for the coming network.

A few small alien starships, most likely traders or explorers.

Actually, that was more than acceptable. It was not the plan to emerge immediately in to a hot war zone.

Naero launched her spyships and a cloud of dispersing stealth drones and exploration fixers. Then she sent a call out to Baeven.

Scouting and Star Charting Data would begin to filter back within a matter of hours. They would analyze that data and proceed.

An urgent response came back almost instantly from *The Star Fox*.

"Naero. We're close. Investigating a serious lead here at these coordinates. Come in secret, stealth ship preferable. Leave the fleets behind for now."

Haisha. She'd just sent out all of her spyships.

Naero turned her flagship over Naero-5 and her XO, the Task Force over to Admiral Yamamoto.

Fleet-1 had a missile frigate, *The Wooly Bully*, that was configured for stealth mode.

She and Khai took that ship, with Ra and Tarim to back them up.

They arrived at the specified location within forty standard minutes, near an immense planetoid and asteroid debris field.

Close up scans brought up evidence of a recent battle, occluded from long distance scans due to the debris.

Jia called out to them, even though they were still cloaked. "Naero. EV and join Baeven and Danjen in the black, around the remains of that enemy ship."

Naero tried to find it. "What enemy ship?"

"If you can believe it, there were originally five of them. An Ejjai battleship, two cruisers, a destroyer, and another of those enemy spyships. You'd never know it. There isn't much left of each."

"Haisha, Jia. What the hell happened to them?"

"You tell us, N. I'll place coded markers on the guys out there so that you can locate them. Join them and see if you can make any sense of this."

They didn't like it, but Tarim and Ra were ordered to stay behind on the frigate. Naero pweaked into her sealed combat armor. Khai then phazed them out the side of the vessel in one of his green shield spheres, zipping them to the markers.

Naero finally spotted Baeven and Danjen in their EV suits, examining small bits of floating wreckage that seemed extremely deformed, melted, and fused.

"Hey guys. You remember Khai."

Danjen nodded. "Big. Green. Cosmic sword. Not many of his kind around, N."

"Hilarious, you furry little freak. What do we have here, Baeven? Was our girl a part of all of this somehow?"

"I'm beginning to fear that she was. I'm guessing the enemy did something that she really did not like."

Naero looked around her and her mouth fell open. "You think our unborn child did this?"

"Either her, the KDM, or possibly both, N."

"What do you think happened?"

"Adjust your range of perception, open to all Cosmic fields."

Naero did so. "Haisha. Holy blazing krap!"

Baeven showed her a chunk of fused slag, with a trace residue of powerful Darkforce energy.

"This is all that's left of one of those enemy Darkforce generators, Naero. From Jia's estimates, there were more than twenty of them. Now all that's left are traces such as this."

Naero looked around her, reading all of the signs. "Something wiped them all out."

"Indeed," Baeven said, "and the enemy warships as well. Annihilated either when they tried to attack or attempted to flee."

Naero made a guess. "Those sons of bitches. They tried to stuff Naero-3 into one of those Darkforce generators. And that was apparently a huge miscalculation on their part."

Baeven grinned through his face shield and even chuckled. "Very much so. Imagine their great surprise."

"Baeven...the raw Cosmic force that it would take to unleash this kind of destruction on this scale."

"I know. No such power should exist. It is as if a small supernova went off, and what's more, the power was spherically directed and controlled."

Naero looked around, reaching out with all of senses, opening her third eye. "If my child was here, and the enemy were all destroyed, then where is she? Where has she gone?"

She was ready to panic. "Don't you tell me she's gone, too!"

"Calm yourself," Baeven said. "Naero-3 is still alive, I'm fairly certain. At least one cloaked ship did leave this area and continued on in the direction of the fighting. The only ships that were destroyed were the alien spyship itself, and the four warships that must have made the mistake of attacking. Once the destruction was over, I think the enemy very carefully retrieved Naero-3, plus her little hitchhiker, and whisked them all away with a healthy new respect."

"Where did they go?"

"That's why we need to track them again. They obviously jumped out of this system."

"Stay on them. Find them, please."

A call came in from the task force fleets.

They had made initial contact with not one, but two other sentient species, and both were involved in at least one of the interstellar wars that was raging.

"Come on, Khai. We need to get back."

15

The first sentient race called themselves the Kodar. Surprisingly, they were about as near human as they could be. About 1.5 to 1.8 meters tall, five fingers and toes, a variety of skin tones, eye, and hair colors. All within the Terran range.

They were spacefaring and had merchant and mining ships with tek that was around Jump levels 3 to 5. Kodar ships were unarmed, even relatively unarmored and unshielded. They possessed no military. On their worlds, they barely had police forces.

The Kodar were uniquely pacifistic, and endlessly diplomatic. They could discuss anything at length, almost forever.

Each of them wore a synaptic modulation chip implanted in their foreheads and their frontal lobes, from birth to death.

Naero was suspect of the chips from the very beginning, but the Kodar clearly saw them as the solution to all of their former problems.

Their leaders expounded the Kodar history with great joy and satisfaction.

Naero, Khai, and a select landing party of her people sat down in a quiet, sunlit conference room on Vertron, one of the six major Kodar homeworlds.

They spoke with a very pleasant planetary diplomat named Mariq. "You must picture the Kodar over three centuries ago. Avaricious, over-competitive, opportunistic–even violent, dare I say it. Our culture was out of control and beginning to conflict with our interstellar neighbors. It was all our fault entirely. We desired conflict so that we had an excuse to make war upon others–to subjugate, enslave, or destroy them, and take their worlds and their resources for our own."

Mariq's voice caught. "Then came the awakening. Some of our leaders convinced others that there was another way, a better way. We could rise above our many flaws, our inner darkness and imperfections, and choose a way that would both promote and ensure right thinking and follow it with right actions. Hence, the modulators."

"It's still mind control, from what I see," Naero said. "How do you know it's all right if there is no choice? No free will?"

"Because it works, and it's so simple. For almost three centuries, we have sustained a perfect, peaceful society. We know outsiders don't often understand. The modulators allow all right thinking, and weed out only negative and destructive thinking. The desire to commit crime, to hurt others, to kill others, and to do wrong."

Naero laughed. "So you've taken a shortcut. But who decides what is right thinking and what is negative thinking?"

"Our leaders decided those matters for us, for the good of all. And since then, the Kodar have been a peaceful and positive culture, among themselves and our neighbors."

Naero was curious. "And world after world just went along with all of this?"

"No, there was a much-needed revolution. The populations had to be persuaded at times to make the right choice. And yes, some were forced to embrace the change for the better."

"If it was forced upon them, then it was not a choice."

"But don't you see? Everyone had to comply. It would not have worked otherwise. Certainly, it is not a perfect system. Show us which system is? But look at what we have now: peace, prosperity, cooperation, and happiness."

Naero shook her head. "Only because you've eliminated all other choices and possibilities."

Mariq smiled at her. "As stated, we do not expect all outsiders and offworlders to understand or accept our ways. But we do ask you to please respect them."

Naero nodded, keeping her reservations to herself. "Of course we will. My people are not here to interfere with or change your ways. But what do you think is going to happen when the great enemy in the distance defeats your neighbors and comes to subjugate your worlds?"

"If they are as great and as intelligent as you say, then we will negotiate with them and come to an understanding."

Naero held her tongue. "Examine the data feeds that we have included in our knowledge exchanges, Mariq. There is a race that fights for the enemy called the Ejjai. Let us know how you plan to negotiate with them."

Mariq merely nodded. "Thank you for dealing with us in peace. We will study the knowledge you have given us."

"Can you tell us about the next sentient species that we are going to meet with next?"

Mariq's face lost color. "You mean the Lish?" The diplomat visibly shuddered. "There is not much to know. The spiders—"

"Spiders?"

"Yes, the Lish are an arachnid race. Quite hideous, actually." Mariq glanced at Ra. "No offense, creature. I am certain that there are good bugs and insectoids."

Ra cocked his mantid head and blinked his eyes. "I am not a Lish. Why would I be offended by you insulting that species?"

Mariq cleared his throat. "Be that as it may. We try to avoid the Lish. They are warlike, even among their own kind. Hotheaded. Competitive. We stay away from them, when and where we can. There is some trade with them in limited areas. Typically, they…do not mix well with regular people."

"I see," Naero said. "Do you know whose side they fight on in the war."

Mariq smirked. "Both or all sides from what we know, which isn't much. There are several factions among the Lish, and many sell their services as mercenaries as well from what the rumors say. The entire situation is a huge, bloody mess from what we hear, and the great enemy merely takes advantage of the chaos."

"Very well," Naero said. "Thank you for meeting with us and exchanging information. We must be moving on. Your peaceful worlds have nothing to fear from us. I cannot say the same for the enemy, should they come against you."

"Thank you, Admiral Maeris. Travel on with our good will."

Khai spoke up as soon as they were heading back up, away from the planet and back to the fleets, most of whom held back, to hide the task force's true numbers.

"Something is very wrong with those people," the Enforcer said, shaking his head.

"I agree, Khai. But that is not our problem at this point. Nor can we save these people from the folly of their own choices. For example: What would keep the enemy from seizing all of the Kodar worlds and reprogramming all of those mind control chips? Those fools have made themselves puppets. Or what if the enemy simply marched them all into the Ejjai meatships?" Naero shivered. "It makes me crazy just thinking about it."

And oddly enough, the Kodar had made several attempts to scan the Spacers and their vessels.

"We can't solve any of this stupidity. Let's move on to meet with the Lish, these spiders as they are called. At least some of them are fighting this new great enemy. Let's see what they are like and what they can tell us."

Quietly, Naero waited to hear back from Baeven. Nothing yet.

*

The Lish were highly evolved, sentient arachnids about two meters in diameter and about 1.5 meters high when they rose up on their eight legs to their full height, to make themselves appear more menacing during negotiations and contests. Yet they were most dangerous when they slunk down low and bunched to attack, or even leaped upon their opponents.

The spy drones had gathered some preliminary data on the fighting that was taking place, onworld and up in space. Initial reports provided evidence of Ejjai, Dakkur, and other unidentified sentients fighting for the enemy–including some Lish, but details were not complete.

Each of the Lish possessed the strength of twenty or more adult humans according to estimates, making them very formidable, especially in large numbers. They were also expert, logical thinkers and mathematicians. They were ruthless and utterly fearless in battle, with no concern for their own lives. Lish fought with a cold ferocity that even the Ejjai and the Dakkur found unnerving, yet they were not invincible. They were vulnerable to fire, cold, and most battlefield weapons.

Their tek was very advanced, on par with that of Spacers and the Alliance, around Jump-7. They used shields for massed units, vehicles and ships, but not for individuals. They did not seem to use tanks or any

105

other armored vehicles. They did use starfighters and gravitics. Their dexterous claws could manipulate almost any tool or device.

Since their dense, armored bodies were naturally resistant to damage, they normally wore no additional armor in combat, unless they were in a vacuum or exposed to toxic environments. They mounted various weapons and weapon systems on their limbs and bodies. They had pods of bombs and micro-explosives that they could drop or fire at foes.

Lish starships and warships were single-minded in purpose, design, and construction. Get to the destination fast, do what was required, and get back just as fast. Do what was needed to be done. The Lish seemed capable of placing themselves into some form of trance or stasis during space travel, and awakening themselves with some kind of signal upon arrival. Their plain, heavily armored and shielded warships and starfighters, just like their podlike starships, had no viewports or blast screens.

All Lish warships were built solely around their powerful weapon systems, and were basically flying cannons and energy weapons, little more. Lish naval personnel had very little in the way of personal items or quarters, and spent literally all of their time at their stations. Food and lix came to them at their posts in measured quantities via tubes. Bodily wastes were just as efficiently processed and recycled.

A fighter had a small weapon. Larger warships had the equivalent of larger weapons with more destructive energy outputs. Lish ships were pods, orbs, ovals, tubes, cones, and even planetoid blobs, or crystalline or metallic cubes and geodes.

The Lish had few, if any, aesthetic sensibilities. They couldn't care less what a ship looked like, as long as it could function and fight as required.

Were they aggressive? Yes. They could be incredibly aggressive. And they were tough negotiators. But once they made a deal, an agreement, or a treaty, they kept their word, to the letter.

Betrayal was not a concept for them. They were neither sensitive nor sentimental, with very little capacity or range for emotion. Yet they still had emotions. They were also incredibly gentle lovers with each other when they consummated their courtships, uncaring as to whether anyone else watched. Lish pairs mated for life, and even languished and died after their mates died.

But more than anything else, Lish were incredibly devoted and diligent parents in the nest, defending their young against any threat, great or small, with an incredible, selfless ferocity. And yet, they sent their children out each day into a dangerous world, to test themselves and their strength and intelligence. Even if they did not come back.

All Lish had to face the threats of their world. Once their own young reached adulthood, the Lish expelled them and then treated them like any other adult in the nest.

The Lish spoke an intricate, subsonic snapping and clicking language that was, in fact, mathematically based. It also functioned as music, and the Lish were beautiful singers. They could approximate and even mimic other speech and communication patterns from other species, but even by their own admission, they found doing so difficult and unpleasant.

They were not telepathic by nature, but telepathy worked on their highly ordered minds.

The Lish controlled two hundred and six separate worlds. Their primary homeworld was Hryxjik, at the core of their empire.

Naero arranged to meet with one of their leaders on Ngvuk, on the outermost rim of their systems, far away from the war.

There were some color variations, but the vast majority of Lish were black and quite hairy, with slight orange-brown highlights in a few places. Their multiple black eyes served in different light conditions.

The Lish leader she was meeting was named Tus, the commanding leader of the main continent.

The Lish had various nests, not cities, and were spread all over the surface of their worlds, where they all raised and hunted various livestock, some of them incredibly dangerous in their own right.

The hunter-warrior Lish apparently enjoyed testing themselves against anything or anyone new. They nearly insisted on it.

Naero went down to the surface in a shuttle, dropping down from a destroyer, bristling with ground-assault-mode weapons. A very formidable display of power.

Tus came out to meet her, Khai, Ra, and Tarim, along with a fireteam of 12th Command armored Marines, looking like the death dealers they were.

Tus clicked and snapped, and thousands of Lish appeared around the landing site. Also a display of power. "We considered capturing you, killing your guards, and negotiating terms over your ransom," he told her.

Naero smiled, not sure if he was joining or being serious. "I'm glad you didn't. It would have been an unpleasant start to our negotiations to be forced to slay so many of you." Naero had taken time to psyonically learn their language, and could approximate the Lish sound ranges enough to be understood.

Tus seemed about as amused as a humorless spider creature could be. "Yes. Amusing. Myself, our leaders, and my warriors want to know how tough you and your guardians are. Let us have one of my soldiers and one of your guards fight to the death. This will be very instructive for both of us."

Naero hesitated. "Emissary Tus. I don't feel that this is necessary."

"Oh, but it is, Admiral Maeris. Come. Just pick one you won't mind dying at the hands of my soldier.

Ra spoke up. "Naero. Allow me to protect you."

"Are you sure about this?"

"Certainly. I understand these creatures. This is but a test. Allow me to fulfill the requirements."

"All right. Go ahead, and be careful."

"Yes, of course."

Tus snapped and clicked.

The biggest, nastiest-looking Lish sprang up out of nowhere. The goddam thing was as big as a tank.

Tus and the other Lish immediately scuttled back, creating a broad combat area for the contest.

Ra remained the same size, but he flashed from red to black, and slammed into the big Lish so fast that the only ones who could follow his blinding attacks were Naero and Khai.

In the space of a few seconds, Ra slew the big Lish almost instantly. Then he proceeded to rip it apart, and even devour most of the body for good measure.

Even Naero hadn't expected the gruesome eating part.

Ra flashed back in behind her, cleaning the last Lish hairs from his mandibles, and silently took up his guardian position once more, his coloration fading from black back to scarlet.

The only thing left of the big Lish were the still-quivering, hairy legs.

"So, Tus," Naero said. "Tell me how the war is going, and let us negotiate. My people have no wish to fight with yours. We would rather trade with you and be your allies."

The leader of the Lish stammered a bit, still sounding a bit stunned. He kept looking back at the remains of his dead champion. "Y-yes, that might be best...for everyone."

16

According to Tus, when he leveled with Naero after their initial treaty was agreed to, the war was not going well at all for any of the original sentients in that region.

Seventeen Lish worlds had fallen to the invaders, who appeared to be Dakkur, Ejjai, a race of humanoids in armor, and waves of deadly robotic gunships and smart drones.

Naero was very curious about the humanoids, and where they came from. Tus said that his people did not know, and that the enemy bodies dissolved after they were killed, denying the Lish a food source on the battlefield. A practice the Lish found very evil.

"The victor should be able to devour his defeated enemies," Tus said in disgust. "That is just common courtesy. These invaders have no honor."

Naero agreed. "We noticed that when we fought them as well," she said. "Tell me about the other races you have been allied with. Those others who also fight the invaders."

Tus handed her what looked to be a basic hand computer. "Here is what we know of them in these data files. But none of the alliances with the others have worked out very well. These others do not understand the Lish, and see us but as voracious monsters. They are stupid and insult us. And none, besides yourself, have taken the time to learn to speak our language, and read our hearts and minds, as you have done.

"The Lish are the way they are. They are not wicked monsters. Our ways are indeed our own, but we can be reasoned with, and trusted to uphold our agreements–better than most. We are willing to allow these other races to live as they choose on their worlds, as long as we are allowed to do so on ours. That is more than can be said of some. Can the invaders be trusted in these ways? No; clearly they cannot.

"Yet even when we have tried to understand each other and help one another militarily, the invaders always seem to know when and where to best attack us. And once the attacks begin, the so-called allies all scatter to defend their own worlds, and will not band together."

"From what we guess," Naero said, "the invaders have cracked your communication systems, and know what all of you are planning. With that knowledge, they know where your forces are and are not, and can play you against each other, in order to keep you divided."

Tus bobbed his head. "That would make sense, then."

"We have communication systems that they have not been able to defeat so easily. Then you can all coordinate your military actions better, and keep them hidden from the invaders."

"Good, good," Tus said. Naero barely detected some kind of subsonic chime going off, resounding throughout the Lish nesting area.

Tus turned to them. "I understand we have different ways, but it is now one of our scheduled feeding times. Will you join me, my mate, and our children? You may bring your own food to feed on if you wish."

Naero glanced back at the others. They were at just as much of a loss as she was. Khai shrugged. "Why not?" she said. "My people will enjoy having a picnic with your family."

Tus looked confused. "I do not understand the word *picnic*, but if it refers to a feeding time, you will be our guests. Come then. Feeding times are when we speak with our mates, our children, and others, exchanging information."

"Good," Naero said. "I still have many questions about your allies, the war, and the enemy."

Naero led her three friends down into Tus's nest. The Marine fireteam remained outside at the DZ, with the fleet destroyer still floating up above.

Naero was surprised. The nest was cool and comfortable down inside, just warm enough. The tunnels, chambers, and various passage ways were neither damp nor dirty or dusty. The Lish tunnels were almost a precise two meters in diameter, allowing them to pass swiftly along the floor, the walls, or the ceiling at will. The nest networks were carefully designed and constructed with precise engineering, reinforced with some kind of resin that was as strong as plasteel when Naero analyzed its crystalloy composition with teknomancy.

They met a few other Lish, going here and there within the nest. They all seemed to be aware of the visitors already, and did not even acknowledge or touch them as they scurried by. Most barely acknowledged Tus.

Their host explained. "Biochemical news of our treaty with you has spread throughout the nest, alerting all of our people to your visit, your different scents, and your presence. No harm will come to you now, as our friends. But if you or any of your kind entered our nests without permission, or acceptance, you would have triggered a defensive response as if you were attackers. You would have been set upon by thousands of Lish, who would have captured, if not slain you."

Tus went on to describe how it was considered rude in Lish culture for one adult Lish to climb over or under another, unless during war or some other emergency, such as flood or fire or some such. The young Lish were exempt from these rules, and mostly climbed all over the adults. Also, most Lish were not very good swimmers without underwater gear, and could drown in deep water because of the ways their bodies breathed. Floods could still be very real calamities for them. The Lish had just begun to use terraforming to control rains and flooding, and they tried not to build nests in areas prone to flooding.

The Lish nests and networks were not completely dark within. They used a system of bio-luminescence and lighting crystals to illuminate their underground areas in a low, greenish-yellow lighting, about the intensity of twilight. Lish had evolved various sets of of eyes to function in almost every type of light, from bright sunlight above ground to near-total darkness.

Tus said that unless they were pursuing mining interests, or defending against attacks, the Lish did not normally dig their nests very deep, for fear of hitting pockets of ground water that could flood their nests.

In temperate zones and colder, the Lish did not do well in the cold. Around temperatures near freezing, the Lish suffered greatly from cold effects and had to wear protective suits to cover and warm most of their bodies. The only time they wore what could be called clothing. They did wear load-bearing harnesses that various tools, gear, and even weapons could be attached to.

Finally they reached Tus's home. It was wide and circular, possessing even a low dome within, and many circular side chambers. There was no furniture to speak of, just raised nodules of stone or resin like rounded tabletops.

Another adult Lish came out of a tunnel within the nest, dragging out a net of what appeared to be various livestock animals encased in webbing and cured into what could only be described as succulent, hams or cured meatpods. With the great strength of the Lish, toting around several hundred kilos of food from their immense pantries was no burden.

"Meet my mate, Gyx. Gyx, these are the alien guests that I said would bring."

She nodded her head. "I am Gyx. Speak with us, new friends. Come, Tus. I have prepared our feeding time. I was about to summon our young. You said our strange guests bring their own food?"

"That is true."

"Then let us feed and talk." She emitted a unique call.

Three dozen young Lish suddenly exploded into the cavern, scurrying and climbing over everyone, including the guests. Naero warned them not to move and to remain still. Then the hungry children settled over the foodpods.

Tus explained that he had released a signal to the young, telling them not to nip or taste the visitors. They were not to be seen as prey or potential food.

"We are grateful for that," Naero said.

Tus and Gyx made sure that their children were fed. Then they grabbed larger foodpods for themselves, dragged them up onto the weird tables, and jammed their mouth parts into them.

Naero and her people nibbled on foodbars and sipped from lix tubes, or simply watched. Ra asked if he could try one of the foodpods. Tus pulled one of the big ones onto one of the other tables. Ra made short work of it, practically inhaling it.

Even the Lish seemed impressed.

"Do you eat your livestock and your food supplies raw?" Naero asked.

"Their meat and its juices are cured, smoked, and flavored very nicely," Ra informed her. "Very tasty. Might I have another?"

"There is plenty, friend Ra," Gyx told him. "My mate says you are a mighty warrior. Seeing you feed, I can well believe that."

"Gratitude, friend Gyx," Ra said. He had managed to learn their language as well, and spoke it now with his own accent from the manipulation of the vocal sounds through his mandibles.

"Some Lish eat their food supplies raw," Tus said, "if there is no other way, or during war. But if possible, we like to prepare our foodstocks so that they are succulent and filled with much juicy flavor. Our smoking facilities compete with each other to create the most delicious foodpods."

"You do not eat your prey alive?" Ra asked.

"Again," Tus said, "such things can be done during war, but we do not normally make our livestock suffer. Suffering and pain taints our meat. That is why livestock are dispatched quickly, and injected with flavorings and necessary preservatives, carefully prepared before they are wrapped and smoked. The best foodpods take about a month to cure properly. We and our children want our foodstocks to be delicious."

Naero watched how the Lish fed. First they sucked out all of the juices. Then their mandibles devoured the jerky-like meat, leaving behind an empty husk of hide and picked bones. The empty food pods were recycled and used as fertilizer to raise food to feed their livestock, who in turn fed them.

Naero listened to Tus and Gyx talk about their children. Lish were not given names until they reached adulthood. Until then, they simply had a number. Lish parents even wrote those numbers on their backs, in their symbolic language. All of the kids were marked so.

"We lost fourteen and twenty-three today," Gyx told her mate.

"I saw that," Tus said. "Did they die well?"

"Fourteen fought a galontok bravely, but was simply unlucky. Twenty-three was hunting along the shore of one of the inner seas and was snapped up by a giant haxgar."

"Haxgar are indeed dangerous. Children, did you all learn the lessons of those among you who perished today?"

Some of the children spoke in unison, while others simply kept feeding. "We learned the lessons of death, father. Our world has many challenges. Each day we must go out and face them. To face the challenges of life and stay alive brings us honor, teaches us many things that we must know, and makes us worthy to be counted among our people."

"Good. Remember what you have learned this day. Apply that knowledge to your efforts tomorrow, so that you will grow strong, smart, and live long."

"Gyx, how many offspring are in a Lish hatching?" Naero asked.

"Anywhere from forty to sixty," she answered. "Life is hard, and each Lish must take their chances in the fierce world and learn to make their way. First they become warrior/hunters. Once they have proven themselves, and earned the right to become adults, they are given their adult names, and can begin to learn how to apply their intellects to helping the nest."

"How many of each hatching survive to become adults?"

"Sometimes none," Tus admitted. "But usually the number is three to seven. Once they have proven themselves to the nest, if there is roomed to expand the nest they will be allowed to mate, and begin to raise young of their own. It is a sustainable system. The Lish do not allow overpopulation."

Now that they had fed, a few of the young Lish wandered over and crawled over Naero and her friends, examining them with great curiosity. The visitors kept it together and withstood such curiosity for a while. Then Naero looked to Tus. Before she even said anything, their host seemed to sense their discomfort, and ordered the young to leave the visitors alone.

Naero let out a slight sigh.

"I meant to ask you, Tus. What about these reports of Lish fighting alongside of the invaders?"

For the first time, both Tus and Gyx stiffened. Naero sensed that her new friends were angry. "No Lish would willingly fight for our enemies," Tus said. "But our foes are cunning and have advanced technology that we do not. They have learned to take control of the minds of our unhatched and set them against us. And they can also clone our kind and program even adult Lish minds to fight as automatons or shock troops. They look like Lish, but there are all but mindless slaves bent only on killing. Their minds are not free to think on their own. Such a thing enrages us. All true Lish have a strong inner desire to be free to live our lives and raise our young as we see fit. None should take that freedom from us. Those who do these things are worse than enemies."

"I agree with you, Tus. Thank you for sharing your feeding time with us," Naero said. "But I must know more about the other sentients who also fight the invaders. I would also like to learn more about the war and the enemies you face."

Tus nodded. "Good. Travel with us to another meeting set up. There you can meet some of them. Perhaps something better will come of it this time. Our ships will launch and lead you to the meeting place."

Naero agreed and contacted Task Force Six.

Skirmishes had already been reported with enemy ships. That was bound to happen. But Naero still wanted to avoid any major battles until they could assess the situation better.

Spacers also made initial fixer contact with the other sentient species in the region.

Naero checked with Tus, and confirmed their findings.

One sentient race were self-aware robots or androids, human-sized, who constructed their own offspring to increase their numbers. They simply called themselves: the Mechans.

Next were the Sa'shom, humanoids with human-range male and female torsos above the waist, with serpentine, snake-like bodies below. Some Spacers were already nicknaming them, the gorgons. And the last race were dragonfly like insectoid with humanoid faces, fighting with multiple limbs.

Naero recognized them instantly. They were the Amavar—S'krin's own people. She needed to contact Baeven right away.

Unable to reach her uncle, she reviewed vid footage the Lish had from the war, watching the Lish fight both Ejjai and Dakkur, and a few other races working for the enemy.

Naero always disliked having to watch the atrocities of the enemy inflicted upon any species, human or non-human.

17

A secret meeting with the defenders of that entire region was scheduled to be held on an isolated world called Muntothon-4 within less than a day. Admiral Naero did her best to position several of her fleets to facilitate proper security.

All the while, data flowed in from the expanding spyfixer nets. Naero and her people did their best to analyze a huge amount of navigation, system, and military data, and sort out what was from the enemy, and what was from the local defenders.

Direct reports from scouts and forward elements also came in.

"Admiral Naero. Fleet-17 reports 183 separate fleets fighting around these coordinates. Seventy of those fleets appear to be in enemy configurations. More detailed analyses to follow."

"Good work, Ima. Get us everything we can learn about those fleets, their actions, and their movements. Knowledge is our best weapon right now. We don't know enough, yet."

Another call from Fleet 86. "Report, Captain Namoori. What's so urgent?"

"Sir, warn all the other fleets and scouts that the enemy is spreading out a defensive screen of four hundred *additional* fleets, on top of their deployed fleets, around their homeworlds and their expanded areas of conquest."

Naero grinned as her fingers flashed, relaying the data through teknomancy. "Done. The enemy knows something's up. A new player is on the field and just like us, they want to learn everything they can."

"The local Mechans and...Amavar are taking a beating out this way. Do we engage? Do we assist, sir?"

Naero didn't hesitate. "I'm sorry. Not yet, Namoori. But that day will come, and soon. Hang back and collect data. We can't tip our hand for now."

"Sir, the enemy just started to attack out this way within the last few days. Could they be trying to lure us into the mix so that they can study us and learn our numbers and capabilities?"

"That's very possible, Fleet Captain. Let's keep them guessing for now. We want to be able to pick when and where we engage them."

That made a total of eight major, separate hotspots now, widely spread out and within an area of over four thousand cubic parsecs. A rough cube of enemy expansion. Each hot zone involved thousands of systems and fleets from different sides, struggling for dominance and survival.

Eight thousand, six-hundred, and fifty-one known enemy fleets and counting.

That was a lot. Even for Spacers.

Any one of these war zones could swallow up her and her 100 fleets with relative ease.

Whatever they chose to do, they needed to fight smart, if they were going to survive and be of any assistance to their new and future allies.

They wouldn't be much good to anyone dead.

Rumors abounded about other alien species, battles, and enemy actions, allies, weapon systems, and overall capabilities.

Truth needed to be separated from rumors and appearances. And they were still in the delicate process of meeting and introducing themselves to the locals.

It was very clear from the outset that no one was going to defeat the enemy on their own.

Then the priority alert went off.

Strike Fleet-50, commanded by Captain Robyn Bucci had triggered an enemy trap. She was cut off by sixteen enemy fleets, five that had been cloaked, and eleven more that had jumped in and piled on.

Naero kicked her command chair down and took charge of her spinning battle holo display. Her hands flew. She checked who was closest and ordered them in to relieve Fleet-50. Herself and Fleet-1, Fleets-4, 12, 22, 33, 41, 43, 44, 45, 46, and 47.

"*Prince of Austria,* 50's in deep. Most of these fleets are yours, Hans. Lead us in and we will support. Slashing death attack arcs on these optimized vectors and you take it from there. We launch all fighters now, and our wings can jump in with us ready to swarm, since it's so close. Tell Robyn to prepare to jump her ships out before they are cut to pieces. We need to gun the enemy down and vanish. No survivors. And no chance for them to pile in on us any further."

"Affirmative, Admiral. Swift death it is then." Vice Admiral Krieger took command as ordered and began shouting orders. "All fleets, all ships, assume these formations. We ride the lightning into battle. Destroy every foe we encounter!"

Five Spacer Navy Fleets jumped in close with the enemy and blasted a way clear for Fleet-50 to jump out.

Half of Robyn's ships were on fire, but they retreated in good order, firing all the way as they jumped.

Krieger, Naero, and the other four killer fleets roared in while the enemy was still reeling.

They hewed through the enemy fleets in swiftly spinning rings of interlocking fire, sending sheets of flame into the foe from several directions all at one.

Then Krieger dropped the hammer. "All battleships! Hard about. Hyperfire! All batteries. Blast their ashes into the afterlife!"

Up close, the massive main guns on almost threescore dreadnaughts and super battleships poured blindly torrents of destroying fire into the enemy bigs.

Shields vanished. Enemy battleships broke apart and exploded, almost instantly reduced to wreckage within that lethal firestorm.

Krieger drove *The Prince of Austria, The Salzburg, The Rheinland,* Graf Tyrol, and *The Deutschland* directly through the flames, utterly fearless, even as the enemy battleships disintegrated and exploded all around them in close proximity.

They punched forward, sustaining their intense fire, ramming the enemy wreckage out of the way with their shields flaring. Krieger proceeded to gut and decimate the enemy formations from within their core, taking out enemy bigs with each passing second.

No enemy warship could endure such concentrated firepower from those massed big guns.

From the outer fields, the superior-piloted Spacer starfighters gunned down the enemy ship to ship and enclosed the foe in a sphere of annihilation.

Anything that attempted to escape that sphere was lit up and blown to bits. Three enemy fleets did their best to close up and blast their way free.

Naero formed up Fleet-1 and took them head on in intercept, Echo-Foxtrot-6 devastation ring formation.

"Hyperfire!" Naero commanded.

The Holy Ghost, Shiva, Thor, Athena, and *Ares* ripped into the enemy fleets trying to escape with the withering fire from their main batteries, enveloping and passing over them. The secondary warship rings finished the job.

The rings of intense fire swept over the foe, tore them up, and spit the shredded enemy pieces out behind Fleet-1.

A hundred and thirty-four enemy warships, obliterated in seconds.

The Spacer formations adjusted and closed in for the kill. So did the starfighter sphere, coordinating fire within the shrinking, collapsing deathtrap.

The Spacer bigs finished off the enemy bigs and carriers. The cruisers and destroyers took out their enemy counterparts, with the help of the Spacer Carrier defensive batteries. The Starfighters owned the black and cleaned up everything else.

The attack and the battle took less than ten standard minutes.

Krieger ordered all fleets out. The Spacer Navy left only death, devastation, and wreckage in their wake.

*

The next day, Naero led Fleets 1 through 25 toward the secret rendezvous with the other defenders.

They were about to go into jump, when emergency alerts reached them from several sources, including Baeven, *The Black Spot*, and *The Dark Star*.

"Naero," Baeven warned, "get out of that area. Retreat. You have over three hundred enemy fleets converging on Muntothon-4 and all of the surrounding systems!"

"Copy that. We need to alert our new potential allies. Do so in this fashion, on my direct orders."

"Affirmative," Captain Tyber said. "We will direct all of them to the designated, alternate meeting location."

Naero pulled her task force back by twenty parsecs to regroup and adjust their defensive positions accordingly.

The Spacers met with each of the five sentient races at five separate, alternate locations. At each of those locations, Naero held back and first sent in hundreds of holodrone decoys posing as Spacer fleets, and the other sentient fleets.

All of the decoys disguised thousands of cloaked, seeker mines, waiting to launch and attack.

They met the Lish at Pyxdymo-3, the Mechans at Menex-5, the Sa'shom at Shasturax-2, and the Amavar at Vamurrii-6.

But when they met the Kodar at Timok-2, thirteen standard minutes later, three hundred enemy fleets surrounded that system and attacked the holodrone decoys, setting off the attacking mines.

Naero conferred with all of the other sentients via holo-projection.

"It would appear," she told the remaining emissaries, "that the Kodar have sided with our enemies and are sharing intel with them."

All of the other four erupted in protests and complaints. Naero even cut the volume for a minute or two while they vented. Then she cut back in. "My people are here to assess the situation in this region of the Gamma Quadrant, and help out, if we can. We are still gathering intel and information. But might I point out from our initial assessment, that combined, even without the useless Kodar, you four races have enough fleets, resources, and firepower to oppose your enemies."

All four emissaries exploded once again with pleas for direct assistance and support.

Basically, each of them wanted the Spacers to take on the bulk of the fighting and drive the invaders off.

"Let me be up front with all you right off," Naero informed them. "Our expedition cannot fight your battles for you. That is not why we have come. But if you join our Alliance, we can support and assist you to the best of our abilities, and help you organize and lead your forces better."

The complaining slacked off, but still continued.

"Or, we can go back where we came from, and you and your worlds can go back to facing these invaders down on your own."

Silence. Finally.

"Let's face what we see as the facts. Your enemies are keeping all of you divided and will defeat your forces in less that three to four standard years. Perhaps less. Remain on you present course, and your eventual and total defeat is but a matter of time."

"What do you propose?" Dexon of the Mechans asked.

"Your overall strategies must adapt and change. None of you will be able to achieve victory alone. That is impossible. Your only chance of survival and remaining free, is to band together, and crush the invader, once and for all."

Sezzim of the Sa'shom raised both hands in frustration, lashing his black and gold, serpentine tail in anger. "And just how do you suggest we do that? We have tried on several occasions to join forces. As soon as we try one thing, the enemy attacks all of our other vulnerable homeworlds. Then all agreements go out the hatch. No one has any desire to leave their worlds vulnerable while they fly off to defend the worlds of another race."

"First," Naero said calmly, "all of you must continue to implement the communications and scanning protocols that we have sent you. Next, your computing systems must be checked for various enemy hackbugs and sleeper programs. We cannot let the enemy know what we are doing."

Some general grumbling followed that, but all four leaders saw the wisdom in such security measures.

"Next, we will form logical defensive zones around all of your systems at risk, and beef them up with massive deployments of advanced drones and seeker mines."

"How will we produce such devices?" Tus snapped and clicked, through his translator.

"How can we manufacture the large quantities we shall need, when our war industries are already producing warships and materials at their limits?" Dexon asked.

"How can we afford all of this with our economies already collapsing from the war?" Sezzim protested. "Where will all of the raw materials come from?"

Ma'triid of the Amavar laughed. "How do we know that all of this tech isn't going to turn on us? You could be another ally of our enemies, only pretending to help us."

"All good questions," Naero said. "Your tek people can study our devices ahead of time. We have ways to assist with their mass production that you do not. The raw materials will come from your worlds and your territories, wherever we can find them quickest and easiest. If you don't trust us, ask us to leave at any time, and we will do so. But you will still be doomed. At least with us helping you, you will have a chance."

Naero paused and took in a breath, as they were poised to start complaining again.

"I was not finished. Third, all four of you and your peoples will double the numbers of fleets you have in the black within three to six standard months."

Naero knew that Spacer fixer clouds were rapidly expanding each day in multiple secret areas. They would be ready. They were ready now.

"Impossible!" Sezzim shouted.

Dexon tried to tabulate how such a thing could be accomplished.

Naero's aides distributed pads to all of the leaders.

"We will make certain that you have your ships. You must immediately implement these intense training programs to make certain that you have the crews available to operate those ships. Yes, it is difficult, but it can be done. Consider how much more difficult it will be to have all of your worlds subjugated and your populations wiped out...except for a few of you left as slaves, food stock, or mind-controlled cannon fodder."

Tus laughed. A very horrific sound, actually. "We must try hard to do these things, if we are to survive and save our peoples."

"Agreed."

"Agreed."

"Agreed."

Naero grinned again. "And yet, I still was not finished," she said.

Everyone but the Mechan slumped forward slightly and let out a very deep sigh.

Dexon did not understand. "What? Has she said something else?"

"She's going to," Ma'triid grumbled. "And somehow we and our peoples have to make it all happen like magic."

"In all of these things, we shall help you," Naero said. "We will coordinate all of our naval and military actions going forward from this point. How we respond to enemy probes and attacks, where we strike back, and in what numbers. If strategically necessary, some worlds may even need to be temporarily evacuated and abandoned, if they are not worth defending. All five of us will have input into our major actions. We must work to find consensus. Everyone of you and your peoples have much at stake. There will be victories, and we shall also suffer defeats, as in any war.

"At times, as during all wars, we must take certain calculated risks and gambles. They may pay off, or they could always end in disaster. There is no certainty in war. We must all share the risks, and take responsibility for our choices, and accept and deal with the results."

Sezzim crossed his arms indignantly. "And I suppose you are going to appoint yourself as supreme leader over all of us, while you are at it?"

"No. I am merely an ally and an advisor. Whoever we agree upon has the better plan of attack should lead us. Is that not fair? But no one naval force should bear the brunt of battle. We must all share the risks."

Tus finally objected. "That is not enough. You expect us to trust you and the others to a high degree. To do much without much in return. What do you and your people offer? What do you bring to us that is of value?"

Naero hit releases on their pads.

"To show our good faith, these are several dozen tek modifications to all of your various systems that will greatly improve your effectiveness in many areas, including combat. I'm certain that once we have a chance to study all of your systems, we will also make further advances. Every culture and their tek has something to offer. Something that the others do not possess or know. We are all in this together now, and we will make each other stronger and more formidable."

"Very generous," Tus admitted.

"And, we can show you how to implement these mods and upgrades in record time. We will play to our strengths and what each of our forces do well."

"We have yet to see your forces fight," Dexon noted.

"Yes, indeed," Ma'triid chimed in. "How do we know that you can prevail against these foes who have given us so much trouble?"

Naero smiled. "Watch our vidscreens. Evaluate this skirmish we recently fought against elements of the enemy who tried to entrap and destroy one of our fleets. My people and I come from very valiant blood. We are warriors, and we are not afraid to fight. But we prefer to pick and choose the time and place that we fight, when and where possible."

No one said anything. Therefore, Naero assumed that they were all sufficiently impressed.

Naero rose up and struck the unbreakable nanotable until it splintered and then healed. "Together we shall crush these foes, because they are our enemies, as well. They have killed countless numbers of our peoples, just as they have yours, and we have pursued them to this place to take them down. We will hit them where they are weak, where they least expect us to strike. We will not let up until they are a crushed, defeated, and dead at our feet!"

"Where should we strike them first?" Dexon enquired.

"I'm happy that you asked," Naero said. She brought up tactical holos with waves of her hands.

"We will bolster our defenses, study the enemy further, and prepare our forces over the next ten days to two weeks. Then we attack these four forward naval bases. That will cut the area that they effectively control by almost half and put them on the defensive with their systems.

Elliott

We will then switch from primarily reacting and defending, to attacking and advancing."

Sezzim protested. "How will launching mere attacks on those naval bases accomplish all of that?"

"Because," Naero said, clenching both fists tight. "We aren't just going to attack those fleets. We shall wipe them out and destroy them!"

18

Their foes did two things in response to the arrival of the Spacers, now that they knew who the new players were. First, they increased their attacks on the four races: the Lish, the Mechans, the Sa'shom, and the Amavar.

All reports from the Kodar said that the enemy began using those fools primarily for food. Yet Naero still felt sorry for the helpless Kodar people. They couldn't do much for them, now. But she hoped that would change one day.

Most likely the invaders would have still done everything that they did in any case. Perhaps they merely moved up their plans.

Next, the enemy began shifting and reinforcing their defensive screens and forces, and shuffled them on a daily basis. They did their beast to keep the Alliance guessing.

The enemy reverted to playing their hand cautiously, not knowing, as yet, how numerous the Spacer fleets were or the full range of their capabilities.

Naero hoped that the days before the main attacks would give her and Khai a chance to finally track down the location of where and how the enemy was holding and containing their unborn child.

Each time Baeven or the others got close, it seemed as if the enemy would get spooked somehow, and move her to some other secret place again.

It became maddening.

In the meantime, Naero also wanted herself and her people to get to know their new allies better. That was going to be very important. Each culture and its race seemed fairly unique.

She had had some initial exposure to the Lish. The other three still remained unfamiliar.

And when they got around to it, the Allies needed to go back and capture some of the Kodar and figure out how deep they or their leaders were involved with the enemy.

The Spacers and their new fixer nebulae were more than busy, improving the system defenses, fleet capabilities, and expanding the fixernet out farther and farther into the Gamma Quadrant each day.

All and all, it was a process, or at best a conglomeration of many series of processes.

Naero and Fleet 1 went with Fleets 2 through 10 to survey and learn what could be learned about the Mechans, their worlds, culture, and the threats they faced.

Not finding Naero-3 was weighing heavily on her mind, whatever she chose to do. Having Khai beside her and being able to be with him and have him near was the only thing keeping her from plummeting off the deep end.

To make matters slightly worse, when she and Khai tried to use the new Oden Astral crystals, they couldn't get them to work. Something was blocking, jamming, or messing up access to the Astral Plane. That in itself was incredibly weird.

There was a schedule to keep up with.

They travelled first to Taekom-7, one of the primary Mechan homeworlds, with a population of sixteen billion people. As one of the Mechan leaders, Dexon explained that his people were not robots, exactly. Nor were they androids.

Dexon himself was 1.80 meters, bipedal, with five-fingered mechanical hands, but no toes. Although Mechan feet were segmented and flexible. They had heads with two complex eyes, a vocalizer mouth, but no nose or ears. Mechan eyes were various colors. Dexon's were deep, cobalt blue.

Could Mechans smell anything? Naero knew they could hear.

From what Naero learned, Mechans were living, sentient machines. They had free will, and they had also developed emotions at some point. They were a very ancient species. They did not eat food, but fed on energy one to three times each day when possible, to boost and sustain their power cores. They also kept their various systems lubricated, clean, and functioning properly through routine scans and maintenance.

"Might I examine you with teknomancy?" Naero asked Dexon.

"You have my permission," the Mechan leader said.

Naero was amazed. Mechans were a marvel of engineering. She merged with Dexon and understood his operating systems and functions. She even had to use biomancy at the same time to perceive the Mechan version of the Lifespark. They were, in fact, alive. And once that Lifespark was lost or gone, so were they.

Did they have souls? Naero was afraid to ask. Would a Mechan soul be released like other sentients and go on to the next journey? Where did any souls go, for that matter?

Secretly, Naero could not help comparing to the Mechans to the Driathans–Jia's people. But the Mechans were neither as perfect-looking or indestructible. They were made out of very durable, but regularly available materials. The Mechans were not as advanced, refined as the Driathans, and looked much more 'machine-like.'

What would they think of Jia if they met her? They were all mechanical constructs, after all. But the Driathans were clearly a more advanced form of intricate life. As different species as Spacers were from early homo sapiens, or for that matter, Cro-Magnon man.

Mechans were also mortal. Their bodies wore out and could also be damaged and destroyed like any machine, and just as susceptible to battle damage as any other lifeform, as the war continued to prove. What's more, the enemy could take them over–if they weren't damaged that much, re-program or hi-jack their mechanical brains and minds, and turn them into robots or automatons.

Doing so obviously robbed them of their unique, individuality.

Naero and Khai and others noted Mechan 'children' of various sizes and developmental ages.

As Dexon went on to explain, "Mechans also reproduce, after their own fashion. They build their offspring as needed. Usually, Mechans have very good friends whom they are fond of, and can even form family groups with. But since they do not have sex, as biological organisms do, they do not mate.

"Although they can pair up to create offspring, and in essence be developmental parents, sharing in both the construction and the orientation and education of the child. Mechans are neuter, again, not being sexual in nature. But they do care for each other and their offspring to a very high degree."

Khai asked. "How long do Mechans exist before they wear out and die?"

Dexon answered without hesitation. "About two hundred of your standard years, before their mechanisms and relays simply degrade enough to make further existence extremely difficult, and even painful."

Naero knitted her brows. "Mechans feel pain?" She knew that Jia did, both physical and emotional–even psyonic and Cosmic pain. And she clearly knew and understood love on many intricate levels.

"My people do have emotions," Dexon said, with conviction. "We are living, mechanical organisms with sensitive, physical bodies. Why would we not feel pain when we are injured or hurt?"

Khai continued with his line of questioning. "With the war, when a Spacer–when one of our people is slain, we experience sorrow and sadness. We mourn the loss of our dead for a time, and know grief. Do Mechans experience such emotions? What do you do with your dead?"

"When a Mechan stops functioning–or 'dies,' as you call it; we do miss them and mark their loss. Before their bodies and their components are recycled, if possible, their knowledge and wisdom is passed among their offspring, companions, and friends, so that parts of them continue on. But their personality remains unique to them and can only be recalled and remembered, not reproduced."

"I don't understand. Why don't the Mechans simply transplant their brains and their minds into a new mechanical body? They do so for their children, until their minds are fully developed and considered an adult. You could all be immortal. You could exist and function forever."

"That is not possible," Dexon noted. "Our minds and personalities are also unique to each of us, just as yours are. The same reason that they cannot be exactly copied or precisely duplicated. Nor do they last forever or continue to function without error. Error creeps in, and the actual mechanisms of our brains wear out, and will eventually seize up on their own and stop functioning, even if they are not shut down voluntarily. This degradation is computed, and the individual selects a date and time to shut themselves down."

"So," Khai said, "Mechans, left to themselves, wear out and eventually choose their own time of death."

"Yes. You could say it that way."

"Can a dead Mechan be repaired?"

"Their bodies can be repaired readily enough, if they are not already worn out. Damage to their brains and minds is much more difficult, and at times–especially during war–impossible to repair."

Naero nodded, understanding completely. "It is the same way with us."

Dexon smiled. Mechans did smile and frown and experience loss and a form of sorrow. "Then we are not so unlike after all," he said.

The Mechans, for their part, were incredibly obsessed with the fixers. Dexon and others could not help asking about them almost constantly, and studying them and their bewildering Kexxian tek whenever they had the chance.

It was not a tek that the Spacers were willing to give over, even to their new allies. They guarded it jealousy. Of course, they would make use of the fixers to assist their allies, to be sure. But as an ultimate failsafe, any fixer that was ever kidnapped, by the enemy or anyone else automatically rendered itself inert and useless, in order to avoid having its amazing tek copied and put to evil use.

They were on their way to meet with the planetary leader of Taekom-7, in order to confirm various treaties and trade agreements.

Khai was still full of questions as they made their way through the Mechan gigacity capital of Mevad, attracting quite a bit of attention as they walked and boarded various transport shuttles and movers. Ra and Tarim came along, as well as a dozen Spacer Marines in full armor and gear. When they all got close enough, they would take an official shuttle waiting for them, that would bring them right to the planetary leadership facility.

Everyone stopped and pointed at them. "Look at the Bios!" many said.

"So I take it the Mechans have no religion of any kind, or spiritual beliefs?" Khai said.

"That is an erroneous assumption," Dexon said. "My people are extremely spiritual, and worship our Creator, who we also call 'The Great Maker,' or just 'The Maker.' We see all existence–the entire universe–as little more than an enormous, complex machine, set into motion by a Creator with incredible purpose and intent. We are a part of that great mechanism, and should do our part to operate and function properly, and maintain order and harmony. Those who are violent, illogical, or threaten our existence or our free will make themselves our enemies and must be defeated."

They reached the shuttle finally and sped off to the leadership facility for Taekom-7.

"I must warn you," Dexon said, "our planetary leader is somewhat…unique. Even eccentric. Petarri is one hundred and eighty-seven standard years old, and has what you humans might call a rare sense of humor, and a penchant for mirth. Please make allowances. Most Mechans are not this way."

Naero smirked and almost giggled. What was the old Mechan going to do? A stand-up routine? She had to get used to them being asexual and not having gender. She still thought of Dexon as male somehow.

Mechan government was very simple. They met in a relatively small building in a normal-sized conference room.

Petarri was short, only slightly taller than Naero herself, about 1.6 meters. Petarri's voice was somewhat higher pitched, and therefore more feminine. Despite knowing that Mechans were neither male nor female, Naero couldn't keep herself from thinking about Petarri as a 'her.' It was difficult to stop assigning such frames of reference.

The Mechan Planetary Leader was polished gold, orange, and white, with copper-plated highlights, and green eyes. Some of those highlights were corroded.

No Mechan had anything akin to hair or clothing. They did carry equipment, supplies, and tools at times, and their heads and bodies and limbs were shaped and designed differently.

Petarri rose up to greet them and quipped right off, "So, what do we have here? Three energy beings, one of them a bug, and thirteen slightly optimized meat tubes? You know, humanoid bioforms are basically complex toruses of meat and bone that only produce carbon dioxide, and what you peeps call urine and poop."

Naero chuckled and shot back, "And Mechans seem to be glorified pocket comps with a head knob, hands, and feet."

"Good one!" Petarri said, roaring with laughter. "Pocket comps…head knobs!" She laughed out of control for a few moments.

Dexon looked slightly nervous; a version of Mechan mortified.

After a bit more jocularity, they settled down to the task at hand, making and securing their agreements, treaties, and trade pacts. It took less than a quarter of an hour to make the Mechans part of the Alliance.

"Depending upon how various battles went today," Petarri said, "the Mechans control 340 worlds. We hope that this new Alliance with you glorified meat tubes is going to keep us all from being scrapped or reprogrammed by these destructive invaders."

"That's what we're here for," Naero said. "We've already begun to help upgrade your offensive and defensive systems. And we will fight beside you and the other three species. "Our allies are more bugs and snake meat tubes. But that doesn't matter. They could be algae scum for all we care, if they can keep us all from being recycled."

They spoke at length on several major issues over the course of the next hour.

"Well," Petarri said. "What are you meat tubes wasting time around here for? Don't you have to go confirm all the same kind of stuff with the snakes, and then the dragonflies and the spiders?"

"I suppose we are done here for the time being," Naero said. "It is nice working with you and Dexon, Petarri."

"Hey, Naero. We are allies now. You don't have to oil us down. Do what you need to and move on. Mechans don't get upset about stuff like that. That's a human thing. You won't hurt our feelings that way."

"Very well then," Naero said, standing up. "We will be on our way. Thank you very much, Planetary Leader Petarri."

"Sure, thing Naero. Stay in touch, and let's get this plan rolling. We're still losing ground each day. But this is the best news we have had in decades!"

Once they were back with the Spacer fleets, Naero had word that an enemy attack was occurring nearby, on a Mechan world called Corvine-3.

A handful of enemy fleets were giving the twenty-seven million Mechans there a very hard time. Corvine-3 had not been fully militarized as yet.

Naero analyzed the situation and called upon Marine General Azkhalatara Walker. "General, I think we could lend a hand to our new allies on Corvine-3. Take a look at this sitrep and tell me what you think." Naero shunted it over.

"Are we talking Ejjai, sir? I really despise Ejjai."

Naero nodded. "Copy that; I think we all do. As stated, I think we can drop down and spoil their fun on Corvine-3 nicely, just like in the old days. But there are Dakkur, possessed, and other threats present as well."

"Very well, sir. Give me a moment to assess."

"Take some time." Naero prepared the fleet raider formations as she waited, and shifted logistics flows to cover such an attack.

The general came back to her in a matter of minutes. "Let's ride, sir. I like your initial plan. Do I have your permission to pweak it a bit?"

"Pweak away, General. Make it your own."

The Mechan forces on Corvine-3 were taking a pounding. The invaders had just barely managed to seize control of the air, and pulled their troops back to carpet bomb a score of the largest cities, including the system capital of Dartin. They also drilled command and control and military bases from orbit.

Several things happened almost simultaneously.

Up in the black, ten Spacer fleets jumped in on optimal attack vectors and caught the enemy napping. The enemy fools were so overconfident, they didn't even have their formations set.

The Spacers hit them ten different ways and chewed them to pieces.

Waves of Navy and Marine starfighters also appeared out of nowhere, and shot the enemy from the skies of Corvine-3, sending them spinning and burning to the surface. Then those same fighters came about and strafed anything else the enemy had exposed.

On the ground, Spacer Marine forces surrounded the enemy forces that had encircled each city in a ring of death. That ring of sweeping fire took the enemy from behind and closed in, driving the panic-stricken invaders before them, right into the waiting guns of the equally astonished defenders.

Naero felt they had set some kind of record.

The Spacers helped defeat a major planetary invasion within the span of three hours.

She went down to the surface, backed up by Khai, Ra, Tarim, and several of her replicants, all in Shetanna mode. Naero personally congratulated General Walker on the victory.

"Great work, Tara."

"Thanks, N. Just like the old days, huh?"

Naero smiled. "Even better, I'd say. What's happening here?"

Tara glanced at her bodyguards. "Perhaps you and your people could lend us a hand."

"Name it."

"Between the Mystic Enforcer and these others, that's a lot of Cosmic juice, I'd say. We have a situation. A few thousand slashers and other assorted goons and slaves have a bunch of Mechan children held hostage in what appears to be a sports arena of some kind. Of course the enemy has the whole place rigged to blow. We have stealth fixers in there disarming the bombs ASAP. But we could use some Mystic assistance."

Naero nodded. "Put us where you need us most, Tara."

Naero and her people slipped in with the Marines and took up their positions.

On the way, they passed several hundred dead Mechans of various ages, cut down and destroyed by the foe. Even though they were machine people, it made it no less grim. Their lifesparks were gone now, and they weren't coming back. All of these Mechans had been unique individuals with lives of their own.

Dead was dead. And in that moment, Naero realized that the horrors of war were the same for all sentients. She saw the same exact tragedies she had seen on countless worlds and in countless war zones.

Helpless civilians had been gunned down, murdered in the act of trying to flee, trying to hide, trying to cover the young and the ones they loved with their own bodies in a futile effort to shield them.

The slashers especially despised Mechans because they couldn't eat them or feed them into the meat ships, but they still had fun torturing them, just like they did everything else. But the Ejjai left the bodies wherever they fell. Given time, the invaders would recycle the dead Mechans for scrap.

Naero and Khai and their group took up their positions and waited for the signal to perform the assault.

They were at one entire end of the arena, where several hundred invaders were herding and menacing the Mechan young, and setting up auto guns and defensive positons.

The signal finally went up.

Two dozen Shetannas took out many of the enemy with multiple Cosmic blast attacks, lightning, and then their signature red swords.

Khai flashed through the enemy right flank, a green blur, Yii hewing through armor, gravtanks, and anything in his path. Everything behind him within a few meters appeared to explode.

Ra tripled his size out in the open and trampled, and churned through everything on the left flank.

Naero charged right down the middle, using her own blades, whirling, smashing, and kicking in true cyclone mode. She transformed into a whirling buzz saw of Cosmic energy throwing off sparks and sprays of destroying force. Tarim flew backwards behind her with his machine pistols blazing, chewing up any threats that still moved or popped up, covering her back.

In a matter of seconds the rescue was over. Marine snipers had done their work also. While she was fighting, Naero saw multiple foes at key positions dropped with clean headshots from afar without a sound. Whispering death came from the snipers.

Like children in war everywhere, the Mechan kids were still in shock. Many of them didn't know what to do. Mechans were machine people, but they did have emotions after their own fashion. They could experience both fear and grief. Naero saw a Mechan child half her size, hugging its legs, cowering under some stands.

She went to the child and held out her hands. "You can come out now."

"Is it over?" the child asked, keeping its head down. Mechans did not have gender. But the poor thing was shaking like any child would under such conditions.

Naero nodded. "It is. My people are allies with your people. We came to help. The invaders here are all dead now."

The Mechan child looked up at her with its large amber eyes. "They killed my parent. They shot my parent to pieces and forced me to this place."

Naero picked the child up in her arms. Its normal reaction was to cling to her. It was about the size of a seven-year-old human child, and it was still shuddering with terror.

"What's going to happen to me?" it asked.

"You're going to be all right. Your people will take care of you."

Naero held onto the child, but there were so many others just like it, and at other ages.

"What is your name?" the child asked.

Naero smiled. "My friends call me Naero."

"That is a strange name. Are all Bios as strange as you, Naero?"

She laughed. "Some of them are a lot stranger."

"Gratitude and appreciation for saving me, Naero. I will remember your name; you, and these other Bios who saved us."

"You're welcome. I'm sorry all of this happened to you and your world. What is your name?"

"I am Taemin. My companions call me Taem." Taem suddenly slumped forward slightly and then caught itself.

"What's wrong, Taem?" She checked him with Teknomancy to see if he had been injured.

"I am...tired," Taem said. "I have not been able to recharge for nearly a day. If we could find a power node, I could replenish my energies."

"Sure, Taem." The Mechans had power nodes all over the place. She took Taem to the nearest one. He placed the palm of his hand over the node and absorbed energy."

"Feel better?" Naero asked, when he was fully recharged.

"I always feel better," Taem said, "after a good recharge."

Naero looked around. Khai and Tarim were giving her the eye.

"Taem, you're going to have to go with the other children with your people."

Taem suddenly clung to her tighter. "I...I don't want to go with them. I want to stay with you. What if the enemy Bios come back?"

"Taem, you can't stay with me. I must go. You will be better off with your people."

Naero never thought she would see a Mechan child slump down and sigh the way Taem did. "The other Mechans will care for me, but they will never know me the way my parent did."

Naero hugged Taem. "The you must teach them to know and care about you."

A large force of Mechans did arrive at the arena a few minutes later, half of them armed, almost completely surprised to see their new allies. The locals were equally astonished to see that the arena had already been liberated, and the enemy taken care of.

The Marines helped the locals secure the young, and begin to transport them out on dropships that came down. Naero couldn't believe how bad she felt when she handed Taem over to the locals. He looked so small compared to the adults. But there was nothing for it. War everywhere multiplied the tragedy and sorrow of orphans.

All across Corvine-3 the story was the same. This world had been ready to fall. The Spacers snatched it back and crushed the invaders in every way possible.

The Mechans cheered their new allies even as the Spacers packed up to leave.

Several Mechan fleets arrived too late, but took over the defense of the system with great thanks.

Naero and her First Contact team returned to Fleet-1 and the rest, now heading toward a meeting with representative Sezzim and other Sa'shom leaders on their outer defense world of Zekad-1.

Yet explosions rocked the command center as soon as they docked.

According to the scanners, some kind of attack between the locals erupted within.

19

Khai called out from the scanners. "Confirmed Naero; it appears to be an internal matter. Sa'shom are fighting Sa'shom, but they are only stunning each other. I see a few injuries, but no deaths as yet. Do you really think we should get involved? We don't know what is happening."

"I still think we need to check it out. What if the enemy is involved somehow?"

Khai snorted. "Then I think we would see a lot more actual death."

That was probably true. "Our superior personal shielding should protect us from the Sa'shom stunning attacks," Naero said. "Ra. Tarim. Suit up and bring our fireteam with us, just in case. We have a meeting scheduled. If this is a coups, let's go see who we're meeting with at the moment."

"What if we meet resistance?" Tarim asked.

"Then we stun them, just as the natives are doing," she said. "No lethal attacks unless they start up. And if things do go hot, we cloak and get the hell out fast. Got that? Make sure everyone understands my orders. We're here to negotiate deals and agreements with whoever is in charge, not start our own war with these people."

They entered the landing bay they had been originally cleared to enter.

Naero noted that their shields began to glow with a red aura. That was odd.

Tarim tapped into the vidcams and feeds for the planet and the area around the Prime Minister's gigatower for the Zekad-1 system. "N, these stunning battles have spread all throughout the system."

Naero teknomanced the feeds and flashraced them through her mind. Thirty-six percent of the planet's population with blue auras around their shields were systematically attacking thirty-four percent of the population with yellow auras around them. They were each doing their best to stun all of the members of the other side in the contest. While the remaining thirty percent, mostly elderly, children, and adults with green auras did their best to stay the heck out of the way.

Some few of the greens also got stunned in the various crossfires. There was no avoiding that. Thus far, the contest between the blues and yellows was a stalemate. Neither one side nor the other seemed to have the upper hand.

Naero and her party kept making their way toward the lifts and movers for the Prime Minister's gigatower.

They spotted some locals over that way and went toward them, also noting several yellows lying stunned on the ground, their snake-like lower halves jumbled about. Scale and skin coloring among the Sa'shom varied widely. Even their humanoid halves above the waist showed a great deal of variety in skin tone, eye and hair color.

The blue aura Sa'shom present were clearly paramilitary, in urban camo fatigues or outright suits of combat armor. With their lower halves being two meters in length, coupled with their upright, one meter torsos, this made them rather threatening and odd to look at.

About ten blues were holding five yellows prisoner who weren't unconscious, and had them trussed up on the ground with plasbinders, and their stunners confiscated.

The blues stared at Naero and her party with great curiosity, talking calmly amongst themselves.

"Offworlders are reds?" the apparent leader remarked. "What the hell do we do with reds? Do we stun them or ignore them like greens? Oh my word—what is that reek? Is that them?"

Naero addressed the leader quickly before they could decide. "I am Admiral Maeris from the Spacer fleets. We have an important meeting with the Prime Minister and your representatives in lest than a standard hour. Can you show us to the meeting areas."

The leader stiffened. He flicked two of his followers with his tail to get their attention. "Hey, snap to it guys. We've got a bloody alien admiral right in front of us!" he whispered. The others murmured and whispered.

"Look, suck it up. I don't care how bad they smell."

Naero sniffed. The Sa'shom had their own odd scent, but Naero did not think that she and her group smelled bad.

The troops came to some form of attention, and the leader even saluted. "Sergeant Vietta of the 731st Tolpaedo infantry light strikers, Admiral. You'll have to excuse us. We're right in the middle of a surprise election. The aftermath is still working itself out."

Naero blinked and had to think on that for a moment. "Sergeant Vietta. If you don't mind me saying, this appears to be more a planetwide coups than an election. Would you mind explaining to me just how your electoral system functions?"

Vietta shrugged, and his troops drifted back to goofing off and taunting the captive yellows.

"Well, sir," Vietta said, and began gesturing expansively with his hands. You see, it's like this. We have these two political parties or factions, basically the blues and the yellows. With the war going as badly as it is, the yellows have fallen out of favor with the population this month."

"This month?" Naero asked, raising one eyebrow.

"Yeah, last month it was the blues who got forced out–almost exactly like this. It's been flip-flopping back and forth for the past year, ever since the invaders hit our worlds. We only have 256 worlds left that we control. But neither faction has really been able to stop or even slow down the steady invader advance."

"But, if the blues have won the elections, what is with these stunning campaigns?"

"Oh, that. I know it seems confusing, but the losing side can still choose to resist and hold out, in a final trial by mock combat. A thousand years ago the rebellions and elections were hot, and fought with real weapons. That caused a lot of death, and even several civil wars. But we aren't that barbaric any longer. Now we just use stunners."

"I still don't understand. The election losers can still try to resist, and fight one of these stunning campaigns in order to remain in power?"

"Exactly. Now you've got it straight. It doesn't always go this far. Often the losers simply concede. But the contests can go this way, and some people even look forward to it and find it fun, enjoyable, and amusing."

"What if one side or both go hot and use real weapons?"

Vietta snarled. "That would be taboo–against all of our laws, sir. Those who did so would be killed or captured and executed as traitors to our political system. No one has attempted a betrayal like that in over eight hundred years. Everyone in both factions would quickly suspend their conflicts and fall upon such killers to wipe them out."

"How does it look for the yellows?" Naero asked.

Sergeant Vietta checked his wristcomp for a few moments. "Things are slowly turning against them. I apologize, sir, but it will most likely take a few more hours to work itself out. You might want to wait back on the safety of your transport."

"What would signify a victory?" Naero asked.

"Oh, when all of our aura's flash the winning color, and then everyone goes back to being green. The first side to reduce the other side down fifty-one percent will usually trigger a victory, or if one side concedes. It's all of the supporters of one side against the other side, all over the planet, in streets, homes, and businesses. Doesn't usually take more than a day. Let the stun fest play out!"

"I see. How amusing. I notice that the aura for myself and my party is red," Naero noted.

"Yes," Vietta said. "You are not Sa'shom, and so, as aliens, you are outside the parameters of our technopolitical system. It probably assigned a color to you at random."

Even as they spoke, all of the native auras present flashed blue, and then switched over to green.

"Wow, that was fast," Vietta said. "Either the yellow leadership just got captured or decided to call it quits for some reason."

The conflict was over, just like that. Everyone was on the same side once more. And to Naero, it all seemed crazy as hell. But the locals appeared to believe in their system and that it worked for them. The former blues released their captives and even gave them their stunners and other gear back. A few of the victors even helped the losers up and went to help the people passed out on the ground.

The levels of tension dropped rapidly, and even though the two former sides did not seem overly friendly, they were no longer overtly hostile and aggressive. Although the former yellows left, and the former blues hung around to take charge of the lifts and movers for such an important political building."

Naero asked Sergeant Vietta if he would check for them, to see if anyone in the apparently revolving government was going to see them that day.

It took several minutes to get an answer. The newly installed Prime Minister actually insisted on seeing them ASAP.

Naero and her group were ushered into a very spacious, official meeting room and apparent press room. It was filled with celebrating formerly blue, now green, troops and paramilitaries.

A very attractive Sa'shom with long, honey-gold hair and glistening jet black eyes slithered over quickly to greet Naero. She wore a very smart tangerine blouse and striped blazer, with a blaster still strapped on her right hip.

She wrinkled her pert nose and her eyes widened slightly.

In fact, more than a dozen stunned members of the former regime in smart, expensive-looking business attire still lay stunned in a tumble about the room. That included former Prime Minister Mevad, lying behind the minister's desk, still tangled up with the Sa'shom weird, bench-like chairs.

The new prime minister extended her manicured hand. "Admiral Maeris. Sorry for the unfortunate confusion, I'm certain that you have many questions. I'd be more than happy to discuss them and the agreements that we wish to confirm with the Spacer Navy and the Alliance of the Alpha Quadrant. I am Jerena, the current Prime Minister."

Naero glanced over. "A pleasure to meet you, Prime Minister Jerena. I'm guessing that former Prime Minister will not be joining us?"

Jerena smirked. "No, I'm afraid not. My husband won't be coming around for an hour or two. Come, let us speak together."

"Husband," Naero said. "You had your paramilitaries zap your own husband?"

"No, not at all." Jerena smirked. "I nailed that bugger myself. You should have seen the look on his face!"

"You stunned your own husband."

"Sure did." Then she whispered behind her hand. "And I nailed him a couple of extra times for good measure while he was still wiggling. Just to pay him back for stunning me the same way last month."

"You and your husband are from the two rival factions?"

Jerena shrugged. "It makes it very convenient to always have members of both factions present. The wheels of government adjust, and barely stop turning." Jerena whispered behind her hand again. "And between us gals, the make-up sex after all of that stunning is out of this world. I call that a win-win!"

Naero had to ask. "Does this same process go on on all of your worlds?"

"Oh, don't worry. The blues now control 189 of our 256 worlds!"

Naero smirked. "I don't think that is my only concern."

She strongly suggested to the Sa'shom that they stabilize their political system slightly more, especially with the threat of an alien invasion that they had yet been unable to slow down or stop.

Even Prime Minister Jerena of Zekad-1 admitted that might be a very wise course of action.

Naero kept noticing the faces of their hosts and the general tittering that was going around. "Prime Minister, I'm sorry that your people find the scent of my people…so unpleasant and intrusive. Perhaps were can find some way to mask or reduce that effect."

Jerena smiled and offered Naero he hand again. "I'm so glad you've addressed that. Our people will work with yours and we'll see what we can come up with. Sa'shom sensory organs for smell are incredibly sensitive. I'm sorry that this is an issue."

"What do we smell like to you?" Naero asked.

Jerena's ever-present smile faltered a bit. "I'd rather not say. It's pretty foul. But we're allies now. We'll work toward a solution."

An aide brought in what appeared to be a large bottle of Sa'shom perfume or cologne.

"Would you mind if we sprayed you and your party with this scent blocker?"

Naero laughed. "How can we refuse? Spray away." Even her own sensitive nose could barely detect anything when they did so.

The aide with the perfume hosed down Khai pretty good with the stuff.

After that slight humiliation, the rest of the negotiations went remarkably smooth and without obstruction, although the Sa'shom had a penchant for talking over every little detail. Naero considered them very legalistic.

After they returned to Naero's Flagship, it was very late, and she felt exhausted once more. She allowed Khai to carry her back to their quarters at a certain point. She liked being in his arms.

"Should I retire to the Admiral's bathroom?" Ra asked.

"No, Ra," Naero said. "I'm sorry. That won't be necessary. I just want to sleep, if that's all right, Khai?"

"I'm a bit worn out by diplomacy, myself, N. A snuggle fest it is then. I'll probably zonk out before you do."

Naero grinned. "Alas, the romance is dead," she said with a laugh.

Khai kissed her, chuckling. "Not dead. Just taking a break."

"I understand…the spirit is willing, the flesh is weak, as they say."

"Who was it who said that?"

"Oh, I don't know. Like all of that Old Earth stuff, someone got around to saying stuff like that at some point."

Naero sighed and they settled in together. "We still have to solidify the final agreements with the Amavar and the Lish. I can't wait to meet S'krin's people, although she sent me a cryptic message both to not mention her by name, and to beware somewhat. That her people could be, as she put it—'a bit much.'"

"Hmmm…" Khai muttered.

"They can't be any worse than the rest. Khai. Khai?"

Her amazing paramour was already asleep, true to his word.

Naero tried to drift off.

Finally she sighed and whispered out loud to no one in particular. "I hope she's all right. We must find them. I just hope they're all right."

Time and time again their ruthless enemies had proven that they were capable of anything, no matter how twisted or vile.

20

Naero and her fleets were forced to heed another distress call, this time on a Sa'shom world called Kudosha-5, that came under heavy attack by the enemy. As allies with the snake people now, it would have not been good form to refuse and simply keep going.

She assessed the situation as they went in and called for back up from Admiral Yamamoto Toshio, assigned as her reserves at that time. Naero had great admiration for her friend Toshi, the oldest son of one of the Spacer High Admirals, who was clearly following in his father's traditions.

A disciplined, cultured warrior poet, who like Naero herself, actually wrote poetry and was a fine painter. He was also a deadly swordsman, as he had proven time and time again during the wars, and at several duels and incidents with non-Spacers who made the mistake of drawing steel or energy blades against him.

Naero always felt safe with Toshi on her side. They had met and become good friends ever since the Annexation War, where both of them had proven themselves to be amazing leaders and tacticians.

As for their current mission, the enemy picked their targets well, going after worlds that were vulnerable and unprepared for war.

They did not simply lay siege to Kudosha-5, but they also attacked the next nearest world over, Sasson-2, that could have normally sent aid to the other system.

Kudosha-5 was a warm, but not hot world, with smaller temperate zones and lots of savannah, prairie, and grasslands. The Sa'shom also had a fondness for swamps and marshes. A thin band of very arid desert surrounded the equator.

With any possible help from Sasson-2 cut off, the Kudoshans were on their own, against a very determined invader. The enemy had the planet completely blockaded by almost two dozen fleets that wiped out anything the planet had to send up against them.

Then the ground attacks struck the hapless cities. The Spacers monitored the enemy chatter and the grim reality that evolved on the ground.

The enemy sent in shock troops of mindless numbers of captured or cloned Lish and reprogrammed Mechans. Then came waves of Kodarian suicide bombers of all ages, drones loaded with explosives, programmed to run in and detonate. The foe even sent in other Sa'shom with control collars around their necks, forced to kill their own kind. The collars exploded if they were removed.

While the defenders were pinned down dealing with the shock troops, the Ejjai and the Dakkur would outflank the Sa'shom and cut them down from the side or behind.

Dakkur liked eating sentient heads. Again and again, they argued with the Ejjai, commanding them to save them the heads, before flinging the bodies into the meatships.

The Ejjai protested, because that was both time consuming and it killed their captives outright. One of the slasher's favorite entertainments was to feed helpless civies into the spinning blades, hooks, and choppers of the robotic meat processing ships to see the bodies ripped apart.

Many Ejjai had to be killed, and their heads harvested, before they were forced by their masters to comply.

Kudosha-5 had a population that was less than one billion, and the small, ill-equipped military forces they did have were quickly worn down, leaving only hasty militia forces to defend the gigacities with whatever weapons they could find. Large waves of refugees and the helpless quickly complicated everything and were caught in the open.

Things turned grim very quickly.

Naero rendezvoused with Admiral Toshi and several Sa'shom fleets, who though competent, would not possibly stand a chance against the twenty-three enemy fleets massed around Kudosha-5. She commended them for their gallantry for being willing to go in on their own, if need be. She asked them if they would accept the honor of fighting beside and with her own ships. They accepted.

Even worse news reached them. Several more enemy fleets joined those around Kudosha-5, and the enemy began broadcasting the atrocities to all of the other Sa'shom worlds, making it clear that they were all next.

Naero despised such terrible displays. She ordered those transmissions jammed as soon as the counterattack commenced.

Although outnumbered, Naero still devised a very daring plan of attack. Toshi disagreed with her on several elements, and proposed ten different attack vectors that were both more flexible, and got them in closer to the enemy much faster.

"Naero, our rate of fire is far superior to that of the enemy, currently," he said. "The sooner we can close with them, if we bunch up their numbers and hem them in, we will devastate them in short order."

Naero smiled at her good friend, as they both folded their arms side by side and studied the holo arrays.

"Look at their poor grouping and lackluster formations," Toshi continued. "They're too bunched up. Too close to the planet. They haven't left themselves sufficient room to shift their naval forces for battle."

Naero nodded. "I see that, Toshi. But it's almost as if they're begging us to attack them. What if this is another of their traps, trying to draw us in? They could jump in and have us cold. I'm just trying to be cautious."

"We have seen this incompetence of the enemy many times before," Toshi argued. "There are always risks. We have a good, solid plan of attack. I say it is worth the risk. If they spring a trap on us, we call in more of our ships and fight our way out. But they do not have the stomach to fight us face to face. We will drive right down their throats and blast out their burning entrails."

Naero snickered. "Well, when you say it like that, it just sets my heart all a twitter, Toshi." They both laughed together.

"This is your show, Toshi. I'm going to help out on the ground. You run things up in the black."

They were on top of the enemy fleets and firing before the foe could react of form up.

Admiral Yamamoto's flagship, *The Musashi*, formed an attack wedge with his other four bigs, The Nagato, The Shinano, The Haruna, and the Kirishima on his flanks, leading Fleet 100, and Fleets 99 through 90 on optimized attack vectors around them.

They uncloaked at attack speed and opened fire.

Shields and entire warships melted before a withering wall of hyper fire from the main guns of the Spacer battleships.

Toshi's assault wedge gutted the packed arc of the enemy fleets like a gigantic, flaming spear of death. He drove through the burning hulks of the enemy and concentrated the fire of his fleets on target after target.

Soon they were surrounded by burning, exploding enemy warships.

Naero and her supporting forces came in the very next moment, as the routed enemy tried to regroup or simply flee, in any direction available. She and her forces closed the legs of their spider formations and effectively cut off and trapped the foe.

The enemy could still fight to the last, but within the hour, those fleets would be annihilated. The Spacers went on the hunt, but pulled back slightly, allowing the Sa'shom fleets with them to take the lead.

When Naero, Khai, Ra, and Tarim joined a Marine armored regiment on the surface, there was still heavy fighting around and in some of the gigacities. They were positioned around the gigacity of Galim, where millions of refugees had fled into the cover of the high grasslands all around.

But a ring of enemy gravtanks and shocktroops was closing in, burning and driving all before them toward the eventual center kill zone. They cut down and killed anything living.

From the huge black circles of scorched earth and corpses visible from the air, the enemy had repeated this tactic several times around Galim.

Three enemy meatships were already harvesting the corpses left on the ground.

"I want those meatships blown completely to hell, as soon as we attack," Naero commanded.

The enemy swept in, continuing to gun down droves of civilians running before their guns.

The Spacer Marines jumped straight down on them hard, face to face, shooting them down, ramming into them hard, and knifing them up close to tear out their guts and spines.

The meatships went up in flames as the enemy advance stopped cold. They even piled into each other, the halt was so abrupt.

Then the Marine meks and gravtanks swirled in counter-clockwise at top speed, pouring deadly, concentrate fire into the packed enemy ranks.

A full unit of Marine meks in battle was a stirring sight to behold: guns blazing, tearing through the enemy lines, and stomping and hurling the enemy in several directions.

As they passed on, more Marine strike teams descended on gravwings, and beat down any of the enemy who had enough sense to try to get away.

Then it was matter of enveloping pockets and arcs of the enemy ring of death and wiping them out. Khai simply chose to go one way, and Ra the other, buzzing through the enemy lines, destroying as they went. Tarim, as always, stayed with Naero to cover her back.

Naero saw a kill team of Dakkur, led by a Dakkur champion begin to transform from the possession wyrms, glowing in the night. They tore into the civilians and began fighting with the Marine gravtanks also.

"Tarim, follow me in," she said.

They fell upon the possessed Dakkur champion. Naero used her blades to slice him into pieces until he exploded.

She transported her and Tarim up into the air above the evolving battle, she opened her third eye and ensnared the thirty Dakkur drones in tendrils and snakes of Cosmic force.

Tarim shredded several Ejjai who tried to spring at them from behind.

"Stand back from the possessed!" Naero warned. Then she detonated all thirty at once, leaving the same number of blackened craters in the ground.

The Spacers took on the enemy wherever they could be found that night and rammed them into the earth dead and bloody, or blasted them to dust.

By dawn, the vast majority of the enemy had been exterminated, and the remnants were being hunted down.

In the aftermath there were countless wounded and dying locals.

Admiral Toshi led a strike force to Sasson-2 and drove off the attackers there with great loss to the enemy. Help finally came to Kudosha-5 from their own people. Naero brought in clouds of medical fixers and other fixers, to help with all of the wounded and the massive damage that seemed to be everywhere.

It was estimated that one fifth of the total population had been killed.

Naero and her people were still helping collect the wounded and the survivors. They marked the dead for later collection. The point now was to save the living.

But she came across the terrible sight of a young Sa'shom girl of about five, with long jet black hair and brown eyes, sobbing and pulling at her dead mother, calling and shrieking to her. Trying to get her mother to get back up.

To Naero who had lost her own mother, and did not know where her own child was, it was particularly heartrending.

She tried to put her hands on the child to comfort her. "Come away, little one. Your mother is gone. I'm sorry."

The small sobbing child shrieked and went into a rage, resisting Naero with a desperate strength, trying to stay with her mother. "No, no! She just fell down. She fell on me when the shooting started again."

"She's gone, little one. I'm sorry. She gave her life protecting you with her own body. You must live on for her sake, and remember how brave she was, and how much she loved you. She wanted you to live, even if she could not."

The shattered child went limp in Naero's hands. Naero held the little one close and stroked her long hair. She was a pretty little thing. Instinctively, the small child clung to Naero's warmth, regressed to putting a thumb in her mouth, and curled her black and green scaled tail around Naero's right arm for comfort and security.

"What is your name, little one. You are very beautiful."

"Zida," the child told her, and then went back to sucking her thumb, and closed her eyes tight.

Another Dakkur champion sprang up out of the ground right in front of Naero.

Before anyone else could react, Naero sent out three concussive beams from her eyes, sliced the Dakkur down its length, and then blew it up, shielding everyone behind her against the force of the blast.

No further harm was going to come to this child while Naero protected her.

Damn the enemy. In her young life, Naero had seen too many scenes such as this play out, with all of their senseless loss and cruelty.

Little Zida was sleeping when Naero handed her off to the Sa'shom aid workers. They took the child from her with great tenderness, and gave her and her people many thanks. "Praise you," one of the nurses said to her. "You are the great leader of the Spacers, many say. Admiral Naero? It is said that you are a legend even among you fierce kind, and that you fight with the strength of a thousand warriors."

"We are allies of the Sa'shom," Naero said. "We were happy to help out here. Together, we shall put an end to our enemies and the terror they inflict upon your worlds."

The nurse smiled. "That is well. Pardon, great Admiral. But the rumors also say that you are a healer, as well. We have many wounded who could use your skill."

Naero sighed. "My skill in healing is only about average," she said. "And I must return to my ships soon, to make sure these worlds are safe once more. I'm sorry."

The nurse bowed, but placed a gentle hand on Naero's arm. "I understand, but please, come with me. It will only take a little of your time. Please help us."

Naero and her people followed out behind the makeshift hospital tent. Under emergency lights that had been set up, the grasslands were covered with dead, dying, and wounded on strips of cloth and emergency foil.

They were everywhere.

The nurse brought her to where most of the children were being kept.

There must have been hundreds, with more being carried in each second.

"Please," the nurse said. "If you can even help a few of them, we would be eternally grateful."

Naero sighed very deeply.

If only she had Shalaen with her.

Over the next three hours, Naero quickly moved from child to child. She startapped and conserved her energy as best she could, using it sparingly to tip the balance and sustain life.

Some of the children were already dead, released from the agony of terrible wounds and injuries. Some were too far gone and could not be brought back, no matter what. Others she could save, just enough so that they would survive and have a chance to recover.

With her biomancy she quickly learned all that she would ever need to know about Sa'shom physiology.

She healed wounds, reknit tissues and organs, and saved limbs. She gave lifeforce to the weak who most needed it.

When she could do no more and all but passed out, Khai took her up in his arms and carried her away, amid the cheering and the applause of the Sa'shom.

Naero wept because she only made it through a few hundred.

But the Sa'shom of Kudosha-5 would remember all that she and the Spacers had done for them, and those tales would spread to all of their other worlds to live in their hearts.

Naero recovered back on board her flagship. Repeated thanks came to them from both worlds of the Sa'shom, and soon from many others.

When they did depart, shortly thereafter, the Spacers left behind waves of defensive drones and seeker mines around both planets to aid in any further defense.

That became SOP for any Alliance world they visited. Naero personally commended Admiral Toshi and his brave fleets, for their outstanding service during the action. But the Spacers had to keep moving.

Naero's continuing diplomatic mission actually took them first into the Lish systems thereafter. The Amavar were even further away from their current location and would have to come last.

Her small diplomatic group went down to the surface of Makryx-5, which was mostly temperate and desert zones. They met near a meganest in one of the more arid regions, yet underground the Lish nests were relatively regular at the same temperature as before.

Their buddy Tus was not there. Their other Lish acquaintance, Gox, introduced them to one who was a very high leader among the Lish— another of them called Sleth, an unmated female who was not only a leader, but supposedly one of their tek geniuses and visionaries.

"Admiral Maeris. I am Sleth, one of the Lish known as the Great Thinkers. Is it true that you understand and can speak our language, without the clumsy translators?"

"That is true," Naero said. "I am doing so know."

"Excellent. Myself and others among the thinkers were very impressed by the data reads, mods, and tech files that you so generously gave to us and the other races. That was a bold and very canny move. You Spacers must be an extremely formidable race, to pursue the enemy here and take them on where they are strongest. That also shows great courage. The Lish are known for their unwavering courage, and they honor and respect that in others."

"Offered," Naero said. "We have offered these secrets, in good faith. The final data only gets transferred once all of the agreements are confirmed. And I thank you for honoring my people. I return that honor to yours, as well."

"I am here to inform you that my people are going to go forward with all of the agreements, and become your allies. We have heard how you helped the Mechans, and the Sa'shom. Everyone we speak to speaks highly of your honor, and your great courage and ferocity as warriors. It is well that we should all join together. We shall fight these invaders of our galaxy to the last, or we shall die."

"My people feel the same way: Liberty or Death."

"Yes. We agree on many things. I am still curious. Is it true that you are a telepath? And that you have Cosmic powers?"

Naero nodded. "I am one of our Mystics."

"As is the green one, your mate, also a Mystic?"

Naero could not help smiling. "Yes, he is. One of the greatest warriors among us."

"More wonders. Then you two are well matched. The sword he carries. We have studied all that we can about it with great curiosity. It is beyond us, and it is a terrifying weapon. Where did it come from? How can your kind wield such powers? We thought that only the enemy wielded such might. We have so many questions. Who are you beings? Who are these enemies? Where do they come from? Why are they here attacking us? We fear that all of this goes beyond mere conquest and violence. The Great Thinkers wish to know and understand. Ignorance shall destroy us all."

"Will you allow me to link with your mind, Sleth?"

"I must warn you. If you try to take over my mind, my guards will attack you, powers or no."

Naero shook her head. "I am an honorable person from an honorable people, Sleth. And you are my ally. I will not betray you. Only the enemy does these foul things of which you speak. Your mind, and your thoughts, and your ways are your own. I do not pretend to know all of the answers, but there are some things which I do know and understand. If I link my thoughts with yours, it is only to impart and share knowledge and understanding–the things I do know–with you and your people. You will know them as I know them, and you will know that I speak true."

"I will allow it. Hear me, my guards. I am going to link minds with this alien ally. You will not harm either of us, on my orders."

Naero came forward and placed her hands on Sleth's enormous head, searching for the right positioning to connect with her mind. Finally she made the link.

Sleth's mind was advanced, alien, and incredibly complex. For one, Sleth was indeed a mathematical genius.

Then Naero noticed something else. All of the components and structures were present.

The Lish simply had not made the evolutionary leap as yet.

Thus far, there had been no need among them for psyonics or Cosmic abilities.

Naero gave their genetics and physical structure in Sleth a nudge.

Sleth's "additional" eye opened above all her others–her psyonic or Mystic eye–the first of the Lish to acquire one. Naero immediately shared with her all the knowledge she possessed concerning their foes.

Then they exchanged other forms of knowledge very rapidly, not with speech, but telepathically.

Then Naero heard Khai shouting at her and abruptly broke the link.

"Naero," Khai shouted. "We just received word from XO Darius and Naero-5, the enemy is springing an attack on Makryx-5 and our fleets. They're moving to intercept, and sending Marine forces down to help protect us."

"Is there any time for us to escape? The enemy is coming after us. If we depart, perhaps they will pursue us and not attack the Lish."

Khai drew Yii and shook his head. "Too late for any of that. An enemy ground assault is already approaching, and will engage us within a minute or two."

Naero turned back to Sleth. "My forces and I will take on the enemy as best we can. More help is coming. We will buy you time to get you people to safety and prepare your defenses."

"We are allies," Sleth said. "Allies fight side by side. The Lish are not defenseless. We shall meet these foes with you. Our forces are already in place. You should join them."

Naero was about to head out when a warning came from the spy fixers. "Khai, enemy phaze troops have penetrated the nest. They're close by, setting incineration charges to take out the nest. They're focusing on the hatcheries and the egg chambers."

"What can we do?" Sleth said. "We sense no foes there."

Naero reminded her, "Recall the information I shared with you about the armor that allows the enemy to become immaterial. They are difficult to detect without very advanced equipment. I have fixers down there trying to disarm the incineration bombs. My people and I will deal with the troops directly. Khai, come with me. Tarim, go with Ra and the Marines and help hold off the enemy ground forces. Help will arrive shortly."

"I will," Tarim said, "but I don't like it."

"Khai and I are the only ones who can phaze," Naero said. "We will protect each other. Now hurry!"

First, Naero and Khai cloaked so that the enemy infiltrators wouldn't see them coming. Then they had the spyfixers paint the infiltrators with markers so that the air molecules around them would show up as flickering, visible light.

She and Khai descended into the nest to the hatcheries and egg chambers, phazed past the startled Lish guards, and went on the attack.

The fixers had managed to neutralize eighty-nine percent of the incineration bombs without detection. But Naero was sensing something else even more powerful.

She and Khai cut down the Dakkur and Ejjai infiltrators with their swords as they hunted them throughout the nest.

Finally they came across an Ejjai mutant, carrying a small atomic within his body cavity, set to go off.

A few lesser bombs went off in the nest, doing some light damage and causing confusion.

"Khai, help me. We need to shield that bomb. I don't know if we can."

Both of them placed their heaviest spheres of shielding around the device, encasing the mutant inside.

"That's not going to be enough," Khai said flatly. Naero—phaze the bomb. It won't hurt anything then."

Both of them unphazed. Naero sat down and focused, opening her third eye. "I've never phazed something else that large. The energy signatures are weird."

"Just do it or we're all dead!" Khai shouted.

Naero just manage to phaze it all an instant before it detonated, killing off the rest of the phazed enemy troops in the area.

But the blast did little else.

Naero and Khai joined their forces up top.

Swarms of racing Lish, some in armor, some not, poured over the arid plane around the nest. They leaped on the enemy troops and tanks and tore them up. Two or three Lish could tear apart a gravtank. They ripped the Dakkur and the Ejjai open like tin cans and swarmed on them.

Naero spotted Ra bulldozing his way through the enemy and focusing on the Dakkur, who he seemed to have a special dislike for. Tarim was guarding his back, just like he did for Naero.

Anything Ra didn't like did not last very long.

Naero's Marines seemed to fight well alongside the Lish and treated them more or less like meks.

By the time Naero's strike forces reached them, she and her allies already had the enemy on the run.

After the battle, the very first thing the Lish did was honor and mourn their dead. This included not only warriors who died in battle, but some eggs and hatchlings who had perished from the blasts in the nest, or were caught out in the open by the enemy.

The dead were laid out, and their names were spoken and honored if they had names. If their mates and children were alive, they keened and shrieked at their deep loss. And then they sang funeral songs. The dead were taken away and buried together beneath battle markers bearing all of their names. And the Lish sang more songs over them.

Even dead Lish made Naero sad, especially now that they were her allies and friends. But the senseless destruction the enemy meted out to all lifeforms indiscriminately only served to enrage her on a regular basis.

The enemy corpses of any edible variety were dragged into the nests in great nets and sent off to be cured and made into foodpods. Dakkur dissolved into nothing but foul smelling goo, and the Lish pissed and defecated on the spots where they died as an insult to such a vile foe.

Naero did not care. Let the Lish do their thing. But no matter what, she still wasn't ever eating an Ejjai turned into a ham. No way. No how. She'd starve first. She didn't care what spices or tasty glazes the Lish used to flavor them with.

To hell with that.

21

When Naero and her group left Makryx-5, the Lish were solidly on board as yet another one of their new allies, against all of the grave threats that their peoples faced.

The final meeting with the Amavar was scheduled to take place at the Rotevvi-9 Naval Base and Shipyards.

The initial fixer nebula had just arrived a few hours before Naero and her fleets did. Sheer Pandemonium erupted.

At first the Amavar, even though they were briefed on what to expect, had even opened fire on the nebula, destroying a quantity of fixers.

They mistook the fixer cloud for some kind of new enemy drone attack.

The fixers absorbed several towed-in hulks that were available, in order to replace their lost numbers.

The first order of business was to upgrade both the shipyards and all of the available Amavar fleets of warships in that region. They would be swapped in and out in shifts for their refits.

Other nebulae would travel from system to system with fleets on patrol. Those fixers would refit still other fleets, revamp planetary defense systems, and sow clouds of new mines, probes, and system defense drones.

Certain primary homeworlds would also get planetary defense shields to help protect them even further.

Naero's counterpart, whom she was eventually brought to, was Admiral Beremel Ziathrah.

The Amavar were similar to each other in form and function, but each was unique and different. There was also some size variations between castes. The only specimen she had known before was Baeven's crewmate, S'krin, the warrior. And like her, all of their faces were more human than insectoid. They had six insectoid limbs with extremely dexterous manipulators–not just claws.

With their manipulators they could do fine detail work, create and operate complex tek equipment, pilot starships, and even fight with six weapons all at the same time. Their tek was very advanced, their energy weapons on par with anything the Spacers had, and they possessed jump-8 stardrives, which they had just recently perfected.

Their shields were adequate, but could use an upgrade. They were experts on gravitics. The Sa'shom and the Lish understood gravitics but barely used them, in daily life or battle. This was an oversight the Allies would need to fix.

The heavier forms of Amavars in certain atmospheres and certain gravities had to be compensated for, to allow them to maintain flight with their dragonfly-like bodies and wings.

Actually, their glistening, shining, iridescent forms were not exactly like a dragonfly, but somewhere between a dragonfly and a damselfly, but definitely insectoid. They were any number of colors, and they were tough and strong, and warrior born.

All Amavar warriors were female, as were their military leaders. Queens gave birth to all of the different kinds. Males were the political leaders, techs, and the basic worker drones. They were also most of the entertainers, singers, musicians, crafters, and artists–who could come from any of the caste types, except for queens. Queens were required to birth up to ten billion offspring in their lifetime, and that kept them a little busy.

From studying them with biomancy, most Amavars lived for about fifty to sixty standard years. Relatively short for most advanced, sentient races.

Admiral Beremel Ziathrah was purple, blue, and silver. Technically, she was a princess. Most leaders were from the royal caste lines. A queen, with effort, could mate with a royal male or prince/courtier whom she chose as her consort. Such pairings became partners and good friends for life. Once her eggs were fertilized, the queen could focus on creating any type of egg, and any type of offspring that was needed–even another queen.

The Amavar were tireless workers, and required only five standard hours of rest.

Their energy, intellect, and drive were nearly boundless. Beremel never stopped moving. She never stopped zipping and leaping about and gave constant orders and instructions to her aides and assistants, who lined up to come to her for new directions and orders.

There was a great deal to do, but the Amavar, for all of their industry were somewhat myopic and could not see the flaws in their organization. Naero spotted it immediately, as an outsider.

For example, Naero observed. Instead of all of these thousands flitting in on their wings to get direct orders from their leaders, a simple series of comlinks, or even basic headsets would simplify matters and greatly speed them up.

Being communal insectoids, they naturally went to and enjoyed the personal interactions. But Naero still had to otherwise commend and respect them for their incredible energy and industry.

Naero had never seen anything like it. The Kexxian fixers were performing their tasks in a flurry, at near-hyper speed–and the Amavar were nearly keeping up with them. An astonishing feat. The only thing faster would have been teknomancing, but doing so would quickly exhaust Naero, and she knew that. She had better things to do than simply conduct upgrades and perform basic construction.

That's exactly what the fixer nebulae were for, an advanced form of engineering and rapid construction, repair, and maintenance.

Admiral Beremel Ziathrah did not slow down, even to eat. Amavar kept food and lix paks on them and inhaled them as they kept going.

If Naero wanted to continue speaking to the admiral, she and her people had to use their gravwings and hustle to keep up.

When Naero asked questions about Amavar culture, society, or politics, Beremel would finish what she was doing, move on, answer Naero's questions succinctly, and continued on to the next task and at a fairly blistering pace.

"So," Naero asked. "I'm trying to understand. Only the royal levels and the leadership levels have sexual relations with each other, but only the queen produces offspring for the entire hive? Doesn't that make the soldiers, teks, and drones more or less sexless?"

Beremel smiled. "I know if must seem bizarre and confusing to an alien mind, especially for mammals. But just remember that the Amavar have lived in this fashion very successfully for millions of years. Soldiers are always female. Teks and drones can be either male or female, and while they will all pair off for temperature regulation and companionship, they do not have sex, even for pleasure.

"The leadership levels have sex for pleasure, within exclusively mated pairs and or with concubines and consorts on the side, but they do not produce offspring. Yes, the queen produces all of the offspring as are needed for the hive. If her consort dies, she can pick a new one, or even choose to retire, turning her reign over to a new queen. If and when a queen dies, several princesses, or potential queens are always held in reserve, in case they are needed."

"Do you have a mate, Admiral?"

"I do. He is a general of our ground forces, and we are very happy with each other. Our duties keep us extremely busy, especially with the war now, but we mate several times each year, and each joining is wonderful."

"Very well. Let me ask about something completely different. How do you see our enemies?" Naero asked.

"I see them for what they are—the greatest threat to our existence that we have ever faced. They see us mostly as food, or to be captured and turned into mindless slaves and shock troops for them.

Beremel shuddered. "I have seen these slaves that they make of our unhatched. They are mindless killers, who cannot be reasoned with, even though they look like our own. We exterminate them with great disgust. That our foe turns our own offspring against us is a crime for which we shall never forgive them. There can be no quarter with such a foe. Either we destroy them, or they will destroy us and all that we could ever be."

Naero took a chance. "I have heard of others of my kind who have met an Amavar female named S'krin. Do you know—"

Admiral Beremel stopped in her tracks and shuddered. She whirled about, her face a mask of emotions, one of them rage.

"You have seen and met with Dellessa Shehanniel Kevatthia S'krin?"

"I have only heard of other Spacers who have, back in the Alpha Quadrant. Who is she?"

"The Alpha Quadrant," Beremel said. "It figures that she would go there to avoid her responsibilities."

Naero didn't follow. "Admiral, you have me at a loss here."

"This S'krin, as you call her, as she now calls herself was the only high daughter of the former Amavar Empress. S'krin was genetically engineered and specially groomed to produce the next leap forward in Amavar evolution. Yet when the old empress was dying, and S'krin was hatched and being trained to assume the mantle of the new empress, she rebelled and fled, betraying her people—insisting on being free to go off on her own to have her own selfish life, without thought to her people and their greater needs."

"And another empress could not be produced?" Naero guessed.

"No, not at all. Not one such as her," Beremel said. "The old empress died, and it had taken almost and entire lifetime to prepare another, even with her assistance. Do you happen to know where this S'krin is?"

"Not currently. They are but rumors I had heard."

"She is considered worse than a renegade. Worse than an enemy. To my people, she is traitor of the highest rank. All of our people have orders to kill her on sight. If you learn of her whereabouts, please inform us, and we will send a fleet after her to bring us her head."

"That all sounds terrible," Naero noted.

"It is. In all our long history, no empress or queen has betrayed our people so utterly. It is one of our greatest shames as a species."

Baeven sure could pick 'em. Apparently, she and Baeven were more or less in the same boat with their species.

No wonder S'krin said not to mention her name.

On their way back, Beremel insisted that they stop off at a nearby moon, to observe a research and mining colony that the enemy had recently attacked and destroyed.

Everything was destroyed, and most of what remained were scorched Amavar exoskeletons of nearly all castes and ages. The enemy had focused on using flame guns, flame cannons on their gravtanks, and incendiary bombs against the colony. The Amavar feared burning to death, and even buried their dead at sea or otherwise under water. They did this because of a spiritual belief that all life originally came from water, and that the dead must be returned to water. Just as Spacers believed that the dead should be returned to the stars.

All that Naero saw on the lost colony were the skeletons and remains of the lost, the slaughtered, and the murdered. Amavar men, women, and children of all castes and ages. Perhaps in a way, the immolated dead had been more fortunate. The other dead and the living who could be eaten had been long since tossed into the enemy meatships.

Naero always looked with horror upon dead children of any sentient species. A murdered child on any world was still a murdered child. And the murderers needed to be stopped and then destroyed.

22

Breakthrough.

The word finally reached them from Baeven.

"Naero; we've got them! Attacking immediately to reach Naero-3. They have her in some kind of high powered shield. Get here ASAP!"

Naero launched every fleet she had available that wasn't assigned somewhere. That also included her and fleets 1 through 11.

This was it.

The Black Spot and *The Dark Star* also converged. They would reach the coordinates before Naero could, but not by much.

If it had been closer, she would have risked transporting straight down to the surface. She teknomanced, and flashraced through the rest of the data.

'Here' turned out to be a top secret enemy research base on Xatrex-3, in an area of dead space.

They arrived into an all-out slugfest between two Spacer fleets, Fleet-86 and Fleet-89, taking on five enemy fleets who had been concealed nearby on other planets and moons. The enemy forces moved in to support the base.

Naero turned command over to her XO, certain that her people would make short work of the enemy defense force.

"We'll go down together in one of my spheres," Khai said. "That will be fastest."

Naero frowned. "I know a faster way, for me. You guys follow on."

Before anyone could protest, she homed in on Baeven's signal, and transported.

She was in the base.

Baeven had just been there and was now somewhere up ahead.

Everything was trashed. All of the enemy were dead. And not just dead...in pieces or reduced to burning goo or slag.

"I'm here, Baeven," Naero called over their link. She tried to follow his signal, but it kept breaking up, with all the enemy tek going wild.

The link he came back to her on was telepathic. "Fighting Danner...in some huge, enemy Darkforce generator mek. Very tough. Almost got him down. Couldn't break through to Naero-3...in that enemy shield sphere. Strongest damn shield...I've ever seen."

"I'm almost there, Baeven. Hang on!"

Several massive Cosmic energy signals flared up ahead.

Transporting was too risky with the energy flows this crazy.

Time for the direct approach.

She startapped and keep startapping.

Naero summoned her Ur-metal swords and formed her Chaos Katanas over them set at full power.

Baeven screamed in agony over their link and then cut off.

Naero surrounded herself in erupting, exploding Cosmic power.

Spinning and whirling rapidly, Naero rocketed straight toward those energy sources, blasting, slicing, and kicking through enemy troops, defensive barriers, walls, and solid underground rock.

A plasma borer could not have drilled through those areas as fast as she fused and melted her way through them.

When she came to a halt, she basically stood within a smoldering crater. All of the enemy lab equipment was melted into slag or completely fried. A massive explosion had blown the entire roof off the complex, from a hundred meters or more beneath the surface.

Naero didn't see Naero-3, Baeven, or Danner. They had just been locked in a pitched fight in that location. Where was everyone now?

The Cosmic energy flows were completely out of control, and unlike anything Naero had ever witnessed.

What the hell was going on?

Khai, Tarim, Ra and the Spacer Marines led the charge of forces pouring into the enemy lab complex. Any surviving foes were put down fast and hard.

Yet the mystery continued.

Then Baeven phazed back in out of nowhere, and he looked somewhat beaten up. Most likely from his battle with Danner.

Naero rushed up to him. "Where is she? What happened?"

Baeven shook his head. "I put Danner down, but the core with him inside escaped in some kind of energy pod that just blasted free and phazed away. Then the remaining enemy teks blasted me with some kind of experimental projector. They were powering the projector with the energy field around Naero-3."

"So they zapped you out of phaze? Were you stuck in the Astral Plane or some kind of pocket dimension?"

Baeven shook his head. "No, you don't get, it, N. They were conducting experiments in *Time* itself. It was some kind of Time gun–a temporal cannon."

Naero examined him quickly. "It didn't appear to damage you. What did it feel like?" She knew that the enemy had been conducting temporal, dimensional, and interdimensional experiments for a long while.

"I couldn't move," Baeven said. "I couldn't transport, phaze, or do anything. I vanished out of sight because I was out of phaze with Time. I was in limbo somewhere–in nowhere. After a few minutes of being frozen like that, I phazed back in to our time."

"Baeven, I want you to tell me everything you saw. Naero-3. How did she look?"

He frowned. "Pretty bad. She was just a floating torso, and she appeared to be in some kind of stasis. She wasn't conscious. All of her arms and legs were missing: burned, blasted, or yanked off. Her wounds were sealed, but it looked as if she had put up a pretty tough fight. She must not have had time or energy to attempt to regenerate."

Naero did her best to suppress her own personal rage. Poor Naero-3. She was suffering in Naero's own place, at the hands of ruthless foes who were utterly without honor or mercy.

But despite all that, Naero would continue her program of making several replicants each day. A growing legion of super soldiers for the ongoing war effort.

Naero contained her continuing frustration and thought upon what must be done. "Pick this place clean and let's get out of here," she commanded. "We depart in fifteen standard minutes. Keep everyone moving! We carpet bomb this place as we go; leave nothing behind for the enemy to use."

They had gotten very close once more. And they wouldn't stop. From what Baeven said, it sounded as if the enemy was siphoning off her unborn daughter's energies, using her like a battery to power their experiments.

That meant that they still hadn't found a way to crack her child's amazing defenses. That was something, at least. But those powerful enemies were nothing if not persistent.

They would eventually devise a way to get past those defenses and get at Naero's child. That was also only a matter of time.

Her XO reported from the fixernet. Hundred of enemy fleets were heading to intercept them at Xatrex-3.

"Do we call more of our forces to fight them here?" Darius asked her.

"Negative. This was a raid, and the raid is over. This is not the main battle we want. Everyone jump out. We'll be gone before those bastards get here. Our fun will start in a few days. Then we'll really put it on them."

Baeven had already slipped away at some point, as Khai pointed out. He never hung around very long once the action was over.

He contacted Naero shortly thereafter in private. "We'll keep trying, N. I'm sorry about today."

"Not your fault, uncle. I know you tried your hardest. We'll get them. Thank you, for all of your hard effort."

The site of the enemy lab complex lit up from orbit, just before Naero and Fleet-1 were the last to jump out and vanish.

*

Two days later, Naero and her new allies were ready to bring the pain and inflict it wholesale on the enemy. First they made several major feint attacks at the opposite end of their enemy's territory, giving all the appearances of the start of a major naval offensive.

As Naero guessed the enemy might, they responded with massive retaliation to drive the attackers back.

Then the foe also mounted coordinated heavy attacks against all four of the Alliance races and their homeworlds, on several fronts.

Those defenses would need to stand firm and hold for the Alliance. There were very few reserves being held back to send to their defense. And they could not be everywhere at once.

The enemy seemed very confident and self-assured about these events. They apparently thought they had the entire situation well-managed.

Next, Naero expanded her attacks in numerous exposed weak areas where the enemy was already rushing most of their forces and reserves.

Then, once it was clear that the enemy was fully committed, engaged, and overextended, the four actual major attacks struck the enemy's forward naval bases and shipyards on the opposite side of the enemy's worlds. The Alliance stormed into those systems in complete fury, with everything they could muster that could fly or shoot.

As soon as the enemy recovered and engaged the attackers, Naero and her Spacers struck like surgeons, each strike force backed by twenty-five hi-tek fleets to gun down the enemy's strongest forces from behind. This was not a battle. It was a slaughter.

The Spacers were there not to fight the enemy, but to wipe the enemy out, destroy the fleets stationed there, and eradicate those four enemy hardpoints.

If they could pull that off, they would collapse over one third of the enemy's overall captured territory, crush the expanding advance, and force the foe onto the defensive.

All four of those battles started off well, but almost an entire day of heavy fighting lay ahead of them.

Naero trusted all three of her very able admirals.

Then, as things continued to go against the enemy on all fronts, as expected, Naero received a call from Captain Tyber and Alala, aboard *The Dark Star*.

"Better be good, Ty. A little busy here."

"We're tracking an enemy spyship similar to *The Black Spot;* Jan's coming to assist us. We are certain by the energy signatures that they have Naero-3 on board. But we're surrounded by ten enemy fleets. What are our orders?"

Naero thought for a second. "Where are they headed, Ty?"

"They're making a dead run straight at the enemy Homeworld of Naggoth. There are over four hundred enemy fleets in between here and there, Naero. What do you want us to do?"

Naero sighed, focusing on her battle displays. "Nothing for now, Ty. I'll send Baeven to assist. If he thinks you can free her somehow, follow his lead. Otherwise, track where she goes and learn what you can. If we win the day, even a stronghold like Naggoth will be in striking range. Stay safe, my friends. Whatever you do, don't get nabbed."

Naero broke off the link. Her duty was to her fleets during a major operation at this level.

She closed her eyes for a second. Even if that cost her the life of her own child.

But she would deal with the pain of that decision later.

Chances were, even Baeven wouldn't see much hope of rescuing Naero-3, surrounded by that many foes. And it was only going to get worse on their way to Naggoth.

But no war was won all at once.

Naero turned her burning eyes to her enemies and focused on the battle holo arrays, fingers flashing, sending orders rapidly and optimizing fleet attack profiles at will.

She was going to use all of her skill, all of her gifts, to make them pay.

Let the enemy come. Bring their fire. It would pale and melt before the hell she was going to unleash upon the foe. Until the moment they drew their last breaths, she would continue to hammer, and punish, and incinerate every enemy fleet that dared to get in her way.

And they would surround Naggoth itself and reduce it to dust, if that's what it took to get her own back.

The Allies smelled invader blood in the black, and closed in like hungry sharks, hungry to throw back their foes with great loss and take back some of their own.

No one that day was in any mood for mercy or to hold back.

All of them had suffered enough.

Mayrun-5 was the first enemy stronghold to fall. The fixer nebulae were even sent in to strip the wrecks clean, the base, and the shipyard. They departed as if giant space locusts had left nothing behind.

Next came Klytasso-2. By the time three bells rang, eighty-seven enemy fleets were left in burning pieces for the fixers to strip and collect.

And as always, before the Allies departed, they left behind clouds of cloaked attack drones and seeker mines to give any other enemies a warm welcome home–to a home that would no longer be there.

The enemy would clearly withdraw and abandon those now worthless and vulnerable forward positions. If they could be destroyed once, they could be destroyed again.

And for the simple fact that there was no longer anything there that was strategically worth defending.

The starbase and naval shipyards at Chomatta-4 took much longer to capture and then destroy. Not only were they more extensive, but the enemy kept dumping reinforcements into those zones that had to be taken out also.

The allies waited, poised like wolves.

Finally the additional fleets stopped coming, and the enemy gave up on Chomatta-4 as another lost cause.

Brattemul-7 was the final hold out, and the closest of all the four bases to the enemy's next most forward line of defensive positions. For an entire day, the battle there had bogged down into a bloody stalemate.

Then Naero sent in all of her remaining ships from the other three locations that could still fight. A quite substantial number of Alliance fleets.

The enemy matched those numbers with five hundred extra fleets gleaned from Naggoth and all of their other systems.

This was the largest, most complex battle yet, stretched out over several nearby systems.

Finally she gave the orders. "We are going to form a death strike. Get all of our largest, rapid-fire ships into Echo-Radio-5 ribbon formation, and we take out all of the bigs that we can. Then we loop back around and shatter the rest. The remnants should break and jump out, if we can make the death zone hot enough!"

Two hundred Spacer and allied battleships came in on a concentrated attack vector at maximum speed and brought the heat. They raked the enemy front lines with devastating continuous fire, and destroyed three hundred and forty enemy bigs with the first pass.

On the second pass, they knocked out four hundred and eighty-one bigs, carriers, cruisers, and destroyers.

No military force could withstand such horrendous losses.

The enemy began to form up and attempted to escape in all directions. In their panic, some even collided with each other and were mutually vaporized.

"Press all attacks with extreme prejudice," Naero commanded. "Send the foe down in flames." The death strike kept twisting around the enemy fleets like a razor chain of flaming destruction."

Naero drew her sword and clenched her fists, hurling defiance at the foe and broadcasting her holo and its message to every ship in the Alliance.

"Drive on, valiant warriors! Destroy these scum to the last," Naero yelled, and then snarled behind clenched teeth. "We're sending a warning to these filth who think that they can take our worlds and massacre our children! These are Alliance systems and Alliance stars, and they will shine free in the black once more. Let the destroyers send their numbers, and their cowards, and their slaves to fall before the might of our will and the ferocity of our guns! Those who know freedom shall always rise up against vermin such as these. Death to the invaders! This is our galaxy!"

Cheering erupted and roared out from the Alliance fleets at their first major victory against the ruthless foe, shouted by countless voices in all of their languages.

"Death. Death. Death!"

"Death to the invaders!"

Naero lifted her head as her fleets swept forward on the attack.

Nothing lived upon Brattemul-7. All was flame and wrath and death.

"So be it," she whispered, sheathing her sword at last.

This was the war that these invaders had forced upon them all.

Liberty, or Death.

23

Naero and her crews did not celebrate. They knew better. One battle did not win any war, and these were canny, unrelenting foes who thought and fought for the long term. They were beyond fanatical, and never gave up, and they always found a way to keep coming at their targets.

The vile spirits of the long dead G'lothc had perished eons before, in a terrible war spread over numerous galaxies. They followed a sick, twisted dream of destroying all life in the universe. So strong, in fact, that even after death these fell beings still would not let go of the universe they infected. They clung to the very edge of oblivion itself, yearning and scheming only to infest the universe with their lethal disease once more.

They sought host bodies to possess, both temporary and permanent, in order through which to work their dark will.

The Alliance shifted into a heavy defensive mode for the time being, alert for any new or old tricks their enemies might try. Naero warned all of the other sentient leaders.

"Every time we have defeated them, they have come back even stronger, and with something more destructive. We must remain vigilant and continue to advance and push forward with all of our plans. We won't be able to surprise them in the same way twice. They would counter our efforts and our new strategies and be ready for us next time. We must continue to adapt and change as well."

Still no word on the location of poor Naero-3, since the enemy landed with her on Naggoth. The energy levels on that Dakkur homeworld were so messed up, that nothing could be detected or tracked near the surface.

Although, if she left Naggoth, Naero, Jia, Alala, and Ty had conspired to devise a way to track her now. Or at least the energies of Naero's child.

If the enemy tried to take Naero-3 somewhere else, now they could follow that very unique Cosmic energy signature, unlike anything in the known universe.

The other sentient leaders still wished to thank Naero and her officers. At an alliance unity banquet, held with an immense WebBall arena, their new allies had a gift for the Spacers.

Hundreds of orphaned children from the four races: Mechan, Lish, Sa-shom, and Amavar, formed a choir and sang for the evening's entertainment. The soloists of the four races sang with voices that were heartstoppingly lovely. Even the spider-like Lish were accomplished singers.

Then Naero was forced to rise and draw her sword, and salute at attention, and every officer with her.

When the children sang the first verse of *The Ballad of the Omaria*, and the rousing chorus.

Janner suddenly cut in with a telepathic high alert.

"Naero, prepare for an enemy phaze attack. Three hundred Ejjai suicide strikers. They slipped through somehow and are penetrating the hull of the arena even now. We're intercepting as many as we can."

Naero sent out her own telepathic call, phazed, and shot up into the air to do battle as the enemy strikers came into view.

Strike force Shetanna—phaze and neutralize these murderous assholes!

Threescore Shetannas, in full combat gear, rose up with her in formation and transfixed the Ejjai on twisting, slicing, exploding blades of scarlet Cosmic energy. Just as the enemy was trying to phaze in and attack. Shetanna Force incinerated the attackers in mid-air, and shielded the crowd below in layered spheres of protective energy.

The children mistook it all for fireworks and a pretty light show display. They laughed and clapped.

The adults all knew better–that a concerted attempt on their lives had just been thwarted, by Admiral Naero and those amazing, deadly clones of hers with the twin red swords.

And they had all done so in the space of a single breath.

Naero ordered the evening's diversions to continue, while extra care was taken to adjust their systems to prevent such and attack from getting that close to them again.

She gave all of the details they had thus far to the Alliance leaders.

"I told you that we would not have long to wait," Naero reminded them all. "This is a foe who will keep searching for ways to strike at us and take us down, any way that they can. The only way to stop them is to destroy them. And that is exactly what we are going to do. World by world. Fleet by fleet. And one by one."

From that day forward, Naero and her leaders continued to have multiple planning and training sessions with all Alliance troops. From her initial strategic analysis, some of their ways of operating and fighting complimented each other, while others conflicted and caused problems in communications, operations, logistics, and execution of tactical efforts.

The Lish and the Sa'shom could make better use of advanced gravitics.

They needed to sort these issues out and continue to find the most efficient and effective ways to work and fight together.

Surprisingly, it was the Lish and the Sa'shom who were more flexible in trying new things. While the Mechans and especially the blockheaded Amavar–as Naero referred to them–who needed to be convinced that there was more than one way to do things. Such had to be proven to them, over and over again, before they would agree to try out new procedures.

That continued to be a hold up.

After several such instances, Naero and her officers held a frank meeting with the Mechan and Amavar leaderships. Naero framed it all under the umbrella of efficiency and unacceptable and dangerous, as well as needless–delay.

Efficiency was like a magical and holy word to the Mechans and the workaholic Amavar. Finally she was able to get them to accept the wisdom of implementing new ways of doing things much faster.

They held war games up in the black, and down on planetary surfaces in multiple environments.

The Lish had a problem with the concept of a practice conflict, without causing injury. But their fierceness in battle was unmatched and unquestioned. All of the races had their strengths and weaknesses.

The Amavar were–surprise–too unyielding and unwilling to adjust their battle plans on the fly, according to the shift and flow of actual combat and events. And as the records of their actions revealed, if a battle did not go exactly their way or conform to what they expected–they were quickly in trouble.

As Naero put it, in the old vernacular–they needed to learn to wing it–to make it up as they went along.

Mechans had similar problems involving logic. They were fierce and coldly mathematical in their operations. Anything that was illogical or counter-intuitive, or simply strange, confused them. And similar to the Amavar in some ways, they did not deal well with surprise attacks and tricks.

First, the Spacers had to help the Mechans not only to simply respond to surprises, but to do so without stopping to try to understand them. That was irrelevant and wasted time. And then beyond mere responding to surprises, the next phaze involved even anticipating such events and learning to expect or even predict the possibility of their occurrence.

In essence, they had to learn to adapt and be ready to respond to various possibilities–no matter what happened. To be prepared for the unknown and the unexpected in general.

The Sa'shom could be overly emotional and sometimes charged in all at once, when they should remain more disciplined and tactical.

And the Spacers were getting far too overconfident. This was an enemy that still had serious tek advantages on them and eventually, that was going to bite them in the ass, and hard.

She needed to try to make progress with the KDM, but she was, frankly, too tired and to torn in several directions to try to find her harmonious, Cosmic center.

Khai and her officers, and even Trudi Cheyenne, her personal physician finally agreed on one thing.

Admiral Naero Amashin Maeris needed a break, some time to relax, and a good night's sleep. Perhaps even two or three. She had been driving herself hard, ever since they arrived in the Gamma Quadrant.

Unofficially, Khai assumed control of the situation. They took *The Flying Dagger* out for spin, only protected by several hundred Alliance fleets within a moment's notice, and secretly accompanied by *The Dark Star* and *The Black Spot.*

Baeven and Crew were still on the hunt, trying to devise a way to crack fortress Naggoth.

Khai insisted that they sleep in the next day. For once, Naero did not argue.

Sleeping in meant that they were up by seven bells.

Naero awoke smelling fragrant, floral-scented steam in the air.

Khai surprised her by programming the nanofloor into a shallow, lighted hot spa. He was already in it, dozing himself, watching her sleep and just waiting for her to awaken.

When they were together, their general rule was that neither of them wore anything. They both enjoyed it that way. Naero sometimes clothed herself–barely–in filmy little things to tease Khai with. But he ended up stripping them off of her anyway. He always followed her intently with his eyes and he smiled at her when they were alone, taking great pleasure in everything she did, every move that she made.

"Why do you look at me the way you do?" She asked him, more than once.

He would always grin and say something like, "Because I like the way you look back at me with those killer violet eyes of yours. It all makes both of us happy."

He was right. She would always smile. Sometimes she just moved around the room for him, stretching and flexing, going about her business, doing the simplest of things. Khai would always sigh and continue to smile and watch like a predator.

In the end, he always came to her.

Unless she grew tired of their little game and went to him first, all breathless and ready to feel his hands upon her. Khai against her body was an extremely good and luscious thing indeed.

Sometimes it was just nice to be a couple.

Naero brushed her long black hair back and wiped the drool from her face, and the crystalized sleepies out of her eyes.

"Join me in the water," Khai said with a deep, tempting sigh, closing his eyes for a few moments more. "The warm water is heavenly...magical. And...I have a surprise for you."

Naero snorted, but with a wide grin. "Haisha...I've heard that one before. Promises, promises, my love."

Khai chuckled. "Suit yourself."

Naero almost raced from their nanobed and dove at him with a giant splash to startle him.

"I just had it installed for you," Khai added.

Now she was curious. "Installed?" Not what she had been thinking about at all. "What are you up to, my beloved one?"

"I know your wants and your needs, my heart."

"Oh, do you?" she said. She came straight at him, flinging her long, glistening hair back behind her like a cape, stepping slowly into the steaming, lighted water, and eventually stretching out and placing her head on Khai's broad chest as she slid in close up against him.

His powerful green arm encircled her petite form and gently drew her closer.

When he bent his head to smile at her with those golden eyes of his, Naero was lost. She surged up out of the water and kissed him, for a very long time.

Khai told her once that his wish was to have a single day to themselves to do nothing but kiss each other, in every way that he could imagine and devise. Naero sighed. What a luxury that would be.

After they broke and caught their breath, Naero took his handsome green face into her hands.

"There are no words, in all the languages ever created, to say how much I love you Khai."

Khai chuckled slightly. "Perhaps such things cannot be proven by words alone," he told her.

She sensed him give a teknomancy command.

Part of her inner hull wall dissolved.

Naero swallowed her own breath and was speechless.

She nearly choked.

Behind the nanoveil stood a brightly lit, hi-tek lix vending machine for Jett soda.

Naero broke down with her face buried in her hands and wept.

They made good use of that Jett machine about an hour and a half later, still breathing hard, sitting back into the hot spa and slugging down tasty, frosty cold Jett.

Naero had even tossed a couple of borbbles into the spacious bathroom for Ra. He had developed a fondness for the lix as well, and like to watch vids on a screen in there. He thought them great fun.

She returned to the spa and sat next to Khai in the fragrant warm water, enjoying herself immensely. "Well that takes care of two very human needs, and now that I'm no longer thirsty, either, I am still ravenous. How about you, Khai?"

"I think I could out-eat Ra about now. What do you have in mind?"

Naero grinned. "How about a late breakfast with some of my crew?"

Khai nodded. "Excellent. And it's not that late. What does the Admiral have in mind from the galley?"

"Hell, I was going to whip up something myself."

"Even better. I love it when you cook. Are we talking brunch?"

"More like an old-fashioned Terran breakfast. You can eat that any time of the day. Come on, let's get to it!"

She jumped out of the water and headed toward the door.

Khai laughed and called after her. "Uh, N... Clothes? I mean–I don't mind, if your crew doesn't."

Naero laughed, teknomancing nano clothing for them both. "No, I don't think my crew is quite ready for that. Although I've heard of a few merchant ships that basically do serve on board naked, with nothing but a nanobelt, just in case."

Ra followed them out to the galley, where Eugene Blooding now ran the kitchen. His former boss, Culinary Chief Specialist First Class Tolen Kothari was now Master Chef on board *The Holy Ghost*, her flagship.

Eugene and his assistant, Ketumi Negawa from Clan Kothari, kept their small staff busy.

They hugged Naero and Khai and greeted Ra warmly. Naero's mantid bodyguard was still new to her crew and wasn't exactly seen as huggable yet by everyone, except Naero.

The admiral took over the mess kitchen, but Eugene and his people assisted.

First she got some red yamtatoes frying, hash brown style. Then she slow cooked a big pan of Spum strips and Huradian thick bacon strips, turning them as needed until they were just the right kind of crispy. Then big Phoradi goose eggs that were as big as her fist and green inside. Khai would enjoy eating food the same color as he was.

She fried those big, glorious eggs over easy and got the bright green yolks just right, transferring them in batches to the warmers. Eugene and Ketumi made a couple of loaves of Laraldan sourdough bread into toast, with Veluvian butter cream spread. They had Churtan blue milk and whiteberry juice from Govania-5.

The last batch of Spum and bacon were finally ready, along with the yamtatoes.

Time to eat.

They had enough for about fifteen people. Eugene and Ketumi ate with them first, and then went into the kitchen to make another larger batch of those same menu items for the rest of the crew for brunch.

Naero and Khai stuffed themselves. Ra did his best to eat as much as them and still hold back. He probably could have eaten everything edible in the galley if they let him.

Enel Maeris and Surina Marshall quickly joined them, and soon they were all feasting and laughing.

Rina was absolutely radiant, with her hyperglam, vidstar looks, her hand and arm looped in with handsome Enel's. Enel had the look of a very satisfied and happy man.

The couple wanted to announce their engagement to Naero, before they told the rest of the crew. Everyone else probably wondered why it all took so long, since the two of them had been inseparable and so besotted with each other for so long. Congrats went back and forth, and soon everyone was in the know.

Then Rendar Nelson, and Passaendra Wild, Piper Fae, Kimbel Allen, Lakara Donovan and Trudi Cheyenne joined the brunch party. Captain Tyber arrived, and brought little Gallan with him. The dark-haired infant was just starting to be a toddler now.

Aunt Naero got him from Ty and did not let go, keeping Gallan happily on her lap while she and Khai laughed and played with him and fed him whatever he wanted. He really liked Spum and the yamtatoes. They got him a straw that he could sip whiteberry juice out of. The kid had an appetite, just like his namesake.

Naero kept feeling twinges of sadness about her and Khai's missing child. Yet this was a happy time, even though Naero kept feeling guilty and those sad twinges of loss and uncertainty. Only Khai seemed to guess her true feelings, and gave her a comforting squeeze every now and then.

The first shift went back to work. Everyone hugged Naero, Ty, and Khai, and squeezed little Gallan's cheeks, toes, and hands until they were pink. That little doll was a bigger hit than their beloved captain...er, admiral.

To them she'd always be their captain, and she did not stop them from calling her that. Despite her major promotion.

Naero-12 came in to eat with the second shift, the replicant assigned to *The Flying Dagger*. She sported bright pink hair half the length of Naero's and put up in a different style. But she still wore her togs and gear the same as the original.

When they hugged, Naero couldn't help absorbing all of Naero-12's experiences with her old crew.

They accepted her and even liked her, but they still didn't treat her with the same admiration they had for the original. But Naero-12 seemed all right with all of that.

In fact, to her mind it was easier, because she was still highly skilled and capable of so many things, and yet there was no pressure on her to be 'the Legend.' Not as much was expected of her, so whatever she did was amazing.

Actually, Naero's life felt richer now, every time she re-linked with one of her copies. Her life experiences were just that much more interesting, sharing in their experiences and memories, and they sharing in hers.

It was a unique, and very special relationship and bonding that they all shared. Each time two of more of them met–especially with the original–they were going to share something new and exciting with each other.

Keldo Ramsey, Chandra Adams, Spenser Gordon, Sying Lii, and Harra Ahmed came in and sat down to eat, catch up, and share stories.

Next came Tommis Barrett, Kayleen Flynn, Prentiss Fox, Fenton James, Juan Keller, and Jima Ortega. It was definitely a full-blown, brunch party by then.

When Chaela and Saemar came over, things went really nuts. The Viking Valkyrie looked like she had swallowed a WebBall, and not just Remy's love child. Fleet Captain Saemar left her all-male bodyguards behind, because she complained she wasn't getting any sleep, from having her body guarded too closely.

"Seriously, sweeties," Saemar said. "Do you think I could borrow one of your empty bunks and just grab a nap for a bit? I'm bushed."

Naero finally gave up little Gallan, and the other two aunties proceeded to spoil that little kid rotten.

Naero had never laughed so hard in so long. Being with her mates brought out the old her. Before the afternoon was finished, she had used the sight to check on Chaela's very healthy boy inside her, and listened to tales of Saemar's latest conquests. Ty started talking shop with her about the implementation of all the new upgrades and possible pweaks to some of their spytek.

By the fourth hour the shindig broke up. Everyone but Naero and Khai and Ra had to face facts and get back to work.

Naero wrapped herself around Khai's big arm and smiled up at him. "I'm still recovering. I think you'd better carry me off and put me down for my afternoon siesta for my own good, Mr. Enforcer."

Khai could be such a dolt at times. He actually looked at her with concern. "Sure, let's go. I didn't know you were still feeling tired."

She bulged her eyes at him. "No, you big green goon. I'm *not* tired…at least not yet. But I will be, when you're through with me. Got it?"

"Oh…" Khai said.

Naero nodded. "Yeah, now you've got the plan. It's a good thing you're so cute, buddy."

"And we can have some more Jett!"

"Aww," Naero said. "I loved your great gift. You really must love me."

"I honestly do, my heart."

Naero looked him straight in the eye. "Then prove it, mister."

Khai grinned, scooping her up. "You know how I love a challenge."

24

Naero felt infinitely better the next day, as if she were recharged and ready for anything. She made eight more replicants and sent them over to *The Black Spot*. Eventually, she wanted an entire crew of them backing up her brother Jan and keeping him and his two new wives safe.

If Jan was happy, that was all that mattered. And he did seem happy. His choices were his own, and he wasn't a boy any longer. He was an accomplished adult—a man now. A fully trained Mystic, and a ship Captain working for her Task Force and for Spacer Intel.

Although if things were really going to get hot, Jan asked both of his wives to either go with Baeven, or stay on the flagship.

Naero asked her brother if she could do a mindlink with him. That way, she could see if he had any Mystic skills that she could quicken or boost.

She also explained that she wanted to study the Cosmic energy patterns and levels in his mind, and compare them to her own to see what the differences were.

She also asked Jan about his own Dark Beast within him. He explained that since it had never broken free, he had managed to keep it suppressed and dormant, avoiding all of those troubles entirely. That was also a huge difference between the two of them.

Naero had no idea if that all had anything to do with Jan being a twin with their insane brother Dan, who was still working with and for the enemy, apparently. Who knew what the hell was going on with all of that?

Baeven had fought Danner most recently, and detailed how whacked out Danner was, but still able to fight his uncle and try to escape with Naero-3.

Then there was the enemy. Everything always came back to them. From what Naero and the Allies had learned from the bits and pieces of data stripped from the enemy lab, even the enemy was stumped about what to do with Naero's unborn child. Thus far, the foe's top minds could only contain those massive energies and siphon some of them off. But that wasn't nearly enough and the enemy was frustrated and enraged. They hungered to crack those secrets and take control of this strange power for their own purposes.

As usual, they wanted to transform it into a weapon. That was all that the enemy masterminds could think of. Whether the child or Naero-3 survived all of these dangerous experiments was utterly of no concern. They were mere things to be exploited.

Naero was finally as ready as she would ever be at this point to go another round with the powers guarding the KDM deep within herself.

Her first few attempts had been humiliating and humbling. Even when she had been given the knowledge to implement the Kexxian cure for the G'lothc possession wyrm plague, it had very nearly destroyed her.

It would have destroyed her, if Jan had not stepped in to share the agony and those energies with her. The fact that she could not have survived it on her own was not lost upon Naero. The knowledge of the Kexxian Data Matrix was currently beyond her own fledgling Cosmic abilities to fully understand or control.

But against such foes as they now faced, Naero knew in her heart that the deep wisdom and knowledge of the Kexx and the KDM were going to be crucial, and perhaps, their only hope.

Even if she perished in the attempt, she had to crack that knowledge and pass that wisdom onto her own people and their allies to use in the fierce battles to come.

Naero meditated and focused as her parents had taught her from a child, trying to center herself as much as possible, to find the true balance and harmony within. All despite what a messed-up wreck she was.

She had always been able to hide that well. Hide the Chaos, and the pain, and make it seem like order and control. She could pweak things at the last instant to make it all appear as if everything was working seamlessly. But things changed, and shifted, and fluctuated within her on a near constant level. And she still did not fully comprehend, understand, or know a way to control it all.

So she kept faking it. That was the best she could do.

Perhaps that was a wisdom in itself.

Maybe that was all that anyone could ever do.

Naero shook her head. She wished she and her mind were more like Jan's. From studying Jan's mind, now that he had completed his Mystic training, his mind was a picture of order and stability, almost an opposite of the façade she put up. That worked perfectly for her brother, but was almost useless to her in her situation.

Still, his mind was balanced. The Cosmic flows were in harmony, the energy levels at equilibrium.

That was all something that Naero had never been able to accomplish since her enlightening.

As she always did, if she could not find that harmony within herself, at least she could attempt to mimic it.

Without warning, Naero blinked and stood before the vast barrier of the KDM. She stared eye to eye, nearly nose to snout with her Kexxian counterpart or liaison–whatever she was.

The enigmatic Orean. Was the Kexx as tall as her now? Before she had been slightly shorter. What did this change mean? Did it signify anything?

"I know," Naero said aloud, or psyonically, or whatever, in flawless Kexxian. "We're still in my stupid head, so why should anything here make sense, right?"

Orean simply smirked her toothy grin.

"What, no questions this time? No booming insults from the great voice of thunders?" Naero waggled her hands for emphasis.

"A fool does not need to be insulted," Orean said.

"Ah-hah! So, I'm right, aren't I? You're not just speaking in questions anymore, are you?"

Orean sighed heavily and rolled her eyes. "You are the one babbling in questions. What an idiot. Now that you have all the answers within you, you're no closer to knowing the right questions to ask. Hopeless. I might as well leave."

Orean turned to go.

"Wait!" Naero called out desperately. "Who…what are the G'lothc? How can they be defeated?"

Orean faced Naero again, but they were still separated.

"You know as well as I, N. The G'lothc are a Cosmic disease, an infection of the entire universe–a dark plague of destruction."

"Aren't they a near perfection of the Dark force," Naero added out loud, "of Destruction itself given the force of will?"

Orean stepped closer, waiting patiently, her face now impassive.

Naero grasped for another point, another question. "What…who are the…were…the Drians?"

"You're stalling," Orean told her. "You won't find what it is that you need that way."

"Weren't the Drians the perfection of the Machine?" Naero asked.

"And they left untold gifts to the universe in their passing, which have yet to be known and fulfilled. Come now, you can do better than all that. That is not your primary concern."

Orean stayed where she was, neither advancing nor retreating.

Naero wracked her mind trying to come up with the key–the proper inquiry.

"What happened to the Kexx? Where did they go and why?"

Orean smiled at her for the first time that day and inched forward. "You're so close, but you still don't have it. Cramming three big questions together won't get you there. You're trying to leap ahead. You must know much more than you do now, before you can answer them."

"The Kexx, they…uh," Haisha! Why couldn't she figure it out?

Orean surprised her by stepping forward and taking Naero's hands. "You're such a paradox, Naero. So full of Love and Hate–the will to create and destroy. The power to choose and not choose. You dance your life upon the razor's edge and still find a way to prevail. Trickster. You even manage to trick yourself. How radiant and terrifying you are."

The Kexx reached up and touched Naero's Face.

Naero gasped wide-eyed, as if transfixed by a thunderbolt.

"We were just like you…and we faced the same fears."

"Who w-were the K-kexx?" Naero stammered, still trying to catch her breath. "What were they like?"

Orean laughed, kissed her on both cheeks, and embraced her. "The truths you seek are in the heart, as well as the mind and the soul. The perfect balance between the three. The Harmony of all things, the Great Mystery which makes us all one, and makes each of us whole as individuals."

Naero embraced her Kexxian counterpart and began to weep. "I'm still ignorant…and unworthy."

Orean pulled away from her and smiled once more. "All of us are, before the sheer might and the eternal majesty of the universe. All are exposed and laid bare, and found wanting. Yet we are also blessed with the eternal power and the freedom to change, to strive to make ourselves into what we need to be."

Naero lifted her head and wiped her eyes.

Then her jaw really did drop as she looked before herself and kept walking.

In her haste and wonder, she stepped right through Orean as if she were but a holo. Then she looked all around her.

"The impassable barrier," Naero said, breathless. "It's gone. There is nothing in my way now."

She beheld the shining wisdom and the knowledge of the Kexxian Data Matrix, laid out before her and organized like an immense library— the size of an entire gigacity.

"Where did the barrier go?" Naero demanded.

Orean passed through her and turned to face Naero again, clasping her hands in front of herself. "I told you before, Naero. There was no barrier; there never was one. It only existed in your own mind, just as myself and all of this does, because for some reason in your head, you needed such at a given time. In your mind, you create what you need, even if that works against you at times. Perhaps you did not trust yourself. Or fully know what it was that you should do."

"I want to know…I want to understand."

Orean smiled and stepped aside, waving her hand the shining city of knowledge.

Naero went to one of the many ornate building structures and walked right through the walls.

She quickly came out gasping for air again as if she had just broken the surface from being deep underwater.

"I glimpsed it, Orean."

"You immersed yourself in knowledge."

Naero had to sit down and place her head between her legs. "Medical knowledge—so much of it. The Kexx cured every disease, once, until the knowledge was lost. For millions of years, they eliminated all sickness. Yet they could not cure Death itself."

"That is because Death is not a disease nor a sickness. Death is a gift to mortal, sentient beings. There would be new definitions of Chaos and horror if nothing or no one in the universe ever perished, died, or moved on."

Naero tried to get up, but fell back to her hands and knees, shaking her head. "It was all so overwhelming, to be so immersed in such overwhelming knowledge. I felt as if I were drowning in it."

Orean nodded. "I will be like that for a long while, yet. Proceed cautiously. Get used to it. Nothing about all of this shall be easy. You must be careful. There is always danger in knowledge. You could lose yourself in all of this and never find your way back. Ever."

Naero felt herself pale and she shuddered. "To hell with that!" But she sensed how very real and possible that danger actually was.

"Haisha...where do I start?" Naero said.

"Start with something small," Orean told her. "Start with something simple. I will be your reference point." The Kexxian girl took her hand. "I will be your anchor. With me at your side, you will never be lost. I can always show you the way out of the Cosmic Labyrinth."

"A labyrinth?"

"Yes, if you beheld the KDM from above, as it is now, you would see that it is a maze-like labyrinth."

"I see, like a complex circuit. An enormous computer. But you know the way out, right?"

Orean nodded. "I do, and just as you found your way in, I will teach you how to find your way out. Here is the secret: The Labyrinth is a shifting mass of hyper-phazic, shifting giga-algorithms. It is never the same each time you enter it, and each time that you leave it. Just as you will be. You change it, and it changes you. It's very nature is Change."

"I don't understand. If it's always different, how do I get out?"

Orean shook her head and laughed. "Because you always know where you are. And you know what's outside. That makes you the constant."

"Inside my big stupid head?"

The Kexx girl smiled at her.

Naero studied the gigacity of knowledge. "Hmmm...you said to start with something easy...something simple, right?"

She picked the smallest structure of them all to approach and enter within.

None of the structures had doors or windows.

Naero just passed through the walls.

Within she was immersed in an ocean of sound, waves and streams which flowed past, through, and around her.

It was music. She had entered a world of—no—a universe of music. She went forward, experiencing every form of music and sound that could be imagined throughout all of the possible galaxies combined.

How wonderful.

But then she began to feel the naked power of it all.

Perhaps she had made a mistake.

Orean rushed in and yanked her out.

"Why did you do that?" Naero said. "What the hell is wrong?"

Orean was trembling–actually shaking. Naero had never seen her so terrified.

"Leave it to you to pick the largest and most dangerous body of knowledge to attempt to penetrate. Of course you couldn't know that you were mere seconds away from becoming lost and destroyed."

"In music?"

"Naero! Things are not always what they seem. The greatest minds of the Kexx had a Grand Theory concerning the Music of the Universe. The Great Mystery of All Things is the highest and most Eternal Harmony of all and exists beyond even all the universes combined. Even the miracle of Creation and our universe itself is only one long song, yet with its own beginning and eventual end."

"Music? Your telling me the basis for all things is music?"

"Think about it. In the end, when even the miracle weapons of the Drians and the Kexx failed to destroy the last and the mightiest of the G'lothc–the Drians withdrew in confusion. But the seven mightiest of all the Kexx–their Mystics, who were called *The Dreamers*–fought with the last six of the enemy upon the very brink of Oblivion. And it is said that they battled not with weapons, but with Songs of Power. All of these legends are part of the Cosmic Prophecies.

"The Six G'lothc were known as the Champions of Shadows, each greater than the one before their number. Their leader was called *Mothroxokul–the Hand of the Great Destroyer*. A dread being. His very words brought death. The other five G'lothc Shadows of the Darkforce were:

Elazethrek, the Accursed.
Asheddethron, the Deceiver.
Nebegtemoth, the Fallen.
Kegrabildimog, the Defiled.
Zokshemarrah, the Betrayer

"Neither side asked quarter. They fought and they slew and they destroyed, until the mightiest three remained on each side, and squared off to decide the fate of the universe. And the enemy did all that they could to flee, to break free, and get away–free to spread all of their evils all over again.

"The last three Kexxian Dreamers clasped hands together and did not hesitate. They sang a song of power that even the G'lothc did not know– *The Song Of Unmaking*–with the full knowledge that it would also destroy them and everything around them as well. Thus the three Dreamers marched forward blazing with the radiance of the pure Lifespark–*The Flame Eternal*, and cast down their mighty foes and made an end of them– the masters of Darkness–who shrank back, and cowered in fear, wailing in terror of that great light at the very last..."

Naero gasped. "And then what?"

Orean shrugged. "They all died; and the universe was at last free from the G'lothc and their direct, poisonous influence for millions of years, free to flourish and burst forth with life just as it has."

Naero let out a breath. "All right, so all knowledge is dangerous, even music, right? Then where do I begin? Is there something that isn't so bloody dangerous?"

Orean shook her head. "All knowledge can be perilous. Go slowly. You can only hurt yourself. You can't make any direct use of the knowledge on the first try anyway. You must give it time. The KDM is part of you, but now, you must become part of it."

Naero gaped. "Why can't I use it? What good is all of this if I can't use it? How do I become part of it?"

"You are not one with it yet. You must see it all and embrace it as the Kexx once did, in order to even understand a portion of it."

Naero lost it. "I can't stand it! This is driving me nuts. I'm speaking in Kexxian–thinking in Kexxian. How can I get any closer to all of this?"

Orean rest both hands on her arms. "Calm down, N. I said 'yet.' Give it time. You are not who and what you need to be...yet."

"What do I need to be?"

Orean walked toward her and through her once again.

A spike of pure Cosmic lightning seemed to split Naero into pieces. She started shaking and convulsing violently.

Her eyes flashed open.

She was back in her quarters.

Khai shook her violently and stood her up on her feet. "Wake up, Naero! I'm sorry to startle you out of your deep meditations, but we have an emergency. Baeven infiltrated the enemy base!"

Naero screamed.

The spike of agony again, ripping through her once more.

Yet that was but an echo.

Somehow she just knew. "The enemy has grown tired of trying to unlock the Cosmic puzzle of our child, Khai." She looked him right in the eye.

"Now they're just trying to destroy her."

25

Naero spoke quickly to the Alliance concerning the situation. She made it clear what their objectives were.

"We are not in a position yet to take and hold Naggoth. But we can hit it hard and do a great deal of damage. But if we hang around too long, the enemy will be able to overwhelm us within a matter of hours. They simply have too many forces nearby that we have not been able to degrade yet."

She paused and brought up screens with all of the sims and projections. "There is time to the hit their homeworld hard, and allow our strike force to go down onto the surface and rescue our objective. Any way we look at this, it is not going to be easy. We'll have to fight our way in, and fight even harder to get back out. And the longer we linger, the harder that will be. I can only ask you for volunteers, do this, and take on this task–for me and Khai."

Not one leader from any race refused, and working together, they quickly gathered their forces by the hundreds, and solidified their plans along the way.

Naero continued to wince and double over, experiencing only part of the actual pain that Naero-3, Om, and Naero's unborn child felt as they were being attacked and tormented. Khai continued to support her.

They drove on at top speed, preparing for battle.

Naero brought all of her available replicants with her, nearly an entire platoon.

Strike Force Shetanna would help lead the infiltration and the main assault.

They met with Baeven and his crew. He gave them all the data he had gathered on the enemy base, a bunker constructed deep within a mountain range.

"I couldn't go in any deeper without triggering their security and their defenses, Naero. I'm sorry. Those hi-tek defenses and troops they have amassed are more than even I could take on alone. It's going to require an elite army to fight their way in and out of that fortress."

Naero snarled and looked behind her. "I just happen to have brought one, based upon your initial reports, uncle. I want you and the others to stay up in the black. If something happens, and the enemy makes a run for it again with their prize, I want you and *The Dark Star* and *The Flying Dagger* to take them down, or at least track them to wherever they go next."

"Are you sure you don't want me with you on this one?" Baeven asked.

"No, I think we can cover the assault. I just want to make sure that they don't get away again. I'll have Jan and *The Black Spot* backing us up on the surface along with our cloaked dropships. I'm hoping to get in fast enough and get back out before they can try to overwhelm us."

Baeven nodded. "That's what I would do." He was hugging her the next instant. "Get back our own, Naero. Devastate anything else that gets in your way."

"I will. All right people, everyone stay cloaked and form up just like we planned. The signal will go up when to phaze, and when to attack. When the fighting starts there's no let up. We destroy anything that moves except for Naero-3. Put her in stasis once we free her. She's probably going to be in bad shape. Once we have her, our primary goal is to get the hell out and make good our escape!"

Naero brought a thousand picked troops to attack the fortress. All of her replicants that she could round up, about sixty Shetannas in number. One hundred and fifty elite Marines. Two hundred each of the finest Lish, Mechan, Sa'shom, and Amavar troops, with the latest phazing stealth armor and the latest advanced weapons.

Her brother Jan and 500 more heavy Marines waited in reserve if they some got stuck.

While up in the black, 4,000 Alliance fleets would surround Naggoth and hold the enemy hordes at bay.

The Alliance struck the enemy homeworld from all sides, sending them reeling in confusion. But that would not last long.

Naero and her forces were already penetrating the base and quickly approached the point where Baeven had held back.

Naero grunted, so close now that she could sense the residual effects of the pain and damage inflicted on Naero-3. The enemy was trying to tear her apart, and Naero's miraculous, unborn child inside of her replicant was putting up a stellar fight.

Hold on, my little duck. I'm right here. Momma's coming, and she's bringing the fires of the Nine Hells with her!

Baeven was correct. Even with all of their gear, if they went any farther, they would raise alarms and start the fight.

Naero startapped, concentrated, and decided to begin that fight on her own terms…with a very big bang.

She centered a Cosmic gigablast right inside the fortress, half a kilometer ahead of them.

It went off like atomics, but without the radiation, and blew one third of the complex wide open into the arid daylight. The blast sheered off one fifth of the mountain and scattered it far and wide.

"Well, they know we're here now, guys. I've cleared the way a bit. Everyone storm in!"

They hit their grav wings and raced ahead at top attack speed.

Naero couldn't make any mistakes. Not with what was at stake. She knew the enemy were certain to have a trap ready to snap her up in. Transporting straight into it alone, like she used to do, wasn't going to get the job done.

This time she had to be sure. And she brought her own surprises.

Waves of Ejjai shock troops hit them, including the big mutants and a few of the psyonic freaks with the big, blue and orange glowing brains and multiple heads.

In seconds her troops were among them and unphazed, shredding them into hamburger. Some of the Ejjai began to transform further under the power of the G'lothc possession wyrms.

The Shetannas made short work of them.

Then came the Dakkur, and with them Dakkur champions and even possessed Dakkur.

Naero transformed first into her energy being form, and from there into the intermediate form of her Dark Beast–ten meters high. Even her own troops shrank back from her at first.

But Naero wasn't done with her surprises yet.

Prince Ra of the Shai swelled up beside Naero in his own advanced energy form slightly shorter than herself, and not just with Chaos Force, but with Cosmic energy also. Naero had been coaching him how to open his third eye and channel those energies for weeks.

Now the Dakkur faced two new Destroyers, and they all clashed head on.

Naero and Ra tore and blasted an entire Dakkur battlehorde to pieces, smearing them and their dust across the rocks, backed up by the Alliance strike force.

Huge blast screens, tens of meters thick, had slammed down up ahead of them, clocking their way.

Naero and Ra burned through them with their eye beams and then ripped them open, peeling the hyper dense alloys back as if they were tearing open ripe fruit.

Her people pulled back to phaze and protect themselves, and then she sent forth another devastating Cosmic blast into the core of the stronghold. They all charged into the flaming breach.

They emerged into what appeared to be an enormous, reinforced dome city, fused under the mountain itself–so immense that enemy warships were fleeing and escaping in the distance through gigantic hatches installed throughout the mountain range itself.

The floor was a broad killing field and battle zone, and more enemy hordes charged in from all directions.

At the far end was the complex's inner sanctum.

That's where they needed to go. "First Team! Naero roared, startapping nearly beyond her limits. Get in close. Form up around me and Ra!" Two hundred troops did so.

"The rest of you cloak, phaze, and follow in like ghosts. Don't fight; just join us on that far side." They vanished and started across.

Naero opened her third eye wide and transported herself and her First Team all the way in front of the Inner Sanctum.

While the enemy hordes were still streaming in the opposite direction.

Another little surprise. Naero, Ra, and First Team were already fighting their way into the complex before the enemy figured out what was happening.

Naero screamed at the pain that knifed and rattled through her.

They were close now. Less than a hundred meters.

She and Ra had to shrink back down in order to go ahead faster.

They tore through the enemy troops in their way.

Suddenly Naero started to feel afraid. As if it all were too easy. Going too fast.

Then the fixers sent out a warning.

The enemy had neutron explosives set all around them, all the way inside. Massive explosions rocked the complex from behind and ahead of them, even destroying the enemy's own troops left down there to decoy any attackers.

Naero punched open a tunnel below their feet and sucked them down into it, shielding them at the last second with a plug of Cosmic energy.

The firestorm sucked all of the air out. They survived on their suit reserves. She did a quick count to see how many troops she had left. Out of 200 troops, she had 164 left. She had even lost a few Shetannas during the fighting and the enormous explosions and felt their life force and their memories return to her.

Once it was clear they burst out of their escape tunnel and resumed the attack. By then the vanguard of their other forces were also rejoining them, right for the main event.

What the enemy didn't count on was the fact that their explosives merely served to clear the way for any attackers who managed to survive them.

Naero-3 was close. Naero could feel it.

They blasted their way into what appeared to be another smaller dome structure–this one only the size of a normal city.

A brightly glowing, spinning orb of white-hot energy was being held up in some kind of gravitic suspension field. Several large Darkforce generator hulks, like Meks ten meters tall poured destroying energy at the glowing sphere. These were the same kind of Darkforce battlemek suits that Danner usually wore.

The sphere that held Naero-3 was slowing down and starting to buckle.

"Attack!" Naero yelled. "Cut them all down!"

But something was very wrong.

The Cosmic energy levels just weren't right. The readings that Naero was teknomancing were all out of whack, registering all over the place.

"Hold back," she ordered. "Let the fixers go in first. I want to try something."

She had them unleash an intense, localized EMP burst right on top of the enemy battlemeks.

As soon as the pulse detonated, everything they saw up ahead of them winked out and vanished. All that remained was a large open power coupling spitting out energy bursts.

Energy bursts being siphoned off of the real Naero-3, somewhere else nearby. They were probably fleeing with her even now.

"Sir, they were all holos?" a Marine Captain asked.

With the readings from the fixers there was no time to explain.

Naero tapped, gathered up all of her people this time, and zapped them as far away as she could, even though she knew that doing so would certainly exhaust her this time.

She needed to get them all out, before the multiple atomics all went off around them. That extreme effort would place her in a regeneration coma for a few hours at the very least.

But she couldn't let them all die in the enemy trap she had led them straight into.

When Naero came to, Jan was holding her. It was night but the sky above her brother was occluded and without stars. Reports and fixer scans recorded that the mountain complex had been obliterated by multiple large, nuclear explosions.

They were now 143 kilometers away from the blast craters, and hiding from the enemy along with their reserves.

"How close did you get?" Jan asked.

Naero sighed. "Not very. They've probably taken Naero-3 somewhere else by now. Maybe even offworld. As it turns out, they weren't trying to destroy Naero-3 at all. I think that was just a ploy to lure me in. It was me they were after, Jan. This was all about taking me down, and I nearly fell for it."

As her Cosmic energy levels began to return to somewhat normal, she suddenly had a very bad feeling.

"Wait…Jan, something is incredibly wrong. Can't you feel it?"

He looked around and winced. "I felt something, but I can't tell what it is."

Haisha. Oh, no…

"Jan, have you contacted Baeven or anyone in the black yet?"

"No, you ordered strict com silence. I knew you had just exhausted yourself getting everyone out. I didn't know if you would want to take another crack at it after you regenerated."

Naero reached out with her Cosmic senses.

Fuck! She was right. Not only was Naero-3 gone, but the enemy had done more than simply trick them this time.

They were probably already completely screwed.

"Jan, do you want to know why the enemy has been conducting all of those temporal experiments?"

Her brother's head snapped up and he stared at the dark, starless sky. "Oh, shit!" He just caught up with her.

"That's right, Jan. That's why we can't see the stars. They've hidden the entire planet of Naggoth in a projected Time suspension field, just like on the Mystic Homeworlds. First we need to figure out what the temporal dilation parameters are."

"They've bottled us up like djinn and marids from those old stories," Jan said.

Word spread rapidly. Everyone grew worried at the news of them being trapped on Naggoth in a planetary time suspension field.

Naero quickly performed a teknomancy analysis with their fixernet that was still based onworld.

"Hmm...about a standard month is going to pass us by on the outside, Jan. To our allies, the planet Naggoth has vanished, and it won't reappear for...thirty of their days."

She looked straight at Jan. "Meanwhile, there are less than fifteen hundred of us trapped here on this world. And the enemy has millions of troops to hunt us down with. And now we can't go anywhere offworld, we can't leave, and they have an entire year inside of this Time trap to track us down and kill us."

And forget about rescuing her unborn daughter, who wasn't even on the planet any longer.

For the next twelve standard months it was going to take everything that each one of them had just to stay alive. There was no longer any choice in that.

26

Naero brought her remaining people to another of their deep underground, temporary safe zones. She had dozens of them established within the planetary crust of Naggoth on all four main continents. These hideouts were usually a few kilometers down in natural pockets that the fixers located.

They had been doing little more than hiding and fighting to stay alive for two weeks. Above them the Dakkur nations and their millions of allies and slaves labored with gigantic plasma borers to reach the small Alliance force again and again and attack them.

Naero and her people could only retreat, fight to get away, and hide once again. Each time they fought, the enemy wore them down and they lost more people doing so.

Just in the past two weeks they lost all of their transports but one, and *The Black Spot*. They hid those ships in desperation and left them behind, concealed underground for a last ditch attempt to escape once Naggoth came back in sync with the galaxy's main Time flow. They had also lost forty-one other troops, dragged down and slain by the millions of enemies who dogged their steps.

The enemy confounded the Allies by possessing some new, infernal way to track and ferret their exact location out. Naero tried to figure out just what it was. At first, when they still had their few ships, Naero worried that they were tracking them by the residual powercore signature echoes.

That was how the Alliance was able to still track enemy cloaked and phazed ships, vehicles, and troops. But that wasn't it this time. The enemy was using something completely different to discover their locations, even without the ships. And it seemed to be taking about half a day for them to pinpoint Naero and company's whereabouts.

Both Naero and Jan tried to briefly go into the Astral Plane to see if perhaps somehow the enemy had placed an astral marker on one or both of them. But they were still blocked from entering the Astral Plane. They could not learn anything.

Naero wished that she had placed such a marker in Naero-3, but there hadn't been time during her trial and the aftermath. And for some reason, this time dilation field the enemy was using also messed up her use of the astral mind crystals from Khai's father's people, the Oden.

So, how did the enemy keep finding them?

Nothing else was suspect. They checked for and found no evidence of traitors in their midst. It was something the enemy was capable of that they were not. No one was possessed, even without their knowledge. Perhaps it was something new.

She feared that it had to be something with her and Jan, and possibly Ra. They were the only beings on the planet who could use Cosmic energy. Perhaps that was how the enemy tracked them.

Janner said that Danner wasn't on world with them; he would know if their insane brother was anywhere near them. At least they caught a break there.

Yet Naero had a general sense of several other powerful sources of Cosmic energy on Naggoth. After a while, Jan could sense them too. But neither she nor Jan could pinpoint where or determine just what they were.

When there was time, Naero made certain that all of her troops knew what they were up against. She described what the Dakkur and their minions were like and how they fought.

But they had yet to encounter the Dakkur queens, who were said to me huge, much larger than the Dakkur Champions–that could be up to fifteen meters in length. And a king Dakkur was rumored to be even larger yet. Both the queen and king Dakkur were also said to be able to use both psyonics and Cosmic energy attacks.

Those creatures might have innate abilities allowing them to track down and pinpoint other beings like herself, Jan, and Ra who also used Cosmic powers. But to Naero's knowledge, only her Uncle Baeven and Ra's father, Prince Gaviok, had ever fought and vanquished Dakkur queens or a king.

And Baeven said that that had been the hardest, closest battle he had ever fought single-handed in his entire life.

But at least Naero knew that such could be done. The enemy were fierce, but not invincible. She tried to encourage her people with the valiant story of how Baeven and the new High Mystic Master Gaviok had once been stranded on just such a Dakkur Homeworld, and vanquished the enemy all by themselves.

"It may come to that," Ra said.

"I hope it doesn't," Naero told him. "All we have to do is stay one step ahead of them. If we can survive a year, I'm sure we'll be able to escape, either in our ships, or by capturing one from the enemy. And I'm guessing that the rest of the Alliance isn't going to sit on their hands during that month. They'll be ready to come help us when the time comes."

"Naero," Jan said. "I think Ra is right. I don't think we can make it just by constantly hiding out and staying on the run. They'll bottle us all up at some point. We'll make a mistake and we won't be able to get away."

Ra smiled wide as only a mantid could. "If we are going to die any way, I think we should stop focus on running and hiding. We should take the fight to our foes. At least we can take down large numbers of them with us along the way."

Naero chuckled. "Haisha...1,378 troops, against a planet of millions?"

Jan grinned. "Sounds like good odds to me. What do we have to lose, N? If we go on the offensive, we can disrupt and upset them, keep them guessing, and even deplete and wear them down. And just think, every day you can make more Shetannas. How many can you make a day now?"

"Nine, on a good day."

Jan jumped to his feet, tossing his hands in the air. "Do the math. That's over 3,000 deadly replicants with your Cosmic abilities within a year's time. More than twice our forces now. We can be getting stronger each day, while the enemy will be getting weaker."

Naero seriously began to consider that option. In a way, Jan and Ra were right. She had just been focusing on keeping them all alive for an entire year, by avoiding combat whenever they could.

And that did not seem to be working very well.

"All right," Naero said. "But we still can't decide this matter on our own, just the three of us. We should put it to the troops. And in either case, we need to find out how the enemy keeps finding us and if there is a way to prevent that."

Jan put his hands on his hips. "Leave it to me and Ra. We'll speak to the officers and the troops and see what they want to do. You need to get some rest, Naero. Every time you transport us away from another enemy attack, I know it takes a lot out of you. You can't afford to get run down. We'll speak with our forces and decide the matter together, after you have slept."

Naero nodded in agreement. Everything Jan said was correct. If she had to be stranded on a deathtrap world, at least she had her brothers Jan and Ra with her.

She could die happily fighting side-by-side with them, if it came down to that.

But she still wished to save as many of her people as she could.

It wasn't their fault that they were trapped here. They had followed her lead without question and they still had faith in her, even with all that had happened.

It was still up to her to find a way out of all of this mess, for as many of them as she could. But she could also see the logic to Jan and Ra's plan. They were all warriors, and even though the odds were beyond counting, fighting was better than slinking, hiding, and constantly running.

Naero had learned that she could rest, regenerate, and even sleep while she also meditated, and in her dream state she walked the labyrinth of the KDM, with Orean, her Kexxian sister and constant guide.

When she was deeply immersed within the dream state she could push her way, with effort, into the nodes or storehouses of Kexxian knowledge and wisdom. Sometimes she would simply thrust her head in, up to her neck, into the confusing, swirling maelstrom of raw data. Ocean after ocean of intense, concentrated knowledge, concepts, and ideas.

She always started with the smallest, but most potent and dangerous Kexxian obelisk of knowledge–the one she had originally chosen and been drawn to from the very first–the node of music.

As she had once discovered from her time among the Tua, so many of the sentient races had been children nurtured by the Kexx in their formative beginnings.

The songs the gentle Tua had sung were derivative or even exact copies of Kexxian songs, passed on with little variation.

Naero recalled those tunes and their Mystical words from happier days upon lost Janosha, when her adoptive family had still lived and breathed, sustaining and passing on their simple ways.

When she was in the labyrinth now she found that it helped her to hum or even mouth those old tunes and songs. And when she did so, she felt and became more at one with the wisdom and power of the ancient Kexx. And her sister Orean would sing beside her as they went about.

Just as the Tua began each day, Naero started each session with the song of greeting–of welcoming and beginning.

SHA NII HAH, AHLUU-NII-HA-AH! MAH NAH-HII, JAH AH-LOH, AH-DII!

And at their voices, all of the vast nodes of the KDM would glow with might and enlightenment, and thrum with the resonance of the Cosmic Harmony.

They came full circle, back to the node of music, and Orean held out her hand. "Come with me, into the source of music once again."

Naero shook her head. "We can't bother with that again, sister. Come, you must help me gain understanding. Show me where to look. I need to learn more about the Dakkur and how they keep locating and attacking us. That is the knowledge that I really need to find this day."

Orean stopped and held out her hand. "Come with me, Naero. I will teach you a new song this day. It is simple enough, but yet it can be one of the most difficult of them all to perceive and use properly."

A new song? The Tua had only taught her nine songs in all, the nine songs of the day, and for all life. A tenth song? What was this song and what would it impart?

"Tell me the name of this new song, sister," Naero said, taking Orean's hand.

"It is called *The Song of Knowing*. And as I told you, and you seldom listen hard enough–it is easy to learn, and yet extremely difficult to master."

Naero shrugged. "Why should that be any different than the rest of all of this?"

Orean stopped, clapped her hands, and burst out laughing. "See, you are learning so much, even if you do not know it yet."

As usual, when Orean said stuff like that it simply made Naero feel like a complete moron. "What did I say? What have I learned? You know you drive me crazy when you do that."

Orean smiled and took her hand once more. "Come, I will teach you the song's words within."

They walked into the small node with much less effort this time, through the walls and into the expanse within. None of the nodes had windows or doors of any kind. One had to pass inside of them by force of will, but yet without effort.

Suddenly Naero gasped, noticing for the first time that outside the node had been the size of a closet. While within it was nearly limitless in its expanse.

Even her first experience with the Astral Plane had not struck her so.

Orean began to sing, and Naero tried to commit the words to her memory.

ANSHA DII, KARANDU HALI, AHLAGO SHANTADU VELLAH, JANASTU LANADO SHANATU!

Orean sang it thrice—three times while they were immersed in the ocean of the knowledge of songs and all music.

Naero felt as if she were in some kind of trance. She spoke, but with great effort.

"Why is it called the song of knowing?" she asked.

Orean did not answer her. Instead, she walked around and passed through Naero like a ghost and kept walking a few steps. She kept her her back turned to Naero and looked straight ahead, holding up both of her arms. "Now you sing the words. Sing them three times as did I, and this time—close your eyes and pass through me."

Naero did not question any longer. She closed her eyes, and sang the words three times, taking a step forward each time as she did.

ANSHA DII, KARANDU HALI, AHLAGO SHANTADU VELLAH, JANASTU LANADO SHANATU!

As she sang the words the third time she stepped through Orean. It was as if she felt something close around her.

She waited, eyes still closed, holding out her arms, despite how very odd and strange she felt.

"What do I do now, sister?"

Then she clasped her hands over her mouth and felt her face.

Naero spoke with Orean's voice.

And moved within the body of her Kexxian sister.

Naero became a Kexx, and only in that form was she able to begin to perceive who and what the Kexx were—and what their vast knowledge was.

It was a precious gift to all of the universe and beyond.

It was knowing. And the simple words of the song were indeed profoundly true.

In an instant, she saw the Dakkur in all their terrible power and fury. Like their dread, dark masters, they had chosen the path of destruction. They had indeed grown very great and terrible.

As Naero feared, there was no way to escape from the keen perceptions of her foes.

The Dakkur would continue to pursue and hunt down the Allies to the death.

Yet she did discover a way to confound them.

Then Naero and her people could go on the offensive, and take the fight to their enemies.

Whether they would prevail or not against so many powerful foes was not certain. Yet if they were trapped on the planet with the enemy, the reverse was also true.

27

Naero opened her eyes and immediately stared at her arms and rubbed them with her hands.

Part of her thought to see green scales and lizard flesh, and dexterous clawed hands, delicate and yet strong. But she was only Orean inside the KDM itself, in her mind. Outside of that experience, she still retained her own form.

Yet another key, another secret that unlocked her advancing understanding.

Only a Kexx could even begin to perceive their intricate and expansive body of knowledge. To learn anything further from them, she needed to become one of them.

Naero sighed. So much knowledge. So very much. It always seemed as if she were stuck in beginnings–going from one to the next. Always beginning, never ending. But perhaps that was best. Beginnings went on. Beginnings started something and kept going.

An Old Earth saying once said to count your blessings.

Endings did not go on. They just ended.

Jan came to her. She heard alarm in his voice. "Naero, I'm sorry to bother you, but the enemy has discovered our hiding place once more. And they're getting better and faster at finding it each time that they do."

Naero nodded. "I understand, Jan. We can't stop them, but I think there is a way that we can confuse them and throw them off."

Jan blinked and raised both eyebrows. "That's great, sib. Let's try it. They'll break through and attack us again in less than two hours."

"Get everyone ready to bug out. Here's what we do." Jan leaned in to listen, right as Naero remembered something else.

"Wait. Jan, what did the troops decide?"

Her brother grinned. "What do you think? If they're all going to die anyway, at least they want to go out fighting!"

She nodded again. "Good. I feel the same way now."

They fled once more, within the hour, before the foe could fall upon them again.

The tyrants of the Dakkur were tracking them by their Cosmic signatures. There was no way to conceal that.

Yet those same signatures could mimicked, and duplicated many times over.

Naero sent out her replicants, over a hundred of them now, each one following her instructions.

She and Jan also went out.

Each of them found a pocket beneath the hardest bedrock of the planet's crust, kilometers thick. There they left behind a flux wave of Cosmic energy, trapped within an infinite, self-replicating loop.

Each decoy would last for several weeks. And each day, or every few days as needed, the Allies could make a hundred more decoys. They would make whatever number it took to keep the foe confused as to their real whereabouts.

Within a week the enemy would be on a wild goose chase, pursuing hundreds of decoy signatures, never knowing which one was real.

Let them bore holes into the planet until it resembled a ball of spotted cheese.

And if they ever did get too close, the Allies could still flee to another. Sometimes the Allies even set traps of water, gas, magma pockets, or even explosives.

Naero could create more replicants each day.

Now they had a chance.

Now they had a way to outlast and avoid the foe. And that gave Naero and the Allies the power to pick and choose when and where they would engage the enemy.

They began to make plans. They analyzed the fixernets to determine where they should strike at the enemy first. Much of the enemy's defenses were still shielded and jammed on all four continents: Shurog, Kolf, Gronet, and Uldrun.

As the data continued to pour in and they actually had a chance to analyze it, several things became very clear.

The enemy had many more forces on world that even Naero and their original intelligence had expected. The rulers of Naggoth had packed it full of armies.

"I'm having second thoughts about all of this," Naero said. "We would need several hi-tek armies just to begin to take all of these forces on."

Unexpectedly, Ra spoke up. "Naero. I have waited to say this, now that we know more about what we're up against. If you recall, long ago, Naggoth was once one of the primary homeworlds of the Ku-Shai. Our people here were wiped out and supplanted by these foes. We have never forgotten that loss; Allondatharru lives in our legends and our memories.

"My father wanted me to eventually take this world back for our people, once it could be liberated by the Alliance Navies. But now that we are trapped here on this planet, and we have no choice, why don't we go for it?"

Naero blinked at and then stared at the mantid prince. What was he yammering about? "Ra, I don't understand. Go for what?"

"Taking over the planet. The enemy is limited to the forces they have on this world. For the next year, they can't call in any help, either."

Naero looked around. "And neither can we, Ra. Look, our current estimates are that the enemy have twelve billion forces on this planet: not population–that's troops. And that number keeps growing. How can we possibly match that?"

Ra grinned. "I admit it's not optimum, but I still have have an entire Shai colony in stasis with me, ready take back our lost homeworld."

Naero blinked again. "Say what?"

Ra took her literally and was about to repeat himself entirely.

"Okay, I heard what you said. Just tell me one thing that is going to make anything like taking over the planet possible."

"Very well," Ra said. "Once I awake my seven fertilized brides, they can produce hundreds of millions of Shai warrior offspring each month.

Naero's jaw did hit the rocky ground. The sounds that came out of her mouth next were generally unintelligible.

"Given a proper food source and clean water supply," Ra added.

Naero's brain still hadn't caught up with her stammering mouth.

"And our offspring can be placed in a dormant state until needed, to conserve food and energy. They can awake for battle or general construction projects."

"So…we could have an army of billions of Shai in four months. Billions more in eight months."

"Given enough food and water."

"Yeah, yeah. Ra, I think it's time that we wake up these brides of yours and get to know them. We'll send teams with them, and find secluded, underground areas where they can spawn, and where food can be collected. During the High Crusade, I learned that huge quantities of food could be taken from the oceans without attracting much attention. The enemy has even bothered to exploit their oceans here. I suggest we get a bit of that going."

Naero's strategic and tactical mind ramped up and began to race.

"Each bride will need her own separate territory for their hive," Ra noted.

Naero nodded eagerly. "There are four main continents and several large island groupings. We will pick the most isolated areas that we can and try to keep them secret until we are ready to bring them online. Like I said, we'll try to feed them all from the oceans."

Ra. Jan, and others started bringing in the other seven stasis containers, similar to the one Ra had emerged from.

Since Shai could compress and expand their size and density. It made transporting a potential nest of them relatively simple.

Each of Ra's brides had a slightly varied coloration pattern, but when they emerged from the stasis fields they looked to be shaped almost identically, like Mantids. Yet even so, with her trained eye and biomancy, Naero noticed subtle differences that could also be used to tell them apart.

Not to mention smell and pheromones. With the highly developed Shai olfactory system, they could no doubt be differentiated solely by scent alone.

Although, until they moved, Naero smiled, musing that they all looked like white and orange ice cream, ready to be dipped up.

Then they stirred, and awoke, tumbling forward out of the compact stasis chambers, unfolding and shaking themselves slightly as they came around.

Ra jumped forward and caught each one lovingly as they awoke in the order he had set. He stood them on their feet and caressed them briefly, obviously very affectionate with his seven brides.

He was very proud, and rightly so, as he announced and introduced each one of his new wives–all sent with their prince on what could only be seen as a very dangerous task.

"This is Shiival; this is Kunali; meet Ishidar; she is called Cliiofarah. Next I want you to meet Pavija; this is Shiibrana; and she is known as Jahenna."

The female Shai mantids were mighty and powerfully built, much like their male counterpart. Their heads were just a smidge larger than Ra's, and their big, blinking mantid eyes were all shades of bright blue or green. Yet for all of their insectoid qualities, they were far from unlovely. And they all moved with the grace and beauty of the most accomplished dancers. Shai were exceptional athletes, unlike any other species known to exist.

The brides all complained to their prince of being famished after their long sleep and even seemed to be in some distress.

Fortunately, Shetanna company returned from the depths of the sea at that moment, with nanonets filled with fresh tuna and a bounty of wiggling, succulent fish stocks.

Everyone looked on in wonder, as the seven brides rushed in and made short work of all of that fresh seafood. Some even pulled back a bit a the sight. Naero had seen Ra eat before.

Even Jan quipped to Naero, "Good thing your replicants brought all that seafood back, sib. Otherwise, these Shai gals would have cleaned us out, and maybe even made a few of us disappear."

Naero laughed. She and her assistants, in their heads and on their comps, and on the fixernet were already trying to find the best places for the seven Shai brides to be squirreled away with enough available food and water to allow their numbers to flourish over the next few months.

The rest of the Alliance personnel would hit the enemy at numerous other points, in order to hold the enemy's attention and keep the Shai from being discovered until it was too late.

Meanwhile, Naero learned a great deal about Shai in a very short amount of time, both from biomancy and observation.

The Shai were an amazing species in so many ways. Not only did they have an extremely healthy appetite, but because their digestive systems were so empty from stasis, they processed their food rapidly. Ra warned Naero and their people about this fact, and a special chamber was prepared and located well out of the way from the main group, allowing the seven ladies to do their business in relative privacy. Then they collapsed that chamber and sealing it all away forever.

Shai poo, as it turned out, was both highly compacted and hyperdense– the consistency of a metal, actually. The smell was also magnified, somehow. Haisha, did it stink. Even the Shai themselves did not enjoy the strong odor.

No wonder Ra always made a big deal about burying his wastes deep onworld, or expelling them out into space when they were up in the black.

The seven brides cleaned themselves up in an underground pool, and after breaking their fast, and having made their toilet, they shifted slightly to an orange, white, reddish coloring combination and followed their beloved Ra around like a shuffling pack.

They were all somewhat shorter than Naero, just like Ra, yet there was some variation to them. Ra informed Naero that a group of Shai was know as a *klath.*

The princesses moved quickly among the Alliance forces, with Naero, Jan, and Ra. They were introduced to all of the troops, and Ra said that they could indeed remember each individual by smell.

The seven Shai females had at the very first taken great pains to imprint Naero and Jan on themselves and their minds as family. They were extremely intrigued by Jan talking later about his wife Vejjah's impending birth back in their main timeline.

When Ra explained to them that Jan's Spacer wife was going to have a single male child, they were all excited, assuming that the single child was being groomed and prepared to be a great prince among the Spacers.

Ra laughed, and a brief explanation was made, about how Spacers were very different from the Shai, and as mammals, they only had their offspring one or two at a time in most cases.

For a moment this revelation stunned the seven young brides. Then they burst out laughing so hard that they could not right themselves or even remain standing for a good long while.

To an insectoid species that gave birth to possibly many billions of offspring an a lifetime, the birthing of one or two children was apparently quaint and completely hilarious to the Shai.

Then Ra began to explain to them where they were, their dire situation, and what their mission was. The seven brides grew quiet and their intelligent eyes fixed and did not blink so much. An intense concentration quickly settled over them, bordering on what Naero could only define as near fury.

Naero had sparred both with Ra, and his mighty sire, Gaviok. Shai were an incredibly dangerous species. She would not want to fight an entire nest or planet of them.

A joy they soon hoped to inflict upon their foes.

It took them all of the next week to find suitable, concealed nesting sites for each of the seven brides. Alliance forces were kept with them underground to help protect and assist them with food collection. One princess was concealed on each of the four continents, and three on tropical island networks or archipelagos.

If a nest was discovered, the princess could be whisked away, and the nest complex collapsed in the usual manner. Then if the eggs weren't destroyed, Naero and the rest could still come back for them at a later time and relocate them.

28

With Ra's seven brides situated and hidden, they started producing eggs and preparing large numbers of Shai to be born, mature rapidly, and be placed in their dormant, hibernation mode.

It took only three weeks for an adult Shai to mature and be fully educated. They were extremely intelligent, yet completely obedient to the parents. The seven brides and Ra could command them without question, even to the death. Shai were communal and very chummy and affectionate with each other, and they adored their mother and father.

The task of feeding them became a major issue. Then more Shai were kept active to assist in the task. They even had the fixers make them underwater suits and submersibles to farm the oceans for foodstocks. That quickly solved the manpower issue.

Naero kept herself extremely busy. By then she was creating ten Shetanna level replicants each day. And when she slept, she dreamed and sang among the KDM nodes of knowledge in her Kexxian form and immersed herself in that endless sea of wisdom and information, just beginning to scratch the surface of it all.

Before the end of the first month, they conducted their first attack on one of the four continental capital gigacities for the Dakkur and their minions.

She wanted to send the enemy a message.

As usual, she began with a massive Cosmic gigablast that rocked the entire region and split the ground around the gigacity wide open, leaving fused black glass and burning craters and chasms throughout the ground zero area, for tens of kilometers in every direction.

Such a detonation of power vaporized all enemy troops and personnel exposed out in the open. And that meant tens of millions of enemy casualties.

The foe meant to hunt Naero and her allies down and destroy them. Well, that put the enemy within that same trap, and also made them vulnerable.

Naero fully intended to teach them a very hard lesson concerning those facts.

When the gigablast effects cleared, Naero and her troops struck pre-selected military command and control, information centers, labs, and research facilities in order to gather important data and Intel on what the enemy was up to.

These hit an run tactics after the shock and awe of the gigablast proved very fruitful, after the allies thoroughly raided and hacked enemy information systems.

Then they melted away once more, to assess all the info that they had gathered.

Yet the enemy response stunned even Naero.

The enemy seemed to go insane. They executed many of their own, including military commanders. Next, because the attack occurred on the continent of Shurog, they pulled all of their plasma borers off the other continents and concentrated on going after every Cosmic energy site that they could on the one. Which was more than half.

Naero and Company spent the next few days muddying the waters further by creating many more fake sites under that continent to serve as decoys. They decided to do the same thing on the other continents, before they made another attack.

The enemy increased searching for Naero and her people worldwide, but because they were transporting, the Allied forces became virtually impossible to trace.

A week later Naero and Company hit a gigacity on the continent of Kolf in the same exact fashion. Cosmic gigablasts could strike suddenly and without warning, even though they quickly exhausted her energies.

Then they fled to a completely different continent, to sift through the stolen data files they added to the others.

Disturbing patterns began to appear. The Dakkur were rapidly expanding their influence in that area of the Gamma Quadrant–as well as five other far flung regions just like it, if not larger.

And here Naero and her people were struggling to contain and defeat just one of the enemy's points of expansion and subjugation. The enemy plans for conquest were industrious and robust.

What's more, the enemy were also working on advanced upgrades for their existing shields, weapons, and tech. And completely new super warship designs and devastating weapon systems–many of them based on using highly destructive and unstable Darkforce energy.

To make matters worse, there was repeated mention in their secret files, documents, and coms concerning *The Armada*, an apparent numberless horde of enemy fleets that were being prepared in the next closest galaxy over.

This was one of the galaxies once completely controlled and almost destroyed by the G'lothc in their hey day.

Projections had this overwhelming wave of fleets being ready within the next one or two decades. Once they crossed over the vast space between the two galaxies, they would bring so much force and firepower with them that all resistance would fall before their might.

The enemy felt absolutely certain that they could defeat Naero's galaxy with these countless hordes. Neither were they happy being idle. Their will to conquer and destroy was restless and could not be suppressed.

While they waited for the Armada, the Dakkur and their minions would continue to soften up the other sentients and do their best to keep them worn down and on the defensive.

This was definitely terrible news, but it was also one to two decades away and could be possibly be prepared for. For now, the problems Naero and the Alliance currently faced were quite daunting enough. These enemies had always planned and plotted both for the short term and the long term.

The only way to stop them was to destroy them.

The next day the Alliance forces hit the continent of Gronet.

The day after that, they struck the largest gigacity on Uldren. Yet this time, the enemy were buttoned up and expecting them. The gigacity there was armored and shielded like a fortress. They still endured heavy damage from the blast, but they did not have as many troops out in the open.

Naero chose not to send in any raiders, and that proved to be a good thing.

As soon the gigablast was clear, enemy armies converged on that city.

Naero wished she had enough juice to zap them again.

She only had to wait until the next day, as all of those troops began to disperse. Naero took out most of them by using two divided blasts, spread out to obliterate more exposed forces across a wider expanse.

After they had acquired most of the information that they could, the data grew repetitive. Naero changed strategies, committing a variety of attacks at random, all designed to keep the enemy guessing, never knowing where she would strike next.

Naero made the lives of the enemy on Naggoth a virtual hell over the next four months.

There were also unavoidable setbacks and disasters for the Alliance.

Troops and replicants were cut down or lost in unexpected explosions from enemy booby-traps and remotely detonated ordnance. There were always chance losses that could occur during raids.

One dark day they lost sixty troops in an op where the enemy went so far as to set off an atomic at one of their own bases.

Naero and the rest of her people swore vengeance to make the enemy pay the highest price for every person the Alliance lost.

Naero grew increasingly worried that the enemy was going to discover one of the Shai secret bases. Therefore, the dormant Shai were spread out over multiple areas in other hidden pockets to better hide their rapidly expanding numbers.

The raiders mixed things up. They boarded and captured an enemy heavy cruiser, modified for ground assault. Then they used it to strafe exposed enemy armies and fleets of starships on the tarmac.

Then as other enemy fleets converged to shoot them down, Naero transported her people away, set the jump drive to activate, and ploughed it into yet another enemy gigacity to explode. The blast took out half of the city.

After that, the Alliance raiders focused on taking out the enemy fleets that were stationed onworld. Cosmic blasts, explosives, booby traps, and stolen ships.

These concentrated Alliance attacks were so devastating, that within three months, they wiped out almost eighty-percent of the enemy fleets on Naggoth. The others escaped further loss when the enemy hid them in the oceans or concealed them by burying them near the poles, or at other remote locations underground.

Next, Naero turned her wrath on Dakkur industry and manufacturing. They degraded that as well, but half of the enemy production capacity was concealed in underground factory bunkers. The enemy even had two underground naval shipyards.

Naero decided to put the emphasis on had.

The Alliance infiltrated those shipyards and blew them straight to hell.

By then Naero and her people had three months to go, before Naggoth came back in sync with the normal timeline. The enemy was starting to believe that perhaps it had not been such a great idea to try to take Naero out, and trap her with them in Time on a single planet for an entire year.

Naero had lost about five hundred troops by that time—about a third of her original raiders. She had many more replicants, and she was up to making eighteen of them each day, but each time she and her forces lost someone else. It was heartbreaking.

Finally, Naero was poised to turn the heat up on the enemy once more, and actually make a serious attempt at stripping the planet from them and wiping them out.

Her main concern was facing down any Dakkur Queens on the planet at the very last. The enemy's slaves would die by countless millions defending them. Naero was counting on that part.

The Dakkur queens remained the wild blade in the fight. Naero had never fought one. Her Uncle Baeven said that they were huge and incredibly tough. She had Ra's help, but what if all four Dakkur Queens came at them at once? Or worse—what if they had a Dakkur King on Naggoth? How many kings were there? Did each Dakkur Homeworld have one, or just Queens?

These were major uncertainties, going into an uncertain war that they could not escape from. Was Naero leading her people to victory, or certain death?

Even if Naero died fighting the queens—and or king of the Dakkur, the Shetannas would save as many of the others as they could. They could even go back to hiding out and escape once the Time dilation went down.

There was only one way to learn for certain what they were truly up against. And to do that, she couldn't send replicants. She couldn't send any of her people in. They had risked and lost enough all along.

Naero's Cosmic abilities remained the most advanced available, despite the fact that she had yet to fully develop them all completely.

Never mind that.

Elliott

But she knew very well that it was her task, and hers alone, to sneak into the lairs of those fabled monsters and scope out the situation for herself.

Eye to eye.

Monster to monster.

29

Naero planned to do her monster recon work through the Astral Plane over several days, while the Allies positioned their forces for the next phaze in the strategy. Instead of exploring the KDM, she separated her Astral form from her body in her dream state. But once again, she found that she could not enter the Astral Plane. Therefore, instead of trying to do that, she sent her spirit form off through the Prime Material Plane like a ghost.

She did all of this while Ra and her people thought that she was getting a normal night's sleep.

The first night she went to the continent of Shurog, and the battered gigacity capital of Nazol. Fortunately, an astral spirit form could not necessarily transport, but it could move from one place to another at fantastic speeds, bordering on the instantaneous.

Other Cosmic beings and entities, however, could still be sensitive to creatures moving around in Astral form, or on any plane. They could even detect their presence. Naero knew that much from her little-big, Kahn-dar dragon friend named Womi.

Naero was already out of phaze with the Prime Material Plane. An astral form already had that much going for it. Now, she was going to attempt something new–something never attempted before by any Mystic.

She was going to use psyonics in astral form to phaze while she was still in that form.

As soon as Naero did so, a horrible, ear-splitting buzzing sound filled her mind and made her head pound.

But as far as she knew, she was out of phaze, and completely undetectable to any entity on either plane of existence.

She passed into the depths of the central fortress of Nazol.

She saw entire armies sealed within a complex that was much larger than anything the Allies had imagined or discovered during their surface raids.

There were even armies in stasis and Ejjai freeze troops, complete with weapons and gear.

She saw hordes of Dakkur drones, with and without combat armor. Layers of physical defenses and blast shields.

Naero's spirit form passed right through them, without triggering any defenses.

The only problem was that her head was killing her. It felt as if it were going to explode.

How long could she maintain this form and endure such pain?

That might have been good to determine beforehand.

Too late for that now.

More Dakkur. Bodyguards now, all of them from the champion caste, twice the size of the drones. And like the drones, over half of them were infested with the G'lothc possession wyrm, giving them the potential to transform into even worse monsters than what they already were.

Then the heavily guarded, heavily protected inner palace, the huge playground and quarters of a Dakkur Queen.

Naero explored the complex birthing chamber where the Dakkur Queen pushed out millions of eggs each day–much like the Shai, actually. Despite the differences in species, the Dakkur were hyper dense reptilioids that were part carbon based, and part silicon based lifeforms. Dakkur were amazing hybrid lifeforms.

The G'lothc could sure pick them. Dakkur were supreme warriors and servants. And like their former masters, the Dakkur shared the same mindset, and worshipped The Great Destroyer of the Cosmic Prophecies with a devotion that was beyond fanatical.

Finally in the deepest lair, fit for such a regal beast, Naero beheld one of the rare White Queens of the Dakkur species.

She was white everywhere, like an immense swirl of new fallen snow. When her eyes flicked open in her slumber, they were the deepest jet, lit from deep within, not only by the Darkforce–but of unlight itself–the deepest, most intense form of the Darkforce.

She was well-over 30 meters long and serpent-like, nearly a snake at first glance, except for her powerful forelegs ending in vicious claws, and her atrophied, vestigial hind legs. The hardened spines on her back were also as sharp as swords, and her lethal tail blade was one quarter of her full length.

Despite her serene slumber, this was a creature of great power who was born to kill and destroy and lead a nation of warriors that she gave birth to.

From the looks of things around her palace, the Dakkur Queen fed each day upon all of her living subjects, even her own spawn. Naero spotted husks and corpses, bones, exoskeletons, and shredded remains from nearly every sentient creature known, and some that Spacers had not yet encountered.

The queen feasted upon them all, sometimes just the heads. She ate them alive, and threw the remains away like garbage. Periodically, the trash probably needed to be swept away–by her other slaves.

This queen was an eater of souls.

A thousand slaves from numerous races waited in a shallow feeding pit nearby, all of them wearing flickering control collars around their necks or whatever. Like droning, mindless fools, they softly sang to the queen, soothing her in her deep sleep.

A fresh meal awaited her, whenever she chose to wake up and dine upon them.

They praised her name softly and spoke it with reverence as if she were some kind of twisted deity.

"Bazretul...Bazretul...Bazretul..."

Naero could only imagine the intellect and Cosmic and psyonic abilities this huge creature might wield.

Baeven was certainly correct. The Supreme Dakkur were indeed quite formidable.

And a Dakkur King was even larger than the Queens, and with greater Cosmic powers and abilities. She could not repress a slight shudder and even experienced a twinge of fear.

One of those things had nearly slain her uncle–it nearly killed Baeven. Baeven. He fought it to the death and barely won, and was nearly left for dead himself. Only his battle brother Gaviok had revived enough to help save him.

Eventually, Naero knew that she was going to face foes greater than herself. She would meet threats that surpassed her abilities in one way or several. That was only a matter of time.

Yet like her uncle, she also had powerful friends allies, and it was not required that she face each an every threat alone.

And, Naero's own strange powers had yet to reach their full limit or potential.

The pain in her head grew unbearable, almost immobilizing.

Naero had seen what she had come to see.

She raced back to her own body at top speed, unphazing as soon as she was clear of the enemy gigacity of Nazol and its mighty queen, Bazretul.

The debilitating headaches nearly crippled Naero for the next day and night until she was able to fully regenerate and heal.

On the next night after that, she went exploring once more, in phazed astral form, moving faster this time to cover two more gigacity capitals, Grux and Dunt, of the continents Kolf and Gronet.

As Naero fully suspected, each capital and continent had its own queen and perhaps something more. But there was, as yet, no exact signs of a Dakkur King.

She did learned the names of the two new queens. At least they were new to Naero. The Queen of Grux upon Kolf was Memetok, and it was said that she was fatter than the others because she was a glutton, and feasted too much.

Akathri, the Queen of Dunt upon Gronet, was almost just the opposite. She was sleek and slender, and dined exclusively only upon the heads of her foodstocks, soaked in special sauces that she found tasty...not unlike grim meatballs.

Naero recovered slightly faster from her second recon ordeal, but she still waited another full day before going to spy out the gigacity of Riyok upon Uldrun.

She did not know why she had such a sense of foreboding about that last enemy capital. If there was a Dakkur King, perhaps she would find him there.

She descended into another Dakkur royal palace. Yet this one seemed even larger and more elaborate. Naero took that as a bad sign.

Naero located the queen's chambers and found her–Queen Golanta, another snow-white ruler, who from the signs of destruction and repeated reconstruction, had a particularly nasty temper.

But perhaps it was not all her doing. Golanta herself regenerated from multiple wounds and grim injuries. What could harm a Dakkur Queen? What could assault and ravage her in such a fashion as this?

Was it even possible to rape such an immense creature?

Yet there were even larger chambers beneath that of the queen, and what appeared to be a vast underground lake.

But it was not a lake of water.

This was of unlight and Darkforce itself.

Something huge, living, and malevolent slumbered beneath the surface of all of that raw, destructive power.

This was a lifeform unlike any other–a creature that did not feed upon mere flesh. Naero could sense it somehow. This thing dined upon raw Cosmic energy. That was its daily food.

And it was filled with lust and violent hunger.

Naero recalled what the Dakkur Queen Golanta had apparently endured.

Then part of a massive, reptilian Dakkur head surface and gazed up from that lake of death. And it thundered in Naero's mind with terrible power.

I CANNOT LOCATE YOU, INSECT. BUT I KNOW SOMEHOW THAT YOU ARE HERE. I KNOW THAT YOU CAN HEAR MY WORDS. WHY HAS IT TAKEN YOU SO LONG TO SPY US OUT? HAVE YOU SEEN ALL THAT YOU HAVE COME TO SEE?

Naero had. She fled immediately. If this creature located her, it might be able to attack her. And if it slew her, her people would be at a severe disadvantage.

Armed with this new knowledge, Naero spoke with Jan, Ra, and all of their forces. They had over two standard months before the time dilation effects came to an end.

They would take another month to adjust and further their plans. Naero would take more time to get them ready for the all-out war they were preparing to unleash.

She wanted to be more certain that they could finish such a war, and defeat the threats that they were up against once it started.

Naero wasn't about to die, and she did not have any wish to lead her people to their deaths, either.

30

All among the Allies appeared ready for their contest to begin.

But Naero still felt uncertain somehow. She wished they had something more, an edge that would give them some kind of advantage, even if it was only in tek.

She meditated and returned to the KDM in her Kexxian form as Orean.

Yet there was danger even in that. As she became more and more Kexxian in that form, it became harder and harder for her to return, to go back to being Naero.

In a sense, her old self as Naero became a guide out of the KDM, just Orean at first had been a guide into it. Now Orean needed Naero to lead her back to become a Spacer once more.

Yet as she became a Kexx–and not just any kind of Kexx–but a Dreamer, or a Kexxian Mystic, her awareness expanded. Everything about the Kexx grew increasingly more familiar and useful: their bodies, their minds, their neural net, their thought patterns, the way they interacted with Cosmic energy. She grew accustomed to their music, their songs, their philosophies and wisdoms, and their tek.

The Kexx could teknomance and biomance beyond anything that she could even yet fathom or comprehend.

The Dreamers could move planets, even entire stars. They could create things–vast things–with only matter and energy. They dreamed or wished them into existence. Just as she could create a handful of near perfect replicants of herself–the Kexx could create entire armies, entire fleets of miraculous machines and weapons to fight for them.

They wiped out all known disease, sickness, and illness.

They could not create immortality. The gift of death was still beyond them, yet the gift of limited life in all of its forms was nearly under their complete control. As long as an injured being possessed a single wink of the Lifespark, it could be brought back from the brink of death and saved from moving on to the next journey before their time.

Naero teknomanced, and biomanced, and studied, and sang every Kexxian song that she knew to keep herself and her mind centered in the Harmony. She came close to losing herself several times, and in the end, Naero had to wrestle with Orean to bring her back to being Naero.

And this time, when Naero Amashin Maeris opened her eyes, she smiled and burst into tears.

She had their edge.

Let the foe bring their darkest and mightiest monsters. Let them bring their numberless slaves.

Three standard days later the great war for the planet Naggoth exploded full force.

It would not let up from that moment forth, until one side or the other lay utterly vanquished and dead.

They struck the continent of Shurog first, and unleashed a lightning assault against the capital Nazol.

Naero and her assault team already appeared deep within the fortress, while Regiment Shetanna broke into three separate battalions and took the core of the gigacity.

Outside, the enemy armies swarmed up out of countless bunkers and holes. As they assembled to attack, the foremost elements of the Shetanna Battalions rained Cosmic blasts upon them.

Then the enemy possessed began to transform into their lethal energized forms–forms that were much harder to destroy.

The Alliance had developed several elements to counter all of that, based on Kexxian tek and weapon designs

With the new advanced phazeshields, Naero's troops could pass through buildings and barriers, fighting all the while. They absorbed energy attacks or simply let them pass through them.

And with the newly modified phaze-pulse rifles, Naero's troops could target and place a hyper fusion phaze-delay round in each tracked target well in advance. Then they could unleash the rounds at random, or time them all to detonate in pattern, sequence, or on command.

Her troops quickly targeted the foremost enemy waves and set them to go off once the enemy approach got too close to the capital. She overhead the chatter of her troops over the secured links. Naero monitored the combat net with teknomancy even as she and her teams descended to take on Bazretul, the resident Dakkur Queen.

"Captain Romanov. Advancing enemy gravtank formations mixed with Dakkur kill teams and drone hordes. We're not getting a target feed confirmation on that wedge, from between the three o'clock and five o'clock positions to our rear. What's happening?"

"Romanov here, Major. We're targeting them as quick as able. We have them seven kilometers out with the phaze shells. That's tens of thousands of confirmed targets covering those areas. But the transfer link is down somehow. The confirmation of the targeting locks are not showing up on the combat net. But we're ready to go, sir. Over."

"Blow them manually if you and your people have to, Captain. Just make sure they burn. And I want multiple phaze cannon rounds in each of those advance gravtank waves. Light them up. They must go down, if nothing else. Copy that?"

"Affirmative, sir. The lead tank waves already have seven or eight rounds in each tank. Don't you think that'll be sufficient?"

Major Donovan laughed slightly. "Don't get cocky, Romanov. That should probably do it. Continue targeting out to the fortieth kilometer arc for your profiles. And get ready for the fireworks. Good hunting, Isaiah. Let's take this goddam rock. Ooh-rah!"

"Copy that. You and the rest, sir. Ooh-rah!"

She smiled. Marines. Naero listened to and tracked the battle above them as it unfolded.

She and her team continued to fight their way down to the queen's chamber. She continued to startap and conserve energy for the fight ahead, using mostly her swords and lesser Cosmic attacks and tricks to help clear the way.

They had to reach the queen quickly and take her down fast.

The earth and rock all around the capital for many kilometers rocked, buckled, and shook.

Millions of phaze rounds activated and exploded up above in well-timed rings of destruction. Each foe or vehicle so-targeted vanished in a flash of pure ignited protonic reversal. Each enemy became a small fusion blast, incinerating them into atomic dust in less than an instant.

Within seconds, multiple enemy armies became scattered dust and chaff upon the rushing winds.

Still more enemy armies rose up to rush in.

But then it seemed as if the entire continent shook and shuddered.

From underground bunkers and sealed caves, digging through and exploding out of the ground, Shai mantid warriors erupted out of the ground from what seemed like everywhere by the untold millions.

Each of them had swelled in size to between three and four meters high, and their bodies shifted from red-violet to black. The ground trembled before their onset until some of the enemy could not even keep their footing.

The coming of the Shai to reclaim their lost homeworld of Allondatharru was in fact an earthquake. The enraged mantids tore through everything that stood in their way: gravtanks, shields, barriers, trenches–even mines. They hardly even slowed down if any of their own fell.

While in the depths of her own lair, Queen Bazretul of the Dakkur Empire came forth in fury to do battle for her realm.

"Look out!" Naero warned her people. Too late.

The enormous queen suddenly lunged at Naero herself with incredible speed and might, clearly hoping to slay the Alliance leader quickly and demoralize the rest.

Naero only saved herself by transporting away at the last instant.

But the Dakkur Queen lashed through many of Naero's command, crushing them or slicing them in half with the energized blades set in her spines and powerful tail. She twisted and flexed, killing everyone that she could.

Ra avoided her attacks by shrinking down to his smallest size, slipping under her thrashing bulk and rising up again behind her. He leaped upon the length of her body. It coiled and snapped and flexed, trying to pulverize him against the hard rock and metal reinforced shielding and supports of the palace.

The prince of the Shai stayed one step ahead of the huge queen, but as he passed over her, he ripped off her spines and stripped away much of her weaponry and blades, causing her great pain.

As Bazretul writhed and screamed, she unleashed a sonic shriek attack, so loud and so powerful that all who heard were dazed or even stunned.

Even in her partial Dark Beast form, Naero took a step back, and Cosmic ichor and vapor poured from her eyes, nose, mouth, and ears.

She attacked the enormous creature head on, slashing at its thick, hyperdense skull with her blades.

Bazretul was still shielded somehow, more than even a dreadnaught. What now? Even Naero's Cosmic energy blades could not slice through the queen's defenses.

The smaller Chaos swords of the Shetannas had little effect, and the queen continued to thrash about and lash out, crushing and killing more, even the replicants.

None of Naero's assault teams had weapons that could hurt the queen in this state.

Naero quickly ordered them all to pull back and defend the area nearby against any lesser foes attempting to come to the queen's aid.

Ra showed Naero the way–raw, direct physical attacks. They pitted strength against strength, power against power.

Dakkur Queens were hyperdense and difficult to kill, especially a large one such as this, with so many Cosmic energy protections. Yet they were still living beings. And if they were alive, that life could be ended.

At first Naero attacked the head, ripping and tearing at its block-like density. No good. The head was the most armored part on a Dakkur, especially a royal.

She switched to attacking the neck at the front, while Ra focused on trying to pin down and sever the deadly tale blade.

But the tough Shai took a pounding as the queen thrashed and lashed her tail every way that she could. Bazretul battered, pummeled, and whipped Ra against the chamber walls, ceiling, and floor.

Chunks of her tail blade also broke off, whether from Ra's direct attacks or her own exertions. The blade gouged deep slices and gouges out of everything in its path.

Naero felt glad that she had withdrawn the rest of her troops. They couldn't have done much but die against a foe this massive and powerful. That tail blade alone would have cut them all down.

The Dakkur queen's neck was still too thick to think of severing it with the weapons she had. No way to cut off the head or neck quickly and nothing to do so with.

While Naero ripped at the thick neck, the queen's powerful foreclaws ripped at Naero. Even in her partial Dark Beast form those claws did significant damage to Naero, draining her form of Cosmic energy as if it were gushing blood.

Naero struggled to get into a position where she could startap and seal her wounds.

The queen tried to crush Naero against the floor.

Before she could no longer move, Naero desperately ripped a large gash through the shields and across Bazretul's neck and chest, filling it with unstable Cosmic energy. Naero transported away from beneath the monster, at the same time that she detonated all of that energy.

The resulting explosion tore out a hideous wound in the queen's lower neck and breast. She howled, but thrashed and twisted, faster than even Naero could guess.

Naero felt both of the queen's ferocious claws close about and begin to crush her, squeezing her tighter and tighter. Naero fought with all her strength to break loose, tearing at the claws and unleashing several Cosmic attacks.

Bazretul dashed Naero against the wall, trying to smash her open, or at least daze her. "I have you now, you annoying spack wretch. You dare to attack me in the depths of my strength? Well, it shall be a rapturous feast to snip off and consume your head!"

Those immense jaws descended.

Naero opened her third eye, but there wasn't enough time.

Then the Dakkur queen pulled away on her own and shrieked, snapping her head behind her.

Ra had just broken off half of the queen's battered tail blade and even ripped out part of the dense spine bones that had connected it.

That must have hurt plenty, because the queen even dropped Naero, letting her slump to the ground, and went completely after Ra. Then Bazretul began to glow, pulsing with Cosmic energy.

She attacked Ra in a rage, driving him back against and even into the solid rock of the wall.

Ra covered up and shielded himself, one of his special defenses, making himself incredibly dense and invulnerable.

Queen Bazretul put that to the test. She lashed her head back and then forward, spraying a thick torrent of Cosmic energy and lightning out of her vast maw in an array of colors.

Ra shielded himself as best he could with his own energies.

Bazretul chortled. "Ah...my kind has not had the pleasure of destroying a prince of the Shai and feasting on him for many an age. Do you like what we've done with the old homeworld of your defeated kind? Join all those others in defeat and death!"

The queen pulled her head back to unleash another torrent strike.

It seemed uncertain whether Ra could withstand another such attack.

Bazretul glowed brighter and brighter.

Then her chest and neck suddenly burst open. The energy within her went out of control, and her entire body first imploded, and then rapidly expanded and burst.

When the dust and the destruction broke and began to clear away, Queen Bazretul lay defeated and dead, her headless, neckless, and lifeless body flung back in pieces and laid wide open, burning and twitching within the shattered domain of her once mighty palace.

Naero hefted the section of the queen's own tail blade in both hands as if it were a huge scythe or cleaver.

With such a blade, she had thrust it into the queen's chest all the way through, charged with Naero's own explosive Cosmic force.

Her blast disrupted all of the destroying energies building up inside of the queen to destroy Ra. Instead, Naero used all of that power to destroy the queen herself.

Bazretul lay dead, and Naero went to Ra to help him recover and regenerate.

After that, together she and her great friend hung the remains of the dead queen from the highest spire in the enemy gigacity, on display for all to see.

The enemy fought stubbornly to the last on Nazol for days. Yet against the matchless armies of the Shai, and with the enemy queen dead, none could stand against the Allies for very long.

They took over the continent and fortified it, seizing the spoils of all of the tek, ships, vehicles, armor, and weapons of their defeated foes. They modified and upgraded everything they needed for their own use.

The Alliance knew very well that the other three enemy-held continents were watching them closely and all that they did.

Naero and Ra went out repeatedly each day to survey troops and newly erected defenses, showing no signs of damage or fatigue. Yet in secret, they were still regenerating from their many grave injuries, and that took several days.

While doing all these things, Naero and Ra made no pretense of consolidating their gains on Nazol. Then they began preparing their forces for another assault.

The Allies did their best to try to keep the enemy guessing about which continent would be the next to fall.

And from the fixer spynet, the foe was very busy fortifying their remaining three strongholds.

Princess Shiival and Princess Kunali, Ra's brides, took command of Nazol, renaming it with its old Shai name of Kala'duan. Each of the brides based their new expanded nests on the west and east coasts respectively, and swore to Prince Ra that they and their children would defend the fabled homeland to the last, whatever happened.

The very next day, another attack would be made on the continent of Kolf, in and around the gigacity capital of Grux. But this posed a problem. Unlike Nazol, which was isolated by large oceans, Grux and Dunt were close to each other and even shared a land bridge–an isthmus between the two.

It would be far too easy for Grux and Dunt and their two queens, Memetok and Akathri, to join forces and support each other.

That could be very bad for the Allies.

And even though Naero and Ra always came back from each major contest even stronger and more knowledgeable. Still, it had taken both of them working together to barely defeat and slay even one Dakkur Queen.

How would they fare against two such monsters trying to destroy them at the same time? And with twice the number of troops to contend against?

Naero and her people took great thought upon these challenges, and did everything they could to come up with various potential solutions.

The war they started was on. They had no choice but to continue to pursue its conclusion, especially when they had the momentum.

31

Scouting told Naero and the Allies that at least to start out, both enemy queens stuck to the Dakkur pattern. Each remained in their territory, apparently determined to defend their nests and hold out to the last.

Therefore, Naero chose first to attack Queen Memetok in the capital gigacity of Grux on Kolf.

Yet when Naero led her strike force into the queen's underground bunker and palace, the Dakkur Queen was nowhere to be found, and the raiders met only token resistance.

Naero got them all out just in time, before the resulting explosion entombed them all deep within the palace fortress.

Above ground, the two queens attacked the Shai directly, causing great destruction and loss of life.

This time, the enemy armies rallied behind their queens out in the open and held the Alliance back. They even drove the Alliance forces back wherever the queens were.

Naero split her forces to keep the two queens separated. The plan was to divide and hopefully conquer. Jan and Regiment Shetanna went after Queen Akathri, to slay or at the very least keep her busy and distracted.

Akathri moved quickly within the battle, lashing and whipping around like a white ribbon of Cosmic power, crushing and slicing up the Allied forces. She had a special taste for Shai heads.

Meanwhile, Naero and Ra double-teamed Memetok.

With her greater, expansive bulk, Memetok could still move plenty fast when she needed to. But she mostly rolled and thrashed around, heedless of which troops she crushed and smashed beneath her weight, as long as many of them belonged to the Alliance.

Out in the open it grew more difficult to contain and control the two queens so as to be able to attack them.

If things got too hot for them in one place, they could quickly zip over to another where their forces could help protect or even aid them.

The fight was grinding down into a lethal stalemate, or Spacer standoff. Naero could not allow that. At this rate, one or both of the queens might even manage to escape somehow.

These two queens both needed to die. That much was imperative.

Naero hated to resort to it all so soon, but she called in her reserves. The sky above the continent of Grux filled with captured, upgraded enemy warships, each captained by a Shetanna replicant, and an able crew of trained Shai.

Most of their ships were now painted a bright, holo-metallic blue, and configured for ground assault and close support mode.

Those vessels began raining death on the enemy from above, circling in tighter and tighter, closing the ring of destruction.

Attacks rose up to meet them. More enemy ships and fleets raced in to fight them, and the battle continued relentlessly.

Any Alliance ship that was about to fall or explode ignited its engines and drives, and ploughed into the foe, blazing a path of destruction, above or below ground.

Jan transformed into his own partial Dark Beast. His form was a titan over ten meters high, composed entirely out of intense, blue flame. He scorched even Queen Akathri with that fire, and she avoided his blazing touch. They continued to duel and spar.

Just hold the skinny one off for a while longer, Jan, while we take out the fat one.

Naero had energized her newfound prize–the tail blade section from Queen Bazretul. She had even gone so far as to transform it into a proper Cosmic weapon with both biomancy and teknomancy. Since the tail blade naturally channeled Cosmic energy, such was not hard to do.

She gave the gigantic sword a name–*Heartcleaver.* She mystically bound the weapon to her own partial Dark Beast form. Whenever she assumed that form, *Heartcleaver* would appear with her, hot and ready upon her back, ready to be wielded.

Naero wielded it now, even though the blade remained a bit outsized in her near form. She still swung it with ease, and it blazed with an even greater intensity of light now, even during the daylight.

She slowly began to slice, and cut, and carve Memetok open like a pan of roasted meet.

Memetok shrieked in fear and rage at the wounds from a weapon fashioned out of one of her fallen sisters.

Naero took wounds and injuries herself while they dueled so fiercely. Whether it was being clawed by those fast, raking hands, snapped at and bit by those cavernous jaws, or blasted by the monster's energy attacks, usually from her maw–Naero and Ra did not come off unscathed.

Ra did his best to strip this enemy queen of her weapons in the same fashion that he had done with the other. Yet he was careful not to fall into her clutches, become trapped in her coils, or beneath her great mass. Then he focused on wearing down that lethal, murderous tail and blade.

Occasionally, Naero and Ra were distracted by lesser enemy troops. They simply ignited these lesser foes up like torches and left them behind to writhe, scream, and burn.

"You fools shall die this day!" Memetok shouted, redoubling her efforts to drag her opponents down and kill them.

Naero flashed in, trying to help Ra sever the thick tail and blade.

But Memetok flipped and snapped at them, spearing at them with her surviving, multiple spines and blades.

Naero tried to reach Ra and transport them both out of the way.

Ra did not understand, and swatted Naero away from harm.

Memetok's long energized spines caught Ra across the midsection, and impaled him up against solid rock, with three of her thick spines stuck through him. Naero struggled to reach Ra, came to his side, and this time whisked them both away before the queen sliced them in half with her tail blade.

They appear right in front of Memetok's block-like head.

"Now, Ra!" Naero shouted. "Combine our attacks."

Both of the Allies opened their third eyes and bored into Memetok's skull, destroying and blinding her eyes permanently.

Memetok fell back thrashing in pain and clutching and clawing at her face and ruined eyes.

Ra was gravely hurt and fading quickly. Naero turned him over to several Shetannas.

Naero went after Memetok with Heartcleaver once again. She severed the tail, both forearms, and the rest of the energized spine blades.

Finally she drove the great sword into Memetok's bursting heart.

After that, she split the Dakkur queen open from breast to groin, nearly cleaving her in two, straight down the middle.

Even as Queen Memetok toppled back and died convulsing, a great wail of terror went up from the enemy forces.

Ra would recover, but Naero could not hesitate. Jan needed her help now.

Many Shetannas had perished in that great contest. And Jan had taken harm also. But he had done what was expected of him, and Akathri, the skinny queen, was clearly wounded in many places as well and slowing down.

Naero joined the fight just in time. Taking a cue from Ra, she first went after the queen's spine blades and tail weapon, hacking them off and doing no small amount of damage.

Naero tried to dodge at first, and then transported, as Akathri reared back her neck for another Cosmic torrent attack.

The gout of energy and lightning shot out of the queen's maw, struck Naero a glancing blow as she winked out.

It still punched through most of her shields and swatted her away–driving her back several kilometers.

Then Naero felt Jan cry out in great fear and pain, and transported back into the battle immediately.

Haisha. Akathri had snapped up Jan in her jaws and was attempting to gulp him down whole.

Jan stoked into an inferno, and the queen tried to spit him out far too late.

Naero looked on as her brother melted the queen's tongue in her mouth, scorched even her teeth and then immolated the Dakkur Queen's brain–boiling it inside her skull.

Flames shot out of the dying queen's stricken, ruined eye sockets.

Jan transported and blew the skull apart from within with a Cosmic blast.

Naero looked around for her brother. Jan was nearly unconscious, and plummeted down from out of the sky like a flickering comet.

Naero shielded herself, assumed her energy being form, and caught her wounded brother.

She healed him with biomancy and brought him to where Ra was being tended.

Bereft of their queens, the continents of Grux and Dunt would fall to the Alliance in a matter of days or weeks at best.

Shai Princesses Ishidar and Cliiofarah came forward to lead the final pacification of the two continents, which they returned to their original Shai names of Anasha'dah and Nu'arrah. These names somehow sounded partially Kexxian even to Naero's ear, but such could well be possible.

The Shai and the Ku were also child races of the Kexx and the Drians.

Once her brothers were healed and had grown stronger, the Alliance would make their final assault on the last enemy capital city of Riyok, on the continent of Uldren.

But there was still much fighting to be completed on these two continents first.

Naero began to wonder if they should attempt to play it safe, consolidate their gains, grow their numbers more. Perhaps they should hold out for the final days or so before the Time dilation subsided. By then they might very well need the help of Khai and the rest of the Alliance.

Naero felt certain that she could defeat another Dakkur Queen now. But the other monster—most likely a Dakkur Dark King or perhaps a prince— was an enormous wild blade in the mix to consider.

32

Naero decided to wait for the planet to come out of its Time dilation before making the final assault. Yet that also meant that the enemy would have time to regroup and further prepare on Uldren for any such future attack.

And they would also have a chance to escape.

Still, there remained many good reasons for accepting such a delay. Many pockets of fierce fighting continued within their two recently acquired continents. Next, both Jan and Ra remained injured and depleted. They recovered as quickly as they were able, yet they still had room to go.

Those were also probably reasons why the enemy unleashed their own all-out attack on the Alliance, with ten days to spare.

The bulk of the enemy surprise attack began at the siege of the gigacity of Dunt, on the continent of Riyok.

The last Dakkur Queen, Golanta, led the attack. Yet she was backed up by some great, Darkforce power that rained down Cosmic death from above. It even blasted warships out of the sky, to fall burning and exploding upon the reeling Alliance ground forces below.

Naero and all of her troops arrived at Dunt, and none too soon, seeing that many of their advance forces had been destroyed, and the rest had been all but routed in the areas near and around the capital.

She looked at Ra and Jan. Both were ready to fight to the last need, but neither was fully recovered.

"I'm going to leave half of the Shetannas here to attempt to complete both of your regenerations. You're no good to us at half-strength. Let me see if I can hold them off."

Jan stared at her. "We don't even know what the king Dakkur can do in combat, Naero. You can't possibly face both of them down."

"Jan is right," Ra told her. "We shall fight and do what we can, even if it means our deaths."

"No, I won't accept that. We can't all die here. That would serve no purpose. That is exactly what the enemy wants. I would most likely get killed trying to save one or both of you. Do as I say. Let me feel this out and stall for time. Let the replicants use combined biomancy to bring you back to full strength ASAP. It might not take very long at all."

Jan was silent, and still brooded. He had made no promise yet to hold back, especially if she got into trouble and was in serious danger.

That was the problem; they were all in serious danger.

Ra finally responded. "I see the wisdom and logic in your plan. We will hold back and allow the replicants to do all that they can. Yet if things go badly, neither of us will stand by and watch you fall."

Naero nodded to them. "Thank you, my brothers. Someone must assess the enemy's strength and gauge more of what we are up against here. If that is a King Dakkur, we need to know what its powers and abilities are. And if I can isolate Queen Golanta, perhaps I can come up with a way to take her out quickly, or at least wound her.

Naero went forward, both cloaked and phazed, doing her best to confuse the enemy leaders somewhat.

She wanted to see if they could sense and track her location, enough to target her for direct attacks.

All the while, Queen Golanta continued to lead the attacks to drive off and crush the Alliance forces.

Naero had already given orders long ago for her people to withdraw in the best order possible, and perform a fighting retreat.

Yet in some hotly contested areas, it was still a rout. The enemy now controlled the air and the ground.

Golanta unleashed torrents of destructive Cosmic energy from her glutinous maw that tore up wide ruts of destruction through the Alliance forces for several kilometers into the distance. Her massive beams even punched into and penetrated hills and the solid rock of mountains.

Darkforce lightning blasted the Alliance from above in screens, sheets, and waves that obliterated everything living that they touched, whether friend of foe. As long as the Alliance people died, the enemy did not care.

Naero attempted to slow down the rapidly expanding enemy counterattack. She commanded the available members of the Shetanna Regiment to launch a combined Cosmic gigablast into the swirling, cloaking mass of energies up in that Darkforce maelstrom growing in power above them.

To her horror, the power lurking within those energies completely absorbed the blast, and then turned those same energies back against Naero's fleeing forces, causing further, great ruin.

We cannot stop them, Naero realized.

In that instant, she saw all of them die.

Then a single, ominous chime, like that of a great deep gong or bell, resounded out from Naero with her as the center. That great note echoed and rippled throughout all of Naggoth in an instant.

Everything seemed to freeze in that exact flicker of time. Naero closed all three of her eyes and attempted to center herself, feeling her Kexxian counterpart come to her at her last need.

"Orean, these powers are too great for us to stand against. Despite all that we have accomplished on this world, we are about to perish."

"That may very well be, Naero. Yet take a moment to study the situation better and see it more clearly. What do you see? What do you need right now to give you and your people a fighting chance?"

"I...I need the ten days to be up. I need the planet to come back into sync with our other forces. We need their help. I'm certain they will have prepared for this. They will not let us down."

"Move an entire planet through a space of Time covering several days? The Kexxian Dreamers could do such things, Naero. Can you do such things? Are you a living miracle?"

Naero clenched her fists. "I AM!" she thundered, just like the voice of thunders, and the power of her words echoed off like a great resonating song.

"I AM!," Naero replied. "All things are possible. If it has been done before. It can be done so again."

"Only a Kexx...only a mighty singer...*A Dreamer* could move the very stars, and planets, and command the Cosmic forces of SpaceTime. Are you a Kexx, Naero?"

233

Naero voice merged with that of her counterpart within the depths of her mind, heart, and soul.

She merged with the Harmony about her, and brushed the outer edge of the Flame Eternal and the Great Mystery of All things with her radiant Kexxian fingertips.

She knew nothing and everything all at once. She shouted to all the universe with *the voice* for a third and final time. "I AM! I am Kexx, I am Spacer, I am one with all things great and small. Naero is Orean and Orean is Naero, and the Great Circle of Harmony and light makes me whole. I touch the Darkforce and I am not destroyed. I hold the Flame Eternal and I am not consumed."

As Orean she had always known the great song of Time and sang the words without hesitation, shifting everything on Naggoth–nay, on *Allondatharru* to the precipice of the exact moment in time they needed to be at.

Then she studied the situation that she as Naero and all of the forces of the Alliance were still in, and all of the fierce threats that they faced. But in mere seconds, they would neither be alone, nor helpless.

Naero noticed two things which might…*might* help to save them.

First, Queen Golanta had a G'lothc possession wyrm concealed inside herself, at the base of her gigantic tail. In a matter of seconds, the Queen would transform and become a thousandfold more strong and deadly. They would be hard put to defeat a creature of that size, armed with such might.

Second, the immense creature hiding up in the clouds was not exactly a Dakkur King, but in fact an immature prince. Who though great in power and raw strength, his full range of Darkforce and Cosmic energies and powers remained woefully underdeveloped, and not within his full control.

From all of her experiences controlling and dealing with her Dark Beast, Naero shared with Orean all of those pitfalls and weaknesses, and how one who better understood such, might go about exploiting them in others who did not.

At least Orean-Naero understood that they had a chance now.

There was never certainty in anything.

The best that one could ever hope for was a chance.

Fortune favor the bold!

Those were her thoughts as she transformed back into being Naero, in their current slip of Time.

But now it was a flow of Time that she as Orean, the Kexxian Dreamer, had adjusted by wishing, dreaming, and singing it so.

When all hell and Chaos broke loose and detonated everywhere around them, Naero knew exactly what to do, and moved to act.

She instantly transformed into her partial Dark Beast form, and drew *Heartcleaver*. Like a surgeon with a scalpel Naero carved out the possession wyrm and incinerated it, before it could trigger.

Then she shot after the Dakkur Prince hiding up that Darkforce hurricane. Time to unleash her Dark Beast in all of its fury once more.

She was never certain if she could ever regain control of it once she did fully unleash it. But this time, she could not hope to achieve victory without its full might.

Below her, Queen Golanta thrashed in agony and began to die. Nothing could save her now. Alliance forces tried to subdue her. More came down from out of the sky as the stars could be seen overhead once again. Everyone was surprised.

Let others finish off the last queen.

Naero needed to focus on the great battle she sped straight into.

33

The dark thing lurking in the Darkforce Typhoon came straight at her, roaring its name as part of its challenge.

"I AM MAHATHRATHRAX, LORD OF WORLDS, DEVOURER OF MY ENEMIES. STAND BEFORE ME AND BE CONSUMED!"

Naero shouted back at him in kind, "NOT THIS DAY!"

They fell to fighting, ripping, and tearing at each other up in the stormy, Darkforce-fueled typhoon swirling all about them.

Naero merged with her Dark Beast once again, yet this time she knew and understood it far more than ever before.

It was not a part of her that she liked or enjoyed, but the truth remained that it was part of her. She was it, and it was her. And even if she could not completely control it, she understood it, and knew what it could and would do.

She and the dark prince of the Dakkur were both creatures born of the Darkforce, and as such, they were nearly consumed and overwhelmed with the deep, intense desire to destroy and to draw in more power.

They saw each other not merely as enemies—but also as competing food sources—each that might absorb the other. Their food was all types of energy and Cosmic energy, even the lifeforce. And that included each other.

They glutted themselves on energy and could never have enough. Left on their own, they would devour all things, even themselves. If they could find a way they would in fact become the Great Destroyer with ravenous glee and consume the entire universe if no one stopped them.

The contest between them became an eating contest, to see which of them could devour the other and absorb the other first, like two snakes trying to gobble each other up by starting at the other's tail.

Naero maintained barely enough control to perceive just how to defeat Mahathrathrax.

First she startapped, something the young prince was clearly incapable of doing, in his brutish, less sophisticated form.

She bloated him with Cosmic energy, and he greedily sucked it down, forgetting even to keep trying to kill her. He fed and fed, until he grew besotted and drunk upon it and for a few crucial moments, he was dazed and vulnerable.

Naero pounced upon him in that state. She ripped him apart the way RA would devour a foe, and swallowed the prince, destroying and consuming him whole.

For Mahathrathrax it was far too late. Yet even as he died, and Naero feasted on his soul, trapping its cringing spirit inside of her just as Baeven had done to a G'lothc spirit, the doomed prince taunted her.

"Your defeat of child of our race means nothing. The Masters still have your spawn, and your wretched simulacrum. Even now, as you struggle and fight on this insignificant little mudball, they use the power of your own child to open all of the gateways well ahead of schedule."

The dark prince laughed as insane as Naero's lost brother Danner, even as he died. "They'll suck her dry and eat her flesh, just for the fun of consuming her, in the end. And the end shall come for all of you petty meddlers. The Armada will leap across the way between our galaxies and conquer you all. And even the Six shall be released once more. The Champions of Shadows shall rise to power again, and there is nothing you can do to stop them!"

As Naero finished consuming the dark prince, she perceived his portion of the enemy's mind and their plans.

She saw where they had taken Naero-3, her unborn child, and Om.

She fully understood what their great and powerful foes were attempting to do.

Khai called her seconds later. But after all that they had been through, there was still no time. She hadn't even time to consider the fact that she had just subdued her Dark Beast once more–this time on her own, and without even thinking about it.

"Beloved," she called out to Khai over their link, with great urgency. "Hear my words. I am teknomancing these coordinates to you and the Alliance. I understand that there is still a hotly contested battle going on around Allondatharru. But listen well. I know where they have taken our daughter, and we must go there immediately. To the edge of our galaxy out this way, to the edge of the universe, at a rare nexus of the planes and galaxies."

"My heart, you've been gone for an entire month. I don't understand?"

"Please, if you have love for me, bring all our forces and Allies that you can, and summon Baeven. Bring everyone. Our dread foes use our own child against us to advance our ruin, and they will drain her energies and slay her in the process. They seek to open up vast gateways to other galaxies and dimensions where their powers and their once great masters hold sway. If they unleash these additional foes upon us before we can prepare to fight them, all shall be lost. We and perhaps all the universe will be doomed!"

"Naero, you speak as if you are leaving. Where are you going? You don't even have a ship. How do you intend to–"

"Please, Khai. I must go ahead and do all that I can to save our girl, even if it means my life. I will die before I allow them to destroy her. I am filled with Cosmic energies from my recent battle. It will be enough to take me there. Follow hard upon my heels and bring all of our allies who can be spared. I have sent word to my admirals to confirm this and assist you. Our foes have had our child too long. It is time we take her back from them!"

With that Naero channeled all of her energies and made the wyrmhole leap across that part of the galaxy to where she needed to be.

There, at the edge of that prime nexus, on the cusp of Naero's galaxy in that portion of the Gamma Quadrant, she saw the G'lothc ship, the large squid-like cruiser with the enormous, writhing black tentacles ending in destructive weapons.

Yet the squid ship was currently heavily damaged from with from within. It listed badly in space, trying to regenerate itself.

Large exit holes were sealed only by emergency shields.

On the edge of the prime nexus, Naero saw about a hundred foes of various species and types, working with enemy teks and a score of various Darkforce generators and powered generator mek suits.

No one noticed her appearance, her approach, or even attempted to scan for her presence yet. All of the enemy focused on what appeared to be a small Dyson sphere that they had constructed around Naero-3.

They used the sphere to syphon off huge quantitates of Cosmic energy and feed those massive amounts of energy into two separate gateway projection screens erected to the left and to the right.

As the power continued to step-up and build, the stars behind those screens flickered out, and other images flashed and blipped into view through their broad length, across those gateways.

Through the gate on the left, Naero beheld what looked to be the interior of another galaxy. Yet in the distance, as she zeroed in, she saw wave after wave and fleet after fleet of G'lothc and Dakkur ships, many of them new configurations, or just larger versions of enemy ships they had already seen. Some of these enemy vessels were carrier and dreadnaught class and size.

These countless warships had to be part of the enemy's Armada. And the enemy was in fact using Naero's child to open a massive gateway between the galaxies, to allow their forces begin to pour through.

Naero had once witnessed the firepower of the guns on the squid ship cruiser during the Annexation War. One blast has taken out dozens of ships, both friends and foe. What could fleets of such warships accomplish?

Yet even worse than the Armada, on the right, the enemy was also opening a gateway to the planes. Specifically, the edge of the Plane of Destruction and Annihilation itself, where the dark spirits of the G'lothc still endured and struggled in their nearby pocket dimension of the Void that was their torturous prison. Trapped within, they still yearned and conspired to find the perfect hosts to house them once again, and allow them to them return to the universe in force and work their will.

Naero saw six large creatures held in stasis tubes out in front of all the rest. The other vessels consisted of about a hundred more sentients in stasis tubes, with all manner of hosts prepared to receive their G'lothc overlords, once that gateway could be forced open.

The six finest and most powerful vessels were undoubtedly reserved for the Champions of Shadows, the six worst and mightiest of the G'lothc who had ever been know to exist. Woe unto the universe if they were ever unleashed again.

Naero could not wait for Khai or any others.

She had to attack, even if she must do so alone.

She had to save her child, and neither of those gateways could be allowed to open.

Transporting took her into the heart of the source.

Naero entered the Dyson sphere feeding off of her daughter, and now, it also drained her.

The mixture of joy and sorrow that Naero felt when she looked at poor, unconscious Naero-3 and her tortured, mutilated body could not be put into any words that existed. And that paled in comparison to the wonder she felt when she sensed both her child's spirit, and her old friend Om.

But they had to make it out quickly before Naero herself became trapped inside with them.

The enemy continued to suck them all dry each second.

She made contact with Naero-3 and did the best thing that she could for the moment–and re-absorbed her, bring her child and Om back within her as well.

So great was the elation of her child, that a wave of energy shot out of Naero's daughter, overloaded the Dyson sphere around them, and shredded it into useless pieces of debris and junk.

They were free, and at first Naero transported safely away from the two gateways. But when she turned back to look, to her horror she saw that the gateways were now fully charged, and beginning to flicker open on their own.

In fact, the first enemy warship would pass through in a matter of minutes, and on the right, the realm of the G'lothc began to split open, in a dark swirling miasma that Naero had seen once before.

The dark spirits of the G'lothc would slip free, and enter into their vessels to live and breathe once more.

Naero could have fled. She could have run and kept running with all that she held dear back within her.

Yet that was not her way, and she knew that doing so wouldn't work.

Such evils had to be confronted, opposed, and destroyed.

She turned back and increased to attack speed, keeping herself as small a target as she could. She swept in to assail the gateways directly this time.

The enemy spotted Naero at last and fought back. Strangely enough, the badly damaged squid ship cloaked as it moved away from the nexus, most likely preparing to jump and escape.

Naero fought and took fire, knowing all the while that she was risking everything she loved. She also knew that she had to do so.

For some reason a song verse rose to mind.

I will follow you to the End of Days!
Side by side we will win our way.

240

Fighting through Love's confusing maze,
With my last breath till our last day!

She blew up the gateway on the left. The nose of a new enemy battleship just emerging got cut off and appeared to implode, sucked back into the other side.

But when she turned to the gate on the right, a long, tentacle like clawed appendage shot out of the void and encircled her neck, burning her with Darkforce and sucking out her energies faster that even she or her unborn child could replenish them.

It was as if Death itself was throttling the life out of them.

A grim menacing voice threatened her within her own mind. *We are coming for you and your kind, meddler. Long have your ilk interfered with our great designs. We shall make you and your children our great vessels, and use your husks to destroy all that you cherish. Those of you that we do not enslave, we shall kill, and make you trophies of our great triumph over all that lives!*

Naero struggled back with all that she had, with everything that she was, and her child battered and blasted the fell thing with her, all to no avail. The thing would not let go off them and continued to murder them each second, siphoning away their lifesparks and feeding upon them, growing ever stronger.

"We will find a way to kill you bastards!" Naero shouted, calling upon all of her reserves, trying to startap and unleash her Dark Beast.

The thing tearing at them laughed. *You cannot kill that which has already died, fool.*

Naero punched, and kicked, and fought in whirlwind of attacks. "What exists can be destroyed, whatever form it takes! We shall find a way. I will find a way. And my children shall never be yours, you foul and nameless thing!"

She tore free briefly and struck and kicked at the thing, trying to drive it off and escape.

But it clamped itself back onto her throat and fed upon her even faster.

What can you do, fool? You think you know much, when you know nothing!

They struggled and fought, but the thing still held her, killing her each second.

Then Naero had a tricky idea.

She flashed a holo of Orean before her and the thing drew back in terror for an instant, unable to control its reaction.

No! They're all gone!

Naero spoke in Kexxian, and then sang in Kexxian after that.

"I…am a *Dreamer*!"

LAH TII AH-VII KAH, SHAI KAH LING JHAH, HAE JELAH SHEVAH! YAVAE LAH SHENAH!

The dread thing shrieked in terror and at first cowered. But then it hissed and flew into a horrendous rage, attacking Naero even stronger than before, ensnaring her in even more limbs, claws, and tentacles before she could get far enough away.

There were legions of these foul things, and they raved at her.

No! We hate your kind worst of all! No more of your tricks! Now we shall destroy you once and for all. Now that we are many and we have you helpless and alone!

Naero gasped and struggled weakly, still trying to fight.

"Not alone!" a fierce voice roared.

Khai flashed in before Naero in all his verdant fury, more welcome than any sight Naero could have wished for.

He was in his energy being form, and Yii rose and fell in his powerful hands, the Sword of Legend gleaming with blinding white flame. Whatever these fell things were, they could not withstand its touch. He cut her free of them and tossed her back to Baeven.

Baeven held Naero in his arms, slaying and fighting off anything that dared to come near them with his own Cosmic abilities, while Jan, Ra, and Jia backed up Khai before the enemy gateway to the Void itself.

They fought and held off the grim, horrific tide trying to flood through and escape. Jia struggled to deactivate the gateway.

A storm of destroying fire came from *The Flying Dagger, The Star Fox, The Darkstar, The Black Spot* and the vanguard of the Alliance fleets massed behind them ripped into the gateway.

The tek of the enemy gateways and those operating it collapsed and vanished in sheets of flame.

Baeven brought Naero into her own medical bay with Trudi, kissed her on the brow, and then vanished with a smile.

Khai shielded the others with one of his protective spheres in the nick of time, and brought them back to their vessels. *The Star Fox* cloaked, but even on her medbed, Naero could sense it nearby.

For now at least, the immediate danger was over.

The enemy Armada was still out there, albeit a galaxy away once more. And the G'lothe spirits still plotted to escape the Void and rain destruction on the universe.

But none of these dire things would take place this day.

By all reports from Admiral Toshi–Allondatharru was now completely theirs, and by rights, was given back to their mighty Allies, the Shai.

The Allies had no intention of giving it back. Naero and everyone else considered all that sufficient progress.

34

While Trudi tended to her various wounds, Naero relaxed and caught up with Om, learning all that had happened during the ordeal with the enemy. Om had learned quite a bit about their enemies also, and had helped out when and where he could.

Really glad to have you back, Om. I can't tell you how much I missed you.

I felt the same way, N. Now we can go back to trying to understand the KDM.

Yeah, we'll need to talk about that, Om. When there's time. I need to introduce you to someone I'm sure you will find very interesting indeed.

Wow, that's sounds great! I can't wait.

How was my little duck?

What the hell is a duck?

My unborn child, you goof. That's what I call her, if you haven't noticed. It's a term of endearment, you idiot. What was it like being with her?

Oh, nothing much. Besides being a completely terrifying and magnificent new life form that's still a complete enigma. No big thing at all.

Well, when you put it like that, Om.

N, I do have to say something. You do owe Naero-3 a great deal, I think. She went through a lot of crap defending and protecting us and was as brave as you are.

She is me, Om.

You know what I mean, Naero.

Already ahead of you on that. You go study all that new tek data, and she and I will have a chat.

You already reabsorbed her.

And I can bring her back around anytime I want. Her mind is still a part of my mine. But you're right, we do owe her, more than we could ever give her. But I'll see what I can do.

That conversation occurred next, once again in her mind.

Naero-3, I'm grateful for everything you've done and I want to make a deal with you. You deserve it. You don't have to serve me. You don't have to do anything you don't want to. You can be completely free to make your own way and have your own life."

"Thanks, N. I might just take you up on that one day, but for now, I'm still feeling very attached to you, Khai, and our child."

If Naero could smile inside of her own head, she would have done so. "Part of that is the way I made you think, Naero-3. I can change that if you like. That might make it easier for you to be your own person."

She could feel Naero-3 protest. "Please don't; that is the way I see myself now. I love this child. I love you and Khai as if you were both part of me."

You are a part of me, Naero-3.

"But there is something I do want, N. Just for once, I'd very much like to experience the depth of love that you and Khai share for each other."

Naero-3, if things go the way I want them to, that wish is going to be granted, and in spades, as they used to say on Old Earth.

"What the hell is a spade, any way, Naero?"

If I recall, it was a small tool-like a shovel, but for the hand. used in gardening. But we digress. And how about this for a deal? When I get around to giving you your repaired body back, we can share our child as she develops when my duties with the Task Force calls me away. You can continue to be her guardian and nanny. And we can even share the experience of the birth together by you merging with me again.

"That sounds great. I accept."

"But after the birth, I want you to seriously consider taking your own name and being free to have you own life. You can find someone for you, and even have your own ship and go your own way. Think about it."

"What if I want to stay? Do you think I would ever be able to leave this child? And won't you and Khai have more kids? You know you're going to need help watching and raising them, with as busy as you guys always are."

That's very possible, Naero-3, but I also want to free your mind so that you can decide all of this on your own. And, I need to square it all with Khai as well.

"Sure thing, N. I'll just rest inhere a bit. Things have been pretty grim, what with getting tortured repeatedly and all. This is actually a nice break, and I can focus on the baby in here, too. It's great. Let me know when you need me, and we can just split off again."

Excellent, now I have something else to attend to.

Naero tracked Khai down in a corridor while he was actually heading to look for her. She tackled him in the hallway and quickly wrapped herself around him.

"Remember that thing we talked about?" she said.

Khai laughed. "Which one?"

Naero grinned wide and kissed him.

"The kissing thing?" Khai said.

"Yeah. There's a window right now, so let's go for it, while we make some other plans." Naero transported them to her private quarters.

She called out to Ra. "My prince, please retire to the bathroom if you could, and take lots of food and lix, and things to do. Khai and I have a lot to catch up on."

"Very well," the mantid said, and closed the door panel.

Just as they once had wished, they spent the next standard day talking over many things and kissing each other all the while, in every way and place imaginable.

Naero made a tactical suggestion. "You know, Khai. We can keep up the kissing and do other fun stuff, too."

Her was busy kissing her tummy and resting his head on her, listening hard. "Working toward that, my heart. Be patient."

Naero sighed. "Khai, I want us to get married,"

"Let's go do it now. I'm sure one of the admirals would be happy to perform the ceremony."

"If all of this has taught me anything, I don't want to hold back or wait any longer. No one else is. My friends are getting married and having kids. Now we have a child. And even though any of us could die the next instant, I don't want to pass up any more chances for happiness. There has always been danger for our people. And yet we have always lived, and loved, and done what we could to be happy, despite all of the wars, and death, and destruction. Look at my parents."

Khai rose back up and kissed her deep an wet on the mouth. "Look, you gorgeous blockhead. Am I arguing with you? I want to spend my life with you, no matter how long it is. But I don't want to die. I want to live. And I want us to live to see our children and our grand children and great grandchildren thrive. And woe to any sonovabitch who tries to threaten us!"

Naero laughed. "Ooh…I like it when you cuss. You've done it like…twice, since I've known you."

Khai shrugged and grinned. "You're a very bad girl, and a terrible influence on me."

"And don't forget it." She burst out laughing with him. She was glad she was so crazy for this big galoot. "What about tomorrow? We'll have a simple ceremony and honeymoon in space, beneath the stars."

Khai smiled. "Sounds like heaven to me, as long as you are there, Naero."

The next day, the short simple ceremony turned out to be a major, instant event held within a WebBall arena and broadcast throughout all of the fleets, to their allies, and back home. All of their available friends and family attended.

Khai asked Jan to be his best man, and Tyber, Tarim, and Enel to stand up with them. Naero had Saemar, Chaela, Surina, and Trudi stand beside her.

No one said anything about Baeven giving away from the bride, and when Jia appeared at the wedding with him, in a gown made of light itself, even the Spacers gasped, and saw what true beauty and perfection looked like.

Most Spacers wore their parade dress whites.

At the last moment, Naero switched into the old fashioned wedding dress that had once made Khai blink and sweat. She had programmed the design as one of her nanosuit presets, and switched to it now, in honor of Zhen.

Admiral Yamamoto Toshio presided over the ceremony and for once, he could not stop smiling.

Then, after some swooching, bride and groom exited beneath an arch of swords formed by many of the fleet captains lined up on either side.

There was a brief banquet and reception, but the new couple slipped away early on, while the Allies partied and celebrated in their honor.

Whatever the future brought their way, Naero and Khai didn't want to waste any time from that moment forward.

The fleet Thiolinists serenaded the couple all that long night, as each bell of the watch chimed beneath the stars.

THE END

Please Post A Book Review Right Now

Please post a review of this book if you enjoyed it. Twenty little words are all that is required. Twenty words that say what you liked about this book while it is still fresh in your heart, mind, and soul. Please do so now before something else makes you forget.

Here is the smartlink for *Naero's Trial* if you purchased it on Amazon:

smarturl.it/NaerosTrial

Please click on the link and post your review now.
Done? The author would personally like to thank you very much.

In this busy world, everyone is pressed for time. Our time is so important, no doubt. It has reached the point now where authors of nearly every stripe compete not only for sales, but to garner reviews from their readers. Some authors even stoop to "purchasing" reviews in social media that some services now offer in bulk.

In the publish or perish work of competitive fiction, book reviews from readers are golden, they have now become a commodity even.

Many in the business even consider book reviews as important, or even more important than book sales in some ways. As crazy as that sounds.

So therefore, trust us in this. If you have authors whom you adore, and you want to read more of their books in the future, please post as many reviews for them as you can in all of the forms of social media that you use.

Doing so will help your favorite authors in numerous ways that you cannot even possibly imagine. Never forget that fact. Book reviews matter a great deal.

And if by chance, if you find that there is something about this book that you don't like, and you really do want to help authors, before you slam them with bad reviews, try briefly contacting them instead with your concerns through their contact info that is always readily provided, or through their publisher. Most authors, especially new ones, are usually happy to get constructive criticism that will make their books better. Only hating, online trolls slam authors with bad reviews without giving them a chance. Real pros and fen contact authors directly with any valid concerns. That is the current, accepted etiquette. Please don't be a troll.

Amazon Kindle Review Link for Naero's Trial,
The Citation Series, Book 2: smarturl.it/NaerosTrial

Barnes & Noble Review Link

TBA

Good Reads Review Link

Please post one or more reviews for Mason and each of his books, everywhere that you can.

Thank you once again.

Cheers,

Mason Elliott.

SF Author Mason Elliott's Contact Information

<u>Please Join Mason Elliott's Readers List</u>

Use either of these links:

http://bit.ly/1L2QpUL

Backup link:
http://eepurl.com/FgQzv

Be among the first to learn about my writing projects and new releases. I promise that I will not share your info or spam you. I will use the list only to inform you about matters directly connected to my writing projects.

<u>About the Author</u>

Mason Elliott grew up loving Science Fiction and Fantasy in all of their myriad forms. That love has transferred into his dedicated writing. Like most writers, he lives a Spartan lifestyle and yearns to devote his life even more to his writing, and someday retire on the Pacific Coast. So be a fan, buy his stuff, and enjoy!

Like and follow Mason on Facebook, where he does most of his blogging at
https://www.facebook.com/masonelliott731

And on Twitter at
http://bit.ly/1nsqOSs

Visit Mason Elliott's website at
www.masonelliott.authorcontacts.com

And for even more information on Mason Elliott and his works, visit High Mark Publishing online at

www.HighMarkPublishing.com

Mason's Acknowledgements

I must forever be grateful to the staff at High Mark Publishing SF.
And finally, let me thank all of my best friends in my beta readers, my
amazing online writer's group, and of course, the rest of my family.

If you have not read Book One of *Mergeworld*, however unlikely that might be, please enjoy this teaser by Mason Elliott and Garan R. R. Faraday. Available now! Here is the Amazon purchase link:

smarturl.it/Mergeworld

1

David Pritchard woke up gasping from one nightmare and went straight into another. A terrible agony tore through him as if the universe twisted him inside out.

Then he snapped back again.

What in damnation had just happened? Something...was very wrong.

Startled, groggy, it only took an instant for his bleary mind to figure out.

Flames engulfed the front of his college apartment building. The stench of smoke, screams, and breaking glass outside only confirmed it.

He was dazed and blinked his scratchy eyes. The first thing he instinctively reached out for was the framed picture of his dead parents.

That was the last picture he had of them from a few years back, right after he started college in South Bend.

They hugged and smiled at each other in medieval garb at the Bristol Renaissance Fair up in Wisconsin. The picture froze both of them happily in time, retired in their forties. Unlike many parents that age, they weren't divorced and they still loved one another. One of their ren-fair pals took that picture for them on their digital camera.

The same camera retrieved from the car accident on the Illinois highways on their way back home from Bristol. A tractor-trailer jackknifed in the heavy rain and took them away.

The same weekend David begged off going with them.

He blew that picture up in Photoshop, printed out an 8 x 10, and bought a nice oak frame for it. He kept it with him wherever he went. He'd die before he'd part with it, fire or no.

All that history and pain flashed through David as he clutched their picture close to him in the dark. He didn't even have to see it, just cling to it in his hands. That picture always sat prominently behind his small alarm clock on his night stand with his smart phone and wallet while he slept. That was how he found it, even in the semi-dark. He also grabbed his phone and wallet.

His clock normally flashed bright green. Power outage, probably from the fire. And the back-up battery must have gone dead. Light switches? Nothing, of course, do to the fire.

The growing reek of smoke triggered his desire for self-preservation. Once he got out, he could call his friend Mason Tyler, who lived in a duplex over on Allen Street. His buddy Mace would help him.

Somewhat more awake now, David struggled not to panic. He staggered out of his room like a robot. His lanky, five-eleven frame stumbled down the hall toward his front door. He stubbed his little toe hard in the darkness. A second later he grunted and cursed the sudden blinding spread of pain, but kept moving.

Oh, hell. No way out the front.

Dangerous ribbons of smoke curled violently through the metal front door frame and snaked up across the ceiling like an upside down waterfall. The paint of the metal fire door already bubbled and blistered. David choked and swallowed hard.

If that door had been wood, his entire apartment might have already been completely engulfed. He might not have even come to. He saw no sense in touching the steaming door knob.

The apartment building stairs acted like a natural chimney, funneling the fire and heat straight up.

A window—climb out a window. He was only on the second floor.

His three richer roomies were already off on spring break for the next week, to the Bahamas or some such. Their parents could afford such junkets. David could not.

He suddenly realized two very important things. The fire hadn't spread to the back part of the apartment building yet.

Next, he was only wearing navy boxers and a gray T-shirt over his shaking frame.

Early April in South Bend, Indiana could be any weather from sun and sixties to a flippin' blizzard.

Clothes. Only seconds to throw some on. Even in the dim, flickering orange light spilling out of the thick curtains, he spotted his laundry basket on the couch.

The smoke in the living room grew thicker. He put his precious picture, smartphone, and wallet down for only a few moments.

Jeans. On. Socks. On. He snatched up his thick blue, gold, and green hoody from the back of the old couch where he usually left it, and pulled into its soft, warm, comfort. Stocking cap. Popped on his head. Wool scarf. Around the neck. He sat down and jammed on his old gray Nike running shoes, feeling a pair of thin gloves and keys in his hoody pockets still, when he bent over.

Ready to ride, or, at least climb out the back window to escape burning to death.

He stuffed his folks' picture, wallet, and smartphone into his dark green Jansport backpack with his pad, gel pens, and a few books. He zipped it all up.

To the back window. He pulled the curtains aside and yanked the big panel open.

He jumped slightly, at some guy who already climbed down the back of the building from the third floor. Their eyes locked, only a window screen between them in the dim, pre-dawn light and the cold morning air.

The guy looked utterly terrified.

"Watch out!" he warned, trying to keep his voice low. "Those things are killing people. They're everywhere!"

"What things?" What was this guy freaking out about?

The guy jolted wide-eyed and then choked.

A bloody iron arrowhead jutted out the front of his throat. In the time it took them both to blink, another arrow punched through the front of his chest, out of his T-shirt. The poor guy's mouth gaped and worked. Then his eyes rolled up white. He fell backwards, head down.

David grabbed for him, but missed, his hands blocked by the barrier of the screen. He tore it away and stuck his head out the window.

He spotted strange movement down in the darkness.

Two dark, twisted, hunched-over figures loped in on bandy legs and clawed feet wrapped in fur and rags. They were smaller than humans, about four to five feet tall and very skinny and wiry.

Whatever they were, they were definitely not human.

One of them slit the dead guy's throat from ear to ear with a long, wicked-looking rusty knife.

Blood spurted bright black in the night.

The other creature sniffed the air and snarled up at David with a greenish-black, twisted, inhuman face. Long pointed ears stuck out of holes in its ragged hood. It had a big warty nose, and gleaming green eyes. It gave full draw to the same kind of short, black bow of jagged horn that the other one carried.

The creature took dead aim at David.

And fired.

Mergeworld, Book One, Amazon Link: smarturl.it/Mergeworld

Please enjoy this teaser for Mergeworld, Book 2:
Amazon Link: smarturl.it/Mergeworld2

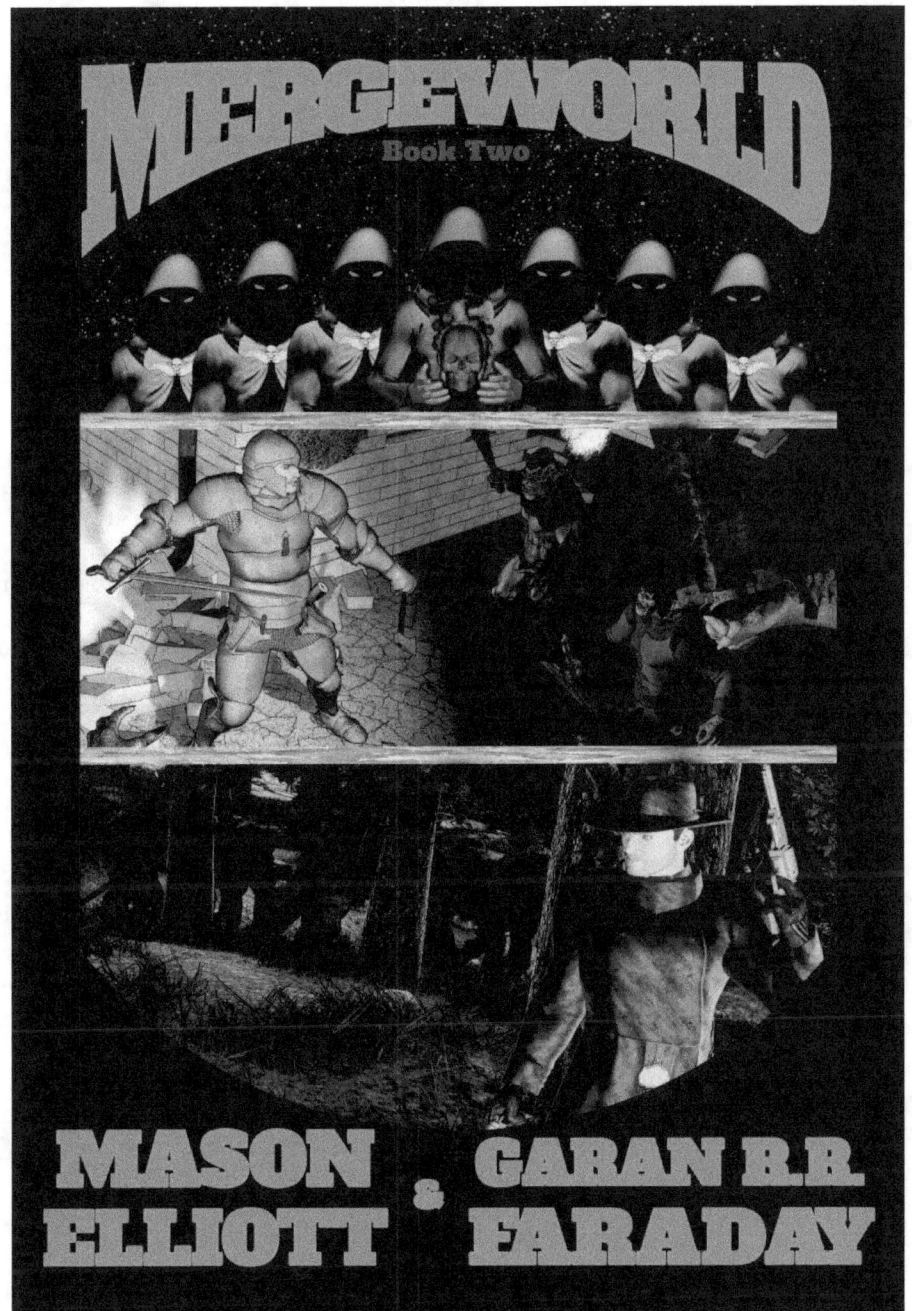

Mergeworld

Book Two

Amazon Link: smarturl.it/Mergeworld2

by Mason Elliott and Garan R. R Faraday

"Several of the enemy mage prisoners have escaped," a runner came to warn them. The young trooper looked terrified.

Mason drew his Spillers. They would have to be enough. After the bath, he didn't have all of his other guns. And there wasn't time to go after them.

It also worried him that he still felt–off his game, somehow. Something was still very wrong with him, but he couldn't figure out what. Perhaps that was merely what sorrow and depression felt like.

Blondie shook the terrified runner. "Calm down. Tell me what you know. Which prisoners? How many of them?"

"S-six, six, I think. They tried to free the rest, but the guards on the scene shot two down. Then the enemy mages fled this way, and started killing everyone they could find with magic."

Troops screamed, and close by to the west, magic blasts went off, and the sounds of battle and further bursts of magical rapidly sped their way.

The runner continued to stammer, "The tall n-n-necromancer is leading them. Five others. I don't know their names. As soon as they broke out, the duty officer sent me after you two and the Thul woman."

Blondie let the runner go. "Try to find the Thul. Go. Keep spreading the alarm."

"Yes, s-sir!" The young runner looked only too happy to keep running.

"They're coming for us, aren't they, Blondie?" Mason asked, hefting his Spillers.

Blondie clenched both fists, and violet magefire flared up to his elbows. "Yep. Just like I said they would. How do you want to do this, Mace?"

"Hmmm…too many to hit them head on. Let's go at them from the flanks. I'll hit them on the left."

His blond friend nodded. "Then I'll take them on the right. The necromancer's going to be the toughest of the lot. Let's peel off the other five, if we can, and then take him on together."

"Sounds good, Blondie. Let's ride."

They skirted around to either side, trying to stick to cover and stay out of sight. Mason quickly lost sight of his friend.

It did briefly occur to him that this would be an excellent time for Blondie to turn on them all, and help the mages make good their escape. But at this point, Mason had no choice but to keep trusting his good friend.

Blondie said that his abilities were returning.

He could tell them anything he wanted. How would they know if it was the truth or not?

From the sounds of things, the militia troops were putting up a pretty good fight and delaying the enemy at least somewhat. Each precious second they could hold them back, more troops would pour in.

Yet even as Mason got into position to attack, the enemy mages continued to push through, causing death and destruction all around them, and leaving many casualties in their wake.

Startled troops could slow the enemy down, but they would be hard pressed to stop six enemy mages bent on a rampage of devastation.

They were lucky that it wasn't all thirteen of the mage captives on the loose.

At Blondie's urging, Major Bill had spread several of the captive mages out to other nearby, secret locations—beyond the limited range of their prisoners' telepathy.

Mason spotted the enemy. The necromancer strode out in front with another sorcerer. A pair of enemy wizards marched slightly behind them on either side, guarding their flanks and watching the rear.

Blondie stepped up and raked the enemy left and the middle with violet lightning that knocked four of the six off their feet, and stunned the two flankers.

The first flanker on the other side turned to attack Blondie. The second one raised his hands and his eyes got big when he saw the Pistolero step out and aim both of his pistols.

Click! Click!

Nothing. Mason's guns wouldn't fire. He cocked and pulled the triggers again.

Nothing.

By then the one mage was charging Blondie, exploding anything that was made of wood around him. He sent the shards and splinters and whirling debris at Blondie, while the necromancer and the other sorcerer still looked dazed and tried to regain their feet. And the mage facing Mason shot greenish-yellow flames out of his hands at all before him.

Mason dove out of the way, tucked and rolled out of sight, and then crouched and ran. The enemy wizard would be on him in seconds.

Finally he came to a building and ducked inside. He scrambled out of sight into an adjoining back storage room and ducked down. He tried his guns again. Still nothing. Why was this happening,? Now of all times?

Blondie needed him out there.

Maybe if he reloaded. Yeah, that would do it.

Slowing his breathing, doing his best to stay calm, he broke out his spare cylinders for his guns and swapped them out. He was fast at it, but every second counted.

He went back out into the fight. As he expected, the fighting quickly turned Blondie's way, and blasts of magic nearby showed where the foes were pursuing Blondie hard and blasting everything around him. Blondie fought back as best he could, but from what Mason could tell, his friend was outnumbered four to one.

He raced that way, not even trying to stay under cover this time. He had to catch up quickly, and take them from behind, if possible.

Mason sped around a building and almost slammed into the same enemy mage as before. This one seemed to be holding back and protecting the rear of the other three while they stalked Blondie.

Mason had intended to shoot them on sight, but he clobbered the mage from behind now that he was right on top of him. The mage grunted and dropped, unconscious.

Pistol-whipping worked better in this instance. Mason dragged the mage back out of sight and quickly gagged him, and bound his hands and ankles behind him.

At this distance, Mason would not have any trouble taking out the other three with one or two shots, once he spotted them again. And their spells gave them away when they fired. Hopefully, Blondie was staying ahead of them.

Mason rushed forward once more, spotted several troops closing in with bows and crossbows, and motioned for them to go around and close in from one side or the other.

Finally he spotted the necromancer and the one wizard, crouched down and making plans of some kind.

Mason took aim at them with both barrels.

Click. Click.

Crap, not again. What the hell was going on?

Even worse, the necromancer turned and locked eyes with him.

"There's the other one. Let's get him!" All of their hands glowed with magefire.

Mason turned and ran for it. Dark lightning and exploding ice covered the area he had just been in.

His foes were right after him. Archers tried to fire upon the mages, but they swept the troops away from their positions with blasts of power.

A stone or outcropping of brick caught the toe of Mason's boot. He hurtled down upon his face, and tried to roll back up to his feet.

The third enemy mage stepped out right in front of Mason.

Now, the three of them had him fairly trapped.

"Kill him!" the necromancer roared.

The wizard still hesitated an instant. Then he prepared a spell, his hands beginning to glow brighter and brighter.

They were only a dozen or so feet away. Mason hurled his useless pistols at the wizard.

One missed as the fellow dodged to one side.

The other smacked him squarely in the face and dazed and bloodied him.

Mason expected to be cut down from behind by the other two enemies any second.

He glanced back just as the two stood ready to unleash their spells.

Amazon Link to *Mergeworld, Book Two*: <u>smarturl.it/Mergeworld2</u>

If you have not read the original Naero Books by Mason Elliott, Please enjoy the following teaser from the first Spacer Clans Adventure, Book 1:

NAERO'S
RUN

NAERO'S RUN

Amazon Link to Naero's Run: smarturl.it/NaerosRun

by Mason Elliott

"We've got more than enough to consider here," Aunt Sleak said. "We'll post our final decisions on the Spacer ClanNet. All crew, take a breather. We're out of jump in less that two standard hours. Everyone on duty needs to be at their ready stations. Dismissed."

Naero went back to her quarters to do some laundry and a little more reading before they emerged. With regular effort, her quarters were less of a disaster than usual. She'd kept her bunk and her floor more or less cleared off, and slept in her bunk regularly now, instead of on the floor or in zero-G or a float bag.

And definitely not in her flex chair, as she had for years because she either couldn't get her bunk panel out or it was too piled up with crap.

Being small had its advantages. She could curl up like a cat and get comfortable almost anywhere for a snooze.

But keeping her quarters in better shape was a promise she made and kept—to herself—and her parents.

They emerged from jump with the customary shuddering of the ship. The fleet spread out into is standard formation, emerging back into real Space-Time.

Naero punched up their positions on one of her screens, even though she didn't have bridge duty for several hours.

The Shinai flanked *The Dromon* on the port side, with *The Slipper* posted starboard. Their two smaller ships, *The Nevada* and *The Ardala*, brought up the rear this time.

A red hot scarlet particle beam, 60mm in diameter, lanced through Naero's walls like they were paper, disrupting her wallscreens.

A direct hit from a big gun.

At the very least, from a heavy destroyer.

Warning lights flashed immediately.

The rupture in the hull led to an immediate explosive decompression.

Naero held on tight to her bunk and went flat on the floor as the hull sealed itself.

All ships were vulnerable coming out of jump. They couldn't activate their shields until right after they emerged.

Someone had been waiting for them.

The Dromon continued getting rocked by multiple hits from what felt like several spinal guns and secondary batteries.

But the big planetoid could take it and give back plenty, her quad main guns humming and whining to life, coming online.

Naero hit her wristcom. All her screens down.

"Bridge. Status?"

"We stepped into it. They were waiting for us. We're under heavy fire. Multiple bogeys."

The general alert sounded.

"Battle Stations. Battle Stations."

Aunt Sleak cut over the com. "All hands. All hands, to your stations. Prepare for battle. All ships, all batteries, return fire. Launch all fighters."

Naero suited up and raced to the drop bay of her fighter. She met Jan along the way.

More intense fire. *Dromon* reeled and fired back.

She and Jan almost got rocked off their feet again.

A security team intercepted them at the launching bays.

Their fighters had already dropped with their backup pilots.

"The fleet captain wants you two at your secondary defense stations, not out in the mix."

Jan started to protest.

"Orders are orders. Get to your stations."

They ran to their remote gunnery stations, small secured cubicles with a chair and a console, operating triple pulse turrets on the hardpoints above them.

Naero brought up her autotargeting displays, weapons already powered up and humming.

The secondary battery gunnery stations operated independently and were well-protected. They were also fully automated, but they still functioned more effectively with a human interface.

Coordinated targeting profiles came online as she watched.

Jan operated a torp turret nearby.

Directly ahead of the fleet. Twelve elite Matayan destroyers, each with a dozen escort fighters.

Half of their number pursued and attacked a convoy of two dozen independent mining freighters.

Aunt Sleak's fleet scrambled, launched, and deployed a total of threescore fighters in a standard Alpha-Charlie-1 defensive screen.

They were outnumbered two to one.

"All batteries make ready. Incoming torps," the bridge com sounded.

Countermeasures took out half of the blips heading their way.

Spacer fighters and the forward defensive batteries blasted the rest.

"That attack's a diversion," Naero muttered.

Shinai's fire control and com computers fixed on and monitored all channels—including those between the hapless freighters and the corsairs.

"Mayday, mayday, we are under intense corsair attack. All ships. Assistance, assistance. Heavy damage and casualties."

"What do you want?" another panic-stricken voice cried out. "We'll surrender. You can board us. We have no goods and few supplies. Please, stop firing. Our ships are full of workers–full of people. You're killing civilians. We're on fire!"

Scanners displayed an awful, one-sided battle among the transports. Most of the old bulk freighters didn't even have weapons.

Each of the heavily armed Matayan destroyers was more than a match for them or most of the ships in Aunt Sleak's fleet.

Except for the 6m quad spinal guns of *The Dromon*.

One crippled freighter broke apart and exploded under concentrated fire from three destroyers. It didn't have any shields, and only minimal armor. Its two turrets either didn't work or had been taken out already.

Static and Matayan battle language rang out in triumph.

Dromon's four primary guns cut loose, lighting up the entire sector. Its blue-white blasts ripped into the lead corsair flagship and its wingships, disrupting their shields.

The starboard wingship took two hits and listed to one side. Its aft section exploded.

"This is Captain Sleak Maeris of Clan Maeris. Enemy vessels, be advised: Cease hostilities and vacate this system or be destroyed."

Matayan curses and laughter her only reply.

"Clan Maeris," one of the freighter captains cut in. "This is Captain Philsen of *The Botaru*. Help us! Our situation is desperate. The corsairs are trying to destroy us. We don't know why."

"Acknowledged. We're coming in. Disperse if you can. You're still too bunched up. Scatter and concentrate on defensive actions. Jump if you're able. We'll try to draw them off. We're boosting your distress call."

Three more corsairs turned on the fleet, with all twelve dozen fighters full front on intercept.

The other trio of Matayan attackers kept after the freighters.

Naero heard the pleading and the screams on the open channel, just before another freighter got blasted to oblivion.

Naero realized she had tears on her face.

Was that how her parents went? Blasted to death by Matayan guns?

The rage she felt nearly overwhelmed her reason.

She checked her systems, gripped the controls of her gunnery station, and forced her emotions to go cold.

Against superior numbers, Naero and her Clan Fleet closed for battle.

Amazon Link to Naero's Run: smarturl.it/NaerosRun

Please enjoy the following teaser from a spinoff series that we call: The Citation Series, Book 1, Naero's War:

The Annexation War

NAERO'S WAR:
THE ANNEXATION WAR

Annexation War Amazon Link: smarturl.it/TheAnnexationWar

by Mason Elliott

Naero's flagship, *The Hippolyta,* was one of the latest, Dromon Class dreadnaughts. These warships were fashioned out of dense, iron-nickel planetoids, not less than half a kilometer in diameter. Incredibly tough and rugged on their own.

It took the most powerful mining plasma-borers–working in precise conjunction with construction fixers and an army of teks–months to hollow out armored crew quarters, lift and transport tubes, launching and loading bays. Next came space for power cores, sublight engines, jump drives, backups, gravitics, life support, sensor arrays, communications, navigation, weapons, main bridge and backup bridge.

Set in the exact heart of *The Hippolyta* were its signature big guns. A quad of the largest production guns ever constructed on any ship of war: Four, *16 meter*, rapid-fire, particle beam cannons.

Cannons any larger than that exploded, melted, or otherwise were not feasible within the limits of current tek and materials. Thirty-six secondary batteries, assorted specialized weapons and gun emplacements, and forty-five advanced fighters.

Seven hundred and forty able crew, including a full Rifle Company of two hundred and forty Spacer Marines, and all of their equipment, vehicles, and gear for ship's security and rapid response deployment. Strike Fleet Six's Marines came from the 3rd Spacer Marine Division–known as *The Death Eyes*–because of their superb snipers and their overall, excellent marksmanship ratings. Marines made up a third of the warship's complement.

Their motto: *If We Can See It...We Can Kill It!*

The main bridge was a massive armored dome constructed on top of the dreadnaught's big metal, rough-hewn orb, protected by heavy blast doors, and the latest, most advanced shielding in the fleet. Within, the circular bridge was laid out in four levels under the huge dome, a dome sixty meters high.

Each bridge tier was separated by the height of a few steps from one to the next. The inner three levels could rotate in any direction, independent of the others.

The fleet captain's command nanochair and station occupied the highest tier. Each bridge station had its own secondary shielding, in case enemy fire penetrated the shields, the blast screens, and the hull.

In combat, bridges were routinely targeted, for obvious reasons.

From that primary vantage point, the strike fleet captain could direct battles in three hundred and sixty degrees, through an advanced, battleholo display surrounding her, full zoom data-feeds, constantly updated by battle AIs. Naero could manipulate the displays by nanosensors programmed into the fingertips of her nanosuit gloves.

The battle display system also recognized her voice pattern, and would respond to voice commands, or commands punched in manually through pads on her command chair, or via other backups.

The next bridge level down from hers held the secondary bridge stations: Helm, Weapons, Communications, Navigation, and Scanning, spaced out equally along their ring.

The third ring held all of the twelve tertiary bridge stations, that monitored, controlled, and coordinated all of the ship's other important functions:

Engineering
Gravitics
Life Support
Power Supply
Security
Shields
Medical
Jump and Sub-light Drives
Damage Control
Alliance Fleet and Intel Communications
Main Computer
Launching Bays

The fourth ring went to the two powerlifts, leading from the bridge to the other movers, decks, and levels of the ship. All lift and access points throughout the ship were constantly guarded by two battle-ready Marines, stationed on either side.

If a warship was boarded by enemy assault craft during a battle, invaders could be cut off and eliminated between decks, before they could reach a vital area.

Today, Strike Fleet Six had a mission–a simple one.

Captain Naero Maeris and her fifty warships proceeded to probe the next system on the outer, port arcwall of the Alliance advance at Beleron-4.

A routine run. Current intel assured them to expect little or no Triaxian presence or resistance.

By any stretch of the imagination, Beleron-4 was a nothing world, in the middle of nowhere, with zero, nacha–absolutely no strategic or tactical value whatsoever.

Checking it off the list on the pacified worlds of the Alliance system-hopping schedule was more-or-less just a formality.

But it still had to be done. And Naero and her lot drew the duty at random.

So why did Naero's sense of warning go bonkers?

After they jumped in, simple three-stack, Delta-India-3 formation, the reasons for alarm grew perfectly clear.

They came in right on top of twenty Triaxian fleets of the enemy's latest warships.

And a gigantic new flagship–as huge as *The Hippolyta*–the advanced design of which did not even register as existing.

It had never been seen before.

Naero shot to her feet, kicked her command nanochair back out the way and sent it down into the nanofloor of her top-tier bridge control station.

She instantly called her battle display holos up in spinning, horizontal glowing ribbons and rings all around her.

Data relays went wild. Her fingers flashed among the highlighted screen arcs, taking control of them and their parameters.

Multiple warnings sounded, and with excellent reason.

Nothing about this was good in any way.

Haisha! Twenty enemy fleets could chop them into confetti–well before any other Alliance forces could even jump in to help.

No strategy, no formation could possibly save them against superior numbers such as these.

"All ships, full withdraw. Emergency retreat on this vector, in Charlie-Romeo-7, cone-ring formation. Shields and all weapons full front and hot. Maximize all targeting profiles on the lead attacking enemy elements–they'll be on us in seconds. Whatever happens–we fight until our carriers and some of our ships can break free and jump out behind us. Get the carriers out first!"

For a split second, everyone braced for the sheets of flame that would quickly overtake and overwhelm them.

Annexation War Amazon Link: smarturl.it/TheAnnexationWar

Please enjoy the following teaser ... an excerpt, from the next Spacer Clans Adventure, Book 2:

NAERO'S GAMBIT

A SPACER CLANS ADVENTURE

NAERO'S
GAMBIT

MASON ELLIOTT

Naero's Gambit

Naero's Gambit Amazon Link: smarturl.it/NaerosGambit

by Mason Elliott

Klyne set the huge Mystic testing room on board *The Kathmandu* to muted gray. Smartwalls, floor, and ceiling, Naero saw no equipment, no padding.

The lights were set low.

From experience, Naero knew that in a training room, just about anything could pop up out of anywhere.

She wore nothing but her black Nytex flight togs.

To her surprise, Klyne and his two adepts wore dark gray Nytex togs also, but with hoods and masks pulled up over their heads. Only their keen eyes showed.

All three of the Mystics appeared to be in top physical condition, including Klyne.

One of the adepts was female, with huge green eyes and light freckles across her nose. The other was male, with the black slanted eyes of the Lii-Kim Clans.

If black was the color of Spacers, the Mystics traditionally wore gray.

They all sat with their legs crossed in lotus fashion, focusing their abilities through meditation, and mental discipline. They formed a triangle, each side about three meters apart, with them at the points.

"Follow our instructions," Klyne said. "Take your place among us. Sit in the center; sit as we do. Face the instructor."

A circle of white light appeared at the center of the triangle. Naero walked over and sat down in it, facing Klyne. Her skin barely began to tingle.

A wider ring of similar light appeared, including the instructor and his two adepts.

Every hair on Naero's body went stiff with electric force.

"You have chosen to come before the circle of Spacer Mystics to be tested for Mystic training. Speak your name."

"Naero Amashin Maeris."

"You agree to be tested?"

"I do."

"I am Klyne, the instructor. My assistants are Adept Iselle, and Adept Makita. We shall refer to you as Adept Candidate Naero. Follow our instructions. Respond only if asked to respond. If you require any medical attention, it will be administered at the end of the testing. Until then, you are expected to endure and continue to do your best. If you understand, say yes."

"Yes."

"The training will begin. Defend yourself."

Without warning, Makita's attack smashed into her.

She blocked one or two out every four or five blows.

A snapwheel kick sent her flying twenty meters, nearly winding her.

The only things that saved her at all, once again, were the experience and knowledge she gained from her training sessions with Baeven.

Makita proved stronger and faster than her, but he still paled in comparison to the outcast's terrifying prowess.

Makita charged her.

Naero met him part way.

She took several punishing strikes, but flipped him hard to the ground.

He swept her legs.

They tangled on the ground, wrestling, slipping out of holds, twisting like snakes. They pummeled each other all the while.

They broke, crouched low, and launched themselves at each other again, like Thellurian fighting blue cranes.

Naero landed a whipkick on the side of Makita's head.

He clipped her under the chin, grabbed her leg and ankle and swung her hard into the floor, stunning her.

She struggled to get up.

For a few dizzy moments, she couldn't.

She rose up and staggered back into her fighting stance.

She half-smiled.

"Come on."

Makita bowed his head, just slightly, and drew back.

"Defend yourself, "Klyne said again.

Naero whirled to face Iselle.

Too late.

An invisible force slammed into her arms and torso, flinging her back.

She rolled with the strike and came back up into her stance.

Iselle fought her from a distance, punching and striking with her hands in rapid combinations.

Naero struggled to advance, to close the distance between them, while heavy, unseen blows rained down on her from every direction, knocking her one way, and then the other.

"Telekinetic combat," Klyne called out. "Try to sense and block the blows. You cannot see them. Reach out with your battle senses, with your mind. Feel them coming. Counter and deflect them. True masters can fight thus, without even moving, simply by concentrating."

At least Iselle still had to physically move in order to project her attacks. That was some help.

Closer. Get closer.

Iselle thrust both hands forward violently.

A wall of force drove Naero slowly back. She pushed against it, slowing it even more.

"Resist. Focus on the energy before you," Klyne told her, "before it smashes you into the far wall. Fight back. Defeat it."

She rolled to one side and then the other. The barrier felt solid.

Naero leaped up four meters, felt the top, and flipped herself over it.

Iselle withdrew a step, cupping both hands loosely on the sides of her face.

Spinning orbs of pure telekinetic force shot out, rapid-fire.

Naero barely perceived them where they warped through the air; they made explosive popping sounds.

She tried to dodge them. One whirred past her head like an invisible ball at high speed.

The next clipped her left shoulder, spinning her aside.

Another knocked one leg out from under her.

She kept her feet and ducked, weaving to either side in turns.

Iselle directed her attack at Naero's feet.

Naero lost her footing, slipping and sliding on what felt like a bunch of invisible ball bearings cast beneath her.

She tried to roll back to her feet, but panes of force battered her from all sides, keeping her off balance.

It felt like being a rubber ball, bouncing around in a box that someone shook.

The sides of the box rapidly closed in.

They tightened all around her, threatening to crush her.

She couldn't breathe.

Iselle released her without warning.

Naero sprawled, gasping, face down on the floor.

"I'm somewhat surprised," Klyne noted. "Preliminary tests demonstrate no psonic aptitude or innate talent to my trained senses whatsoever. That in itself is very rare. After your battle with the former Danner entity, we simply assumed that you would exhibit some kind of psyonic ability."

"I burned myself out dealing with the entity. I burned both of us out. I'm a nud once more." She admitted it openly. "None of my former abilities have returned."

So she wasn't psyonic anymore. Not even a teknomancer. Disappointing, but not the end of the universe.

"Yet I sense something incredibly strange within you," Klyne said. "What could it be?"

Was it Om? He was still inside her somewhere. He had not emerged again either.

"Take your place at the center of us once more. Face me again."

Naero did so, resisting an urge to massage several bruises.

Klyne positioned himself directly in front of her, sitting lotus fashion just like her and the others.

"I'm going to attempt to merge directly with your mind telepathically, one of my gifts. I'm also an Auralcognitor. Once I link with your mind, I can sense any type of psyonic energy field you might have, active, passive, or latent. I might even be able to trigger or bring them out to the surface. There might be some discomfort. Shall we proceed?"

"Sure."

"Do as I do. I will show you how to place your hands to effect the mind merge."

Klyne cupped his left hand firmly behind the base of her skull.

Naero followed his lead.

He placed the fingers of his right hand on precise spots on her face.

Thumb on her forehead, directly between her eyes.

Index finger on her left temple.

The next two fingers curled slightly in front of her left ear. His smallest finger hooked at the point of her ear and jaw.

As soon as Naero placed her right hand the same way, she gasped slightly.

Thin hairs of what felt like burning hot energy threaded their way slowly through the layers of her awareness.

She could feel Klyne connecting with her thoughts, joining their two minds.

The dull ache continued to grow.

"You should be feeling the initial discomfort. Hold still. Keep focusing. Almost there. Almost…"

A spike of pure agony exploded within her skull.

Naero screamed, transfixed as if by lightning.

Through the torment, a voice awoke in her mind full-force.

Protocols unlocked and engaged. We...are.

Interface...partial.

Om awoke, reacting instinctively with fear and vast power.

Threat detected...Protect all access.

Neural net...INTRUSION. UNWARRANTED.

LEVEL 1.359 DEFENSIVE RESPONSE.

An intense blast wave of white-hot psyonic energy fanned out rapidly from the epicenter of her immolated mind.

Naero continued to scream.

As if far away in the distance, Klyne and his two adepts also shrieked.

*

Naero blinked, her eyes and mouth frozen open.

She lay with her head to one side, in a puddle of her own mixed blood and spittle.

More pain struck her when she attempted to move.

Blood continued to stream from her eyes, ears, nose, and mouth–a bloody mess.

It felt as if a fusion grenade had blown her head open.

She reached up with her hands, to make sure her skull was still intact.

Some kind of noise.

Warning alarms sounded.

A ship. Yes, they were on a ship. The Spacer Intel Ship *The Kathmandu*. She was...being tested, for the Mystics.

Something had gone terribly wrong.

Naero focused, getting to her hands and knees.

She heard other voices, groaning and whimpering.

Makita lay sprawled in a broken tangle, blasted across the room. His gray clothing had been shredded and scorched into tatters. He choked and coughed.

To the other side, Iselle fared little better. She lay convulsing, blasted, scorched, a yellow-white bone of her forearm sticking out of her wrenched flesh. One side of her face was blistered, her red hair burned, some of it still smoking. She trembled and shuddered in pain and terror.

Naero looked around for Klyne, and found the instructor in a burned, bloody heap, lying beneath a dark red smear on the far wall. His hands were charred black, and he was missing fingers.

Naero could not walk. She couldn't even stand. She crawled to Klyne as quickly as she could.

He still lived, just barely.

Then she noticed the intense effects of the blast, all around the room, less than a meter up.

A massive expanding ring of Cosmic force had sliced into the duranadium hull of the smartwalls, punching a deep crease right through them where they buckled, all along its full diameter.

The force of the strike disrupted all systems. The entire training room was compacted, crushed, and heavily damaged.

Rescuers struggled to force their way through the various ruined doors and access panels.

Please enjoy the following teaser from the next Spacer Clans Adventure, Book 3:

NAERO'S
FURY

NAERO'S FURY

by Mason Elliott

Naero still hadn't done it much, but going into a direct trance to enter the Astral Plane shouldn't be all that difficult. Master Vane had shown her how once. And she had gone there lots of times in her sleep, in her mind, to speak with Khai, using their astral crystals.

Before her friend Khai had vanished without a trace.

Yet she had never been completely trained in astral travel, and didn't know that much about exploring or moving around. Master Vane had taken her there once, just to teach her the basics and give her his marker. Many other times later to spar with her.

If nothing else, she could probably focus on his marker and locate him.

Zhen had roused Naero and reminded her it was time. And that she and Shalaen would monitor her while she was in the astral trance.

Naero focused her mind and abilities, controlling her breathing. Remembering the little she had recently learned.

Within several minutes of focused meditation, she open her eyes and found herself floating in the Astral Miasma, the nebulae of energy. She hugged her knees to her chest in her astral form.

Om spoke to her, even more easily here than in her own mind before.

I have accessed some of the Kexxian Matrix's data files on The Astral Plane. Like everything else, they explored it quite extensively.

Om, I'm naked here. I'm not complaining–but just tell me–how do I put astral clothing on again?

You control everything here by imagination, and force of will. Concentrate on your favorite clothing and they'll appear.

That's easy.

She looked down and saw her favorite Nytex flight togs, programmed just the way she liked them.

Naero blinked, spinning and twirling in one spot, turning upside down.

Why can't I move more than a meter at a time in front of us?

You're not used to this reality. So it's not clear to you.

The air around her looked opaque. Not mist. Not smoke or vapor. And it glowed slightly with its own bluish-gray light.

In the twilight she glowed softly blue-white with her own light. From within.

"I once heard rumors that the Mystics could travel and send messages this way, but I thought it was all just a myth."

Since the other planes are entire universes within themselves, it is said, they are all nearly infinite. Thus, it is difficult to pin point any kind of location or person unless you already know them.

Naero instinctively tried to stand up, but there was nothing to stand on.

Then she recalled Master Vane's Marker, and it appeared right before her. Where she found him, she would find the other High Masters.

At least she deserved a chance to be heard by them all. To try to explain herself and her actions. What happened with the obelisk was clearly not her fault.

But they would still blame her for it–especially Mater Vane, who seemed to blame her for everything since Hashiko's death.

Naero could not simply stand by and let the High Masters decide her fate without herself being present at her trial, in some way at least.

She focused on the crimson and black star more and swept forward, seemingly at great speed.

She came to an abrupt halt, like a starship coming out of jump at its destination.

The opacity around her partially melted away. She proceeded forward, opening her visual field far wider. She made out the area around her as the miasma peeled back.

Slightly below her, she saw spheres within glowing spheres, all spinning within greater spheres.

Her own sphere, glowing white-blue, suddenly surrounded her like a glittering soap bubble.

Yet it did not pop when she poked at it.

One sphere in particular, the largest, glowed and pulsed blood red, containing a withered old man with a long beard, pacing impatiently.

Burning eyes vanished and re-appeared at random all over his bald head. The red sphere absorbed Master Vane's marker.

Was this his true form? What he really looked like?

His scarlet sphere was also flanked by two smaller spheres with figures inside them.

Om made a calculated guess.

His current guardian adepts, no doubt. The ones you rescued from the enemy Darkforce generators on Janosha.

I think so, Om.

At most times, every High Master had at least two champion adepts protecting him or her, each of them very close to mastery themselves. Just as Hashiko had been.

Naero studied Vane's new guardians for the very first time, and tried to see into their spheres.

Something about each of them did seem strangely familiar.

One of Vane's adepts, the male, appeared to be so deep dark black, he could be a singularity. This adept's sphere was flat black on the surface and barely transparent.

If Naero had been able to breathe, she would have gasped.

Instead she simply raised her hand to her mouth.

She recalled that she had seen many of these adepts long before.

In her dreams, nightmares, and crazed visions. Perhaps even on the Astral Plane somehow.

Vane's other adept was the white female, the exact opposite of the other. So brilliant and blindingly radiant, she could be a pulsar. Her orb was like a high intensity bulb, blinding and almost completely crystal clear.

It occurred to Naero that during her initial testing, Klyne had male and female assistants as well.

She couldn't guess what the significance of that pattern was all about. Perhaps just some weird Mystic, egalitarian tradition.

Then why weren't any of the High Masters female?

Everyone seemed to ignore her where she floated.

The next larger sphere, farther away, glowed silver-blue.

If she focused intently on it, she discovered she could zoom in with her third eye–her mind's eye.

Within that silver-blue sphere, a silver man sat serenely, neither young nor old. Master Tree, in his purest form of order.

Two smaller guardian spheres flanked him.

Master Tree's female adept glowed with intense blue energy in a deep blue sphere.

The male likewise glowed with vibrant green force within a green sphere, a shining sword sheathed down his broad, athletic back. He seemed very familiar somehow.

Naero did a double-take. Long blond hair. Green skin. Big glowing sword.

Yep. In the flesh–or–astral form at least.

It was Khai! She was sure of it. He was alive.

Had he actually succeeded in his great task of forging his mystic sword in the heart of a gigantic pulsar? Was that it on his back?

Naero gasped again. Now that she knew what he looked like, Khai was also the dreamy green hunk from many past, pent up nightmares. The one who kept sticking his astral sword through her head.

What did it all mean? She wasn't nuts enough yet?

Now she knew for certain she needed serious help.

And to do some serious dating at some point, once-and-for-all.

If the Mystics continued to let her live.

Khai must have sensed her inner turmoil, or thoughts, or maybe just her concentration on him.

Mr. Green-god even glanced her way for a second, looking just as confused and puzzled by her sudden appearance.

Neither of them had ever met the other in person.

Naero covered her face with one hand and looked aside, withdrawing her sphere suddenly further away.

How fricking embarrassing.

She crept forward again. Slowly.

The third and final sphere glowed golden, and contained an equally golden child within, energetic and bristling with lightning. He bounced back and forth inside like a gigantic electron.

Master Jo of course.

Two flanking spheres.

One of his adepts had no clear form, eyes gleaming within a shifting, flickering miasma like the Astral Plane itself. His female counterpart shifted shape from one fantastic creature to another.

When she suddenly made out their voices, she could sense that an intense debate had been doing on. One that still continued.

"We cannot be certain in this matter," the golden child insisted. "We do not dare act in any rash way."

"Agreed, High Master Jo," the serene silver man added. "She might yet be another Trickster from what I can tell."

"Yes. Quite possible, High Master Tree."

The old man in the blood red sphere blustered impatiently. "Fools! Always conspiring against me. Taking positions opposite of mine for no reason but to anger me. I've been telling you all along, this child is clearly the Great Destroyer—long foretold. Our duty is clear. She is a threat to all existence. To multiple dimensions. She must be eliminated, at once, before she can grow even more powerful."

"High Master Vane," Tree said. "None of us can be sure of that fact. Including you."

"I am."

"You are always certain when it comes to destroying someone," Jo added. "Your pure Chaos answer to everything. Destruction or Creation."

"It works."

"No. It doesn't. It only delays and worsens the inevitable," Tree said. "The Universe shall have its way. We all know this. You were mistaken with the last savant when he appeared, and now he remains at large–a renegade beyond even our control."

Baeven? We're they referring to her uncle?

Vane rolled his eyes. "Idiots! The Renegade is the Trickster, I say. This child must in fact be the Great Destroyer. Just look at the powers roiling within her. They will surely corrupt and overwhelm her entirely and drive her mad in the end. She will go berserk on a scale that makes her recent outbursts feeble and puny by comparison. She must perish now, while we have a chance to put an end to her. While the only crimes she has committed include destroying an entire planet, and another of the vital obelisks!"

"We still don't understand the purpose of the ancient obelisks. And we've studied the mysterious disappearance of Janosha, and we still cannot be certain in any conclusive way, that she had anything to do with it."

"Really? Who else could it be then? Planets like Janosha aren't in the habit of just obliterating themselves suddenly for no reason at all. Everywhere she goes, destruction follows!"

I cannot allow this.

Quiet, Om. Don't do anything. I'm trying to listen.

Naero…they're discussing our destruction. The Chaos Master means to destroy us.

Master Jo continued to protest. "You can't just kill off every entity that manifests Cosmic Abilities such as these. Our universe is peppered with them. We must continue to locate and guide them–not find excuses to execute them. Like the Others have told us, Tricksters often appear to oppose Great Destroyers. Without the former, final victory is never possible. "

"High Masters," Tree said. "This young woman also possesses the Kexxian Data Matrix. We cannot destroy her without destroying it. Intel and The Spacer Council of Elders value our wisdom, but even they would not agree to such action."

"Regrettable," Vane said. "Yet I cannot take the risk. I have decided this matter on my own."

"You have no such authority on your own," Tree insisted.

"Idiots! I cannot stand by and allow our galaxy–perhaps our entire universe to be destroyed–just to satisfy your foolish, philosophical, and theoretical whims."

Master Vane turned to his adepts. "My finest students, obey me. Delay these fools. Keep them occupied whilst I act for the good of all existence."

More rapid than thought, the male dark ensnared the blue sphere and its satellites in coils and tendrils of darkness. While the bright female enveloped the golden sphere and its companions in waves of of pure light.

Naero tried to pull away, but in her panic she did not know where to go.

High Master Vane sped straight at her with impossible speed.

I must act, Naero.

No, Om. Please, this is already bad enough. Don't do anything.

I cannot comply. I must defend us!

Naero went down on her hands and knees before Master Vane. She called out, using *the voice* to project her words.

"Please, Master Vane. Do not attack me. I only wish to be trained to control my abilities. I have struggled hard to do so. I still don't understand what happened with the obelisk."

Vane bore down on her, arcs of pure scarlet energy bristling around him.

"Far too late for that, monster. Nothing is ever your fault, is it? Now, you must perish for the good of all. I told you this hour would come."

Instinctively, Naero drew back again, trying to evade his attack. She rose within her receding sphere.

Vane closed in once more, gathering his powers.

"Don't do this," Naero begged. "Please. Help me. I know I can't fully control all of my abilities yet. I'm trying as hard as I can. I can't be responsible for what will happen if you attack me. I can't control myself."

"Yes, and look at the results? Countless lives crushed and eradicated. Janosha vaporized–an entire planet. You must never be allowed to reach your full potential. Now–monster–hold still and embrace your fate."

Naero put her hands out before her, holding her palms out defensively. Pleading.

"No. Don't. I can't–"

"I know, Maeris. You can't help yourself. That is why you are *an abomination!*"

Vane smashed into her, piercing all of her defenses as if they were shattering glass.

In the distance, she sensed that Master Jo and Master Tree finally broke free.

Too late.

Master Vane attacked, trying to overwhelm her with raw power.

He pummeled her with impossible blows.

In the end, he beat her up badly, but only succeeded in knocking her around once more.

Om roared in their mind.

Kexxian defense protocols unlocked and on line.

An energized, glowing armor of some advanced origin formed around Naero like a hi-tek battle suit.

Naero saw out of her third eye as it awoke and burst into radiance like a blue-white star.

Master Vane came at her once more, all of his powers focused through his primary scarlet, burning eye, centered in his forehead.

All of his other flaming eyes closed as he concentrated, his skull wreathed in weird cosmic flames like a mane of cosmic fire.

"See how powerful you have already become? No adept could have withstood those lethal attacks. We must finish this now, before the others can interfere."

"Please, Master Vane. Please–I'm begging you–please, don't do this."

"Maeris, just as I foretold–you shall fall before the greatest of all Cosmic attack techniques. And I am one of the few who have ever learned to master it: The Eye of Annihilation!"

The same Chaos technique that had destroyed Hashiko–even she couldn't control it properly.

A massive blood red beam of destroying Cosmic force shot straight at her.

It all happened so fast. Naero heard Om screaming.

Reflection defense. Analyze incoming cosmic assault. Duplicate and reflect attack tenfold!

Just before the incoming blast vaporized her, a blue-white beam shot out of her own third eye to war against Master Vane's powers.

The Cosmic flows flared intensely.

Naero screamed as if her body and soul were being sucked through the eye of a black hole's needle.

The wide blue beam quickly drove the red beam back to its source.

At the last instant, High Master Vane cried out in terror.

"Impossible! There can be no such–"

The destroying energy ignited on contact.

A massive detonation on the Astral Plane blinded the area within a few light years.

High Masters Jo and Tree barely managed to withdraw and shield the others. All of their spheres shattered.

Pure cosmic energy punched into High Master Vane right before Naero's eyes.

It drove him back like a white-hot comet.

He struggled against it with all his might.

To no avail.

The reflected attack obliterated High Master Vane to glowing ash and dust, screaming in the wake of his own annihilation.

Vane's dying force of will echoed off into the universe.

Naero would have caught her breath if she had any.

The outcome left her completely stunned for a shuddering instant.

Om…what did we just do?

We had no choice, Naero. My sole purpose is to defend our current form.

Naero stared down at her hands in terror. Tendrils of Cosmic energy rippled and still curled off of her body and her sphere like smoke.

Om…*Haisha!* We just killed a High Master of the Spacer Mystics!

Amazon Link to Naero's Fury: smarturl.it/NaerosFury